Dear Reese and Liliana,
I hope your lives are full
of adventure!

Daughter of the Ancients

Donna Van Braswell

DONNA VAN BRASWELL

D1563881

CHAMPAGNE BOOK GROUP

Daughter of the Ancients

This is a work of fiction. The characters, incidents and dialogues in this book are of the author's imagination and are not to be construed as real. Any resemblance to actual events or persons, living or dead, is completely coincidental.

Published by Champagne Book Group
2373 NE Evergreen Avenue, Albany OR 97321 U.S.A.

~ ~ ~

First Edition 2020

ISBN: 978-1-77155-987-4

Copyright © 2020 Donna Van Braswell All rights reserved.

Cover Art by Melody Pond

www.champagnebooks.com

Version_1

I dedicate this novel to my dearest husband Jim,
who has made my dreams come true so
many times, I only dare to dream again.
Nicholas and Jessa, my children, you always
amaze and inspire me.

Dear Reader,

I am humbled that you show an interest in this thrilling adventure had by two flawed but wonderful young women. We all know someone like that, don't we? You may be passionate about learning, travel, love, forgiveness, and history. If so, may this book touch your heart as it has mine. I miss the characters already.

Donna Van Braswell

Author's Note

Visiting all the glorious places I mentioned while on the island of Rhodes and the Palace of the Grand Master, in particular, with brilliant friends who shared their knowledge, was the biggest inspiration for the book. So, details are quite specific and accurate to the best of my recollection.

The Colossus of Rhodes, which no longer stands, was of the Greek Titan Helios, one of the seven wonders of the ancient world. It fell in 654 ce to Arabian forces. It was eventually dismantled and the metal sold for scrap.

Many artist renditions depict it standing tall and mighty in the main harbor. Some paintings date back to the time it was in place. I invented the gold covering the fiery torch held by the god, although many pictures depicting the wonderous metal beast showed the torch having a goldish in tone.

I wasn't able to visit Scotland until after the first draft of my novel was completed, but I spent innumerable hours online researching each location I described. (Except for a tearoom, which I made up. Guess what, they're not on every corner!) I cried when I actually saw Dalkeith Castle standing tall and bleak before me. I walked around the building and viewed the library, remembering the funny things the women did, the students, the bad guys, and Aubrey—let's not forget him!

I have done extensive study on the lives of Scottish lords and ladies, thus the descriptions of their connections to the Knights Templar in the book, and so many other tiny details, are accurate.

I've spent months researching the blockade of Rhodes by Suleiman the Magnificent, and mafia activity in New York City. Can you guess doing so might have been the most fun?

Chapter One

The Odyssey Begins

Some echoes are magical, soft and distant. Some are haunting, a cry in a shadowy forest. In this case, the echo reverberating in Dr. Katina Bason's head was as pleasant as a braying donkey.

"You need to get your life in order. Publish. Soon." The strident voice of Professor Cara "The Terror" Crenshaw, chair of Medieval Studies at Emory University, warned Katina after a traumatic end-of-year review.

The Terror thrust a bony finger in her face. "Your career is drying up like the last moldy grape in the bottom of my fridge. You're going to get cut from the staff soon, girly."

If Katina hadn't been dumbfounded by the unexpected attack on her career, she might have snapped that finger in two.

Moldy grape. I'm thirty years old. Not a gray hair anywhere.

She paced in front of the lead glass windows of her home, checking the bottom of her braid for signs of a traitor. Her hands shook with anger at a system that didn't value a teacher's ability to make the people, places, triumphs, and tragedies of medieval history come alive.

Through her living room window, Katina expected to see her father's antique Aston Martin career down the boulevard at any moment. All was still, except for three squirrels that skittered up a magnolia tree in front of the Butler-Tate mansion next door. They had as much nervous energy as she did.

She left her post and sat on the chaise longue upholstered in a yellow, oriental silk brocade. Her father's imminent gift thrilled her. She would soon hold a diary full of wonder and woe from the land of her people, the Greek island of Rhodes. It described the famous 1522 blockade by none other than Sulieman the Magnificent.

You need to get your life in order. Publish.

Katina gritted her teeth as echoes of that acid-filled voice interrupted her thoughts. Although, she had to admit the evil woman lit a fire under her that singed her drawers.

Well, Cara, I'll do just that.

Summer had finally come. The next few weeks would include travel and in-depth research. Her plan to attack the world of royalty was masterful and bound for success. *I hope.* She walked to her powder room off the foyer and inspected her reflection in the mirror. Why her father compared her to the goddess Hera, she didn't know. *Ridiculous. I will never be like her. I don't even want to.*

Katina continued to grouse as she checked the hint of blush across her cheekbones. She pooched her too-full lips and dabbed off some of the pale, coral lipstick. The smidge of mascara over her blue-green eyes was adequate. No flakes. No smudges. *Good enough in my book.*

A crack of an engine as it backfired announced the arrival of her dad. She smoothed the pleats of her simple, white silk dress.

Her father yelled as he opened the door, "Hello, daughter. Your loving papa is here."

The announcement made Katina smile despite all the aggravations troubling her. That brilliant, demanding man was notoriously silly.

"I brought your present," he called. "I thought you'd meet me at the door with your hands ready."

Her spirit lifted as she entered the foyer. "It's about time." Her smile turned to laughter.

There he stood, the famous Dr. Peter Papamissios, as Atlanta's scorching July sunbeams outlined his body in the arched doorway. He wore a purple and gold turban tipped at a jaunty angle. His short physique was enveloped in a gold brocade robe, tied at the waist with a droopy, purple sash. He completed his outfit with pointy-toed slippers with tassels on their tips. He looked around as if he owned all that surrounded him: her inlaid marble floors and the classic landscapes that hung on her walls.

"What have you gotten into now?" she asked.

With a wily laugh he threw his shoulders back, balled hands on hips, and announced in his heavy Greek accent, "I am a sultan! Where is my harem? I can afford forty wives, and I'm feeling randy!"

Peter's remarkable imagination could spin a story out ten minutes longer than any normal adult could tolerate.

She played along. "They ran away. I was outnumbered. Couldn't hold 'em back."

"You are a funny one." He eyed her in a nonchalant perusal.

Katina's humor melted like butter on a hot skillet. Though his scrutiny was more of a habit brought forward from her childhood, so too were her dread and avoidance of it. She recognized her fruitless irritation and his inability to change. He was a typical Greek man in this one regard. They judged their daughter's perfection.

Peter, unaware of her turmoil, bent to pet Pippen, the smallest and most persistent of her two Pomeranians. "You are as silly as I am, little doggie. I will bring you back a tiny turban another time. Okay?"

"Speaking of which, where'd you get that?" Katina indicated his outlandish outfit with a wiggle of her index finger. "It's awesome. I want one."

"A yard sale at the Pearson's. His wife always gets rid of his good stuff while he travels." In a conspiratorial tone, he went on, "As I was paying for this marvelous robe, a man tried to take my case." He nodded toward his old, leather briefcase by the door. "He apologized, then said he thought it belonged to him. You cannot trust anyone anymore, daughter."

"Not one of my strong suits anyway, Dad. So?" Katina patted his robe where pockets might have been. "Where's my present? You promised it would change my life, for goodness sake."

"You are such a child sometimes, but I understand your excitement. It is not misplaced." He pulled a plastic bag, containing a paper-wrapped package, out of his case. He laid it on Katina's outstretched hands. "This has much that is worthy of publishing. You will make associate professor soon. I promise."

"I'd better."

Her heart fell like heavy raindrops out of a black cloud as another emotional storm approached. The diary within the bag was too light— heavier was better. The odds of finding something good increased if there were more pages. More content. Her disappointment eased as she remembered that a single sentence in an innocuous document had changed the lives of many historians. The thrill of discovery was what she craved. That and what it would bring.

"You hold a small treasure. Why does my flower seem so droopy now?"

Rats. Nothing escapes that man. Usually guarded, she gave in to the need for comfort that only her father could give, when he was in a paternal mood. "I've had some serious issues at Emory. Even though I received my PhD summa cum laude, I doubt myself. Maybe, enrollment in my classes isn't as good as it should be."

She cast her gaze to the floor, afraid her eyes might reveal the depth of her distress. "I'm surrounded by success. You. My best friend, Celeste, made associate professor at NYU *last year*. We're the same age."

He chuckled. "Not keeping up, *koukla*?"

Even though he used the Greek term of endearment, doll, it didn't lessen the skillful jab he'd delivered.

"Daddy be nice. I shouldn't have said anything." Katina shot him a pointed glance, then opened the seal of the bag and removed its contents as she entered the living room. "Let me examine this in peace."

He followed her into the room's cool confines. He snickered, picked up a saggy-bosomed Nairobi fertility statue and held it out for her to take. "Rub this."

"Stop it," she scolded. "Sit with me and behave."

Making a tsk-tsk sound of parents everywhere, he returned the statue to its position among other object d'art he'd given her over the years. He joined her on the couch facing the marble fireplace fit for a small castle. "Grandchildren will bring new light into my otherwise dreary life."

"Said the man who just came back from a dig in Egypt that was attacked and ransacked."

She got a pair of ultra-thin latex gloves from the end table and peeled back the small diary's protective cloth wrapper. She inspected the rough leather cover as she half-listened to her dad telling her, again, how he'd gotten it from his brother's out-building on Rhodes. That story would become a favorite. One he'd tell everyone he knew or would meet.

She sniffed its musty odor.

"Your very-distant relative, Katha Papamissios wrote it." He continued with the familiar story of the famous Ottoman sultan and the Palace of the Grand Master.

As Katina inspected the thin strips of leather that bound the diary, his words were lost.

"So. I'm out of touch. Is Jim still in the Dominican Republic? He's doing a superb job researching Christopher Columbus's involvement with the Taino people. Not a well-known subject with the North Americans, you know."

Yes, she knew. Her husband was a genius. Emory snapped him up for their archaeology department as soon as he completed his dissertation. No one was surprised that he made full professor by the time he was thirty-two. Some people even believed he could carbon date a piece of charcoal by tapping on it. Not true. Not true.

Katina said, "He sure loves it. He came back three weeks ago and left two days later to look for dinosaur bones. He should have been home yesterday."

"Little boys like dinosaur stories. I didn't know this hobby took up so much of his summer." His frown matched the one she tried to hide.

Failing to hold her emotions in, she blurted, "Me neither."

She blamed her surprise on their short courtship, just a few months, but Jim was brilliant and funny, six-foot four, sandy-haired, and had a jaw that'd make a Marine jealous. He'd knocked down her protective barriers like Suleiman did to the stone walls of the fortress around the Old Town of Rhodes. He was kind and serious, but best of all, he was thoroughly entertained by her foibles.

Katina said, "Thought I'd see him by now, but I leave in a half hour or so. I'm visiting Celeste in New York."

"Well, if he's like me, he will turn up sooner or later with a grand story."

"That's true but, I was on the phone with him a few days ago. The connection was bad. I said, 'You have to get back or I'm...'" She bowed her head and shook it. "I was yelling so he could hear me better. I needed to tell him that Lexi was still here on summer break and would watch the dogs until he got back. Then the connection dropped. I haven't been able to reach him since."

His aqua-blue eyes, so like her own, were sympathetic, so she continued to confess her worries. "The last thing he heard was me yelling that he had to get back or I would do something. He thinks we're in a fight, I bet."

"Stay here and be a good wife then."

Ha! So much for sympathy. I should have known. "I would, but I lost that book you gave me, so no."

Peter cocked a brow. "What book?"

"The one titled, *You Too Can Look Elegant While Cooking and Cleaning.* Published in 1950, by Just Kill Me Now Press, Inc."

"Okay, daughter, I get your drift, as they say. Tell me you and Celeste will not sneak into the English nunnery again." He growled, "You'll embarrass the Papamissios name if you get arrested."

Katina took in his outfit. "Really," her tone dripped with the sarcasm that women raised below the Mason-Dixon Line have mastered—three syllables instead of two. "No promises, but if I do get arrested, I'll keep it between me and the nuns—"

Mister Perfect straightened his tassels, then gave a grin of acknowledgement.

"Celeste and I found a manuscript," Katina said. "We'll search the archives of the New York City Library to find some corroborative Templar documents."

"You thought that trip would give you something so fantastic the department would have to promote you, correct?"

"Yes, I did. That manuscript was written by a French Templar Knight in the 1400s. It documented the existence of icons that disappeared from the island of Rhodes. Definitely goosebump-worthy, in my book, but—"

"But you were mature enough not to tell the panel what you only *might* have. Correct?"

Wow, during the interview with the most judgmental people I'd met in years, I felt infuriatingly inept and impotent. I couldn't stand up for myself. He thinks I was being mature.

She avoided the truth. "The fact remains that there was no corroborating documentation. Yet."

"The diary is better." Peter checked his watch, quickly rose and rearranged the flow of his robe. "I guarantee it. It talks about a golden cross and something even more spectacular for you, personally. I shall let you discover what that is as you read it." He kissed the top of her head. "Your beautiful mother is expecting me. I spent too much time shopping at the yard sale."

He started for the door. "I translated the diary. I suspect you haven't used Meta-Byzantine Greek in a while. Do you want me to bring it in from the car?"

"No thanks. I'll have way more fun working through it."

The focus of his eyes seemed distant; his mind was already onto another adventure. He gave a back-handed wave of farewell. "All right my darling rosebud, I'm off then. Enjoy your new adventure."

Katina turned her attention to the first page of the diary and called out, "Love you…" She sighed at the sudden silence in the room and shook off a chill. His presence was powerful. His absence was too. She pushed aside her unexpected loneliness and became engrossed in the words in front of her. The language of that period came back to her like muffled voices behind an old, heavy door as she struggled through the first few lines.

Her three-year old rescue dog, Sadie, jumped on the couch and nuzzled under Katina's hand. She caressed the tan, plane of fur where an eye once had been. Soft as silk.

Sadie looked back with her remaining brown eye in adoration. Pippen, the five-pound black and white pest, soon joined them, and together, they sat scrunched on one cushion. As three dark dog eyes observed Katina's every move, she translated the first page. The wording was distinctive, formal, and sometimes complicated. Over a decade of practice allowed her mind the smooth shift from the dated dialect to more of a 21st century approximation.

> *My name is Katha Papamissios. I am 19 years of age and live on the magnificent Island of Rhodes. The year is 1522.*

I will write of my harrowing days and my troubles caused by one powerful man of great dishonor. He calls himself the tenth Sultan of the Ottoman Khans, son of Sultan Suleiman Khan, Sultan of the Ottoman Empire. He was determined to conquer all that the brilliance of the knights have built. Our shores have been blockaded. Starvation has begun in earnest. The living are surrounded by death.

Katina was thoroughly rooted in the sixteenth century as Katha's tale unfolded.

...One was most important and most secret.

I must say that I was loved by our knights, whom I loved dearly in return. This will help to explain why I had the special knowledge of this area in the palace.

I had been taken there when I was but a precocious child, by the Knight Pierre Longuestress. He was very old and trusted by the Grand Master himself. He had often sworn me to secrecy about the treasure. I laughed each time at his silliness for his treasures were the rooms full of honey wine, stores of grain, and tins of spices.

However, to my great surprise, real treasure, there was. One day, Sir Pierre took me to the wine room and pushed down on a corner stone. A two-meter area of the floor lifted. I was shocked beyond comprehension at the massive counter-balanced hinges and a staircase that led into darkness. He lit a torch on the wall and his eyes held infinite pleasure as he took my hand and led me down the stairs.

Beautiful icons, Catholic and Orthodox, lined the walls of the room we entered. Sir Pierre pointed out the Orthodox paintings, but I could easily tell the difference from the others. Ours had dull tones and the figures had indistinct, narrow faces. Only a mere suggestion of the Saints they represented. He said the knights found them many years prior.

Sir Pierre has hidden them so they may remain safe from the Ottomans who indeed for centuries have yet again been attempting to gain control of this island, as I have previously mentioned to emphasize the importance of the fact.

I thought the icons were the only treasure. I was much surprised by my error because he handed me a golden cross, heavy, and bright of color. He told me that he was dying and I, the Daughter of the Ancients, was to take custody of this cross, the Holy Treasure of Rhodes and the painting of St. Paul. I must return them to the...

Katina struggled to translate the next word, "remains ... remnants ..., the remnants of Saint George church and the people of Rhodes." She searched her memory. *The remnants of the underground Orthodox church of Saint George, built in the 1300s. The Knights of Saint John built the Monastery of Panagia Filerimos on top of it in the 1500s.* "That must be the place.

"That I, as the Daughter of the Ancients, would know when the time was right. I worry that Sir Pierre has too much trust in me. How am I to know when I should do this?"

Katina sat up straight and stopped reading aloud to let the discovery sink in. "This is it. I can't believe it." Her puppies cocked their heads, as if asking for clarification. She told them, "The reference to the antiquities I found in the Templar manuscripts must have been *these* Catholic icons. The gold cross and these icons are in the same room!" She showed Pippen the page. "Is the cross the Treasure of Rhodes or is there something else?"

Pippen's ears perked up, and she tilted her head almost sideways.

"What? You don't know either?" Wonder still muddled her thoughts as she read:

On the morrow, I was summoned to Sir Pierre's chamber. All other goodly knights and dearest friends had been asked to leave him. The room smelled sour. I was beset with fear. My stomach sickened when I saw my favorite friend and teacher ensconced in bedsheets under which he shivered fretfully.

My brave knight smiled and handed me the key to the hidden room with a weak and shaking hand. He showed me an inscription of an owl. In addition, there were letters and numbers on one side. He whispered that they were to remind me of the treasures' location.

I studied the owl on the key. I understood then. There was indeed a medallion of an owl carved into the floor on the way to the secret chamber. My mind became bright with flashes as I pictured the way we walked there and understood the meaning of those letters and numbers.

I scoffed at the need for the hints and told him that the palace was not that large, and truly I would never forget the way. There would be no reason to doubt such an important matter. He said that I may not, but there might be another. This girl would not know the way to the room.

What girl was this? Is she of the village? If not, how would anyone know to trust her?

I was desperate to know though why I was not told of this before. He became so weak he labored just to breathe, so I kissed him a last goodbye and cried. I left the chamber feeling as if I were a mere child, for my mind was filled with trepidation, willing itself to reject my new responsibility.

Hours passed as slowly as candle melting in a closed room with no wind to hurry its extinguishing. I finally accepted the enormity and inevitability of his words and last wishes. Then I was assailed with yet another confounding thought. When would my new purpose be fulfilled?

Katina laid the diary on the end table. She'd spent years researching the Knights Templar and the Orders of Knights. *Good Lord. If the information in the diary is true, I will have something inordinately good enough for a book, even if I never find the icons or the cross themselves. God, please let there be actual evidence in the archives to back this up.*

She stood and paced to ease the tension. She checked her watch. *Almost time to go to the airport.* She walked to the sun-drenched solarium next to the living room and kitchen to calm her nerves and think about Katha's words before she had to leave. Marble planters, overflowing with blooms in shades of reds, yellows and lavender, filled the spaces between the comfortable furniture. Stained glass transom panels, patterned with hummingbirds in flight, diffused the light streaming in above the large windows. The cooled air was alive with molecules of color.

Unlike the formality of the living room, this room contained items of Katina's second passion, puzzles. They required a love of discovery and a good dose of deductive skills. A square table tucked against the corner had a 5000-piece puzzle scattered on top. The pieces were turned picture-side down; only the shapes of pale gray pieces would guide her.

Katina had just started sorting its edges when Alexa walked into the room. Lexi was a beauty. She was five-feet ten-inches tall and had the same mahogany colored hair as Katina's. Lexi was her some-time dog-sitter and the daughter of her cousin, but they thought of each other as aunt, *thea*, and niece, *anepsia*.

That morning, Lexi oozed attitude. The nineteen-year old Vassar student dropped onto the crimson chair and crossed her arms. She flopped a pair of clunky Doc Martens onto a footstool. The dogs leapt on her legs, attempting to get into her lap. She patted their heads. "Simmer down. They can hear you in Alabama."

Katina said, "Fantastic. You're here. I needed to talk to you." She became wary of the palpable silence emanating like a sonic boom from the teenager. "Um…Good morning, darlin'. Have you eaten yet?"

"It's nine frickin' thirty in the morning." She yawned. "My stomach doesn't wake up until noon."

"I'll get you some coffee." Katina told Lexi about the diary while in the kitchen. On the way back, she recounted the short version of the Templar document and her trip. She placed the tray of coffee and muffins on the table. "Here you go, sweetie. Thanks for coming. I don't know when Jim will be back, and I can't find out. His phone is going straight to voicemail."

Lexi lifted the mug to her lips and took a sample sip. "He's in the Dakotas, right? I think he's in a dead zone. The coverage out there is ridiculous. But hey, there's only about a hundred people living in those states, so the cell company probably doesn't care."

Katina gazed at the 200-year-old oaks in her backyard. *Well, she's right about one thing: the coverage is terrible. But, a hundred people? Apparently, being a computer whiz and knowing anything about geography are mutually exclusive.*

"I wouldn't worry if I was you. I bet Uncle Jim'll get into town tomorrow."

Katina tried on a winning smile and held out the instructions. "Thanks again for stepping in. I'll bring you back a little sumpin' sumpin' from my trip."

Lexi put the mug down and took the paper. "Rappers haven't said that in years." She read the first of three pages. "Good grief. They're just furballs. All you have to do is throw some fancy food in a bowl every now and then and follow 'em around with a lint brush."

"You're awesome, blossom." She checked her watch again. "I've gotta go now. The car service should be out front."

Lexi followed her to the kitchen and grabbed Katina's phone from the counter. "What's your password?"

That smarty-pants rarely did anything without a good reason, but that reason might not reveal itself until months later. "Why?"

"I want to make sure it's charged."

Katina doubted her altruism, but what harm could Lexi do? "My babies love me. All in lower case."

Lexi continued to slide her index finger across the phone's screen, typed with two thumbs, then tapped some more.

"Give me my phone if you're done hacking it. I hear the car horn. Can you hold the babies? I don't want them running out to the driveway after me." She hurried to the front door and grabbed her suitcase and hand luggage on the way. She yelled, "Thank you. You're the best almost-niece anyone can have."

"I only work for the good of humanity."

A nice thought, but Lexi sounded like Dr. Evil when she'd said it.

~ * ~

An hour and a half later, Katina sat in her favorite spot on the plane, seat 2A. She surrounded herself with a paisley cashmere wrap to ward off a chill from the overly air-conditioned cabin and sipped a mimosa.

Through the plane's window, Earth's vast horizon could have been a perfect metaphor for the array of possibilities that awaited her. However, she put them aside because her heart was a little broken.

Jim? What are you thinking, sweetheart? She held her breath for a few moments, but as expected, there was no answer.

What she heard was a man's voice with a New York accent ask

a busy flight attendant, "Stewardess. When can I get some food here? It's been a long day."

She'd seen him eat barbeque and French fries just before they boarded the plane. When he passed, he still had the ketchup-stained paper napkin hanging out of his soiled shirt. He needed clean clothes— she wrinkled her super-sensitive nose—and a bath.

She whispered, "That wasn't nice, Katina. Shame on you," and removed the diary and a fresh pair of latex gloves from her purse.

> *Today is July 17. It has been many days since Sir Pierre died. I still have no sign that I must act on his wishes. I watched Papa and three men bury my friend Nelly. I cried all night. I, within my deepest regretful heart, confessed to my father that I desired the eyes of my enemies, for I would hold them aloft and call, 'Regard what you have done to the righteous.'*
>
> *Papa said I was a young woman and should control my anger. Death will come to us all, he said. His mind must be breaking from burying people, for he should be as filled with anguish as I am.*

The view of the earth and clouds that moved deceptively slowly under the plane's wing, despite traveling at hundreds of miles per hour, was peaceful. People in the United States, all over the world really, die as if under siege by drug dealers and gangs. The need for power never diminishes. *Katha made an important point. How much can someone experience without losing their sanity?* Katina shook her head in sorrowful wonder over times past and present, then continued to read the horrific experiences of the sad, young woman.

~ * ~

The time flew by as fast as the plane itself. Before she knew it, her ears popped as the plane descended. She returned the diary to the protective bag and slid it into her purse. A few minutes later, something tickled her ankle. "Holy crap. What was that?"

She pitched forward to investigate the unwanted touch, but the seatbelt only gave a few inches. Her purse spilled its contents around her feet. She silently cursed the mess while unlatching her seatbelt and bending to see what the heck was happening down there.

Hairy fingers wiggled around, touching the filthy floor, searching for something. She sat up, twisted around, and gave the hunched back of stained-shirt-man her most hateful glare. "What are you doing? You scared the pants off me."

"You ain't wearin' no pants," stained-shirt-man said in a low, gravelly voice.

"What?"

He looked at her nonchalantly. "I said, you ain't wearin' no *pants.*" His New York accent was as thick as the grease in his hair. "I didn't grab you or nothin'. Just lookin' for my pen."

"Oh. Okay." She noticed the stares of the other passengers and waved at everyone. "It's fine. Nothing happened here." She picked up her lipstick and sunglasses and shoved them into her purse with a hot face of an embarrassed over-reactor.

The plane screeched and thudded across the tarmac. After the final lurch of the brakes, Katina shot to her feet and retrieved her carryon bag from the overhead compartment. Her excitement grew. The next segment of her research project was about to begin, and she couldn't wait to tell Celeste about the diary.

Katina clutched her purse to her chest and started to leave. She took one step up the aisle and stopped dead. "Oh my God—"

She knelt and searched under the seat that was in front of hers. With a groan of relief, she retrieved the diary and put it and a few more errant things into the side pocket of the carryon. She chastised herself for the careless treatment of the priceless document as she exited the plane, then berated herself the entire way to the luggage carousel.

As she turned the corner, anxiety turned to joy. "Celeste."

Celeste Daly stood out in any crowd, even though she was barely above five feet tall. Her father was American-Irish, but her beauty was that of Nefertiti, complete with pupils in shades of amber from her Egyptian mother. She down-played her 14th century look-alike by wearing designer clothes. That day she wore a pink Prada suit she'd gotten secondhand a few years before.

Katina liked their mix-matched friendship. It spoke to her love of puzzles—odd pieces that combined to make a complete picture of interesting possibilities. Their need for balance and wholeness was strong. They found it in each other.

"I've missed your face," Katina said, kissing each of Celeste's cheeks.

"Tina. I've missed your face," her best friend looked at Katina's feet, "and your tennis shoes too." Celeste grabbed Katina's hand and all but dragged her to the edge of the gathering passengers. "Your luggage'll take forever, so sit with me. I'm pooped. The traffic was ridiculous."

She joined Celeste on a hard-backed chair and glared at stained-shirt-man who invaded their space. New Yorkers either ignored each other or got in their business like he was doing.

The man cleared his throat. "Excuse me. I just wanted to say I'm sorry I scared you."

"Forget about it," Katina replied, using a mafioso pronunciation for her own amusement.

He nodded and turned his back but didn't walk away.

Celeste leaned in and murmured in her half-way-refined New Jersey accent, "As you know, Jonathan Ridgewald allowed me into the archives a few times over the last month. I was able to find a few promising manuscripts." Her voice rose as she said, "This search reminded me of our trip to England. Remember when we sneaked into the archives of St. Mary's?"

Her friend's exuberance made her heart happy. "Of course, I remember. My father brought that semi-disaster up earlier today."

"We are very, very wicked sometimes, but I love that about us."

"Me too." Katina sighed with sweet happiness as she stood and moved toward the luggage being disgorged in rhythmic clunks onto the carousel. She lowered her voice as she said, "My father gave me an old diary this morning." She wiggled her brows at Celeste as she pulled her suitcase off the belt. "It's incredible."

"Fantastic. Is it in English or Greek? Shoot. It could be in French or German too."

Katina noticed stained-shirt-man again. He followed them out but seemed too intent on finding his ride. "Greek. My dad wrote a translation, but he left it in his car. Anyway, I'll give you the gist of what I read so far later. You'll be amazed."

Chapter Two

Accidents, Heroes, and George Clooney

Katina was afraid of a few things: knives, spiders, Celeste's driving, and other near-death experiences. While they traveled on the Van Wyck Expressway from JFK into Manhattan, Celeste weaved from one lane to another as she tried to get into the city before the traffic got even worse. Blaring horns set her nerves on edge. "You know…we don't blow our horns in the south."

Celeste said, "What're you talking about? People honk in Atlanta."

Her fingernails dug even deeper into the leather passenger seat of the old Mercedes. "Yes, well, did you see an accident almost happen when you heard a horn?"

"I guess so. Why?"

"Horns are a warning of impending disaster, not an announcement of 'get the hell out of the way.' Stop honking." She tore her gaze from the insane traffic ahead. Celeste bobbed her head to the uneven tempo and melodic dissonances of the jazz that played on the stereo, as if she were at a club in the Village. When Maria Andretti wasn't yelling at the cars, she controlled her vehicle with a cool and calculated expertise. "Is the radio playing Felonious Monk?"

"This, girlfriend, is *Thelonious* Monk's "Straight, No Chaser." You can turn it down if you want. In fact, do that then tell me about the diary. It'll take your mind off the honking."

Katina grimaced. "That's impossible. Can I find a different station? I need something soothing or I'm gonna get a headache." Without waiting for approval, she turned the knob. The squawk of the channel search filled the car with the happy beats of Latin music, rap's staccato pulse, then gospel. She settled on the dulcet tones of a classical symphony.

"Ahh… This is nice. Vivaldi's Four Seasons, with Bela Banfalvi conducting." For a few minutes, Katina closed her eyes and moved her fingers, pantomiming the conductor, as the music filled the car's interior. "I feel better now. Sorry. I'm a terrible passenger. Anyway, what's new with you? How's your good-looking brother?"

"Bobby?"

"Um… do you have another good-looking brother I don't know about?"

They were well into Manhattan and a few minutes away from their lunch destination. Celeste's car inched ahead at the pace of a crippled caterpillar. "Of course not." She checked her rearview and side mirrors as if she were going to make a break for freedom. She'd have to hit some hidden button that turned the car into a helicopter because no one moved more than an inch at a time. "He's fine, I guess. I saw him last Friday. We had a family dinner at Buvette's. Yummy, yummy, yummy. I had the Coq au Vin."

"You always were a sucker for a good Coq."

Celeste did a double take. "You say the most shocking things, my friend. Remind me again what boarding school you went to?"

"The same one you did, darlin'."

Celeste gave a knowing smile and turned her attention back to the stop-and-go snarl. "He pulled the double homicide at the Met. He'll be working a lot of overtime with this one. Mayor de Blasio is—"

"Oh—" Katina moaned.

"What's wrong?"

"I don't know." Katina rubbed her temples, but the gentle motion did little to ease the pain.

"Poor thing, we're almost there. Do you want me to pull over or can you make it to the restaurant?"

"No, it's not a migraine. I'm not going to be sick, for goodness' sake."

"What is it then?"

She shook her head to clear the cobwebs. "Do you ever get weird feelings? I think it's my Dad. Something's happened. I'm gonna call him."

As Katina reached for her purse on the floor, the car lurched as if hit from behind and she was thrown forward. In a split second, she hit her forehead on the glove compartment and was tossed back by the airbag. She cried out, coughed, then used her hands and forearms to push the rumpled bag back and flatten it against the car's dash. She wiped a powdery substance off her mouth. Her face was hot and sore. "What the hell happened?"

Celeste rubbed the area where the seatbelt had grabbed her and regarded Katina. "I haven't seen an airbag deploy in person before. Wicked." She brushed some hair off Katina's face, then looked over her shoulder. "Some jerk just rear-ended me."

"Your airbag didn't work. Are you okay?"

"Yeah. I de-activated it. I'm too short." Celeste twisted in her seat to get a better view of the car in back. Her eyes became angry slits. "Can you believe it?" She turned to Katina and gasped. "Oh man. I'm sorry. Your forehead's bleeding."

"I'm okay, I guess. You're relatively fine." Her perusal was interrupted by pounding on her side window. Startled and confused, she tried to figure out why George Clooney stood by the car door and caused such a racket.

She said, "George?"

"You need to get out," came his muffled words.

After she opened the door, he reached in to unbuckle her seat belt. He took her hand and pulled her out of the car. With little grace, he navigated her to the sidewalk.

All she could think was, *Movie stars always have great hair. He's handing me his handkerchief. Who has those anymore? What am I supposed to do with it? I can't blow my nose, for heaven's sake.*

"Miss." He thrust the handkerchief into her hand. "Here. Put it on your cut."

Look how his lips move and his eyes crinkle when he talks. She was fascinated by the subtle dimple on the right side of his face. Her gaze traveled to his lips again, too shapely for a man. *They're perfect above that chin groove.* She wanted to put the very tip of her finger in it. She stopped her hand just in time. That small movement caused the handkerchief to slip over her eyes. When she put it back into place, he was gone. Well, not gone, but taking lengthy strides away.

She waved the makeshift bandage and sang out, "George... you forgot your hanky. Yoo-hoo..." She gave it one more wave for good measure then turned toward the scene of the crime. Celeste stood behind the car risking life and limb to inspect the damage. "Get your heinie *back* in your damn car or over here. You've lost your mind. There might be a chain reaction and you'll be smoosh—"

"Do you see what that jackass did to my car?" Pointing to the small green sedan that had rear-ended them, Celeste yelled, "And on top of that, the idiot got out of his car and started screaming at *me*." Pacing back and forth safely next to Katina, she groused, "He's the one that caused the accident." She gave the green car the finger.

Katina stifled a laugh, then a groan. "Well, where *is* the jackass-idiot?"

"Oh my God, he's gone." She scanned the street. "He was going to get his information. His friend was checking on you." She threw her arms up in pure, unadulterated frustration. "Are you *shitting* me?"

"You gonna call the police? Did you see George?"

Celeste took stock of the grim and noisy situation. People cursed and fists waved out of almost every car window like angry flags. She marched to the driver's side door. "Forget about stupid George. Let's go. Everyone's ballistic because I'm blocking traffic. I got the plate number."

"You might be dead meat if your brother finds out you left the scene of an accident." Katina scanned the sidewalk ahead. "That nice man took such good care of me. I've never had a man give—"

"Tina. No one was seriously hurt. Get in the damn car. You can tell me all about your hero after we get out of here."

Katina cleaned some of the debris off the seat, then slid in. "Yeesh. He should have honked his horn."

"Yeah. That would've solved everything." Celeste started the car. "Your forehead stopped bleeding. It's just a scratch."

Katina checked her reflection in the mirror and gently explored the area of the cut. "If I have to hire a plastic surgeon, I'm gonna sue."

"You're okay, toots. We can go back to my apartment now and clean up, eat there, then go over to the archives. Or, we can go straight to the restaurant."

"I'm good. I'll just re-braid my hair. Let's go on. I'll tell you more about the diary while we eat. That'll turn this chicken egg day into a custard pie."

~ * ~

Celeste pulled into the valet parking section of Crème de la Crème. The red and white uniformed attendant ran over and opened Celeste's door. "Ms. Daly, it's wonderful to have you back. Let me help you," he said. "Ma'am, your interior's a mess."

"Yeah, thanks," she said as she took his offered hand. "We're ignoring it for now."

"My purse isn't here, Celeste. Check the rear for me, will you? Maybe it flew back there during the crash."

Celeste searched the car floor closest to her. Jon ran around to the other side. Katina exited rear-end first and checked under her seat. In a muffled voice, she asked, "Is it back there?"

Celeste conferred with Jon, but he shrugged a negative. "No. It's not."

"Damn it to hell. Everything I need is in that purse."

"I'm sorry about that, ma'am," Jon said. "Could it have fallen out during the accident?"

Katina tilted her head back and closed her eyes. "Let me think... Well, when that man helped me out of the car, I was pretty scared and a bit disoriented after the crash, so, I probably wouldn't have noticed if it fell out." The blood drained from her face. "O. M. for the love of G. Do you have your purse? Maybe the guy that hit you was a scammer. They slam into people and steal p-purses and computers or claim neck injuries."

"I have mine, see?" Celeste said. "Calm down. It'll be okay."

"How am I going to get on the plane now?" Katina said, wringing her hands. "My passport's gone, my wallet and driver's license, my phone, everything. Oh. My. God. The diary was in there too. I'm such a complete idiot."

Celeste took it back—losing all that was a big problem. "You're not an idiot, one. And two, we can work this out. We'll go to the library and do some shopping on this trip. We can rearrange our schedule and go to Rhodes some other time."

"Summer's almost over and I've been put on notice to publish or I'll lose my job. So, no. I need to search for that manuscript in the archives and go on to Rhodes this weekend. It can't wait, damn it."

This was a side of her personality Celeste hadn't witnessed often. Sure, Katina was feisty, but this? *That girl found some chips for her dip.*

A melody drifted from the trunk. Muffled notes of the *1812 Overture.* Katina said, "Oh my God. I'm a genius. My stuff's in the carryon. Thank you, Lord."

Celeste opened the lock and unlatched the trunk lid.

Katina pushed it up and dragged her bag out. "I got it. Hold on." She unzipped the top while doing a happy dance in celebration. "For once, I'm glad I'm clumsy. I dropped this stuff on the plane." She waved the diary in one hand and showed the contents of her other hand—the wallet, phone and passport— like a child showing off her candy at Halloween, then stowed everything but her phone back in the bag. She swiped the screen just as the music stopped. "Rats. It was my father. I should call him back, but I need a drink and lunch. I'm starving." She gave a huge Julia Roberts smile. "Let's eat."

Celeste tossed Jon the keys, and Katina started an excited babble about the archive search as they entered the building. For a southern girl, she could talk as fast as a New Yorker.

"Did you remember to bring—" Celeste's cell phone blared a jazzy tune. She pulled it out of her purse and held up a finger to quiet Katina. "Yes?"

"Good afternoon. This is Jonathan Ridgewald."

"Hello," Celeste said. "We should be there in an hour."

"That's why I'm calling. I'm afraid I must go home. A bug or something. The staff is in a meeting and won't be able to help you. Can we reschedule for tomorrow?"

"We can absolutely come tomorrow but…" Celeste gave Katina a this-isn't-good-news look.

Katina gave a try-harder look back. She even pointed a demanding finger.

Celeste mouthed, "I *am* trying," then said, "Are you sure no one will be available later today?"

"Well." Ridgewald paused. "I should be in tomorrow. Let's meet then, shall we?"

There was no arguing. He was the gatekeeper at the archives. "Sure thing. Hope you feel better." She rang off and cringed at the frustrated set of her friend's mouth. "I guess you heard. Tomorrow morning. I'm so sorry."

Katina sighed. "The gods of discovery are making this a challenge. Drat."

"We can have a good afternoon anyway. I found a great secondhand shop last month. I know your mom buys you the new stuff, but you may find some goodies."

"My mother knows I'd rather wear sweatpants, but okay, I'll go. We'll devote the evening to the diary."

Celeste cheered and added, "And drinking wine."

Chapter Three

Behind-The-Scenes Bad Guys

Peter Papamissios did not walk away from his accident. What remained of his vehicle was being lifted by a Liberty wrecker. Though his head was bandaged, and his chest ached, he attempted to make a call from the ambulance gurney.

"I need to tell my daughter that her mother will meet me at the hospital and not to worry." His hand shook as he tried her number one more time. As it rang, he told the EMT, "I'm having trouble breathing."

"You took a beating. Steering wheel, I think. I'm going to hook you up to one more monitor. It'll track your oxygen level."

As the phone went to voicemail, he regarded his once-beautiful silver car. "It's a 1970 Aston Martin DBS V8 Muncher. It came in seventeenth in the 1974 Le Mans, you know. It has—had—modified cylinder heads and revised camshafts." He rubbed his chest and winced. "I'll miss that car. A present from my darling wife."

"It kept you pretty safe. Relax and keep your oxygen mask on. We're going to get you to the hospital."

~ * ~

Black clouds rolled across the Atlanta skyline. A man in a cop's uniform drove a black SUV with counterfeit cop decals on the side. He was in trouble. He called Robert, his *sometimes* boss. "Hey. I'm just gonna tell ya. You may want to fire me on the spot. The car went up in flames."

Robert fumed, "The hell you say?"

"Yeah. Sorry. We were in traffic and going pretty slow. I did a modified PIT maneuver to the back bumper of the Aston Martin. I never done it to a sports car before, so I gave it just a tap. Enough to get him to pull over, but the damn thing swerved and crashed into the median barrier. The guy wasn't killed. He was pretty shaky, so I called an ambulance. I took off when the other rescue vehicles showed up. It would have been too suspicious, ya know, if I just left."

Robert yelled, "What about the diary?"

The man took a moment to control his frustration. "The car and everything in it was destroyed by a fire. The fuel line musta cracked."

"Why didn't you get to the car before it went up?"

"Because flames were shootin' outa the bottom of it." The man shook his head. Robert was either desperate or just plain stupid. "I mean, it is what it is."

"Unbelievable. You'd better hope Joey had better luck."

The man said the only thing that was left to say. "Shit."

~ * ~

In a cheap motel room in Queens, Joey Biscotta, a part-time wise guy, rolled off the rumpled bed and walked to the rusty bathroom sink. His socks and the rug were grungy enough that they stuck together for a millisecond with each step. A loud rush of gas erupted inside his gray sweatpants.

Dalilah, his favorite red-headed hooker, rolled onto her stomach and looked in his direction. "Men make odd noises."

"You just finding this out?" Joey snarked.

He wore a stained shirt that stretched across his stomach. His gut filled half the sink as he brought his face close to the mirror. He inspected his nicotine stained teeth as he ran pudgy fingers down his cheek. "Hey, get outta here. I gotta make a few phone calls and it ain't gonna be nice."

Dalilah gave the grunt of an infirm person as she rolled over and off the bed in one motion. "It don't matter to me. Go 'head which your phone call. *I'm thirsty*. There a minibar in this place?"

"Does this place *look* like it got a minibar? Get your clothes and scram."

Dalilah picked up her black pleather leggings. "Ain't you sweet." As she pulled and wiggled into them, her pendulous boobs swung about wildly. "Joey, don't make me leave. It's hot outside, and I'm not gonna get anymore tricks. My place ain't got no air conditioning."

"I'm serious. *Please* get your crap and go." Joey attempted to be nice and polite. He went to the toilet and started to pee, not caring that the thin door remained open. Peering over his shoulder, he said, "Take an extra ten and get a cab. 'Cause I'm a nice guy, ya know? Crap. I pissed on the damn floor."

Dalilah said, "If your dick wasn't so short you wouldn't have that problem."

"What'd you say?"

"I said, no problem." Dalilah snatched up his wallet and took an extra twenty, then gathered the rest of her things. "Bye, asshole. I'll see you later."

"Hey, nice talk. Your drapes don't match your rug, lady." Joey grunted in satisfaction. "And your rug is gray." He laughed. "You owe me ten. I saw whatcha did there. I'll call ya tomorrow."

"Yeah. I'll be sittin' by the phone with weighted breath."

As the door slammed, he shrugged, not knowing what she meant. He'd delayed the inevitable long enough. He dialed and spoke with a toughness he hoped would hide his pansy-assed panic, "Boss, it's Joey."

The boss, Maxwell Blackmarr, was supposed to be a Harvard-educated man, but he had sketchy origins. Joey was told that he was known in the art world but not necessarily respected. None of that meant shit to him. What mattered was the money he'd get if he turned this thing around somehow.

Joey hated Maxwell's smooth, upper class New England accent.

"I should have heard from you two hours ago. I've been trying to call. Did you get it?"

He expected the question. The answer was gonna get him into some bad shit. "Umm... my phone got on silent somehow." As he paced, a pee-soaked sock made a sticky, wet noise every other step. "But to answer you direct, because I'm a direct kinda guy, uh... I didn't get it. Sorry."

"Let me state the obvious. You failed on the plane. You failed while she was getting her luggage. Now you say you failed in Manhattan?"

"Umm ...yes ... yes ... and sort of," Joey answered.

"What in the *hell* does that mean? Either you have it or you don't."

He started to sweat. "Well, you're right. I couldn't get it on the plane. She never left her seat, but I saw her put it in her purse when the plane was landing. I told you I couldn't get it at baggage claim because she and her friend must be lesbians or somethin'. Those skinny bitches were stuck together like a peanut butta sandwich."

"You have a disgusting way to describe things. Can't you just get to the point?" Maxwell demanded.

He looked around the room. "I did get the purse from the car." He tossed clothes and kicked a shoe clear across the room but couldn't find it. "The fuck?"

"Do you or do you *not* have the purse? What the hell is going on?"

"I *had* the purse, sir, but it's gone."

"What did you do with it? I am God-damned tired of asking all these questions."

"Boss, I guess the purse never had the diary thing *in* it." It dawned on him that he should've started with that.

"Where—is—the—diary?"

Joey jerked the cell phone from his ear and spoke into the bottom of it. "That I don't know, sir."

"Find it."

~ * ~

Maxwell Blackmarr paced his office, cell phone to his ear, and yelled at Robert. "He should have anticipated a fire. The goal was to get in the car, not save an old man. Joey screwed up, too."

"That's all true, but I got an update. They're going to Rhodes."

"You're good for one damn thing anyway—"

Maxwell dialed the number to the airline.

Gotta get there in time to salvage this or everything I've done so far will be a fucking waste of time and money.

Chapter Four

Katha's Pain, Katina's New Understanding

That evening, as the sun fell behind the tall buildings of Manhattan, Katina and Celeste sat close together on Celeste's loveseat, the only large chair that could fit in the apartment's tiny living room. The tall windows were shut against the heat of the summer night. Soft jazz played in the background, and white wine sat on the coffee table.

Katina was about to translate the diary again, but her muted phone buzzed on the couch's armrest. She picked it up, elated to see her dad's number. "Hi, Daddy. I've been trying to call. You've been busy."

"Good evening, *koukla*. Don't be concerned. Your old papa will get out of the hospital tomorrow morning."

"What are you talking about? Are you okay? Is Momma okay?" Katina's hands shook.

Celeste took Katina's outstretched hand and mouthed, "What's going on?"

Her father's jovial voice commanded, "It is all okay. Calm yourself. I am just fine. I have a few bumps and bruises. That's all. My poor baby didn't fare so well though. I—"

"What do you mean your baby didn't fare so well. You were in a car accident? Daddy, what happened?"

"Well, yes. Sometimes little accidents happen, even to the best drivers."

Katina pulled her hand from Celeste's and balled her fingers into a fist. She wanted to punch something because her dad was being so evasive. "Yes, but people in little accidents don't end up in a hospital."

"Very true, but it's okay. Your mother is here. I am sad about that. She wouldn't let a pretty nurse, named Sapphire, give me a sponge bath. Your momma never lets me have any fun."

"Stop being silly. What happened to the car? If you're in the hospital, it must have been totaled." The panic in her voice escalated with each word.

"That's the thing, daughter. It shouldn't have been. I was driving into the city, and a car hit me. A while later, my car blew up!"

"Blew up? Holy cow. Tell me everything that happened." Katina stood and paced the small room.

"I was on the side of the road. I watched the engine smoke, and I heard this muffled mmboosh sound. I can't describe it. The next thing you know, my car is burning. Not big flames, but it took a few minutes for the fire truck to get there. I shouldn't have ignored the backfiring, I guess. It needed a tune-up. It's either that or the fuel line ruptured. Listen, I'm okay. I promise. My ribs are bruised. It hurts a bit, but the medicine they give me makes me very happy."

"Oh, Daddy. This trip is jinxed, I swear." She walked to her bedroom and opened her suitcase. She almost burst into tears as she pictured her father: the turban askew, the robe dirty, her father crumpled inside the car. Her chin quivered when she pictured flames flickering around him. "Papa…," she sniffled, "I'm coming home tonight."

"No, no, no, Tina *mou*. Don't be upset. All is fine, I promise. Stay. Have fun. Exciting things are waiting for you— What's this you say about the trip? What happened? Are you okay? Is that why you didn't call me back?"

"Yes." She sat on the bed and controlled her fear. Her father did sound fine, until he sounded worried about her. Maybe she shouldn't have mentioned the stupid jinx; Greeks were ridiculously superstitious. "It's nothing."

"Let me decide what is nothing."

"Fine, but you'll see." She described her rear-end experience to him. "He wasn't George Clooney, of course, but—"

"*Koukla*, this George Mooney is not important. Are you okay?"

"Yes. Sorry. Just a cut on my forehead, and my purse was stolen."

He took a quick intake of breath. "Katina." He switched from English to ancient Greek and back. Code switching when necessary because things like cars weren't invented yet. "This worries me. We both had accidents."

He spoke quietly, "The translation was in the car, but the fire destroyed it. Now your purse seems to be stolen. You may think I am a silly man sometimes, but I work in a very competitive world. Some people are unscrupulous. Do you still have the diary?"

Katina answered, "*Nai*, yes, I have it."

"Use ancient Greek, daughter. No one must understand. I think you haven't read to the end of the diary yet, correct?"

"*Oxi*." Not as proficient as her father with the ancient version, Katina continued with a few stammers, "W-Why? What should I know?"

Peter said, "In the writings, Katha alludes to the treasure of ancient Rhodes. Remember I told you about that? People have been hurt, even murdered, with talk of these things. I do not exaggerate. This was to be an exciting quest for you, but I think people have hurt us trying to get the diary. Now I think that you should not go."

"Okay. That's freaking me out," she blurted in English again. "How would anyone know about any of this in the first place? All of the books, the different archives, the papers I read about the knights—everything was all so convoluted. On top of that, how would anyone know about the," she switched back to Greek, "diary, if that is what they are after?" Katina shook her head in disbelief.

He murmured something unintelligible and was quiet for a time. "I might have to agree with you. I could be wrong about the danger, but we should keep it in the forefront of our mind— Perhaps you should not cancel your trip altogether. But for the sake of your mother and me, please be careful."

"I will. I'm the least brave person I know." She sighed with relief, closed her suitcase, and placed it in the closet. "Is Momma there?"

"No, she's getting another cup of terrible coffee and hounding a nurse, I am sure. I will have her call you later."

Still torn, Katina considered getting the case out again. "Are you sure? We can reschedule—"

"No, no. Tell Celeste you both must be on guard but have fun."

"Okay, Daddy. We'll search the archives tomorrow. If we don't find anything concerning the manuscript, or about the Templar knight, I may just come back home. I love you."

She sat on the bed and slumped. *Daddy. Hurt. My research. My future. Moldy grapes.* She planted her feet on the floor. *Okay. Enough.* She stood and straightened her change of clothes, loose, linen slacks and soft shirt, and marched to the living room. Celeste was pouring herself yet another glass of wine.

"My dad was in an accident. Or. Someone tried to kill him."

"That's freaking nuts. Was it bad? Do you need to go home?"

"Yes and no." All the bravado she'd tried to present, the fixing of her clothes, the stomping into the living room, was just that. Her hands still shook like someone who finished their final meal on their last day on death row.

"Tina, look at me. Yes and no to which question?"

Celeste seemed as frightened as Katina felt. "Yes and no to both. He was hurt pretty bad, but he'll be fine." She relayed the near horror-story as told by her father. "I think it would be better to go home, but he said we should go on with our plans and just be really cautious. What do you think?"

Celeste leaned back and tried to clear her throat. She rasped, "Sorry. Went down the wrong pipe." She waved her hand in front of her neck, hacked a few times, then wheezed, "It's up to you, I guess."

Katina sighed as she sat. "I'm going to listen to my dad on both counts. We'll go and be careful."

Worry mingled with determination as she picked up translating where she'd left off:

> Today my mother died of a disease that I am sure she would have survived had there been more food. She was everything that the wife of a priest should have been. Many times, villagers would bring scarce vegetables to our door, so loved were my mother and father. Even on this last day that her soul remained with us, she asked that a recent gift of a tomato and two eggs be given to someone more deserving. I begged her to use this food to nourish her emaciated body.

> She asked how her soul would be better by ignoring the tears of a mother and child. I wanted to demand how her soul managed to ignore the pleas of her daughter.

"That was so sad. Wasn't it? I bet my mother would have done the same thing, too."

Celeste's eyes softened. "I've never met a more self-sacrificing woman than your mother. She's wonderful."

Her mother, Diane, was rather perfect, in appearance, deportment, and temperament, for the most part. "Yep, she is. I wish I were more like her, though I doubt I could do all that volunteering *and* get tenured."

"That's just it, Tina. She doesn't have a Ph.D., and she doesn't have a *job*, job."

"Your brother told me you've volunteered at lots of places in Harlem and you still managed to make associate professor."

"Don't forget I got lucky with my last book. Remember. I was Professor Ó Dálaigh's assistant before he died. He willed me the research he'd worked on for the last ten years."

"How did you get to know him anyway?"

"He was my dad's cousin, the last of his line in Ireland. Guess that's why I got his work; that and he knew how much I loved the subject. I just needed to tie up a few loose ends and write the darn thing. It's not like I started from scratch. Anyway, you never know what'll fall in your lap sometimes. Like the diary."

Katina gave Celeste's shoulder a quick squeeze. "It was lucky for you and I'm glad you got the promotion, but I'm sorry you and your dad lost him." She crossed herself at the thought of a dear one passing.

Celeste waved her glass of wine toward the diary. "How about you read me some more."

Katina remembered her mom's voice, soft and Greek. She sighed and continued, wistfulness tinging her words:

> *During the last hour of my mother's life, my heart tore apart as I cradled her head in my arm. I spooned a weak broth into her mouth. Her breathing became ragged. She coughed, spitting up the meager nourishment she was able to swallow, then still completely. Without a whimper. Without another blink of her eyes.*
>
> *My father came into the room just as foam trickled down her chin. His black robe and leather wrapped feet were caked with dirt from the hours of walking while he ministered to the sick and dying. He fell to his knees and wiped her chin with his sleeve.*
>
> *I wanted to tell him that it was not clean enough. I could neither move nor cry because I could not believe that she had just died.*
>
> *Blessing my mother, my father prayed, first for her soul and redemption. He prayed next for strength to be given to the Knights and our people. I was angered when I heard him next pray for the souls of our attackers. I asked him how he could ask for salvation for our enemies. I wanted them to suffer for all of eternity, for my misery would surely last the equivalent.*

Katina stopped reading. "I'm with her. I'd want them all to die in a fire." She hoped Celeste was a partner in anger.

"War is hell, Tina. I hate that it happened but…"

They came from different backgrounds. They spoke and acted differently. Despite it all, they forged a strong, lasting relationship, not of similarities, but more for preservation. In the world of old New England families at ritzy schools, they were the outsiders.

She accepted their different viewpoints and read on:

> *My father broke my heart further by saying that God*

does not see one sin as greater than another. He reminded me that we have all sinned. Therefore, would he not need to pray for all of God's children? He pleaded for me to understand that they, who do not believe in Christ, are equally, if not more worthy, of our prayers.

I was humbled by his faith which was greater than the oceans that surround us, but my sorrow began to overwhelm my soul. I told him that I am only a daughter, who loves her parents more than I love myself. I said that I cannot forgive my enemies as he does.

I saw his eyes tear when he told me to love God more than any life in this world. If I did, I would not have a moment of trouble in praying for another child of God.

To this, I could not respond. He lowered his head and pulled something gold from the depths of his robe. As he handed it to me, he told me to always wear my mother's earrings. The dolphin would remind me of freedom, and the owl would remind me of the wisdom I needed to gain. I hoped her earrings would grant these wishes so that I could be as he wanted. My doubts that anything could do this were great, for in magic, I did not believe.

Today is August 28. It is wet, and we all are suffering. I helped carry water to people in a nearby village. I am sometimes angry, but mostly I am more dead inside than alive. Once, I looked back down the path toward the fortress. I thought I heard my mother call me. It was just the wind.

My father, being an Orthodox priest and son of an Orthodox priest, has fasted most days of the week, for his entire life. I thought that he would survive this famine. The sickness spreading throughout our people had no respect for his piety.

This morning, I listened to the faint beating of his heart and the fluid gurgle with each breath.

I asked him a question that I was sure he answered a thousand times since the blockade began.

Father, if God is love, how could he allow such suffering?

His hand was gray and shook as if the ground rattled from its core. I held my head still as he rested it on my neck and pulled me close. He whispered that people decide their own course.

As his last breath left him, I prayed for his soul and for courage, but even in this horrible time, I am sure my words and my belief failed to meet as they rose to God's ears. I was now completely alone and frightened. When the invaders become our captors, will I be struck down like a sheep by a butcher?

Performing the final act of love and respect before the priests took his body, I poured fragrant Holy oil over his feet, cleansing them for his journey to Heaven. I wondered then as I do now, why have I not died, for part of me surely has. My legs are but bones and knees. My chest is skin and ribs. Where breasts were making a mature appearance, they and the health of my womb are surely gone forever. I believe I will never be able to carry and suckle the baby I had once hoped to bear.

Today is September 4. After five weeks of artillery fire, of repeated assaults and bombardments, after a large portion of our great wall crumbled into the moat, we thought the battle was lost. Using the tunnels, the brave English brothers under Fra' Nicholas Hussey and those of the Grand Master Phillippe Villiers de L'Isle-Adam repelled the attacks of the Janissaries.

Today, I attended meetings with the villagers and town leaders. I listened as our leaders met with Villiers de L'Isle-Adam, convincing them that a truce should be agreed upon. A brave delegation was successful in the negotiations. Suleiman will be given the island.

December 22. It is over. I complete this testament of my life now, as I have pledged to do, as the Daughter of the Ancients.

It is time for me to reveal the final words of Sir Pierre. There is a small painting. It is the most Holy. It is the painting of the Apostle Paul and blessed by himself during the time he spoke at Lindos, on this very island. Will generations after us understand the significance of this?

Though the painting of the Apostle Paul is a magnificent treasure to Orthodox Christians, there is an even greater secret I have held. The cross was made from only a small part of the gold that once covered the massive torch held by the Colossus. The remaining gold must be found and given back to the people of Rhodes in their time of dire need.

"Are you kidding me?" Katina exclaimed. "Celeste, she's talking about a lot of gold. Tons?"

Celeste's eyes widened in amazement. "I have no idea. How big was the Colossus, anyway?"

"Thirty-three meters. One hundred and eight feet tall." She pictured the most popular depiction of the statue. "That would make the torch about ten feet high. I don't think that would equal tons."

Celeste shrugged, but didn't seem too disappointed. "Who needs a ton?"

"Yeah. You gotta point there. No one person needs a ton of gold. On the other hand, remember the state of Greece right now. They might, now that I think about it."

"Let's table that. Move on with the diary."

The time has finally come for me to act. As instructed by Sir Pierre, if all goes as hoped, I will take the cross to the ruins beneath the Monastery of Panagia Filerimos.

There are symbols on the back of the cross. I will hold it up to the mosaic of the icon of the Resurrection of Christ, which I was told, also has symbols of a different nature, within the area that depicts our Lord trampling upon the Gates of Hades. These symbols, joined with the illustrations on the icon, will show me the location of the rest of the gold. I do not know how this mystical event will unfold. I cannot imagine the mysterious process that will take place. I will trust that the Lord will show me the way.

I am safely in the hidden chamber now. While I rest my nerves, I will complete my final telling—

I sought the fate of my most favorite soldier, Gerard La Fontaine, in the Palace of the Grand Master. Many men walked around. I was so fearful as I climbed the courtyard stairs. Blessed was I as no one bothered me while I checked each workroom on that level. Finally, I went into my dear Sir Pierre's office, second to the left of the stairs.

Worry left me, for Gerard was there, unharmed. He was bent over the desk, writing. I wanted to hug him, so great were my feelings.

I built up my courage. I was finally able to tell him that I believed the Ottomans would murder me and asked for his assistance. I took him to this secret chamber and revealed the existence of the cross.

I will give this, my last testament, to him also. I will ask him to hide it well in our family home by the seaside.

I will commence my mission to return the painting of the Apostle Paul to the church immediately. My quest may take me days or months, or even years, depending on the Ottomans. If I can escape the city alive, and perform my duty bestowed upon me by one who had too great a belief in me, I will one day retrieve this testament and the key to keep as my only personal treasures.

If not, I pray that in the future, when peace prevails on our blessed land, she, a Daughter of the Ancients herself, will complete this mission from God.

Gerard and I leave now, each with a different duty. May
God, in his wisdom, guide and bless our actions.

"Okay. Let me think a minute." Katina stared into the distance to settle her thoughts. "My Metabyzantine Greek is far from perfect, but I think Katha says next that she told Gerard to take the key Sir Pierre gave her and hide it in plain sight in his chamber."

"She trusted that young man? I wonder if she was in love with him."

"Those knights were celibate, so—"

"So, what? She could still be in love." She groaned. "Never mind. This is too much. I don't know what emotion to feel. So much suffering, so much loss for such a young woman. Then all the talk about that gold? Wait— Gerard took her diary and gave it to her relative. So that means—"

"Oh my God, you're right. If we're reading it, it could only mean that she didn't retrieve it. My dad found it at my uncle's house."

Celeste's expression filled with awe. She whispered, "Katina?"

"Hmmm?"

Celeste repeated Katha's words, "'If not, I pray that in the future, when peace prevails on our blessed land, she, a Daughter of the Ancients herself, will complete this mission from God'." She lowered her hand and was utterly still. "Katha is a Daughter of the Ancients, and you are her distant relative. You are about to go to Rhodes to find the cross—"

"I'm the next Daughter?" Katina pondered what they just discovered. "I'm—overwhelmed. I'm going to bed. You don't mind, do you?" Without waiting for an answer, she continued, "I'll try Jim's number again. I need to share this with him."

"Wait a minute. Jim's missing, and your father's in the hospital. This is mega humongous, granted, but are you absolutely sure you don't want to go back to Atlanta? We can do this another time."

"Sweetie, I know he's not really missing per se. I just don't know where he is, exactly. There's a difference. And Dad said he was going to be fine. Just fine."

"If it was my husband…" Celeste bit her lower lip.

"Jim lived in the wilderness for the fun of it. He spent most of the two summers we've had together out west for God's sake. We aren't attached at the hip, and I'm cool with that."

Celeste poured the last of the wine into her glass and tipped it toward Katina to emphasize her point. "Damn, girl. Your words say one thing, your voice, on the other hand, sounds annoyed."

Katina pushed aside thoughts about the diary and her father. She dreaded what she was about to do, but she came back to the room and sat on the edge of a side chair. "You're right. This has been bothering me since Christmas."

She slid onto the cushion and settled back. "Jim was never much of a romantic, though I have to admit he's way more than I am. Just what I thought I wanted."

"But?"

"Well—" How could she describe the jumbled feelings that stemmed from the perspective of a confused kid? A child that grew into a woman determined to avoid the disquiet of events out of her control. "I think my parents play into this somehow. That's typical, right?"

"Probably." In a hushed voice Celeste reminded her, "By the way, I know you avoid talking about your *issues* like a pap smear, so good job here." After a moment, she continued, "You did say your mom sent you to Dana Hall because she thought you'd be happier away from the Atlanta snobs."

"Ha. Out of the fryin' pan and into the fire. I traded them for even bigger New England snobs." She realized a second too late that's where she met Celeste. With an apologetic grin, Katina added, "You excluded." The foot in her mouth caused embarrassed heat to rise.

"Anyway, I was sent to that school because my father thought my mom and I would eventually kill each other." She slapped her knee in remembrance of harsh arguments and hard feelings that had softened over time. "Two Greek females in a house can be *loud*. Dad used to stomp out of his study and yell in Greek, Ειρήνη. He'd repeat it in English for good measure. Peace! He even slammed his door. Boy, he got mad."

Celeste giggled and took a deep sip of wine. "So, you weren't a well-adjusted child. You know, it's not just Greek girls. There are arguments up and down my street all the time."

Katina pictured the blue-collar neighborhood where Celeste grew up. Brick brownstones with small porches. Cars honking. Kids playing. "That makes me feel better."

"What about Jim? What do your parents have to do with your relationship with him?"

Katina arranged her hair to hide her face, then parted one side to reveal an eye. "Damn girl. This is tough. I guess it's a role model thing. I wasn't around them much. Dad traveled all the time, and Mom volunteered a lot, remember? When I was there in the summer, the house was empty and quiet. When I wasn't arguing.

"Anyway, I marry Jim. He cleans fossils in the evening. I read my journals. He puts up with my dogs. I put up with his dust."

"Sounds normal."

Katina thought about it for a moment. "It may be normal, but I'm kind of *sad* in my own house." Frustration roiled inside her as she struggled to be accurate in her portrayal while avoiding the melodramatic. She regrouped and tried again. "When he leaves for his summer trips, he's perfectly happy to say goodbye, and I'm pretty much okay with it. Doubts set in. I ask myself, is this what marriage is? Are we a good match? We are, aren't we, Celeste?"

"Well, never having been married, I'm not an expert." She twirled a silver ring on her pinky and held it up to the light so the amethyst sparkled. "This is how I see it; there are two questions you need to give some serious thought to. First, who else have you told about your parents and your childhood? And second, who else have you asked if you and Jim are good together?"

I guess she's asking if I talked to Jim about all of this. Walking to the windows that gave an enjoyable view of Manhattan's busy streets, Katina thought about the buildings and the windows which receded ever-smaller down the street. Big to small.

It's like studying the history of something. You start with the big event, a fire burning a house down, and work backward to figure out how it could have happened. If you start in the middle, you might be able to understand the path of the flames but not the cause of them.

Still confused about her life with Jim—if the cause of her unhappiness was Jim, herself, or the rhythm of their marriage—she rationalized that perhaps she was only looking at the middle of her own story. She needed to be patient.

"Let's get ready for bed. We have serious research to do tomorrow. I bet our lives are about to change. Big time."

Chapter Five

The First Clue and a Letch

The drive to the New York City Library was without accidents or George Clooney. Katina admired the skyscrapers and expensive apartments up 5th Avenue toward Midtown East. The Stephen A. Schwarzman Building, also known as the Main Library, was a four-story structure made of white, Vermont marble and was a colossal 390 feet long. She thought this columned building, fit for an ancient Greek city, was a true monument to knowledge as she marveled over the marble stairs and magnificent main entrance.

They parked blocks away and Katina was hot and annoyed by the time they climbed those stairs. Celeste's uneven gait indicated her shoes were uncomfortable, but she didn't utter a peep of complaint as they made their way down the hall to the main reading room. Katina read the inscription above the entrance:

A good Booke
is the pretious life-blood of master spirit,
imbalm'd and treasur'd
up on purpose to a life beyond life.

The message was wonderfully obscure, and she loved it as much as the rarified quality of the room itself. Massive yet quiet, the room had dark mahogany tray ceilings at least thirty feet high with impressive frescoes and proportionate chandeliers. Stone walls and oak bookcases surrounded dozens of oak tables. Researchers, some wearing dark business suits and others in jeans and hoodies, sat with shoulders hunched and heads bent to copies of books or computers.

Katina and Celeste walked through and entered the Brooke Russell Astor Reading Room for Rare Books and Manuscripts. That was the room where well-connected researchers could study the actual documents.

The women approached the center desk and a man who looked like a creepy undertaker with gray hair, myopic gray eyes, and an ill-fitting, off-the-rack gray suit. He extended a gnarled, arthritic hand. "Hello, Dr. Daly, and you must be Ms. Bason, is it?"

With reluctance, Katina extended her hand. "How do you do, Mr.—"

"Oh. Pardon me. My name is Dr. Seymour Fritz. I work for Dr. Ridgewald. He's still under the weather, so I'll be, at your beck and call, as it were."

"A pleasure to meet you, uh, Dr. Fritz." She tried to extricate her hand, worried she might hurt his bones.

Dr. Fritz continued to hold it and pat away as he gave her the once over. "Tell me about yourself, Ms. Bason. I hear you're good friends with our lovely Professor Daly here. She tells me you have been very helpful, as an assistant of sorts, over the years."

Katina glared at both of them.

Go with me on this, Celeste's eyes pleaded.

Dr. Fritz waited for Katina to answer by staring at the way she filled out her cashmere sweater. "Do you enjoy working for her? She seems like a lovely young lady."

"Well, it's *Dr.* Bason, and I don't work for her. Celeste and I met at school."

"Did you share a room at college?"

A disgusting speck of drool clung to his lower lip. *This man is gonna get it. I swear to God.* Instead of playing Whac-a-Mole on his bald head like she wanted, she took a cleansing breath. In. Out. The good-girl mantra kicked in. *Be nice. Be sweet.*

Celeste stepped forward and touched Dr. Fritz's arm, steering his attention from Katina's chest to the matters-at-hand. "So, you have some material for us?"

Showing a bit of disappointment in the change of view, he grumbled, "Well, Miss Bason, it seems we must end our nice chit-chat. It would be my pleasure indeed if I can help you in assisting Dr. Daly."

Celeste looked over her shoulder; her amber eyes bugged out at Katina.

"I'm your assistant? Are you kidding me?" Katina mouthed.

She shrugged.

Again, Katina mouthed her reply, "He's a jerk."

Dr. Fritz interrupted the silent exchange. "Your manuscripts have been brought up and are over there." He indicated a more private table on the side of the room. "Is there anything else you might require?"

"We're fine from here. Thanks a ton," Celeste said.

"Dr. Daly, Dr. Ridgewald assured me that you are on the complete-access list, so I'll take a break now."

Katina chuckled as she made her way to the boxes. "Lordy Peter. What a letch." She dug around in a box labeled *Italy, 1200 to 1250.* "These are enticing, apparently not as enticing as I am according to that creepolla, but I think they're too early. The manuscript we found mentioned the 14th century. We need something written by a Scot nobleman."

"Yeah, I know. I asked him to put out a few unimportant things this morning. I knew you'd want a bit of misdirection in our requests." Celeste pulled a box forward and two pairs of latex gloves from her purse. "Didn't want anyone to know what we're actually after. Here."

"What is it?" Katina took the proffered gloves.

"I believe *that*, my dear Sherlock, is what you've been hunting."

"Why thank you, Dr. Watson. You are indeed invaluable."

Katina joined Celeste in giggles as they spread the contents on the table and began to read.

~ * ~

Celeste murmured an apology for her growling stomach. "How long have we been here? Let's stop and get something to eat at Butter's. I love their dolmades. Those lemony, stuffed grape leaves rival my love for a good New Jersey pork roll."

"We'll be getting plenty of that when we get to Rhodes. Butters' has a great salmon though."

Celeste lunged toward a small sheet of paper.

"What've you found? There's been nothing in my stack."

"I think this is another of John Sinclair's manuscripts." She rubbed her fingers on the paper and held it up to the light. "The paper seems to be milled by John Tate, so that fits."

Katina sat back in her chair and crossed her arms.

Celeste looked at her with the squinting eyes of Chris Hemsworth, only hers weren't at all sexy. "Tina, if you're mad because I found it and you didn't, I will knock your block off. You are the only one who can determine the significance of it."

Mollified, Katina took the paper and recited from memory three Middle English lines, "'And John Tate the Younger, Joye Mote he broke; Which late hathe in England doo make this paper thynne, that now in our Englysh this boke is printed inne.' Do you remember that? Bartholomew the Englishman wrote it as an epilogue celebrating the arrival of paper to England. Tate's paper was used to print Chaucer's *Canterbury Tales*. I've seen one of those printings."

She studied the page. "This paper's qualities are the same as Tate's." After a moment more of consideration, she said, "By Jove, old girl, I think we've got it."

In unison, she and Celeste raised their arms and whisper-yelled. Celeste's tiny pumps and Katina's tennis shoes did a quiet happy-feet dance under the table.

The harsh rattle of a cart pushed by Dr. Fritz caught their

attention. "Please. There are a number of people here now. I'm moving you to a different room," he said with a surprising amount of surliness. "You can carry on your research in private."

They followed him three doors down the hall. The room was a small office with little more than a table and two chairs, almost devoid of decoration, as if it lost its purpose or tenant.

Dr. Fritz left with a firm, yet quiet, shut of the door.

Katina wondered if the room was soundproofed against further squeals of delight. "This is awesome. Had I known we could have scored this place I would have made some noise earlier."

"I may have lost my status on the complete-access list."

"Hey, he let you bring the documents in here. You may be even higher on the list than you thought. Let's get started."

Food became inconsequential as they poured over the document, shoulder-to-shoulder, with their heads close together. Katina translated the Middle English aloud:

> *The year is 1400. I am Henry Sinclair, 1st Earl of Orkney. I am the son and heir of William Sinclair, 1st Earl of Caithness. My family and I have been bound to the Knights Templar from the beginning of their existence.*

They continued to read in silence for a few moments.

Celeste pointed to a paragraph. "This part confuses me. I know for a fact Hugh De Payns was married to Elizabeth de Chappes."

"Hmmm. The Middle English doesn't translate well, does it? Roughly, it says that Henry was related to a man named Henri De St. Clair, Duke of Champaine. Then he writes that *Henri* is related to Hugh De Payns. Apparently, Hugh de Payns was briefly married to the invalid sister of the duke."

Katina indicated a new section. "She could never bear children and was not long for this world. Henri, the duke, truly believed that De Payns was anointed by God to be the Grand Master of the Knights Templar. Henri wanted his sister's...inheritance, I guess, to be rightfully passed to its founder. So, Hugh had to marry the sickly sister for her money. It happened all the time in those days."

"Okay." Celeste gazed at the wall in front of the table. "So, this earl lives in Scotland. His name's Henry, and he's related to Henri, who was related to money-hungry Hugh, the founder and first Grand Master." Nudging her way closer, she concentrated on the text. "He goes on to say, 'I will not be the traitor and give over the location of the centuries-old Orthodox icons, created for the glorification of our Lord, except to the recipient of this letter.'"

After making lightning-speed connections between people, places, and actions, Katina whispered, "Oh my God, Celeste. There's a verifiable link between William and Henry Sinclair and the knights. That would give credence to Henry Sinclair and his descendants knowing about icons hidden by them. Could this be true?"

"Why not?"

"Because things like this don't happen to me. I research links and travel around Europe, visit the beautiful sites. Rarely finding anything that matters. This is different. This is actual confirmation of what we found last year."

Patting Katina's hand, Celeste said, "Hey, are you going to hyperventilate? Put your head between your knees." She then tried to push Katina forward.

"Knock it off. You're excited too, and you don't see me shoving *your* face into your crotch."

"Okay, okay." Celeste stopped with the patting and pushing. "If you say you're fine, we can keep going."

Katina harrumphed her displeasure but continued reading Henry Sinclair's manuscript. "I've left the Riddle of Rhodes in the crypt of my manse."

"He's switching between Old and Middle English here. Anyone doing a quick read would probably miss that."

Katina paraphrased the next section. "We need to look for the slab— *'losenge.'*" The next line was tricky. "I think that says it's the 'slab of the knight.'"

She declared, "Good grief all mighty and a hundred ducks. He switched again, and it gets whack. In Middle English, night is 'nyght,' and knight is just 'knight.' You remember, in *Old* English, night is 'niht' and knight is 'cniht.' So, given the mishmash of Middle and Old English, he says to find the image of the crossroads— *'cros.'* It's the guide to the slab of the *night.* Geesh. A devious trick, Sir Sinclair. I wonder what it means."

"Maybe a carving of a night scene or a moon?"

"Sounds good to me, but I could be very wrong about the order." She turned back to the document and found where she left off. "He switches back to Middle English. Having might—*mightand,* to push— *'possen,'* the slab. Celeste—he says the riddle will be 'writing on the wall.' Doesn't that sound ominous?"

She glanced at Celeste for confirmation. "Now he's says that the message containing information about treasured Orthodox icons, kept on the island of Rhodes by the knights, was sent by a man named Cordon, in 1310."

"So, Rome wouldn't want them, the style was too different. The Greeks would though. Hey, at least the Sinclairs understood their value and the knights honored the island people enough to keep the paintings safe—" She nudged Katina's shoulder with her own. "A couple of hundred years later, they hid their Catholic icons with the Greek ones, according to Katha's diary."

Katina nodded, barely listening. She was too wrapped up in his words. "He says that the message maintained that the residents of Rhodes declared that the icons were meant to be found by *Archaeo-Dehtren*, the Daughter of the Ancients. The legend said there would always be a righteous daughter of Rhodes. They were descendants of a single family.

"Henry changes the subject back, saying he searched for them for five years. He queried residents and local priests until his health failed, which caused him to return to England.

"Lordy Peter. He mentions the Daughter of the Ancients in future tense. He died the year he wrote this, 1400. This coincides with what Katha wrote because she lived on the island in the 1500's. My Lord, now we have proper verification of Katha's story. Hand me the pad and pen, okay?"

She wrote: *The domed room is in the crypt. To find where the secret is buried, find the crossroads, the guide to the slab of the knight. Push the slab hard. The riddle will be writing on the wall.*

She trembled. "Damn. I kinda wish he'd just tell us what he knows, but this is fun, isn't it? We have to change our plans and go to Scotland first. There's a manse we need to break into to find yet another path in the enigmatic trail that leads to the icons. Though he never found the treasure himself, this guy seemed to have an idea about what part of the palace the hidden room was in. Oh, good grief. It just dawned on me that we didn't know where in the palace *Katha's* room is. It's a huge building. She just mentioned an owl on the floor and a key with some more hints on it. His information might narrow our search considerably."

A moan escaped as Celeste stretched. "Man, this hunt has officially fallen into the ridiculous column."

"The chances of all this happening are remote, but by God they did. This turning out successfully is more astronomical. But just think. We have Katha's diary. Now, a confirmation and linkage from the extensive line of Sinclairs and their connection to the knights who took over Rhodes." She rubbed her hands together, then shook them, trying to relieve the sudden return of excitement. "Scotland, here we come."

Chapter Six

Katina, lover of medieval times, never traveled to Scotland. It should have been at the top of her list to explore the mysterious and glorious fog enshrouded landscapes and spired castles filled with delicious history. A sovereign state since the Middle Ages, until James VI became the ruler of the new Kingdom of Great Britain, his court was surrounded by scandal. The man's reign was mired by acts of bloody rebellion.

The plane flew over the angry waters that surrounded two-thirds of the country. She wanted to feel the cool air blow across the craggy Highlands of the north. Battles were fought over the rocky stretches of land in the west and the hills and broad valleys of the south. Remembering events like the Battle of Dunnichen, the Jacobite Uprising, and the Battle of Killiecrankie struck her imagination like a match to tinder. So much domination. So many factions.

Her love of research, and a good old internet search, yielded Katina and Celeste's destination. They would go to what was left of Sir Henry's ruined castle. Its location was two miles south of Loanhead and off a lesser road called Chapel Loan, close to the town of Dalkeith.

Surprised to learn that there were very few lodgings in the area, Katina eventually engaged a single room in a quaint inn within walking distance to the castle.

As they exited Edinburgh Airport's main door, they were met with a miserable, frigid wind, not the nice cool air the website described. Katina checked her phone and sure enough, the average temperature in August was about 60 degrees. They had packed for summer in Rhodes, not summer in Scotland. Celeste, who liked few things better than to shop for a great outfit, at a steep discount of course, wasn't unhappy.

Katina acknowledged the inevitable as they found a cab and asked the driver to head to the closest clothing store. Edinburgh was only five miles away. They drove past the round International Conference Center and other cream-colored stone, high-rise buildings of the financial district. Then the fun started. As they drove closer to the core of the city, the architecture transformed from modern to old, then to something out of a J.K. Rowling book, a large and exciting fairytale at its best.

The driver turned right on Princes Street, with its lovely garden many blocks in length. It was so large, in fact, that it surrounded a most magnificent castle that sat dark and ominous atop a huge green hill. Katina didn't know where to look first; she wanted to explore every building.

The driver said, "Here we are. This be Jenners. You'll notice it's a massive building established in 1805. They call it the Harrods of the north. We're very proud of it."

The structure had an ornate Victorian edifice complete with female sculptures that took the place of pillars and stone cherubs gracing other surfaces.

Celeste and Katina entered through the uninspired doors. They stopped. Katina focused on the enormous central atrium and its spectacular glass ceiling, as a smile of appreciation stretched across her face. The chills on her arm was a reminder it was time to get down to business and find a woolens department.

Celeste searched rack after rack of blouses, slacks, and dresses. "There's nothing but summer stuff here. Armani and Sara Pacini, for God's sake. These Scots must do better in the cold then I do. Let's get out of here."

They strolled the downtown area asking for suggestions and directions. Katina was chilled to the bone by the time they found an outdoor store like a Patagonia in the U.S.

Celeste compared prices for an hour.

Grumpy, Katina said, "Darlin', I'm paying for the clothes, so pick whatever you want."

Celeste's stride faltered. The skin around her eyes tightened. "No. I've got it."

Her need to build a world of economic and emotional stability around herself had always been apparent. As a young teen, Katina learned that Celeste had a mother who clung to her Egyptian upbringing, a dynamic brother who clung to threads of past success, and a father who clung to a bottle of Irish whiskey.

As they shopped, Katina remembered to be gentle in her statements and cognizant of their economic divide. Celeste made decent money as a professor, but her tiny Manhattan apartment, a great investment, used up most of her budget.

Katina came from wealth, plain and simple. "Scotland was an unexpected detour. It would be nice if you'd let me splurge a little."

"All right, but I'm buying dinner," Celeste said, with veiled relief in her voice.

"Nope. Food is always on me." Katina's response was automatic. "You know the rule. Greeks must feed people. It's in their genes."

Her friend pretended to be disgruntled while she picked out a few less expensive items. The battle of the clothing-cosmos began, for finding outfits that matched the scale of her proportions was indeed a war. She insisted on her usual pastels, choosing a heavy, handknit sweater, a pair of slacks, and a silk scarf in shades of pinks, yellows, and pale greens. Shoe shopping was a miserable challenge too.

Celeste and her tiny feet.

Katina paid for their bundles, relieved to avoid the delicate, financial minefield as they left the store.

The fresh Scottish air invigorated her, while Celeste drooped with jet lag. Katina wanted to grab a hamburger and start their adventure—searching for the hidden document.

"I need to concentrate just to put one foot in front of the other, and I'm really hungry." Celeste yawned as if to emphasize her plight.

They decided to have a nice dinner of smoked salmon, *Forfar bridie,* a pastry stuffed with meat, kale, and potatoes. With her stomach full, Katina and Celeste took a taxi the short distance to the village.

Katina's blood ran hot as she planned the research she would complete while Celeste slumbered.

~ * ~

Katina googled the history, a detailed layout of the area, and how to get to the manse from the inn. She stopped to take a quick shower. The scent of lavender soap wafted through the suite as she toweled her hair.

Celeste was already in bed, curled up under blankets like a hibernating bear cub.

"Celeste, have you ever gotten out of the shower and realized that you forgot to wash your hair?" Getting no response, she continued, "Well, I just did that. I was daydreaming. I can't believe we're in Scotland. We're supposed to be in Rhodes right now."

"Tina, we left JFK at ten this morning. It is now ten at night, about 300 hours later with the time change." She yawned. "You should be tired, for cripe's sake."

"I've got more research to do. I'll see where the stores are around here. We may need to buy a pick and hammer or something."

"I'm *trying* to sleep." Celeste plopped a pillow over her head.

"We'll have to rent a car," Katina whispered.

Celeste lifted the pillow a smidge. "I'm not sure you get the concept of letting someone sleep. I can still hear you. You're worse than a kid."

"How would you know? You don't have one."

"I don't need one. I have you. Goood niiiight, Tina."

Katina poked the bear with a stick. "*Oidhche mhath leat.* That means good night in Gaelic."

Goofy pleasure filled her as she ducked Celeste's thrown pillow.

~ * ~

The next morning, Katina and Celeste enjoyed the change of scenery during their taxi drive to the hardware store named Bits and Bobbs, Katina found online. The vistas had gone from Manhattan's monolithic buildings to Scotland's lush, rolling hills and oodles of old-world buildings. Many had gray slate roofs spotted with moss and other greenery. Hand-cut stone was everywhere. As they approached the town, Katina was delighted to see an unusual three-story brick tower.

"It looks like a lighthouse, but we're not even close to water." Little kid excitement filled her. "This area is fantastic. Isn't it?"

Their taxi driver, who wore a gray and green tartan hat, said in a pleasant Doric accent, "*Ach*, young bonnie lass, you say that, but ye daen't hae to put up with the muckle traffic problem Dalkeith has. It's a real scunner. This town is on the way to Edinburgh, it is, and the *briefs slaw* and it's a *sair fecht* to get ben town. I was after taken a fare from dare in jist forty-fife minutes. It niver takes less than an hoor, noo. It's the devil, it is."

Katina turned her eyes from the hat to the amused face of Celeste.

"What did he say?"

She laughed at Celeste's confusion. "I studied up on this a bit last night. I think he said, there was a train between the village and Edinburgh. It took people five minutes. Now, they have to drive, and it takes an hour."

"Ah, I see." Celeste mouthed, "No, I don't."

The driver said, "Okay. I'll be after daein' the translatin' 'en from noo on."

Celeste whispered, "What?"

He looked at Celeste in his rearview mirror and chuckled. "I said, young lady, that I'll be doing the translating from now on...there was never a train. I was just telling you both that it was once quicker to drive between the village and Edinburgh. I should hae guessed ye ur nae a Scot with the looks of ye bonnie lassies. And when ye are done at the store, where will you be then?"

Celeste said, "A manse close by."

"Well, that's fine. Are ye after needin' a ride back?"

"We'll need a ride to the rental car agency. It's the Condor Self

Drive at 30 Eskbank Road. Our car should be ready in an hour," she said.

"Right ye are. I'll be after picking ye up in an hoor 'en."

"That would be nice. Thank you so much, uh…"

As the driver pulled to the curb in front of the store, he said, "Call me Scotty, lass."

"Right. Thank you, Scotty." Celeste's smile fell. The store had a brown, red, and white realtor sign filling the front window. "Oh no. It's closed."

"Oh dear. Right ye are."

Katina asked, "Is this even downtown Dalkeith? The area is awfully rural."

"No, it isn't. This is East Dalkeith, more of a suburb, ye say in the U.S. Are ye sure the Google told ye right?"

"Crap. Guess not." She didn't count on stumbling so soon off the block. "Do you know another store that might sell hammers and such?"

"I dinna know of any but let me see what I can do." Scotty called one person. Then another. Then a third. All the time sending reassuring nods to the back seat. "We'll find somethin'."

It took a full ten minutes for one of his contacts to call him back with an address. He started the car and drove back to Dalkeith proper. Fifteen minutes later, they passed the city limits. A few shop fronts with 'To Let' signs were displayed in dusty windows. Like most towns in Scotland, it had not rebounded from its economic woes.

He stopped in front of a business called Dalkeith Handy Store.

"Handy Store?" Celeste asked.

"Aye. That's what we call it."

Katina grumbled, "Had we known that, it woulda taken thirty seconds."

Celeste and Katina gathered their purses, gave their thanks to the driver, and entered the establishment. They meandered up one row and down another. Both brimmed with home improvement doodads.

Katina noticed a man with wavy, auburn hair that fell to the collar of his yellow, oxford shirt. He was staring at Celeste and eyed her jazzy hair and the shape of her body. Katina grinned at the poor man. Celeste rarely dated, but when she did, her date was always a smart and sharp New Yorker. This man looked…nice.

Katina browsed the aisles for the hammer and pick, until her attention was drawn by a tinkle bell that hung at the front door. She wondered why she hadn't noticed it before, then was startled to see Celeste and Mr. Handsome together, outside, talking. Katina snuck up to the front of the store, using a few shoppers and a broom for cover. She tried to read their lips until he turned and bumped into a green-haired teenager as he hurried away.

Rats. What the heck just happened?

Celeste continued to gaze at his back and swiped at her cheek. She pulled her sweater close and rested her body against the store window.

She dropped her head as if she heard some sad, sad news.

Good lord. What the heck's happening out there? Katina paid for their robbery gear. *Does she need me? What should I say? Why am I so damn ill-equipped to handle normal girl stuff?*

She went with her instincts, sorry as they were, and joined Celeste outside. Katina stood close and raised her face to the bit of sun breaking through the cloudy sky. "Who was that?"

"Just someone I once knew in England. His name is Aubrey Wells."

"You were upset."

Celeste shifted. "Let's just say we didn't end up as friends."

"Oh, was he your *boyfriend*? You never told me about him. He looks like that guy that said, 'As you wish' in that movie."

"*The Princess Bride*." With sad eyes and an even sadder voice, Celeste said, "He teaches here. My God." She pushed off the building and searched the street. "Can we talk about it later, Tina? I need to process this. Where's the cab?"

A hundred and one questions filled Katina's head, but she held her tongue. She'd never seen her best friend this upset over a man. "Sure. You're pale. You're never pale. Let's get tea and scones at the Sun Inn."

~ * ~

The high tea experience started with one piece of bread, a large amount of butter, and strawberry dip.

"I hope this isn't all there is because we have a big evening ahead." Katina was relieved when, after the bread course, a sweet waitress gave them an assortment of sandwiches in the shape of flowers. She held back a squeal of delight as a surprise selection of cakes on a miniature picnic table was set before them.

On her best behavior, she sipped her tea with a pinky extended, hoping Celeste would cheer up. "We should save some of the cakes for our late-night excursion. You know, adventures are always better when goodies wait at the end. Preferably, bite-sized pieces in cute containers. And maybe a bow or two."

"Um, about that, do you think you can handle it by yourself? I need to meet with Aubrey."

Katina licked at a single sweet drop on her teaspoon, then placed it gently on the table. "I can, but I don't want to. You can meet him another time. Remember what the warning said? 'Go at night to avoid danger.' It said danger..."

"According to the website, the manse is closed while they turn it into a B&B. So you shouldn't have any problem sneaking in." Celeste turned pleading eyes to Katina. "Please let me do this. I *need* to talk to him. Tonight."

"Who is this guy to you?"

She said nothing, and a sudden and mysterious aloofness engulfed her.

"Why is he so important that you can't come? This stinks Celeste."

The air stilled as if a huge revelation was about to be told. Katina clutched a fork like a child waiting impatiently for Christmas pudding.

She leaned forward...

Raised her eyebrows...

Cocked her head and smiled...

She gave up.

"What the hell. If it's that important." Katina tossed the spoon onto the saucer which caused gasps from the other guests. "Let's take the goodies back to the inn. I'll rest a bit before I change into my breaking-into-ruins clothes."

Celeste's expression shifted from stubborn, to relieved, and back to good-old happy. "That's the spirit. You've got this."

Katina hated both of those phrases. She had a sinking feeling she did not have *this* and would regret trying to get it.

Chapter Seven

Passages Found in The Manse

Katina dressed in dark colors from her turtleneck and new leather jacket down to her sneakers. Her black satchel bumped against her back as she walked across a ditch away from the inn. To get to the rocky cliffs of Roslin Glen and the manse would take fifteen minutes or so. The moon's glow was too dim, but she didn't dare use her flashlight for fear of someone peering out the inn's window as a beam of light danced its way across the ground.

Her excitement for the adventure drained with each step. Gone was the thought of an old ruin to explore, replaced by the thought of Celeste and her conversation with a man named Aubrey. Katina's nerves got the best of her; she wished her best friend was there.

I need a lookout man. Celeste's super at that.

Katina screamed as she pitched forward and fell to her knees. She jerked her hand back from whatever had brushed it. Two innocent cotton-tailed rabbits beat a hasty get-away.

"A rabbit hole. Cripes." She sat, forlorn, on the damp earth. "I'm asking for trouble. I just know it."

She cleaned off her knees and continued the journey. The urge to gripe some more was huge. Instead, she got a grip and worked through her plan for the tenth time. The internet was amazing—Bits and Bobbs withstanding. Not only did a website show the land, but she found the layout, along with another site that diagrammed the rooms, halls, and stairwells as they were first built. She used pencil and paper to draw the two plans and overlaid the sketches to determine which stairwell led to the burial chambers.

Something new needed to be added to her list of scary things: exploring unknown burial chambers. *Worry about that later. Just get there, Tina.* She slapped blades of damp grass from her pants and focused on her plan of action while she hiked the short distance.

Cross the stone bridge that replaced the drawbridge. Go through the ruins of the gatehouse. Head toward the remaining part of the original structure—the East Range.

At the main building, find an open window and the stairs to the three lower levels. Then locate the vaulted room on the lowest floor, furthest from the stairs. That's where there should be a hidden door to the remains of the building.

Right. You know what to do next. Try not to scream. I'm such an idiot.

But there's gonna be dead bodies under slabs of granite. Don't forget the ghosts of the men that died in the battle of 1303 and the 1544 War of the Rough Wooing.

The Rough Wooing. During that horrible time, the original structure was wrecked, so they built over it. Then the rebuilt manse was attacked by Cromwell's army in 1650 and by the mob of Reformers in 1688. *Good lord, so many battles over this place. So much rebuilt. The basement better be in good shape.*

She was comforted as the beautiful, old stone bridge and the road between the walls, lined with red bricks came into view.

Fantastic. I made it. Celeste was right. I can do this. If the spirits don't take me away, for God's sake. Don't think about it. Spirits don't take anything. Maybe...

All was quiet. No lights shone from windows, and no cars were parked in the courtyard. Katina took a steadying breath and followed the path, flanked by tall, thin bushes that reminded her of sentinels standing guard.

The building was like a pink-bricked Tudor, with its steep roof, pitched crow-stepped gables, and gray slate. Just like the picture.

As expected, a window was located twelve feet to the right of the back door. Her heart began a Jamaican beat as she approached. *We're not supposed to be able to feel our organs.*

She yanked the left wooden shutter. It scraped the stone casement with such volume the hairs on the back of her neck stood up. She leaped back and uttered an involuntary squeak.

Satisfied there was no other movement or sounds, Katina pulled the right shutter and shoved the window frame, surprised when it gave way. She peered into a room paneled with dark, rich woodwork. Its ceiling was decorated, and as the internet site had shown, near-devoid of furnishings.

Good to go, girlfriend. She whirled her arm about like a pinwheel as she fell off the ledge onto the floor in a heap. Her satchel lay half on her head; the heavy stuff missed her by inches. *Blasted freakin' idiot move, dummy. Couldn't just drop down like a ninja. No. You had to be humpty-damn-dumpty.*

She rose on shaky legs and rubbed the pain in her hip. She retrieved a small flashlight out of the bag and used it to light her quiet progress to the hall. With a limp, she went left toward the main part of the building. An oak door was midway between the entry and the Great Hall.

This should be the stairs.

As she opened it, her breath caught at the unexpected darkness of the stairwell leading to the lower floors. The seventh-century scale-and-plate stairs were steep. Cool, musty air flowed up toward the warmer main hallway where she stood.

Using the oak railing just in case her big feet messed up on the small steps, she eased herself down. After what seemed like five minutes, and two more flights later, she stepped onto the bottom floor.

She used her sleeve to wipe the sweat from her forehead before it could get into her eyes. Sweat belied the cold that emanated from the stone walls causing her to shiver. She flipped the light switch up and spoke to an imaginary Celeste. "Don't you ever wonder why cops continue to use flashlights after they crash into a perp's house? There are light switches everywhere, for God's sake. Why don't they use them?" She strode quietly to the furthest room as planned.

This is it. Almost there. Please be right, Henry. I promise I will honor your secret. I'll find the icons for you. When I'm finished with Katha's mission, I'll return the Orthodox icons to St. George's and the others to the Catholic church.

The large, empty, square room she entered had granite slabs across its floor and up the walls to the domed ceiling. Nothing screamed, *Yoo-hoo. I'm what you're looking for.*

According to Henry's message, her first task was to find a slab with a map showing crossroads. She hoped it would be a mosaic with a big X marking the spot. Scanning every foot of the room, she expected to see *something*. Granted, she didn't know what that something was, but she found nothing at all.

Time was not her friend. She ran her hands across the walls and found only expected surface roughness.

Ten more minutes passed.

Katina gave a frustrated sigh. "Drat. It's never easy, is it?"

She switched off the light, turned the flashlight on, and held it flat against the stones of the walls. *There must be... Maybe... just maybe...* She used the beam to create shadows. What were normal variations in the two-foot by two-foot stone blocks now showed a vast number of carvings. She studied the faint images which turned out to be shapes of people. Given the strong adherence to Western Christian dogma in those days, they were probably important saints and wicked sinners. As a pleasant relief, the stones were also etched with cloud-like swirls.

Time was running out. *What did I forget? That's right. The lower three floors were cut into the rock face of the cliff, so there can't be a hidden chamber in that direction. I have to search the wall and floor closest to the interior, away from that face.*

After carefully studying stone after stone, she found herself at the middle of the wall, to the right of the door.

There. A carving of a Templar Knight. She could even make out a large cross on his chest.

She checked the time. "An hour left until daybreak."

Her excitement diminished by the string of rotten frustrations and lack of progress until she studied each edge of the slab. "Wait—I forgot."

Her breathing quickened as she remembered that the word knight was the ruse. *God, I could have wasted hours more.*

I need to find something to do with night.

The stone wall directly above the cliff might have some sort of night scene, a moon, stars, owls maybe. In the top left corner, a small opening let in a drift of cool night air that chilled her skin. *It's cut like a cross. How does that fit? The crossroad he mentioned would be shaped like its namesake, I guess.*

But why would he tell me to go at night? Because of danger? What if it was daytime? There would be light streaming in. Wouldn't that highlight a place on the wall? *That's it.* The sun has a different trajectory across the sky than the moon. It would be defused coming in and would cast light on the wall with the knight at certain hours. The moon would be specific and shine on the floor.

She got down on her knees. *Damn.* "Where's the moon when I need it? I'm going to have to study every stone."

Sitting on the floor, Katina studied the cross and followed a few paths that a beam of light might possibly make. She set the beam of light at an oblique angle on the three-foot by three-foot stone on the floor. She smiled with relief. "There it is. A half-moon, close to the knight."

After studying every crevice around the edge of the slab, she remembered the text. Mightand. So she pushed on the first side with all her might.

Nothing happened. She went to the second side—nothing. Her frustration grew. The third side didn't budge either. With a great grunt, she pressed on the side closest to the knight on the wall. Still nothing happened.

"Damn it. The stone should move away from the cliff and toward the wall next to the center of the building. You have to be the right one." Crossing herself three times for a bit of good Greek Orthodox luck, she turned on the light and got out the pick and hammer from the satchel.

Putting the pick into the crack on the fourth side, she gave it a few good whacks. She was rewarded as it gave way.

She repeated the process on every edge one more time. "It's moving!"

Much time had passed, but she didn't care. Strike after strike, the sharp noise hurt her ears, even as she continued until a significant space showed. She gathered her strength and heaved with all her weight.

The slab inched toward the wall, and with each shove and inch moved, her sagging hopes vanished. When opened fully, it revealed at least twenty stairs that led down to the pitch-black vault.

"Fantastic."

Her hands shook as she put her tools back into the satchel and lifted it on her shoulder. She spotted a torch attached to the wall at the top of the staircase. She wondered if it had been lit since the 1500s. Turning the flashlight back on, she put it into her mouth.

I can't believe I'm here, doing this.

Taking a ragged breath around the flashlight, she slid her feet and bottom down the steps, not daring to stand until she reached the bottom.

She was startled to see three marble crypts in the middle of the small vault room. "Yoo-hoo, any priests in there?"

Katina panned the light and revealed two other rooms. She inspected the interiors of each. Beautiful religious murals decorated the walls of all three rooms. More saints. More sinners. All painted this time.

She was drawn to touch the face on the icon of St. Catherine. Winged angels held a bright halo around her head. A spike-edged wooden wheel lay by her side, books painted in muted colors with plain gold-leaf pin-striping were at her feet.

Katina's gaze returned to the delicate face. "*Buon fresco.* Hello, beautiful." She studied each inch with an expert eye. "Your lovely, red robe looks brand new, doesn't it?" The fresco seemed uneven in places, as if the surface beneath was not prepared well, or had suffered a modicum of expansion here and there due to dampness.

"According to the text, there should be writing on the wall." She read the words across the top, St. Catherine. "I'll be right back. Let me check the other icons."

After wandering around the rooms, looking for anything that was different, Katina came back and said, "Y'all are pretty much alike. Talk to me. What's special about you?"

The books. Of course. Happy-feet-dance time. After a quick jig, she shook the nerves from her hands and studied the painted books. *No writing on them, so what could it be?* An idea hit her. *Is it worth marring part of the icon?*

To be sure, she scanned every surface in the rooms one last time. "Nothing. It has to be you, Catherine. I'll be gentle."

With that said, she drew her penknife out of the satchel, raised her hand, and bit her lower lip. Ever so carefully, she touched the tiny blade to the fresco. She snatched it back and clasped it with the other hand. "I can't."

"Only tiny changes, I promise." She checked her watch. "Dawn is in ten more minutes."

After crossing herself, she put the blade to the edge of the books and made a few slight flicks. A bit of white plaster fell as a fraction of the book's edge peeled off. She lifted the knife and whimpered at the specks of falling dust. However, the painting itself wasn't damaged at all. She bit her lower lip and slide the knife against the wall with greater confidence.

Inspecting her work, she gave a whoop of excitement. *I was right, there's an edge. The books aren't part of the fresco. Oh, thank you, God.* She scraped around all four edges.

Her hands shook as she peeled back what was actually a painting of books on canvas. A delicate piece of paper fluttered to the floor. Her heart pounded as she bent to pick it up. She swayed. The flashlight fell, clattering toward the wall. She dropped to her knees and put her forehead on the cold stone floor.

Breathe... In... out... In... out.

After a few moments, her senses cleared. Straightening, she grasped the flashlight and read the first sentence, which seemed like yet another riddle, written in Middle English.

Are you kidding me? Katina scanned the document and groaned. "Here we go again."

She rolled the thick paper and slid it into her satchel. She was thrilled to see a fresco version of the books beneath the canvas she'd removed. No real damage done. *Yay.* She spread the bits of dust around, leaving as little evidence of her presence as possible.

Katina made her way back and replaced the stone of the secret opening but was not happy with her results. Grout was missing, even after sweeping as much of what she'd chipped out back into the cracks. Her time was up and there were no other options.

It took a few more minutes to get outside, careful to close the window and shutters behind her. She turned to make a clean getaway.

Oh no.

Across the lot and almost to the tree line, a beam of light bounced back and forth. Someone carrying a flashlight, maybe forty feet away, strode in her direction. She stood still, with her mouth agape like a dolt.

"You there. Hold," a baritone voice called.

I'm holding for God's sake.

As the man approached, she hoped he was a security guard, not a policeman. She freaked. *Holy crap. The bag.* She eased it from her shoulder and let it drop into the bushes. "Ummm. Hi." She was hit with a rush of nerves and nausea.

"Fit ye doin, Ned?"

"Hmmm? What'd you say?" *Brilliant comeback, Tina.* A harsh light scanned her face and body.

"You American, then?"

"Mostly."

"*Weel.* I said, what are you doing here?"

What to say? The truth? Nope. Holy crap. Some internal, goofball voice told her to play drunk. Having only been drunk once in her life, she wasn't sure she could pull it off, but she gave her best shot at word-slurring inebriation.

"I went for a walk and got losht. I was hoping shomeone was here and I could ask them the way back. I hate getting losht. It's one of my big time—"

"Awrite. I noo need your life's history. Why are you all in black? You're a might suspicious now, aren't you?"

Katina looked down. *Blast. Didn't think about that, did you?* "Umm." She paused. "I come from New York. Thash's all we wear." She stumbled for no reason, just for good measure.

The guard said, "Christ," as he moved forward with a hand to catch her, then murmured something unintelligible but nasty sounding, as she righted herself. "Where do you need ta go?"

"The inn." She waved an extended hand around like she didn't know what continent she was on, let alone the direction of her lodging.

He pointed the flashlight up the drive toward the road. "You go back ta way you came and turn left at t'road."

"Sure. You bet. I'll do that. Thanksh." Katina weaved up the drive with her hands tucked under her armpits to quell their shaking. Halfway up, she turned backward and pretended to stumble. *Cripes. He's watching. Stop it!*

With a quick wave, she continued a drunken stroll, left at the road. Out of his sight, she ducked into the tall bushes that lined almost every byway in the region. At least ten minutes later, the guard was still on the premises. Her whole body spasmed in muscle cramps. Hiding was not her best suit.

The guard's car started after another ten minutes.

She crouched deeper into the hedge as the tires crunched on gravel, and the car sped past in the direction of the inn. She exhaled the breath she'd held, crossed herself, and sent God a truly heartfelt thank you.

Between stretching her frame and giving little moans as she stood, a little mouse or bird scurried away sending her senses reeling. Moments later, after a quick scan of her surroundings, she was back searching under the last section of bushes, still filled with exhilaration for getting away scot-free. "There you are. Come to momma."

With her bag shouldered, Katina started a slow jog to avoid rabbit holes, remembering a joke her father had told her, which might explain the term scot-free.

A newly widowed Scot was on his monthly train trip to the city and complained to the fare collector about having to pay for his wee son. "Hee'll no take up enough space for anyone ta notice, now weel he?"

The collector yelled at the man named MacTavish that he was too cheap for words. That made MacTavish madder than a baby coo being taken from its mam. So, the next month, he refused to pay altogether. Ooh, the fare collector had it with MacTavish, so he grabbed the man's trunk and threw it out the door, telling him to get off at the next stop.

MacTavish screamed, "First you insult my thriftiness. Now you trow my son off the train. How dare ye man!"

She panted and giggled as she reached the inn's front door. She entered their room to find Celeste asleep, her breaths soft against the pillow. As Katina put her pajamas on, she wondered how someone would explain away burglary tools. *That was way too damn close. Gads. I may never fall asleep. Ever. Again. Dad would have a bloody fit and surely make good the threat to send me to the nunnery.*

She wiped the mirror and tiptoed to the bed wondering how Celeste's night had gone. Seconds after her head hit the pillow, Katina thought of Jim. *What are you doing? Why don't you call me? Dad couldn't make long distance phone calls from Egypt, back in the day. I get that, but times have changed.*

Katina pictured herself on an overseas flight. Beyond her window was a night sky, black and starless. All the passengers and attendants were asleep. The cockpit door was open. The pilot and co-pilot chairs were empty. Only the quiet, constant drone of the engines could be heard.

She gathered the covers close to her neck. The chin wobbles started. *Why didn't Celeste come with me? She could've had dinner with*

Mr. Wavy Hair anytime. Katina took a deep breath and rubbed her eyes. *Buck up. You're a lion, remember?*

A faint light came through a crack in the paisley curtains and the bed sagged as Celeste shifted; she breathed in and out with quick soft gasps as if she were crying in a sad dream. She mumbled incoherent words.

Katina didn't know if she wanted to be mad for being ditched or be a sweet friend and wake Celeste up. She turned on her side and closed her eyes. *I'm going to be both. I'll figure out which one I'll stay in the morning.*

Chapter Eight

Celeste and Aubrey Meet for Dinner

Celeste thought Katina, who loved to sneak into places, would have far more fun than she was. Instead of meeting with Aubrey, she more than half-wished to leave with Katina. The whole experience evoked a profound sorrow, one felt innumerable times over the last ten years. Regret lingered as Celeste entered the pub of the Jamison Inn.

Laughter, conversations, and the tangy smell of ale engulfed her. She scanned the room and found his solemn face. He stood as she approached.

Her instinct of self-preservation urged her to turn around and never see that man again. A broken heart that needed to heal encouraged her to see what might happen.

He tilted his head to kiss Celeste's cheek, but she reared back.

"I apologize, Celeste. I didn't mean to offend you. It shan't happen again. Please, sit." He touched the chair across the small oak pub table. "Let's start over. Hello, Celeste. As I said at the store, you are pretty as ever. How have you been?"

How would a happy person describe themselves? She slid into the offered seat, picked up a napkin, and dabbed at her nose to stall for time. She needed a convincing lie. *Had a thrilling life…with tons of lovers. Anything's better than the truth.*

"Hello, Aubrey." She bit her quivering lower lip. "And as *I* said, you look pretty good yourself. I've been fine. You?"

It split her in half to see the plane of his cheek, in need of both a caress and a slap. She clenched her hands together under the table to prevent either.

You disgust me…

Her heart shifted, and her mind grasped an unexpected possibility. *I might still love you…*

She remained silent as an overriding truth reasserted itself. *You destroyed me…*

"Well, I've been grand. Very busy," he said with a jovial English accent she used to find endearing. "Let's order a fine pint and food, shall we?"

She steeled herself to the task at hand and managed to say,

"Sounds good. I like the pub, by the way." She ran her fingers across a narrow pearl and diamond choker, a gift from Katina. "Do you eat here often? I guess I should ask: do you live here now?"

He glanced up from her neck. "Yes, I do. I've, ahh, been teaching full time for three years."

"Nice. At a primary school?"

With a deep chuckle, he said, "Now, Celeste, please. I'm a professor."

She rubbed her arms and avoided his teasing gaze. "Are you still into computers?"

"Exactly. My passion has become cybersecurity. I want to teach the future hackers of the world how to defeat themselves."

I used to be your passion. "Aren't you worried they'll, I don't know, hack the government?"

A waitress, in a tight T-shirt and tighter jeans, stood mere inches away from Aubrey. "Hello, Professor. Be ye after wantin' sometin' from the kitchen or jist the bar t'night?"

"From the kitchen, if you please. What's good?"

"*Uch*, notin' if ye ask me. I'm a bloody vegetarian. I hear the lamb and beans is passable though. What do you want t' drink? I'll get Callen t' start you a pint. Miss?" Francie gave Celeste a brief glance.

"Celeste will have a chardonnay, and I'll have my usual. We'll order more in a bit. We have some catching up to do, don't we, Celeste?"

He just orders wine for me? What if I wanted a beer? "That'll be fine, I guess."

"So, my dear. You didn't tell me how you were. What have you been doing since we last saw each other?"

Do you want to go there? How about, filling my days with academia. You know, cold, dry, lifeless.

"Well, let's see. I finished my doctorate, and I work in New York. You? I mean, I know you teach…" Celeste was too conflicted to continue. She searched the room for something to take the focus from herself.

"Brilliant. Brilliant." He cleared his throat and grimaced. "Um, I do apologize. Maybe this wasn't such a good idea. I seem to be making you dreadfully nervous."

She couldn't find any words to help him or herself out of this complicated situation.

"I am so pleased to run into you again." As he waited for a response, his expression changed from uncertainty to disappointment, "I see you don't feel at all the same, do you?"

This is it. Say what you need to say. Be done with it and be done with him.

"Aubrey—"

"Here ye go, loove." The waitress interrupted with a tray filled with pints of ale and a single glass of white wine. "What are ye after havin' ta eat?" She bent her knees and brushed her breast against his cheek as she put the drinks on the table.

Aubrey's face stayed turned toward the waitress's chest a few seconds too long. "Right." He shot a guilty glance toward Celeste and another back to the waitress. "Yes, to eat. We'll have the lamb and beans. Thank you so much."

"Tank ye, me loove."

The waitress sauntered off with a flirtatious glance over her shoulder.

My love? Have you hurt this girl too? By the swing of those hips, I'd say not yet.

Celeste braced herself against the power of those blue eyes that used to follow every movement she made. Thick eyelashes gave butterfly kisses from her breasts down to her belly. The top of his head covered with soft, wavy hair, tickled at his progress. Crinkles fanned out from the corners of those eyes now.

He has laughed a lot. He's been happy. Damn him. Damn me. I was the stupid one. I was the only one who got hurt. Well, I pray I was the only one. Melanie Rose. My flower. How are you, my darling daughter?

Without a word to Aubrey, Celeste, eyes blinded by tears, got up from the table and tripped her way to the ladies' room. She opened the door with a strong shove and hit a girl with long, pink hair. Celeste managed a brief apology and found an open stall. Her chest heaved with anguish.

She wrapped her arms around her head and rocked. She turned and sat down on the side of the toilet seat, bent over as if she had been hit in the stomach. Silent screams came out as quiet rushes of air.

Why? Why does it still hurt so badly?

She thought of the pain as she pushed the baby out and away from her love and protection. She remembered the cord being cut, her final connection. At that very second, her darling daughter was someone else's baby. She moaned as an ache in her empty womb filled her, just as it did years ago. At last, the sobs began. She cried so hard she thought she would throw up. She knelt by the edge of the toilet and waited for the nausea to pass.

I can't do this. I should be stronger by now. Her sobs softened. *Please be happy, sweet Melanie Rose. Don't hate me for what I did.*

Hate. A coldness came over her heart—a familiar feeling, almost comforting. This she could deal with.

She blew all kinds of wetness from her nose into a wad of toilet paper and wiped her eyes again, hopefully for the last time.

A small tap, tap, tap came from the stall door. "Are ye okay, now? Do ye need me to gie someain fer ye?"

"No, thank you. I just heard some terrible news about an old friend. I'm fine," she stammered. "Thank you though."

Celeste opened the door, still sniffing, and washed her hands in the sink. She dampened a paper towel and laid the coolness on her red, blotched cheeks and neck. Two women looked at her askance: an older one with a knowing sadness and another with a face toughened by time and experience.

I need to be like the second woman. She took a cleansing breath, acknowledged both women, and left. She squared her shoulders and felt her heart harden. *He's a horrible man. I let him break my heart back then. This is now, damn it.*

As Celeste approached the table, she noticed that Aubrey was miserable and lost in thought. *Be strong.* She sat down and regarded the steamy food on her plate. It was the most disgusting excuse for meat and vegetables she'd ever seen.

She pushed it away and took a hefty sip of her wine. "So. Tell me, do you ever think of our daughter? Once a month? Once a year? Ever?"

"Jesus, Celeste." He leaned closer and murmured, "Yes, of course. Am I that despicable?"

She thought her face must have revealed her opinion because his eyes transformed from sadness to desolation.

Aubrey nodded resignedly. "I see." He looked away as if he couldn't bear the truth. "So, you still hate me, do you? Perhaps you have a right."

"Well, good. Thank you for admitting that." The New Jersey girl still inside her wanted to slap his pretty face right off his shoulders.

"Please, Celeste. You don't know my pain, do you? How could you? We haven't spoken in years. Not since the hospi—"

"Don't say it. Do *not* go there." She half rose.

He lifted a hand in a silent request for her to stay. "I'm sorry." In a gentler voice, he said, "I'm sorry. Stay."

He drank some ale and wiped the foam from his upper lip. "You're right. I know. But don't you think we could—should—talk? About the baby? I don't have anyone to talk to about her. My parents have never mentioned her. There's been this awful, complicit agreement that she is not to be discussed. I felt I needed to honor their needs too."

"First, the baby is ten now. Her birthday was three and a half weeks ago."

Aubrey's eyes brightened. "Yes. Yes, I knew that. I remembered."

No, you didn't. I bet you rarely remember her. You don't have the thin white scars crisscrossing your belly. You didn't stay long enough to see her strawberry blonde hair and smooshed little nose.

"She was beautiful. She had your hair."

"I'm sure she was. You were her mother."

Celeste was quiet, staring at her drink. A quick peek showed Aubrey tracing the curve of his handle.

"God, Celeste. We can barely look at each other. So intense." He cleared his throat then continued, "I must say, I *am* sorry. We were young. My parents were horrid. I haven't spoken to them much since that day. The day she was born."

"Her name is—was—Melanie Rose."

"The day Melanie was born."

Her voice cracked as she responded, "No, Melanie *Rose*. That's her name to me." She glared at the man she had loved with all a young, virgin's heart could love.

"A lovely name." A deep blush rose from his neck to his cheeks. "So, um, have you thought to contact her in some way? Never mind. Stupid, stupid question."

"How was that supposed to happen? Your parents arranged the adoption. A closed adoption, remember? Because I'm biracial.*" Oh my God. I've finally said it.* Admitting that dreadful fact should have released something within her, but nothing came.

"Is that what you have been thinking?" Dumbfounded, he scratched the back of his head. "My parents are a lot of things, but racist isn't one of them. Believe me."

She raised her chin and turned her gaze to the wall beside her.

"Look at me." He waited until she complied. He braced his shoulders and took a slow, deep breath. "Celeste, I need you to truly hear me now. You had—," he cleared his throat again, "you gave birth to our child in England. Sweetheart, open adoptions are rare in the UK. I'm a fool for even bringing it up. I was thinking about how things were done in America when I said what I did. More to the point, it wouldn't have been something my parents would have even thought about."

"I have a hard time believing that." Her mother's words about not being African and not being black would always be close to the surface of her Egyptian identity. *I don't know what to think anymore.*

She wiped a tear and studied the person he'd become. She glimpsed a bit of that handsome, young Englishman filled with hope.

He wants me to understand and to forgive. We were young, he said. Our first time in love. We flopped around in bed, laughing and experimenting with what felt good. We trusted that everything would be okay.

"Everything wasn't okay, Aubrey."

"Pardon?"

"We thought everything would be fine, but it wasn't, was it?"

Tears filled his eyes. She had broken through his shield.

His voice was rough as he whispered, "No, my love, everything wasn't okay." He leaned back in his chair.

His stare became so unyielding Celeste grew frightened.

"It hasn't been since you left without saying goodbye or leaving a note. You cut me to the quick. I'll admit I wasn't as attached to the— Melanie Rose, but how could I? You barely spoke to me while you were pregnant. To save my soul, I made excuses for you. Maybe you wanted to spare me, that kind of thing. But Celeste, I loved you. We could have gotten through it together, finished college, married. Call me a fool, but that's what I thought would happen. I never expected you to disappear."

She had not expected to hear that. She needed to defend herself. "I hated you. I didn't want to give up my baby, our baby. You were the cause of the very thing from which I could never recover."

He took a gulp of beer and slammed it onto the table. "So. I am the cause of everything that happened to you? I guess I was the only one having fun, mucking about in bed, fucking. I was alone, right?"

"Don't be so crude."

"Why not? You don't bloody get it, do you? You don't *want* to. I told you the truth, as *I* see it, but you seem content to wallow in your pain." He pointed a finger at her, emphasizing each word. "As I've admitted, you weren't the only one in pain, Celeste."

"*We* loved each other. *We* had sex. *We* had a baby. *We* gave it up for adoption. You were alone in this because you chose to be alone."

She gasped. *Oh...my...God.*

Memories flashed one after another. The times he had visited. Sweet bouquets of flowers he picked from gardens on his way. Her yelling. His anger, because she'd sent him, with his flowers, away.

Her stomach lurched as she recollected their last night. She'd called him a coward.

I was horrible.

In a hoarse whisper, she said, "I have to go now. I'm sorry, Aubrey." She left the pub more confused and hurt than when she'd come in.

Could he be right? Had I shut him out? Misjudged his parents all these years? Can pain, loss, blind a person to the truth?

Chapter Nine

George Sinclair, Fourth Earl of Caithness

The aroma of strong coffee and rashers of fried bacon filled the air. Visitors to the inn ate breakfast in a dining room just large enough to hold eight café tables, barely large enough for two people. The room was filled with bright sunlight. Katina and Celeste raised their mimosas and clinked their glasses.

"To another beautiful day and a successful mission," Celeste declared. She took a big bite of runny egg and moaned with pleasure.

"To a successful mission," Katina returned. She dipped a toast point in her yolk. "The coffee is fantastic, but I can't get used to the cold toast they eat here. It's dry and soggy all at the same time, don't you think?"

"Yeesh, yes. But if you're hungry…" Celeste laughed, and a bit of egg shot out of her mouth and landed on Katina's hand.

"Young lady. You wreck my image of the fairly perfect you, talking with your mouth full like that."

Celeste finished chewing and dabbed her napkin on the corners of her mouth. "Well, you've seen me do a lot of things like that. I'm still a New Jersey girl with regular-person manners most of the time. Now tell me all about last night."

Katina replaced her worry with childish exuberance. "I did my normal excellent recon—"

"You mean you looked around?"

"Yes, then I approached my target with stealthy confidence—"

"You mean you went to the back of the building?"

"Uh huh, then I risked life and limb by crossing the threshold of possible doom—"

"You mean you were able to get into the window?"

"Damn it, Celeste. I'm telling the story, now knock it off." Katina stamped her Keds and crossed herself at the same time.

"Tina, I enjoy your dramatic raconteur, but can you get to the good part?"

"What's the matter with that? Anyway, I got to the basement and found this." Katina held the corner of the parchment up. "Ta-daaaa."

Taking the paper, Celeste's face broke into a lopsided grin. "I'm sorry. I didn't mean to ruin your fun. Please, tell me *all* about it. Should we be wearing gloves?"

"Rats. You're right. I didn't bring any. Our hands are clean. Maybe just hold the edge."

Katina gave the blow-by-blow of her movements and hooted at Celeste's expression when she reached the part about the guard.

"Girl, you are one lucky thief. I'd get taken to the station and booked."

"They would not," declared Katina. "You're the cute one in our gang of two."

"If you say so."

"I do. Now I'll tell you more about the best thing ever: how I found the letter." She described the fresco and her process in detail. "All I had to do was separate the canvas from the wall. I'm a genius, aren't I?"

"Absolutely, you are. Did you read it yet or did you save it for us?"

"I saved it, of course." Like a school kid, Katina bounced in her seat as she took the paper back. "I got a little mad when I saw it, but I've settled down. This is going to be so cool. I'll read it now, and we can dissect it later if it's too complicated. The text's in Middle English, by the way. Here it goes, 'You, who have found this, are indeed the clever one. Henry Sinclair hid his riddle well, did he not? The location of the icons will not be easily found. Alas, the seeker of the riddle, and all the answers thereto, must now pass my test of God's desired outcome. Presumptuous, am I not'?"

She peeked over the top of the paper. "This better be good because it already sounds like it's going to be a lot of trouble."

She found where she left off. "'I have had a respectable life of privilege and adventure. I regret that my time strolling the green dells, hearing the drone of the bagpipes in the distant village, comes now to an inexorable end. I desire a few more years for repentance of my sins, a few more years to love God and all his glory, a few more years to test God's plan for me. My mind protests that I was not worthy of finding the treasure, and my heart breaks at my failure.

"'Generations since, I, George Sinclair, Fourth Earl of Caithness, found the riddle from Henry Sinclair. As did my revered ancestor, I commenced the quest for riches but was also thwarted in its retrieval. I have been vexed by continuous skirmishes for power and favor in my homeland'."

Shaking her fist at the god of pretending and trickery, Apate, Katina said, "Darn you, George."

Celeste shook her fist too. "Yes. Darn you, George."

"He had to have written this before the island was taken over by the Ottomans, so we're talking the 16th century here." Katina laid the parchment on the table and continued reading:

"'I was not able to travel to Rhodes. It would have been my great honor to join my fighting skills with that of the Knights of Rhodes, in defense of their powerful seat and more so, to fight off the evil intentions of the Ottoman ruler, Suleiman. However, I was but a lad.

"'I wept for the lost but was pleased that the remaining Knights of Rhodes were relocated after their failure. One of those was young Sir Gerard, a relative of my friend, Archibald Douglas, 4th Earl of Morton. He bypassed France, returning, instead, here.

"'He was a saddened young man, no longer enamored to the knighthood. Months of battle broke his mind. Gerard spoke of a mysterious tale of marvelous icons, a treasure he left behind.

"'The knights and citizens of the island were told to leave immediately. Fearing certain death if he stayed, Gerard left with the other knights within hours of being granted permission. He said that he did not reveal the existence of the treasure or its location because he did not want anyone to attempt retrieving it, for even a good man may have been tempted.

"'Archibald scoffed at the story and attributed the young man's ranting to the shock of war. I knew the truth of it but have been powerless to search for it. I will never tell Archibald of its veracity. He is not deserving.

"'My reputation as a cruel and vindictive man is overstated. I have been entrusted with many high offices. I have fine sons to protect my rich legacy. However, being a man of Godly intentions, despite what the Protestants charge, I trust that these icons were meant for another to find.

"I have dreamed a dream of a destiny not my own. It must have been part of God's plan. If you decipher the following, my test, I believe you are truly destined to find the treasure of the ages.

To save the queen, castle the king.

The night was not the knight; you learned that to be truth.

The night is the knight now. In the castle, he dwells.

For inside the keep of Clan Graham, the book of old remains.

Regard the knight, the king, and queen,

on the edge of gold, the dark of truth is shown.

You will find the first chapter of the story of your destiny.

You must prove to me now, that you have the gift and persistence of a true believer'."

Celeste said, "That's quite the tale. If I understand this mess, he failed in finding the treasure and set up another task for us? To prove we, I mean you, are *the one*?"

"It's apparent that we, my friend, are supposed to find a book. A book with a gold edge," Katina added.

"This is like a dream."

She put down her mimosa and regarded Celeste.

"Speaking of dreams." Katina leaned her forearms on the table and steepled her fingers. "Who's Melanie Rose?"

Celeste spewed her drink. "What?"

"Who's Melanie Rose? You talked about her in your sleep last night."

"Well." Celeste wiped her chin and placed her napkin on the table. She folded it in half. Then folded it again. "Melanie Rose was a beautiful baby that Aubrey and I put up for adoption."

In that moment, it became too clear that her life was far from perfect. Katina was stunned by the revelation. *My best friend had a baby? Tiny, pink booties and bows on a bald head kind of baby?*

Tears welled in Celeste's eyes.

Katina used her softest voice, the one that brought out all her years of living in the South. "I bet she's the most darlin' girl in the world."

Chapter Ten

Your Past May Guide Your Present

Maxwell Blackmarr got off British Airways flight 632 to Athens at one thirty-five in the afternoon. A pregnant woman behind him threw up every twenty minutes, and her snotty-nosed kid cried the entire three hour and forty-minute flight.

He threw a leather satchel onto an empty chair in the waiting area and jerked out his cell phone. He tried to punch in a number, but was bumped on all sides by British tourists, a group of pushy Russians, and a few excited people speaking Greek.

The sickly mother crooned, *"Po-po-po,"* and patted the bottom of her crying toddler.

"Po-po-po, my ass. Your kid needs a good whack."

In a heavy Greek accent, the mother asked, "What deed you say to mee?"

Surprised he had spoken his thoughts out loud, he replied, "I was wondering if your handsome boy wanted a snack."

The woman glared and threw out her hand as if to stop traffic.

Knowing he'd just gotten the Greek version of the finger, he grumbled, "You must be from the village."

Being called the equivalent of a peasant, caused her to burst into tears.

He turned his back and finished dialing Robert's number, then moved away and growled into the phone, "They weren't on the God-damned plane."

"They were supposed to be."

Maxwell yelled, "Where are they?"

People turned to stare.

"I don't know. Like I said, they were *supposed* to be on that plane."

Maxwell picked up his satchel and pushed through the multitude milling around. He scanned the various arrivals and departures listed on the flight monitor, wondering if the women had chosen another possibility.

Perhaps, a connection through another city other than Athens. It irked him to no end that there were three that day. One of which had come in forty-five minutes before his arrival and left twenty minutes ago. The second connected from Turkey, not a great prospect. The third came from Egypt, an even less likely option.

In a quieter voice, Maxwell chastised Robert, "I pay you a lot of money to know what the hell is going on. When you get off your ass and find out, please be good enough to let me know. There's some sort of delay here, a ground worker strike maybe. Damn Greeks are always striking. I have a room at the Mitsis Grand Hotel. Find out when they're getting to Katina's apartment."

Maxwell Blackmarr sat on a cheap yellow chair at a small bar on the second floor of the terminal to wait. He tapped his index finger on the plastic table and tried to be patient. He jerked his chin in the waiter's direction. The waiter jerked his chin back and kept walking.

Swearing under his breath, Maxwell stood and went to the bar. He smiled with as much graciousness as he could muster. "May I have a Tanqueray and tonic, please? Do you serve food here?"

The waiter continued to wipe glasses.

"What the hell is with these people? I just want a damn drink." He stormed back to his table and waited. "Why is everything so difficult?"

He stopped grousing and remembered a time, many years ago, when he'd said those words. The youthful self-pity, rare nowadays, stood out in the annals of his mind.

The year was 1985. Thanksgiving break at Yale started the next day. His parents picked him up at the fraternity house to take him home to Queens. The roads were wet and slick. Their car was hit, all but destroyed. His mom and dad died instantly, they'd said.

His resilient heart hoped his studies would lead him to a great career. He would show his parents in heaven, or wherever good people go after they die, that he was worthy of their love and sacrifice.

The reality of his new life crushed him. Poverty didn't drive his friends away. His bitterness did.

Everything was so damn difficult after that.

Chapter Eleven

A Walk in The Park Can be Hard on The Heart

Katina and Celeste planned to make a plan. Celeste said she didn't have the emotional energy to rush into the next phase of their project, while Katina was desperate to move forward. Together, they decided to figure everything out during a hike in the countryside. Maybe. She and Celeste walked down the main street of the village to a grocery store and ever-important snacks.

From there, Katina lead the way from one path after another, passing small cottages with gardens full of vegetables and flowers so bright and colorful most people might be tempted to pick one or two. The final destination was an old cemetery within a verdant valley that sloped toward town from unremarkable mountain peaks.

Celeste interrupted the silent walk. "Did you know that the poet William Wordsworth had a sister? Her name was Dorothy Wordsworth. She wrote, 'I never passed through a more delicious dell than the glen of Rosslyn.' Isn't that beautiful? A more delicious dell. My goodness."

Katina nodded. "I just love it when people use the word delicious for non-food descriptions. It's like using 'thingy' for all things technical."

Celeste gave her a sidelong glance. "Here I am waxing poetic, and all you come up with is *thingy*?"

"I can be as romantic as the next girl—"

"No, you can't," Celeste countered.

"I can too. It's just that I think I'm more of a fun-slash-serious person than romantic. Romance doesn't get you anywhere."

"Well, you're right there. Romance has never gotten me anywhere, but I'd like some now and then, I guess." Celeste paused until Katina gave her full attention. "It's not something you have ever talked about."

"Hey. You had a major romance without a single mention. You could've given me a CliffsNotes version." As she approached the graveyard, Katina held her arms wide and twirled a slow circle. "We are so lucky, don't you think? I wonder if the poor inhabitants of Atlanta and Manhattan are sweltering?"

"Probably." Celeste buttoned her sweater and shivered.

"Speaking of Manhattan, my brother called this morning."

Katina bent to pick a wildflower with translucent white petals and purple pistils in the center. She murmured, "How's the investigation going?"

"He's done. 'Caught, bagged, and tagged,' he said."

Katina tucked the flower in her hair. "Yuck. They killed the bad guys?"

"No, just cop humor. Their way to relieve the stress." She raised an eyebrow and pointed a finger like a ten-year old tattletale. "You wouldn't know anything about *that* would you?"

"Yeah, I guess I do that when I'm, um, upset or trying to get out of trouble." She gave a sheepish grin. "But enough about me. Was Bobby checking on you? I thought you were supposed to keep track of *him*."

"I do, sort of." Celeste gazed at the trees which were swaying in a breeze. "Let's sit here for our picnic. I found another article in the *New York Times* this morning. I keep a collection he's mentioned in. I'm going to print them out and maybe make a scrapbook of his career one day."

"I'd never think about that," Katina said as she placed a bottle of white wine and snacks from her satchel onto the ground.

"Well, he had one when he was a football star in high school. I just want to make sure he knows what he does now is, and will be, more important than anything he did back then."

"You're an amazing sister. Know that?"

"Maybe. I guess." She searched the Kindle. "Anyway, I'll read the article. It's awesome.

"The alleged mafia-style hit on Jacoby 'Jersey Man' Jameson was solved Wednesday night after a raid on an apartment in a 1950 low-rise on 8150 102 Road in South Ozone Park. This was the infamous location where the FBI dug for a body in the former yard of the notorious and powerful mob boss, James 'Jimmy the Gent' Burke, who was a major player depicted in the movie *GoodFellas*, portrayed by Robert De Niro.

"Mr. Mario Banino, the alleged shooter, was led out of the building in handcuffs, wearing a T-shirt and boxers. He was resisting arrest—arms flying and legs kicking. He yelled in the direction of the two detectives in charge and a number of residents standing close by."

Celeste yelled in a male *basso profundo*, "You owe Vito on two counts. You gave me up. Now you're a dead man." She continued as a fake-broadcaster, "This reporter believes that Mr. Banino referred to the local mob leader, Vito 'The Lender' Leonardo. Mr. Banino is held pending payment of a $150,000 bond in the Metropolitan Correctional

Center in Lower Manhattan."

Katina leaned over to see the accompanying picture. "There's Bobby. Good grief, he's photogenic, isn't he? His face is fierce. See his hand? He's about to draw his gun. And look at that gangster's face. It's in mid-yell. I'd be terrified if I was one of those people. Your brother must deal with 'em every day."

Celeste accepted an offered apple. "Thanks. It didn't seem to shake him up or anything. He asked if we were having fun in Rhodes. I told him we detoured here to visit friends, and we'd go there in a day or two. I wonder if he'll join us this time. He needs a break. You know, he loves the island and the beautiful women who walk around in bikinis."

"I think he likes the women who wear half a bathing suit and the food." Katina took a sip of wine. "Umm, are you going to see Aubrey again?"

Celeste put her head back and slowly chewed a small bite of apple. The corners of her lips turned down to a frown. "There's so much there, Tina. How complicated could my life get, in what, twenty-four hours? I meet the father of my child, the one man I've ever loved and hated. I've held this anger in my heart for years. Then I find out I've been wrong about almost everything. I don't know. He hasn't asked to see me again. We'll see, I guess." Celeste let that thought linger for a moment. "I wasn't prepared to deal with him. I've never even talked about it…to anyone." She looked at Katina with aching, sad eyes. "Secrets are a bitch."

She has no idea.

Celeste messed with the Kindle again and took a few sips of their dry Chardonnay. "Let's get down to the reason we came here."

"Please God, yes." Katina grinned with relief. "Spending hours of following internet rabbit holes is one of my best favorite things to do."

"I know."

"But I have a new least favorite thing. Rabbit holes in the *fields*. They're way too heinous."

"But that's where the rabbits keep their babies safe." Celeste grinned at Katina. "You joke when you're scared too. Seen it a bunch over the years. You can be kinda cute."

She flashed her biggest cheesy smile. "Tankyouberrymush."

Celeste chuckled and continued her research.

After a few minutes, she held out the tablet to Katina. "Archibald Douglas is descended from the Clan Graham. So, we need to find a Clan Graham keep. There's the Lennoxlove House in East Lothian. It says it's the home of the Duke of Hamilton who is also the Marquess of Douglas. It's preserved."

"Maybe. Is there anything else? We need to identify, then rule out as many as possible so we don't have to sneak into, I mean, visit more than we have to. Man. I really shouldn't plan to break the law in advance. I hear the jail time's longer. And besides, it's just wrong isn't it?"

"You're such a goof. Let's focus on what we can do, not incarceration. There's the Tantallon Castle. It's also in East Lothian." Clearing her throat, Celeste continued, "The stronghold of the Red Douglases. Sounds so cool, doesn't it? Aww. It's partially ruined. Never mind. Hey, they owned two more in East Lothian. One's the Whittingehame Tower. Oohhh. And there's Kilspindie Castle." She read a bit more to herself. "Nope. That one belonged to the Douglases of Kilspindie and is just a bunch of ruins now. And the tower just seems too small."

"Does it have a statue?" Katina wondered.

"Statue? I don't know. Maybe on the grounds somewhere."

"We need to find a statue of a knight, in a building. Right?"

"Yeah."

"Geez Louise! Lothian encompasses Edinburgh and land all around it. Let's narrow it down to anything around here and work out if we have to." Inspiration hit Katina like a sugary glaze on a hot Krispy Kreme. "We need a building that has a direct connection between Archibald Douglas *and* George Sinclair."

Five minutes later, Celeste raised her eyes. "Damn. This website says there's a place right here called Dalkeith Palace. It's also referred to as a castle. Hmm. Anyway, the owners are descended from the Clan Graham, and a Douglas was one of the previous owners, shall we say. It seems the Sinclair and Douglas families knew each other very well so George would have easy access to it too." She all but shouted, "George Sinclair must have been talking about this one, don't you think?*"* She scanned some pictures of its interior. "This one has a huge statue of a knight."

She and Katina did a few fist pumps and giggled, as birds flew away from the tree above in a panic.

Moments after resuming a search for more specific information, Celeste said, "George Sinclair died in Edinburgh but was buried here. That puts him in the region when he wrote the riddle. Given that, I'm all but sure this place is our best bet. If not, we're screwed." She shook her head. "I feel sorry for people. Half of the references on the internet call the building Dalkeith Palace. The other half refers to it as the castle at Dalkeith. The third half calls it Dalkeith College. How do people keep anything straight around here? Take Trenton. It may have a population of over 80,000, but they keep their damn name straight."

Katina laughed at the third reference. "I love how the names have been changed over the centuries. You know it just depends on how the building was used. Castles were for protection. Palaces were posh houses. Now it's used as a college. I *bet* people are confused."

Celeste tucked a highlighted chunk of hair behind her ear. "Do you think we should just march in and say, 'Here we are. Give us the keys to the castle?'"

"Of course not. Silly girl. Where'd your imagination go. We absolutely need to break in. The question is, what tactics will we need to employ to be successful?" She wrung her hands like an awesome not-too-evil genius. "You're too short to scale walls, so that's out. My hip bones would bruise if we had to crawl on our bellies across ice cold stones. So that's out. Oh, heck. I don't know. Whatever we do, we're gonna do it together this time, though."

All pretense of humor over Katina's ideas disappeared, replaced by a pall of dread in Celeste's eyes. "I think we could get the keys this time."

"Do tell, *ma belle*."

"Aubrey said he was a professor around here. That means a college or university, doesn't it? If it's the same one, he'll have the keys."

"What? That's fantastic. He'll be our knight in shining armor."

"The very location we would need next. You know I'm not religious, but that just seems like divine intervention. Problem is, I don't even know if I want to speak to him again, let alone ask for a favor. One that might get him in trouble at that."

Katina finished crossing herself at the mention of divine intervention. "If you ask him and he helps, it will be a testament to his good-guy-ness. If he gets in trouble, it's just karma."

"Tina, your line of logic is both amazing and troubling."

"If it works, don't question greatness. Will you ask? Pretty please?"

With a face drawn with concern, Celeste stood and put her Kindle away.

Katina joined her as they meandered into the small graveyard, abandoned by families and forgotten over the centuries. Rounded, moss-covered stones marked a few grassy plots. Others had Celtic crosses standing at odd angles, as if the ground beneath them had compressed. She noticed one that was tilted so far to the left it looked like a brooding mourner.

Celeste studied the words of a newer gravestone. "Listen to this. 'Here lie the remains of a brother, who died saving another. He was a farm hand. He was a good man, but the Lord saw to save t'other.'"

"Now that's a strange epitaph."

"I love the potential of stories. Ya know? I like to imagine their lives." Celeste hummed some Felonious Monk for a few minutes. "I think I need to come to terms with Aubrey. He seemed open to seeing me again. I was awake all last night thinking—remembering. He was right, you know. I was the one who shut him out. At that time, I agreed with his parents that we were not in any position to raise a baby, emotionally or financially."

"That period was overwhelming, Tina." She squatted next to two tiny headstones. "I know you think I should have talked to you, but I didn't think you could understand. I didn't even want my parents to know. God, what a disaster *that* would've been."

She brushed dirt from the name on one marker. "So, I just...handled it myself. Not very well at all, though."

Tina, keep your mouth shut for once.

"I look back on my life, and I see a lot of, I guess I could call it, aloneness."

Katina understood that all too well. "I remember you telling me your mother had three miscarriages trying to have a boy. Once Bobby was born, they were consumed by him."

"I get that. On the one hand, he struggled with academics. On the other, he was a football star. Every aspect of him demanded that attention, even if he didn't demand it himself. Our purpose was to make Bobby successful, and I was okay with that because life, school, they were easy for me. I jumped at the scholarship to Dana Hall Prep school. It was my ticket to success." Her gaze softened. "And I met my goofy buddy, Tina. Who knew?"

"Fate indeedy."

"What all that didn't do was teach me how to handle failure. Not that Melanie Rose was. I just never had to deal with anything that momentous."

"I understand what you're trying to say, sweetie. You don't have to defend your actions."

Celeste's gaze flew to Katina. "I'm not." Her voice rose with shock and disappointment. "You don't understand at all, do you? I'm *trying* to say Melanie Rose wasn't a mistake, but almost everything that surrounded her was." She swiped at a tear. "I refused to see my part in any of it. I refused to accept my guilt because I was crushed by it."

She took Celeste into her arms as if consoling a child. "I understand now. You needed to grow up enough to start your own life, right?"

"I was immature on all fronts." Celeste pulled away and sighed deeply, as if she'd exhale all the bad thoughts and anger and lonely years from her mind and body. "Well, I guess I'm growing up. I'm taking responsibility for my part. I'm not proud of what I did."

Wiping the tear tracks from her cheeks with the heel of her palm, Celeste said, "I'll talk to Aubrey. He may or may not help us, but regardless, I need to apologize. Can we go back now?"

Scratching at ant bites on her ankle, Katina said, "Gather the goodies!" She jumped from foot to foot. "The devils hath found-eth us-eth!"

"Run for your life. They're going to eat you alive."

"I can't believe those stupid ants. And your laughter isn't helping me a bit, oh by the way." She settled down and shoved the leftovers into her satchel.

"Tina. They didn't have you in their crosshairs or anything. They're just bugs."

"They did so." Katina pointed to the ground. "They planned a siege on my left flank and scuttled my jib."

Celeste covered a smile with her hand and said through her fingers, "You're unhappy. I'm sorry."

Uncomfortable with Celeste's pity, she shrugged and smashed a few confused ants with the toe of her boot. She was inordinately pleased with her destruction upon the biting creatures. "You're just going to call?"

"I don't have his number, so I'll call the college. See if he works there. Do you want to go back with me or continue the hike?"

"I'll stay. I'm going to call home again, if I can get a signal, to see what's happening with my dad, Lexi, and Jim. I sense he's okay now. I bet he just isn't used to checking in because he hit it big."

"Jim hits it big?"

"You know, finds dinosaur bones. It takes him to some of the most God-forsaken places on Earth, time after time. It's *his* treasure. I understand that now. I'm driven to carry this mission through like nothing I've ever felt before."

"Yeah. You're a regular Lara Croft in a real-life *Tomb Raider* now."

Katina shivered and gave Celeste a sheepish grin. "Umm. She didn't die in that movie, did she?"

"Heck no, toots. She rocked it, just like you will. Let's send a prayer that I rock it too."

Chapter Twelve

Mending Fences

Celeste sat on the edge of the bed. Her hand shook like a Floridian in an arctic snowstorm as she opened her cell phone. She wasn't cold. Nope. Nervous as hell. To stall, she thought of ways she might repair a small tear in the wallpaper, maybe cover worn areas on the faded velvet armchair in the corner with doilies, and clean hints of mold off the ceiling.

Enough. It was time to get it done. She googled the number and pressed the call button. She took a deep breath and released it in a slow exhale, while she listened to the ringing. She gasped when someone answered the phone. *Of course, they'd answer, dummy. Can't change your mind now.*

"Dalkeith," said a cheerful, female voice.

"Oh, hello. My name is Celeste Daly. Does an Aubrey Wells teach there?"

"He does indeed. Can you hold a minute, love?"

"You bet." *Love? Must not be Francie.*

Her leg jiggled until all movement in her body stopped. *Get a grip—*

"This is Professor Wells."

His deep voice sent a chill through Celeste. "Hello, Aubrey—"

"Celeste. How are you?"

"Fine. Good." *Yeesh.* "How are you?" She cringed at her unease.

"Splendid. You?"

"Marvy." She rolled her eyes at herself. *Who says marvy?*

Celeste deepened her voice and tried to sound like the professional she was as she said, "Aubrey, the reason I'm calling is, um, I think we should get together. I mean, not permanently. Not that it's out of the question." *Mother of God, shut up.*

Aubrey chuckled. "I'm glad you're open to the possibility."

"I'm flustered."

"It sounds like it." His voice was so gentle her heart fluttered.

"I'd like us to talk and get to know each other as adults. Maybe you'd let me ask for forgiveness?"

"Well. I would love to see you again. We had a difficult

discussion that didn't end as I wanted."

She held her breath, for fear it would fuel a whimper. "I've come to understand some hard truths."

"As have I. Let's mend these fences, shall we? I can be there in twenty minutes. Is that good for you?"

She didn't remember if she mentioned the inn. How had he known she was twenty minutes away? She shrugged her acceptance of weird things that happened when people were freaked out. "That'll be fine."

"Can we talk whilst dining?"

"Oh, no thanks. My friend Tina and I had an eventful lunch at a graveyard." The memory of the crazy ant attack eased the tension in her core. "I'll explain when I see you."

"That sounds intriguing. See you soon, my dear."

"See ya." After hanging up, she rose and paced the room, wondering how she should fill the minutes and stay calm-ish at the same time. Unfortunately, her ideas for potential hotel repair were exhausted.

"I sounded like an idiot," she grumbled, as she went into the bathroom to redo her makeup. In mid-stroke of her mascara wand, a noise startled her. She peeked out the bathroom door as she wiped an ugly brown smear from under her eye. "Hi, Tina. I didn't hear you come in. Give me a sec."

After a moment, Celeste came out to find Katina picking up discarded clothing off the floor. She rolled them in loose bundles and put them into her suitcase. Celeste lifted her brow.

Katina answered the silent question, "I'm packing to leave. Just in case things didn't go well with your phone call."

She emptied her satchel across the bed, repacked her tools in a better order, and put the document in the outside pocket. She smiled. "However, I'm getting the breaking-into-places bag ready just in case things *did* go well. So. Tell me. Are we coming or going?"

Celeste was struck by how Katina's brain worked. "You seem okay with either option."

"Well…"

"Ha. I knew it." Celeste went back into the bathroom and called out, "The talk didn't happen yet. I'm meeting him for drinks in a few minutes."

Katina appeared in the door. "Do you want me to come? I can be your wingman."

"Why would I need a wingman? I don't need to pick anyone up," she said, applying a dusty pink blush across the top of her cheekbones. The frost in the powder shined against her dark skin. She nodded her approval.

"No, of course not, but I may need to rescue you." She stood behind Celeste pretending to fix her own makeup. Her elbow bonked Celeste on the head.

"Tina, I'm a big girl."

"You're short," she said, then burst out laughing.

"Knock it off. You know what I mean. You can come, but you can't sit with us. The pub's called The Jackal's Tale, and it's just down the street. Go in a few minutes after I've gotten there. When we get to the part—I guess I should say, *if* we get to the part about the castle, I'll wave you over. Just stay out of sight."

"Okay, but if he does or says anything to hurt you, I'll be there to hurt him back. Somehow."

She regarded Katina in the mirror. "He might, but it's time I look at things through grownup eyes and deal with this. Aubrey was a nice man. I can't imagine he would have changed much."

She put her makeup in a small travel case and pushed her way out of the bathroom. She slipped on a cozy, peach sweater over a pair of heavy linen slacks. Selecting her favorite Prada heels, she gave Katina a nod of encouragement. "Here I go. Wish me luck."

~ * ~

Aubrey's self-assured smile both set off warning signals and warmed Celeste's heart. *How can he be so happy? Last night was horrible.* She couldn't stop staring and couldn't say hello. *He's still so handsome.*

He put his hand on her back and led her into the pub. "I'm glad we could get together." He indicated a booth by the bar. "Let's sit here."

The place had cozy, hunting-lodge-inspired décor. A few young people chatted quietly. Three booths led to the back where bookcases lined the walls. "There aren't many people here. Are they from your school?"

He regarded the patrons. "There aren't many students attending summer term. These kids might be locals. I don't recognize any."

"Weel, awrite noo, Aubrey. Thes will be twice thes week, noo willnae it? Anither swally fer ye?"

Celeste turned to see Francie leaning into Aubrey. She shifted away to place paper napkins on the table, while regarding Celeste.

I think she's jealous. Oh-oh…

Aubrey replied, "Good day to you. I'll have a Guinness. And a nice chardonnay for the lady." Rubbing his hands, he turned his attention back to Celeste. "Well, here we are."

"Here we are." He looked so sweet and hopeful at that moment.

She wondered how long it would last, before recriminations would fly.

Her vision blurred. *Rats. I'm crying already. This isn't going to go well. Would ya look at that, his eyes are tearing too.*

"Let me start by saying, I've missed you, Celeste. Did I forget how beautiful you are, or have you *become* the stunning woman who sits before me now?"

"I—"

"Before you say anything, I want to apologize for my horrid behavior last night. I was unforgivably unkind. With that said, please forgive me."

She couldn't draw her eyes away from his. They were sad, and sorry, and hopeful, all at once. She tried to read his mind, to understand what his face revealed. It dawned on her that she hadn't answered him. She stammered, "I'm sorry. I wasn't expecting an apology from you."

"No? What did you expect me to say?" he challenged.

"Aubrey, I'm a little shocked. I called you today, not to ask for an apology, but to offer one. I'm the brute, not you."

His face transformed from insult to enlightenment. A twinkle lit his expressive eyes. "Well, I must say, I never called myself a brute. I had planned to save *that* for later, if you didn't forgive me right away."

So dry. She adored his British sense of humor. And how he spoke, such flowery words. *You haven't changed, have you?*

He sighed. "There you go again. You don't look angry, but a few words might save my soul from destruction."

"Don't self-destruct. I-I," she stammered again. "I can't seem to get two words out, and I'm the one who asked you to meet *me*. I'm so sorry, Aubrey. There are a million things to tell you, but I'm saying them in my head. I have to figure out how to get them out, don't I?"

Celeste took in his deep, masculine chuckle. The hairs on her arms rose. Other parts of her body tingled in a familiar response. Euphoria, like a deepest breath taken while experiencing a great joy, filled her. It took a concerted effort to say, "We haven't seemed to— I mean, I haven't gotten over how I feel about you."

"Nor I you, my love."

She closed her eyes. *He called me his love.*

Fully acknowledging the possibility of a rekindled relationship, she let the ever-present destructive anger go. "Thank you... Frankly, I'm amazed at how we're responding to each other. It seems we have a mutual desire to forgive and forget."

"I could never forget, Celeste. I wouldn't want to."

"Of course not." She leaned in. "Not forget everything. I mean that we'll start *again*. Almost fresh. You know?"

Happiness filled his handsome features. He started to slide his hand across the table to take hers, only to have a frothing beer put into his palm.

"Haur ye are. Haur's jist what ye bin wantin'. Drink up," the waitress bellowed. She smacked the glass of white wine down in front of Celeste which caused a spill down the side.

Both she and Aubrey grinned at the back of a smug Francie as she sashayed back to the bar.

Celeste giggled. "Well, me thinks she's sweet on ye, Aubrey. Ye've made her a mite mad."

The tension was broken. Celeste and he'd had a good laugh, and conversation became easy. They reminisced about college life and spoke of the possibility of new times to come. Most healing was the lovely conversation of their baby girl, a thread woven from Celeste's heart through his, pulling them closer.

Evening approached with silent speed and a dullness settled over the bar. Staff turned on lights, and dinner aromas filled the air. Celeste stretched and sniffed, trying to decide if she smelled fried potatoes or broccoli when someone jolted her shoulder.

She squeaked and turned to the offender. "Well. Katina. Fancy seeing you here."

Chapter Thirteen

Katina Couldn't Stay Away

Katina was annoyed. She used her best, I'm-friendly-but-I-may-bite-you voice to say, "Hi. I just happened to be sitting in the back. Did you know they have books and magazines for the patrons? Anyway, I was reading some fascinating information on the importance of proper sheep husbandry, when I noticed you here. Let me tell you, I didn't see any mention of weddings between a girl sheep and a boy sheep."

She crossed her arms and tapped her foot. She raised her brows at Celeste and waited for an invitation to sit.

"Okay. Okay. Okay." Celeste sighed. "Aubrey, may I introduce you to my dearest friend, Katina Bason? Tina, this is my first boyfriend, Aubrey Wells." She bit her index fingernail like a mischievous child.

Watching the play of emotions across her friend's face, Katina accepted the inevitable. "How *lovely* to meet Celeste's first boyfriend. I'm Katina."

He shot to his feet, a warm smile on his face. "I'm chuffed to meet you too. We've been catching up." He offered a seat next to Celeste. "Would you join us for dinner?"

Katina sat with grace and arranged herself to take up more room on the bench than Celeste offered. "I've heard you eat Spotted Dick. Sounds awful. Celeste? What do *you* think?"

"I think, *Katina*, Spotted Dick is now called Spotted Richard, where it is served in England. You'd hate it because it's raw beef fat and dried fruit. So maybe a stew might appeal to you."

Is my hair on fire because I think I smell something burning.

"Oh, well, there you go. Aubrey, is it? What do you suggest?" Katina gave her most innocent expression to him, knowing it wouldn't work on Celeste.

The hairs on her arms stood up at his deep chuckle. She turned to face Celeste, raised an arm to show the tiny bumps and gave a what-the-hell-just-happened look. Celeste grinned and raised her own for inspection. In unison, they turned back to a baffled Aubrey.

"Well then. Right. Maybe we can get Francie over here. You're in luck. Tonight is steak night. They serve locally sourced meat. It's always tender and flavorful because it's grass fed. It should appeal to your American sensibilities."

The smile he tried to deliver was less than impressive. His previous reference to the phrase "join us for dinner" didn't sit well either. Us meant them, the two women there that have been buddies since middle school. Not him. "American sensibilities? What, exactly, do you mean?"

"Katina…" Celeste transformed her angry gaze into a sweet expression as she shifted her gaze to Aubrey. "Don't mind her. She has gas. Must have been some Dick she ate for lunch."

Katina and Aubrey's laughter rang out.

"I'm…I'm…" Celeste stammered.

Katina couldn't stay mad, though she tried hard. "You're the best. Isn't she, Aubrey? She's funny, and brilliant, and beautiful, and sassy as hell. We're lucky she puts up with us, don't you think?"

"Absolutely. I hope she'll consider putting up with me often in the future."

"Well, speaking of the future, Aubrey…" Katina sought Celeste's approval with a flick of a glance. She received the affirmative. "We will be busy."

"Anything fun?"

"Absolutely. We have some research to do here in Dalkeith." Katina waited to see if he would take the bait. Celeste rolled her eyes but didn't help with the conversation. *Chicken.*

Katina focused on Aubrey. *Reeling you in.*

"Anything I could help with?" Aubrey said. "I know my way around here pretty well now."

Gotcha. "Well, I don't want to waste your time." She rarely tried manipulation. So much thought on how to influence people hurt her head.

"I would love to help. What can I do?" His handsome face was sweet and eager.

"Now that you've offered, it would be just wonderful if you could, um, give us a tour."

"Dalkeith?"

"Um-hmm," she murmured.

"Of course."

Success. "How about later today? Are you busy?"

"Well, no, actually. I hadn't expected to give a tour, but I'm sure it would be fine. Celeste?"

Katina spoke before Celeste could. "Perfect. If we finish up today, we can continue with our travel plans. We're heading to Greece next."

"If steak is too much, let's order a light meal, and we can work this all out, shall we?" Aubrey got the attention of the waitress, who'd sent dagger-eyes in their direction for the last five minutes.

"We ate at the cemetery, remember, Tina?" She looked at Aubrey. "We'll have a glass of wine and tell you about the attack while you eat."

He laughed with gusto. "I can't wait to hear about this. Francie!"

Chapter Fourteen

Hidden Closets Beckon

Katina viewed the rolling green hills shaded to muted hues from the setting sun through the window of Aubrey's tiny sedan. Her bench seat had next to no padding, and her legs started to cramp. He'd said the castle was a short distance to the northeast side of the village, but good God, she needed to stretch out. She wished she had the front seat but didn't want to break the bond forming between Celeste and Aubrey. He did have a few good qualities, like his voice and awesome auburn hair. *Auburn. Aubrey. Auburn. Aubrey. His parents must have known he'd have—*

"So, ladies, what in particular has drawn you across the pond?"

Katina gave Celeste a he's-your-guy-so-you-decide look.

"Well, you know my major was medieval studies. Tina's also a historian, of sorts. The Knights Templar and the Knights of Rhodes."

"Bravo, Katina. I've loved the subject myself. This area of Scotland is rife with associations to their illustrious past. There are many references to the Masons, which as you know, have indelible ties to the Knights Templar."

Unsure of the root of his enthusiasm, Katina said, "Of course. We want to find a document that was left there. We'd appreciate your help."

"The town's library has a display of minutes from Grand Lodge proceedings. In 1723, the London Lodge elected the Earl of Dalkeith as their next Grand Master. I'll take you there another time."

Celeste added, "Really interesting. We've researched a much earlier period, around the 1400s. A fellow named George left a message for us. Well, for *someone*."

With a nod, Katina gave consent to continue.

Like a spy, Celeste gave an almost imperceptible nod in return. "Katina found a document in Sir Henry's old crypt."

Aubrey's voice rose an octave as he said, "Brilliant."

Katina glanced at his reflection in the rearview mirror. Bemused horror came over his face. "You broke into Sir Henry's manse?"

"It's not the first time an explorer removes a find. You make me feel a little guilty." She had to figure out a way to get him so interested he'd be willing to steal the Hope Diamond. Let him in on a bit of their activities. *Okay. Step one, appeal to his ego.* "You know everything about the area, and I guess a lot about the families. What they did. Who hunted with whom."

His brow wrinkled for a moment. "I know the Sinclair clan owned property here for generations. The Douglases gained their lands, which contained Dalkeith Castle and other properties, toward the end of the medieval period. I'm sure they all attended each other's parties and such."

Step two. Get him excited. "Exactly. This is deep so hold on to your kilt."

He said, "I'm not wearing a—"

"We think George Sinclair, 4th Earl of Caithness, and friend of the Douglases, left a riddle in the castle during the 16th century."

"What are you about, Katina?" He turned to Celeste. "What's going on here?"

A full minute later, she gave Aubrey a good rundown of their last few days.

His raised brows rose higher. "So, you're not interested in a tour of the area in general. You want to find something where I work?" His gaze vectored between the road, Celeste, and Katina. "I must warn you both the building has changed a good bit over the years."

It worked. Katina did a mental woo-hoo. "We suspected as much. In fact, a website described it in great detail. We know there's a library. Is it still intact? Are there pieces of original furniture?"

He swerved around a rut in the road. "Blast. Sorry. The library's still there. It's next to the computer lab where I do most of my teaching. There are a few chests in the ballroom dating from the 1600 and 1700s."

She picked at the bottom of her cashmere sweater while trying to picture the interior of the building. "No, probably not."

The dinky car made a bumpy turn to the left. Her head smacked the side window. "Criminy. Slow down."

As with Celeste, Aubrey was also oblivious and continued to drive onto the blacktopped courtyard in a helter-skelter fashion. "Some people call it the Dalkeith House now, because it's been converted into a school."

Good grief. Another name for the same place. Katina was captivated by the stately property. Her imagination put bricks on the courtyard pavement and formal, gloriously-colored gardens, inviting aristocratic visitors, dressed in elaborate finery, to stroll in the direction of the stone Montagu bridge.

As they parked, she turned her attention to the looming three-story, block U-shaped, Georgian building. "It's still beautiful." Just as pictures had shone, sandstone slabs surrounded a multitude of windows. At least twenty chimneys shot above the dark-gray, slate-tiled roof.

Aubrey slammed the car door. The metal report echoed off the building and into the night sky. "The original castle was built in the 12th century. Sacked and rebuilt again in the early 18th century. This was an important military stronghold, thus the repeated attacks. Did you know Bonny Prince Charlie, King George IV, and Queen Victoria slept there?"

"No, I didn't know that. Imagine the pomp and circumstance those occasions brought. The maids cleaned, the cooks cooked, and the butlers butled for weeks," Katina said.

Celeste chuckled at Katina's made up word, and they continued to follow as Aubrey gestured and talked as if he was a tour guide and not a resident professor. He needed one of those little flags they carry to complete the picture.

"It had a moat and four massive stone walls. Later, a tower was built where the royals lived and kept their riches for safe keeping. You can see the outline and some remains of the tower on the western side."

The internet had informed Katina about much of what Aubrey said, but she didn't interrupt for Celeste's sake. That girl looked at the man as if he was royalty himself.

"At one point," he continued, "King James VI of Scotland, the son of Mary Queen of Scots and King Charles I owned it. There are stories of treasures remaining somewhere on the grounds or in the walls. I suspect there are many secret doors I've yet to find."

"Perhaps there are treasures behind one of them, just waiting for me," he added, with a wink to Celeste.

Katina's skin tingled at the thought of hidden rooms. She wanted to do a we're-going-to-hit-the-big-time dance but didn't want to embarrass Celeste. *Oh, the lengths I go to be a good friend.*

Walking toward the stone steps to the entrance, Katina asked, "You said the library's still there. Does it have books from the 16th century?"

"Some." He punched a code into the outside lock. "I've been here for a few years, and I just can't get used to this modernity." He opened the door that led into a large square room.

The walls had wood paneling from floor to ceiling. Carved cherubs lined the crown molding, and a set of moose antlers hung in a prominent location.

"Isn't there a huge statue of the Duke of Wellington in the Marble Hall? I googled it. He's a knight wearing a robe."

"This is the Great Hall. Marble Hall, with the statue, is through there, to the left." Aubrey led them through the indicated door. "These huge black and white agate floor tiles are a sign of wealth. The *hugely* wealthy have things like this castle's massive column made from one piece of marble."

The reception area was more formal than what they'd previously seen. The stairs had blue, black, and green checked runner. "That's the Black Watch tartan pattern on the carpet, isn't it? Interesting history but not very attractive." She glanced at Celeste and crossed her eyes.

"Yes, of course, but the battle tartan of King George IV, laid in honor of his visit, is an immense source of identification and pride."

King George, aka George Augustus Frederick, and King of the United Kingdom of Great Britain and Ireland, stood in the very space she stood. Particles of his dust and breath might remain. She filled her lungs. That he was extravagant in dress was an understatement. His coronation portrait showed him wearing layers upon layers of heavy, brocaded robes under more layers of necklaces, fobs, and fancy doo-dads. She was sure his feet were full inches smaller than hers.

She shook herself from the reverie and caught up with a ridiculously happy Celeste who was asking Aubrey, "What are those AB crests? They're on the walls, the furniture." She pointed to the ceiling. "They're even up there."

"That is the crest of Anne Scott, 1ˢᵗ Duchess of Buccleuch."

"How'd I not study her? What's she known for?"

"Her extreme wealth. In fact, she was the 4ᵗʰ Countess of Buccleuch and had three 5ᵗʰ Baroness titles. Let's continue on to the library."

His chest actually seemed to puff up. Katina thought she might be wrong but rolled her eyes anyway.

The library had a wonderful view of the grounds and the Montagu Bridge in the fading light. Katina would have spent her time daydreaming about knights and horses practicing on the lawns if she'd had to study there. Bookcases jutted at regular intervals around the walls. They were about four feet wide, four feet deep, and oak paneled. Compared to the New York City library, from where they came a few days before, those shelves held a paltry few books.

Aubrey shut and locked the door then led the way to a bookcase situated between one set of floor-to-ceiling windows. "Watch this." He pushed the middle shelf toward the back, which caused a slight, audible pop. The whole front swung open with ease. "I discovered this bit of genius the first year I was here. I don't know who knows about it, but I will keep it as my secret joy until I have to leave. Then I'll ensure the current duke is aware of the treasure here."

"There's a current duke?" Celeste asked. "We missed that somehow."

"Yes. He's the 10th Duke of Buccleuch. I must add that he is the largest private landowner in the United Kingdom."

Katina and Celeste said together, "Richy-rich-guy." Giggling, they peered into a tiny room no bigger than a cleverly hidden closet. Inside was row after row of old leather-covered books and parchment-type documents.

"This is amazing. Your own private archives. Pull out anything that has to do with knights, kings, and queens," Katina said with glee. The hunt was on.

She and Celeste entered the small enclosure at the same time. They bumped shoulders and reached for the same brown and gold leather-bound book.

Katina nudged Celeste out of the way. "This is so much fun."

Celeste said, "I'm sorry, Aubrey. There isn't much room in here."

"The two of you are adorable together." He chuckled. Deep. Charisamtic. "I can tell you've been friends for a goodly while."

Katina and Celeste paused long enough to look at their arms.

Katina murmured, "That laugh..."

Celeste poked her finger into her side.

"What can I say?"

Celeste poked her again.

Aubrey leaned in at Katina's squeal. "Are you all right?"

She snickered. "I guess you haven't felt the wrath of the princess here."

"Not that I can recollect. I'm not sure if I would love it or—"

"Okay, folks, let's get back on task. Put the contenders here." Celeste indicated an empty spot on the closet floor. She opened a small journal and read aloud, "'I decided to return to my estates after the beheading of my dreadful husband. I have grown weary of all the intrigue of court. I shall return to Dalkeith and manage my property from there. I plan to rebuild the castle into a fine palace. My architect has determined the remains of the fifteenth-century tower will be incorporated into the new design. I plan to take the finest furnishings and art from my other estates. This will be my palace.'"

She looked up from the book. "You learned about this from her own writing?" Her voice was all but a squeal.

"Yes. The Duchess Anne. I mentioned her earlier, if you'll recall," Aubrey replied.

She stepped out of the closet to give him a quick hug. "You're so lucky."

He gave a humble head nod.

Expecting a proverbial tug of a lock of forehead hair next, Katina said, "Geesh."

Celeste stayed close to him and perused the journal. "It doesn't reveal anything about kings and queens."

"Her dreadful husband was the first Duke of Monmouth. Very famous, or infamous, I should say. The eldest illegitimate son of Charles II. He was executed in July 1685 for treason."

"But that's neither here nor there. Can't turn it off sometimes."

Katina understood that all too well.

"Anyway, she put so much money into the exquisite design and furnishings that it became a true palace. If we have time, I'll give you a proper tour."

"That'd be awesome but," Celeste checked her wristwatch, "it's getting late, and we haven't even found—"

"By Jove," Katina cried, "I think I've got it." She held out a black, leather-bound book. "It's called *The Interior Castle*, written by St. Teresa of Ávila in 1577."

Celeste hurried back into the closet, and she and Katina examined each page. They sighed and said in unison, "Nothing."

"This big one's called *A Book of Royal Decrees*. I'll put it aside just in case," Celeste said.

Katina also found a contender. "How about this one? It has a chess board and players on the first page. I won't be able to translate it though."

"Put it in the maybe spot. If we can't read it, it won't do us much good." Celeste handed Katina a beautiful book, entitled *The Bishop's Bible*, written in 1568. "Where's the document you found? We have a bunch of books about knights and queens now."

Aubrey joined Katina as she got her satchel. As she pulled the Sinclair writing out, he leaned in and snatched it from her hand. "Brilliant. Is this what you were referring to?"

What is he doing? He's being a pushy jerk. "Yes, it is. May I have it back?"

"You don't mind if I take a gander, do you?" He ignored her request. "May I take a picture of this? It's fascinating."

She grabbed for it, but he turned his back to her. He used his cellphone's camera and checked the results. "Blast. That didn't work well now, did it? I need a bit more light." He turned on a nearby desk lamp and took another shot.

Frustrated, she crossed her arms and sent daggers to Celeste, who in turn silently pleaded for calm back.

Everyone jumped as the library doorknob rattled. A muffled voice said, "Hello?"

Katina took the few steps toward the secret room and gathered the books. With care, she placed the keep pile into her satchel. She reached for the Sinclair document, but Aubrey folded it and put it under his tan corduroy jacket.

After ensuring the closet was shut, he opened the door. "My goodness. I don't know how this got locked."

Two young people, mouths agape, stood on the other side.

"Come in, kids. Meet some fellow Americans. I gave them a tour. Scotty, Jeannie, meet my friends Celeste and Katina."

Celeste said, "Nice to meet you. Where are you two from?"

Scotty spoke first. "We're both from Wisconsin. We're real lucky we got to come here."

Jeannie continued, "We are part of the study abroad program. I've been here a year. I talked my parents into letting me stay the summer because I aced all my classes, didn't I, Professor? I loved his programing class. I may change my major, but I'd have to complete all new..."

Katina wasn't the least bit interested in the barrage of words about the friends she'd made or joyous descriptions of the high caliber school.

Aubrey said, "Very nice, very nice. Well, if you'll excuse the three of us." He extended a hand to indicate the library door. "Off we go, ladies."

She took the suggestion and grabbed Celeste's arm, almost dragging her out of her little pink flats. "It's been hours since lunch, and I'm starved. Let's get some spotted—I mean some steak and kidney pie, without the kidney part."

"I'm not very hungry yet." Celeste waved a farewell to the students.

"I almost always hungry from the pursuit of treasures," Katina whispered.

Celeste gave an enigmatic smile as a response.

Aubrey led them to his office, opened the door and flipped on the light. He moved computer manuals, spreadsheets, and books to the edges of his desk. He laid the Sinclair document in the center and moved two straight back chairs closer. "Have a seat. Let's figure this out. You can put the books here too."

Katina was torn between the subject at hand and the rumbling of her stomach. She got a few books out and put them under the riddle. "Do you happen to have any snacks in here? Is there a kitchen we can raid?"

Aubrey did a doubletake. "Pardon?"

"I'm worried about Celeste. I could go days without food. I'm Greek Orthodox, you know, and fasting is our middle name."

Celeste tried to poke Katina again.

With a quick turn, she avoided the attempt and smiled in triumph. "Aubrey? Food?"

"Right. It's not quite the thing to do. However, I can imagine Celeste, the little bird she is, may need a bit of sustenance."

She mumbled something about lightning and death.

Katina crossed herself and strolled away humming *God Save The Queen*.

Chapter Fifteen

Aubrey is Going to Die

After some warmed-up lasagna and garlic bread disappeared in less than five minutes from the plates of Katina, Aubrey, and Celeste, they all stretched their waistbands. The dinner was surely a nod to the tastes of the American students, and not regular Scottish fare. Their cook deserved a Michelin star.

Katina didn't care. *Maybe it is their mushrooms, the butter and cheese produced from happy Scottish coos, not normal, boring cows like we have in the states. Whatever the secret is, it was delicious.*

"Thanks for not making us eat the kidney pie. I feel... I mean Celeste feels better. There's color back in her cheeks," Katina said as she entered Aubrey's office.

She shuffled papers around on his desk. "What?" She tossed a few in the air, heedless of where they landed in frantic search. "Oh my God. The riddle's gone. And so are the books."

He nudged her aside and searched drawer after drawer. "What the hell happened to them?"

Celeste scanned the floor layered with stacks of papers. "I can't imagine. Aubrey?"

"Who stole our things?" Katina's snarled. "You locked the door, didn't you?"

"I don't believe so. I remember being ushered out of this room, if you'll recall."

"Don't blame this on me," she countered. "You wouldn't give me the document back. Your students might have taken them."

He slammed out of his office. His voice echoed down the deserted hallway as he yelled, "Jeannie. Scotty. I need you in my office immediately."

"It'll be okay. Aubrey will find them, I'm sure," Celeste said, as she took Katina's hand.

"I followed the Sinclair document for a year and a half. Whoever took it can't have any idea how important it is. I can't believe it just disappear—"

"Tell Celeste and Katina what you saw," Aubrey said to the trailing students.

Scotty stammered, "I don't know. I… uh…"

Jeannie offered, "Well, an American-sounding man said he wanted a tour. We let him in because he said he was visiting his daughter and had an appointment."

Scotty added, "He left your office about fifteen minutes ago. We thought his appointment was with you and—"

"Damn it to hell and back." Katina crossed herself and sent an I'm-gonna-kill-him look to Celeste.

That idiot just had to take control, didn't he?

Celeste looked to Aubrey for answers.

His gaze fell to the floor, running a hand through his hair. "Um, Scotty, Jeannie, thank you for the information."

"We're awfully sorry, Professor. He seemed like a regular person, you know? He wore a gray tracksuit and tennis shoes. Just a regular American dad."

Aubrey took a deep breath then said, "Thank you both. You've been very helpful, but in the future, remember, there is a lock on the front door for a reason. There are still a few valuable paintings and many historical objects here. I'll have the resident leader talk to the remaining students. It may be a relaxing summer, but we absolutely cannot relax our security. Did you see him leave the premises?"

"Yeah. We did," Scotty said.

"Fine. Off you go now."

Katina shut the door on the departing students. "So, some nefarious man came in here and stole our books and my riddle. Is anything else valuable missing?"

"Unless you think a two-year-old version of Matlab holds any value." He picked up a well-used textbook. "Nope, that's still here."

They found a somewhat empty surface to sit. Katina grew uncomfortable as the room warmed with their collective deliberation.

"Oh good grief. We've been sitting around stewing, but the answer's been here the whole time. Aubrey. Your phone," Katina snapped.

"Pardon?"

"Your *phone*. You took pictures, remember?"

"Right." He drew it from his baggy trousers and searched for the pictures. "Got them right here." He squinted. "I can read every bit of the part when he talks about castling the king."

Celeste beamed as if Aubrey had saved a drowning child. "Well, that's a terrific start. Could you send it to the printer?"

Katina sat on the edge of the desk. Her leg bounced with agitation as she waited for the printer to spew out the message.

"Here it is," he said as if he was the hero of the hour.

You're an idiot.

He read from the page:

"'To save the queen, castle the king.

The night was not the knight; you learned that to be truth.

The night is the knight now. In the castle, he dwells.

For inside the keep of Clan Graham, the book of old remains.

Regard the knight, the king, and queen,

on the edge of gold, the dark of truth is shown.

You will find the first chapter of the story of your destiny.

Should God decree that you are the one.'"

Katina groused, "I guess I'm not *the one* or we'd have the books we need."

"I'm sorry, sweetie." Celeste put her arm around Katina's shoulder and gave it a consoling squeeze. "You were so close."

For a moment, they leaned their heads together as they often did as girls. Katina shifted away and with a sad sigh, picked up her satchel, clutching it to her chest for additional comfort. She raised her brows and gave the bag a squeeze. Her breath quickened.

She whispered to Celeste, "I'm a genius. I do have a book."

Her friend locked gazes with Katina. "What?"

She furrowed her brows and almost growled for Celeste to shut her trap. "I *said*, let's have a *look*."

"Surely," Aubrey replied.

"On second thought, can we take this?" Katina snatched the paper without waiting for an answer. "It's late, and I'm tired. This has been a challenging and incredibly disappointing evening." They could come back the next day, but she prayed they had what they needed.

"Sure. I'm sorry about the dreadful turn of events. I guess it's a goose's chase now, I'm afraid. I'll take you back to the inn."

~ * ~

The drive was fifteen minutes but seemed like an hour. She opened their hotel door with a bang. She placed the copy of the riddle and book on the bed and tossed her satchel in the corner. "This is the chess book. It has the king, a rook, which is shaped just like a castle of course, and the queen chess pieces on the cover. I had a hunch this was the one we needed."

Celeste clasped her hands together. "Brilliant."

"You sound like Aubrey. I don't know if I like that."

"Don't be mean. Speaking of Aubrey, why in the world didn't you mention the book at the school? We could have just continued the search."

"Because I don't know him. You don't know him very well either. Maybe he's in cahoots with the thief. He seemed super grabby. I'd forgotten about my father's warning. Weird things are happening around our search. I'm starting to think he's right."

Celeste took off her clothes, folded her silk blouse and slacks then placed them back in her suitcase with care. "Why would you think he has anything to do with it? He didn't even know we were coming."

Katina tossed her clothes into the corner. "Hmmm. I see your point. We don't know what's going on or who to trust. Do we?"

Celeste tied the sash of her robe. "Well, no. But think about it. Who would know we would be here *and* have someone ready to steal what we found?"

"No one, I guess. Aubrey irritated me when he hogged the riddle, though."

"He is just as enthralled as we are. He doesn't spend his spare time searching for Templar manuscripts and ancient treasures, does he?"

Katina found her pajamas under the side chair, put them on before she climbed into bed. "No, I guess you're right. That doesn't change the fact I'm worried." She put the book and riddle into her lap. "Come here."

Wearing a warm night gown, Celeste slid in beside her. "I wish we didn't have to share this bed. You take up most of it."

"Yeah, well, tiny towns in Scotland don't have a lot of choices. Everything else decent was booked."

"Don't hog the covers tonight."

"Celeste, if all goes well, you'll have to get used to sharing a bed with your English hunk. Not that I approve. Now, pay attention. The riddle says, 'The knight is the night now, and inside the castle, he dwells. Inside the Clan Graham.' After finding all those books, I'd have to say we were correct."

"Me too. If it weren't for Aubrey—"

"So, the riddle went on to say, 'On the edge of gold, the dark truth is shown.'" Katina was done thinking about that man.

"The pages are gilded. I don't see anything out of the ordinary, do you?"

"Nope. Well. Wait a minute. I just remembered fore-edge paintings. I'm sure you've heard of them, haven't you?"

"It's a small painting hidden on the edge of the paper. It became popular in the 1800s."

"Right. They might have become popular in the 1800s but existed at the time this was made. Go ahead and fan the book."

Celeste depressed the pages with her thumb. "I don't see

anything." She bent over the book, biting the tip of her tongue in concentration.

Instead of taking it out of her hands, as everything in her screamed to do, Katina encouraged, "Maybe if you angled it more. Every book was made differently."

Excitement lit Celeste's eyes. "Tina," she whisper-yelled. "There it is."

"Woo-hoo," Katina whisper-yelled back.

Chapter Sixteen

Joey Continues His Streak

The door of room 115 crashed into the wall. "These Europeans should get a God-damned doorstop," Joey Biscotta grumbled. He was desperate to examine the old books and paper. The smell of sweat and fear still emanated from under his grubby clothes.

He'd run the rental car into a ditch on the way back to his inn. The police let him off with a warning because no other car was damaged. The Toyota Aygo was a different story. The cheap front bumper was now tied to the hood with a rope the cops gave him. They made him put chunks of soil back into the large divot.

"It's just dirt. Who the fuck fixes dirt?"

He tossed the stolen items onto the ratty, dark green bedcover of the single bed then strode to the sink— the only bathroom fixture in the room. He used a toothpick he got from his jacket pocket to clean the filth from under his fingernails.

That was close. I guess no one called the police yet. Shit. Maybe they were on their way to Dalkeith when they found me. Holy crap, what've I gotten myself into now? People oughtta drive on the right side of the road. That's why they call it the right side.

What's Mr. Blackmarr up to, anyway? I don't know what the hell I'm doing here. I shoulda stayed in the States.

The tiny mirror above the sink showed a tired, stressed out, and red-eyed man. Seeing nothing out of the ordinary, he took a deep breath and picked up the old piece of paper. He had no idea what this all meant.

Hopefully, Mr. Blackmarr will know.

Joey wiped his forehead with his dirty sleeve, sat on the bed and started to read.

"You who have found this blah, blah, blah. Yeah, I found it, didn't I? Holy crap. A treasure? George, whoever the hell you are, you sound like a friggin' jerk. Get on with it. More bullshit. Yadda-yadda. You weep for the lost? What an ass. Sounds like it's a God-damned war going on there, for fuck's sake."

He picked up the phone and dialed.

"Mr. Blackmarr? I flew in here a few hours ago and got a piece a shit rental car. It needs a new bumpa', by the way. I drove right to the school and followed a couple of kids to the front door and watched them put in the code. It's a cheap locking system.

"Anyway, I was talking it up as we went to the door together. You know, 'I gotta kid who wants to come here.' Shit like that. Piece of cake. They even showed me where the computer teacher's door was. Can you believe it?

"I went into the office, thinking I was gonna have to give the same excuse, but no one was there. I found this old stuff, like you were hopin' I'd find, laying right there on a fuckin' table. I took it and ran. Well, I walked fast at any rate. Didn't want to draw—"

"Good, good," Mr. Blackmarr said. "Did anyone see you leave with the items?"

"Don't think so. I don't know if it's what you wanted, but I got what I could. I didn't wanna push my luck. I'll read it to you, and you can figure out what you want me to do next."

"What'd you find?"

"I gotta piece of old paper with some stuff about kings and shit and a few books. Like I said, Mr. Blackmarr, I don't know what—"

"Not to worry. I wasn't sure you'd find anything. So, you have a document and books. Tell me about the document."

"The paper is yellowed, and the writing on it is fancy and tough for me to read. It's short though."

"Try and read it to me then." Mr. Blackmarr sounded encouraged.

"All right, here it goes. 'You, who have found this, are indeed the clever one. Henry Sinclair hid his riddle well, did he not? Alas, the seeker of the riddle, and all the answers thereto, must now pass my test of God's desired outcome. Presum... Pre-something, am I not?' I don't know, sir. I'm not used to these words."

"I think the problem is that you are not used to reading. Let me think a minute." Mr. Blackmarr cursed under his breath.

In response, Joey paced the small, dilapidated room. The possibility of another failure that made him sick.

Mr. Blackmarr barked directions as if he was Patton during a battle. "Take a few close-up shots of the document with your phone. Evaluate them closely and send the best pictures to me. This sounds better than I could have hoped for. You did well. I'll read it here and call you back with instructions."

"Don't you worry, boss," Joey said, then disconnected.

He sat on the bed, slouched over, and pressed the phone against his forehead. "Okay. I can do this."

He laid the pages on the bed and took the pictures with shaking hands. The results were shitty. He cursed and steadied the frame by planting his elbows.

"What I need is a stiff drink. They gotta have some whiskey in this stupid town." He checked the new shots. "Good enough."

He dialed feeling more pleased with himself than he had since the whole operation started. "Sir? I just sent them off. I'm going to go find some food and a drink. I haven't had time to eat since I got here."

"You'll do no such thing. You stay put until I call you back," Mr. Blackmarr snapped.

Joey tried not to sound like a whining bitch, as he said, "If you say so."

"You're damn right I say so. We're not finished. You have to tell me about the books."

"The books. Yeah. I forgot about them. Sorry. Maybe I can find a takeout menu or somethin'."

"I doubt it," Mr. Blackmarr said.

Chapter Seventeen

The Bad Guys are at it Again

Maxwell disconnected as Joey spewed some foul curses on the other end of the phone. He went to the balcony that overlooked the azure waters surrounding the remarkable island of Rhodes. Part of him wished he could be a tourist and enjoy its beauty. The other part planned to divest it of a national treasure.

He dragged a tanned, manicured hand through wind-tousled hair, as he scanned the horizon and admired the late-summer setting sun. Maxwell leaned over the stainless steel and glass railing and enjoyed the vision of two oil-slicked females reclining on chaises. They sipped freshly-squeezed orange juice, as richly-colored as a yam. He'd noticed far too many fruit trees with oranges rotting on the ground. *Why aren't these people setting up drink stands? They don't have jobs. Lazy.*

He poured himself a glass of mineral water and drank the salty, bitter flavor in one swallow. Feeling a modicum more refreshed, he checked his email.

"Fantastic." He opened the attachment, and his amazement grew with each word. He was shocked as he read, "…Young Sir Gerard, a relative of my friend, Archibald Douglas, 4th Earl of Morton, bypassed France, returning, instead, here…"

"The same Gerard I know about? How the hell did you get into this document?"

He continued reading. "…Gerard spoke a mysterious tale of marvelous icons. A treasure that he left behind."

Shock turned to horror. "Who else have you told?" He wanted to punch the computer screen. "…Young Sir George said that he did not reveal the existence of the treasure or its location because he did not want anyone to retrieve it.

"Okay." Maxwell put a hand in front of his mouth, signaling a long-since dead man to silence.

"Now we're getting down to it." He read the remaining lines. "…Regard the knight, the king, and queen, on the edge of gold, the dark of truth is shown."

"This is it." Adrenaline drove him out of his chair. It toppled to the marble floor with a crash. With steps as powerful as his pounding heart, he paced the room.

Maxwell's cell phone chimed. He all but yelled, "Tell me about the books now."

"There's three of them. The first one is *El Castillo Interior*. The second one is called *The Book of Royal Decrees*. The last one is called *The Bishop's Bible*. I can't make heads or tails outta anything."

"Get on with it."

"Okay, like I said, the first one is *El Castillo Interior*. There's a date here that says 1577. It's in some foreign language. Don't know what though."

"What does the book look like?"

"It has a rough leather cover. Plain brown."

"Keep going. At this rate, we'll be at this all night. Describe the edge of the book."

"It's the same brown leather as the front and back."

"No. The edge of the pages. For Christ's sake, I should have sent someone else."

Joey's voice rose as he said, "No, sir. I can do this. I just need a bit of training. I've never seen shit like this before."

"Enough. Get on with it."

Joey continued, "The paper edges are kinda gold-colored, I guess. Not real shiny or nothin'."

"Are there any specific pages marked?"

"Can't see any."

"What about the other books?"

"The *Bishop's Bible* has the same kind of cover. It looks almost new. The page edge is goldish-brown. With the emphasis on brown. I opened it up, and the first page has a bunch of frilly stuff, women wearing long dresses and a fancy-pants man in the middle."

"Not the one. Go on. What about *A Book of Royal Decrees?*" Maxwell cringed at the grunting on the other end.

"I got it here. It's a big book. Expensive maybe. Good condition. Leather cover. The paper edges are gold-gold color, not brownish-gold."

Maxwell said, "Interesting. Now listen carefully. Do you know how to fan the book's pages?"

"I guess I don't, sir. I know what a fan is though."

He suppressed a string of foul language and explained in simple terms what to do.

"Got it. That makes a lot of—Holy crap!"

"What is it?" Maxwell yelled. "What do you see?"

"I see words, sir. The first word is spelled A – L – L – E."

"Good. Then what?"

"Then I see the letters W – I – T – E – N."

"Got it," Maxwell said. "It's Middle English. It says, 'You must.' There has to be more instructions."

"Sir, it has one more word. It's spelled S – W – E – L – T – E – N."

Maxwell translated the word "*swelten*" into the verb "to die." *You must die.*

"Fuck—I just got stabbed!"

"What the hell do you mean, you got stabbed?"

"A razor or a knife-like thing shot outta the edge of the cover and sliced my hand."

A string of profanity and rustling came from the other end. Maxwell assumed Joey was getting a towel.

"I'm back," he said, breathing heavily.

"I'm sure it's nothing."

"The blade went deep. I need to get stitches. I got it wrapped tight."

"Joey, if you're not in too much pain, could you tell me about the blade?"

"There's writing on it. It says 'poison.' In English." Joey then yelled, "I've been poisoned. I'm gonna die in a godforsaken rat hole."

What an idiot. Too bad the word for poison is the same in Middle and modern English. Whatever was put on that knife, four or five hundred years ago, isn't going to kill him though.

He could hear Joey bang around in the room and a faucet turn on.

Joey shouted, "I'm washin' it out. I gotta get to a doctor."

Maxwell ran a hand down his face and punched the phone's end-call button. *Now this, I did not expect.*

With a sigh, Maxwell strolled onto the porch for some much-needed respite. Searching the sea for signs of water-life, he rolled his shoulders and tilted his neck from side to side. With no dolphins or fish to be seen, he laid on the chaise and closed his eyes. He remembered the evening the search for the icons started. He'd spent it with one of his British suppliers, Franklin Woolcote.

Maxwell and Franklin had decided to eat at his hotel's pub, The Fox and Anchor. He was comfortable with the Victorian décor. The public rooms were paneled with paintings of hunting scenes and battles. The small rooms had fireplaces, lit for warmth and ambiance.

The Englishman droned on and on about this subject and that, all of which Maxwell had only the slightest of interest. Until Franklin lit on a new topic. He leaned in. "I beg your pardon. Would you mind starting again? What was that about a treasure?" He tried to give Franklin a look that implied amused interest and not the loathsome greed he thought surely had crept onto his visage.

Franklin relayed a phone conversation he'd overheard by a man named Professor Papamissios about a diary and a medieval treasure left by the Knights of Rhodes.

After that conversion, Maxwell's humdrum activity that month turned into full-blown computer research into Dr. Papamissios and the person he was talking to, his daughter, Katina.

She was enchanting, with sea-blue eyes and a beautiful body. I think it's time to go back to plan A. Seeing her again will be a pleasure.

Chapter Eighteen

The Diamond Bracelet

Katina sat next to Celeste on their bed at the inn. It was late, but neither she nor Celeste were the least bit sleepy.

"Tina, I'm having one of the best times of my life." The spine of the chess book pressed against her lap. Her thumb pushed the pages' edge. "I see an image. It's the inside of a beehive." She held the fore-edge painting for Katina to see.

Pleased with herself for letting Celeste be the hero, Katina huddled close. "Good job, babe. What the heck is it?"

"You got me." Celeste shrugged. "If it's not an actual beehive, it's the weirdest room I've ever seen. Judging by the ordeal we had to go through, this room, if that's what it is, should be in Dalkeith Castle. We need to call Aubrey. He has to show us what or where this beehive structure is."

"Do we *have* to? I might knock his block off and I hear that's not lady-like."

"I know you're mad at him, but I don't want to sneak in there. Or look in every nook and cranny. It'd take years."

No, no, and please God, no. "All right, but I wish we could do this by ourselves."

"Don't scrunch your face like that. It'll get stuck."

Celeste's laughter eased Katina. She relaxed and tried to open her mind to the possibility of *Aubrey* joining them.

"That's better," Celeste said. "He knows the place inside and out, *and* he can explain our presence if anyone sees us."

Katina understood but couldn't let go of her lingering distrust. "I just don't want to. He could take what we find and throw us out of the building."

Celeste adopted her stubborn, head-rocking mad expression. "He's a teacher. Not an international assassin. He didn't know what we were after." Up came the hand. "He is a nice man, and I trust him, God-damn it." Out came the finger, poking the air with each word.

"Geesh. Go ahead and call him," Katina wanted to curl into a ball and protect her vital organs. "Let's do this tonight."

"Oh my goodness, this is exciting." Gleeful Celeste had to dial twice. "It's ringing. Hello, Aubrey. Hi. How are you? Yes, we were a bit shaken. Umm, Tina and I have made a wonderful discovery. Yes. Tina had one of the books in her satchel, and we used it to figure out the riddle. We did. So, I know you're as interested in this as we are. Do you want to help us search for treasure?"

"I thought you would." Her eyes were full of happiness as she gave Katina a thumbs up. "Can we drive over now? I know it's late, but we can't wait. You will? Fantastic. We'll be over in a few."

Since presence was inevitable, Katina decided to let herself enjoy the hunt. She jumped out of bed and grabbed a pair of pants off the floor. "This will be great. Do you want to drive?"

Celeste was already dressed in a warm but stylish outfit. "I'm too nervous. You're better at driving on the left anyway. Let's go."

~ * ~

The landscape, mysterious in the moonlit night, flew past as Katina drove from the inn to Dalkeith Castle. Her speed was as fast as the narrow, empty roads would allow.

Celeste had been whisper-talking on the phone the whole way. She hung up as their sub-compact rental fishtailed into the entrance of the courtyard. The headlights captured Aubrey jogging down the steps toward the car. He opened her door and helped her out, then spun her in mock formal dance. His joyous laughter joined her squeals.

Katina's jaw dropped as his mouth covered Celeste's.

She stepped away and giggled like a young girl after a first kiss.

Katina groaned and walked toward the door. She glanced back. "Hey Aubrey," she called, trying to break up the love fest. "If we show you a picture, could you tell us where it is?"

He grasped and kissed Celeste's hand as they walked to the door. "Probably." Moving passed Katina, he punched the code into the cipher lock and ushered Celeste into the hall. "This is bloody marvelous, isn't it?"

Katina stood on the landing, off to the side, as they shared an excited exchange.

"Come on, Tina. Where's the book?"

She dug into her satchel and handed it to Celeste without saying a word.

"Tina and I figured out that the edges are painted. See?" She fanned the edge. "Here's the picture. It's pretty small, but distinct. Looks like a beehive."

In the Great Hall, Katina lifted a small chain and dangling sign out of the way. She sat on an antique chair, heedless of the 'Do Not Sit' warning she'd just moved. The change in circumstance between Aubrey and Celeste caused a loss she hadn't anticipated.

Well, I did tell her last night that she might be sharing a bed with him soon. I just wanted her to stop whining, though.

Celeste was jubilant, her eyes alight, her laugh soft. Strands of her hair clung to Aubrey's shoulder as they studied the image.

Aubrey said, "I know what this is. It's the very bottom room of the treasure tower—one of the areas that's remained relatively unchanged. I'll show you."

"There's a treasure tower here and you didn't think to show us?" Katina asked as she followed them down four paneled hallways and two flights of industrial stairs. Metal doors ran the length of the next hall.

Her question was ignored, so she said, "Why are there bars on the window of this door?" Still unheard, she yelled, "Aubrey. Back here. What's with the barred window?"

His smile faded and a puzzled look replaced the goofy one. "What? Oh, that's where they held Polish prisoners during World War II."

"This was a prison?" She peered through the small set of bars, but it was too dark to see anything within. "Can you imagine the plight of prisoners here? It's so dark and dreary." She shivered, thinking of all the times she'd gone into restricted places but had not gotten arrested. "This place gives me the heeby-jeebies."

"Pardon?"

"Guess you don't have that expression in England. It gives me the creeps."

"Hmm? Oh, right. No one was tortured. No one died. Many of the captured Polish remained after the war, in point of fact." He hurried down another hall and stopped at the end. He grunted as he shouldered a wooden door open. "Here we are."

Celeste and Katina caught up and entered behind him.

"It does look like the inside of a beehive." Celeste put her hand over her heart. "The room's even honey-colored." She walked at least twenty feet across slate slabs until she was in the middle of the round room.

"This is amazing." Katina took in the thousands of tiles, the size of small bricks, lining the domed walls. "The last time I've seen something like this was in Italy. Those rooms were used to store weapons and explosives."

"That's indeed what this was used for." Aubrey sounded as if he'd designed it himself. "It provided easy access to the arsenal from within the castle. There are tunnels that men would use to move ammunition to the outer defensive walls. I don't know if they're still intact though."

Celeste said, "All the tiles look the same."

Katina pointed to a tile in the center of the ceiling. "That one's a little different."

"It is the odd man out, as it were. I'll get a ladder. If a student wanders in here, tell them you're waiting for me to, um, bring a camera. You two are architects studying domed rooms."

"Will do." She didn't believe for an instant that an architect would be allowed there at that time of night, to take a picture. She sat on the floor and leaned against the wall. She tugged on a string from the inseam of her jeans and took a deep breath. "So, you and Aubrey seem cozy. You two must have had a nice visit."

A blush spread across Celeste's cheeks. "I don't know what's come over us all of a sudden."

Love is strange. "A hormone wash of the brain?"

"A wash of what?"

"A hormone wash of the brain. *Love.*"

"I still don't understand."

"It's a naturally occurring phenomenon." Katina explained with the patience of a kindergarten teacher. Enjoying the topic and killing time, she gave Celeste an indulgent smile. "Did you know that anger does that also? That's why some people explode and become violent. Explosive anger, explosive sex—"

"Are you saying this is temporary? That tomorrow or next week, the chemicals will just go away? I'm not buying your supposition." Celeste frowned.

"Look at it this way; you guys acted like friends for a minute. That's the initial giddiness. Then sexual attraction flooded your brain. So, if you guys breakup, there'll be this terrible devastation. The brain, used to regular inputs of the chemical, goes into withdrawal. That's the sadness. Wow. We figured out your present and future with Aubrey in the span of time it takes to get a ladder. We're awesome."

"Don't be so damn pleased. You have us being friends, having sex, and breaking up in one fell swoop."

"Not in the same day, for heaven's sake. It may take a week." The play of emotions that crossed Celeste's face broke Katina's heart. "You're right, sweetie. There's much more to love. And your relationship with Aubrey might be full of boundless joy, for all I know." *Criminy, that sounded so stupid.* "I don't know why I get so analytical and ruin a perfectly nice time. I think my brain was flooded with something when I saw you and Aubrey together tonight."

Celeste cocked her head. "What flooded *your* brain?"

"The jealousy chemical." She hated to admit it.

"Poor baby. You're not used to sharing me on our vacations." Celeste patted her leg like she would a wounded dog.

"Yep. We've always been the dynamic duo. Kim and Khloe."

Celeste gagged.

Katina laughed. "All right. I'll shut up. I don't know why you and Jim put up with me."

The mock-sympathy returned. "Ah, don't be so sad. We love you because all your faults make us look great."

"Thanks. Friend." Katina got up. She brought her hair over her shoulder and braided it. "Where's your Englishman? We need to get this done and go to Rhodes. Times-a-wastin'."

They both turned at the sound of metal scraping and banging.

Aubrey dragged a ladder into the room. "This better be good. I had to go all the way to the bloody greenhouse. Any visitors?"

"Nope." Katina secured the braid with an elastic band. "Celeste and I bonded while you were gone. Then she ruined it."

"You didn't try to figure out what's hidden up there?"

In unison, they said, "Of course we have."

"We think the answer to the riddle can't be anywhere else." That might not be true, but if they believed it enough, maybe it would make it so.

Relief flooded his face. "Brilliant. I thought I was the only one made a bit daft by this whole book and riddle."

"Of course not." Katina set up the ladder after a few fumbling tries. "I'll hold it while you go up there and poke around, okay?"

"I'm ridiculously afraid of heights, but I shall be brave." He gave her a sheepish smile and climbed. His legs shook in harmony with the wobbling ladder as he ascended.

Celeste chided, "Hold it better, Tina."

"I'm doing the best I can. He's fine. Good grief."

"Not to worry. I've got my balance now," Aubrey reassured them. "The tile has a drawing or an etching on it. Two more steps and I'll be able to see better… It's three figures on a cloud. Odd."

"For God's sake, don't push it yet. It might be a trick." Katina looked around the room, expecting spears to fly like in an Indiana Jones movie. "Get the riddle from my satchel."

Celeste rolled her eyes but got the paper. "'This dream must have been part of God's plan.' Blah blah blah… 'Find the knight in the castle he guards.' We did that. 'For inside the keep of Clan Graham, the book of old remains.' We did that too. Blah blah blah… 'on the edge of gold, the dark of truth dwells.' That's it. The edge of gold was the edge of the book *and* this gold room here. What do you think?"

Aubrey stood at the top and studied the unusual tile. "Well. It's all we have. I'll give it a push."

"When he does, duck," Katina whispered

"Okay, here it goes." Nothing happened. He balled his fist and gave it a good punch. It popped somewhere into the dark void within.

Aubrey yelped, Katina crouched, and Celeste laughed as dust sprinkled down around their heads.

"That was easy enough, I suppose. Did a secret door open anywhere?"

All three scanned the room. The ladder rocked, causing him to cry out.

"Oh dear. Are you okay up there? I know it's probably the scariest thing you've done in years." Katina steadied it, trying her best to be helpful and sweet. Sort of.

"He's fine," Celeste snapped. "Aubrey? Nothing moved. Is there anything in the hole?"

He peered inside. "No, it's too dark."

Katina repeated the last line of the clue, "'On the edge of gold, the dark of truth dwells.' Can you put your hand in there and feel around?"

"I can try." Half of his hand fit through the small opening. "No, I'm afraid I have fat hands." He grinned at them. "What about you, Katina? You're almost as tall as I am, and you're slender as a reed. I bet your hand will fit. As the poem said, you are the one truly destined to find whatever's in there."

"There better not be any spiders." She let Aubrey descend, then ascended herself and stuck a trembling hand into the hole. "Wait... There's a piece of paper. Celeste, I cannot bear another riddle. I'll rip it to shreds."

Celeste clapped her hands. "Come on, Tina. This is it. What'd you find?"

When Katina reached the floor, she unfolded the paper with extreme delicacy. Aubrey took it from her and began scanning.

"Be kind, my ass," she barked. "Give me that back. Immediately. And be gentle about it or I'll knock your nicely coiffed English head off."

His brows shot up. "I beg your pardon?"

"I thought I was quite clear. I *said*, give it back. Our hands are filthy. Neither of us should handle it."

"Aubrey, the paper." Celeste shook her head and pointed a hesitant finger. "I'm sure you're interested, but Katina needs to see it first. This is her discovery."

His cheeks became a bright crimson. "I've made you mad. My mother said I can be quite boorish. She's right." He lowered his chin as he handed the paper to Katina. "Here. Tina, forgive me. I've—"

"Just give it to me. Celeste can do the forgiving." Katina knelt on the floor, cleaned her hands with sanitizer from her bag, then wiped them on the inside of her shirt. She inspected every finger before retrieving the paper.

With her back to Aubrey, she addressed Celeste, "It's a drawing. There's a note around the side, in Middle English." She turned the paper as she read the edges. "It says, 'This shows the years of my labor at the fortress. The building is the Palace of the Grand Master.' There are markers on the map. I think the section drawn is in the northwest quadrant. It goes on to say, 'Return the icons to their origin, for you are the destined one.' He signed it 'Henry Sinclair, First Earl of Orkney.'"

Celeste addressed Aubrey, "We thought we could find the room from Katha's diary. We had no idea what part of the building the room was in. This map, coupled with Katha's directions will lead us right to it."

"Brilliant. When will you leave?" He took Celeste's hand and led her a few feet away. As they made eye contact, he touched his forehead to hers. "I'd love more time with you, of course. Would you consider staying here? Or perhaps returning after your trip to Rhodes?"

"I'd like that, too." She sighed and turned a pleading gaze to Katina.

Katina fumed. She didn't trust him, but she'd never, ever seen such light in her friend's eyes either. Had her eyes lit that way when she'd fallen in love with Jim? "Fine. He can come." *Crap. Shouldn't have thought about Jim. He brought out the nice in me.*

Celeste's face was full of joy. "How'd you know what I was thinking?"

"Give me a break." *Who can say no to such ridiculous happiness?*

She clasped her hands together like a child seeing a kitten. "Can you come with us? It's summer. You don't have classes."

"I'd love to. I'll make arrangements in the morning." The "kitten" was giddy.

As Katina climbed the ladder. Aubrey asked, "What are you doing?"

"I'll put the tile back. We always remove evidence of our, um, expeditions." She touched the opening. "The tile's in here somewhere."

Her wrist disappeared inside the void. "What's this?" She pulled out a slender, gray leather case and presented it to Celeste. "Jewelry." She jerked it back from Aubrey's outstretched hand. "Not a chance, buster."

Katina unclasped the tiny hinge and lifted a sparkling bracelet. "Diamonds. Gorgeous." She found a piece of paper and handed it down to Celeste. "There's another note here."

She set down Katina's satchel then went through the hand cleaning process before she read. "It's from George Sinclair."

"Come again?" Aubrey asked.

Celeste patted his arm. "I know there are a lot of names. It's hard to keep them straight too. This is the George I mentioned. He wrote the riddle about the kings and queens. He also put the painting of this room on the side of the book. That was about 1582. *Henry* Sinclair, his great-great-great grandfather, went to Rhodes, wrote the *first* riddle, and drew this map of the interior of the Palace of the Grand Master. That was around 1400."

Katina about laughed at Aubrey's dumbfounded look. "Celeste, what does it say?"

"You're not going to believe this. It says the bracelet is his gift to the next Daughter of the Ancients. He used the same word as Henry Sinclair, *Archaeo-Dehtren*."

Shaking her head, she said to Katina, "You did it. You *are* the next Daughter of the Ancients."

"Put it all in my satchel, okay?" Katina secured the tile as best as she could. "I don't think it'll hold very well. If no one pokes at it, it'll be all right."

Back on the ground, she said, "Let's go before someone comes."

Celeste nodded her agreement. "Aubrey, let's go to your office and coordinate our travel plans now. Is your passport up to date?"

"I do, and I have a month's worth of leave saved." He grasped the ladder and beamed.

Katina glared at the ceiling. *Please God, don't make me spend a month with him.*

The ladder banged on the floor with each step as he continued down the hall. "Perhaps you two can return. We could search for the nearly forgotten treasure of the tower."

At the top of the stairs, Celeste said, "That sounds fab, but we don't know how long we'll be in Rhodes. Do we, Tina?" She held open the door to the main floor landing.

The noise he was making would wake the dead, so Katina helped Aubrey angle the ladder through the door. "No, we don't. Maybe next year."

Celeste cooed, "I'm glad you're coming though. We can get to know each other even better."

Katina dropped her head and shook it. *Defeated again. I forgot the English have at least a month of vacation time every year.*

"Splendid."

"Yes, splendid," she muttered.

Celeste gave her a don't-start-trouble look.

"We have some serious work to do there. This is historic. If we find the treasure, the impact on the people will be huge," Katina reminded her.

Celeste's joy deflated like a popped balloon. "You're right. Don't know what I was thinking."

I do. You want to explore something as rare and important as this treasure is to me. Katina put her end of the ladder on the floor with a decided thump. "All right. Call your agency. Maybe he'll be helpful. Who knows?"

Geesh. It's hard being such a wonderful, sweet, loving, generous, faithful, helpful, magnanimous, and plain-old good friend sometimes. I bet it leads me to more trouble than I ever thought possible.

Chapter Nineteen

Momma Has No Idea

The diamond bracelet was small on Katina's wrist. She wondered how tall the original owner was as she moved it under the lamplight. Its sparkles traversed the walls of their room like stars in the night sky. "It goes beautifully with my pajamas, doesn't it?"

"Umm, hmm," emanated from below a rose embroidered duvet and pillow.

Katina compared its diamonds to the center stone of her engagement ring. "They're around a half carat each." Celeste's lack of enthusiastic response was not a deterrent. "When did jewelers start using the phrase carat?"

Celeste's covers continued in an even rise and fall.

"I don't know how you can sleep at a time like this. Even though some of our stuff was stolen, we came up with remarkable discoveries." She regarded the jewels at her wrist again. "Should I keep it? I'd feel awful if I did." Katina paused for a moment. "You know what? He left it for me."

She got a brush from her bag and stroked the tangles out of her hair. *I found it in the duke's castle. So, it's his. But what if my uncle left a bracelet in his friend's house for me? Complete with a note, for heaven's sake. Then it wouldn't be the friend's, would it? I should keep it. No, I shouldn't. I should buy one like it, for memory's sake. Blast. I'll ask Daddy. He's found tons of stuff on his digs.*

She sat on the bed as her father's home office phone rang.

The bed shifted as Celeste repositioned herself. "I'm trying… sleep…"

Holding the phone closer to her ear, Katina said softly, "I'm lonely, Daddy. Pick up."

His recorded message played, "I might be sorry that I missed you, depending on who is calling. If it's Joanna, you are a fine assistant, and I know you will make the right decision, so handle it, whatever it is. If you are Tina… *Koukla.* Leave a message, and Papa will call you soon. If you are my beautiful wife, I love you."

"Hi, I need you guys to do something. I love you and hope you're getting better, Daddy. Please don't pester your nurse, if she's still there.

I'll call Momma now. *Adio.* I love you." She made kissy noises into the phone and ended the call.

Katina made a desperate humming noise while she dialed Diane Papamissios, a stay-at-home mother, who spent little time at home.

"*Yassas*?"

"Momma, I'm so happy to hear your voice."

"Tina *mou*. How are you?"

"Worried sick. I called Daddy's office phone but, he didn't answer. Is he still in bed?" Her words were so rushed she sounded unhinged. She took a breath and slowed her speech to say, "I didn't want to bother him if he was asleep. Should I call his cell?"

"My dear, I'm on my way to volunteer at the mission. I'll tell you, the last time I saw him, he was out in the backyard playing with your dogs. Lexi brought them over. I was surprised of course. Your father and I aren't the biggest dog people." Her voice was filled with resignation. "But it will be okay, I guess. Lexi said she was taking a short trip. All very rushy-rushy. I bet she thought we'd say no if she gave us enough time."

Katina pictured the scene in her mind and sighed with longing. *I miss them so much.* "I wonder where she's going." She paused. "Holy cow, you said Daddy's well enough to play with the dogs. That's terrific."

"He takes an ibuprofen in the morning, and he seems good to go."

In her mind's eye, she saw the wide smile on her mother's face, always amazed at her husband's spirit. "Fantastic."

"What are you about, Katina? Weren't you traveling to Rhodes?"

"We're having an adventure for sure. We stopped off in Scotland, but we head there in a few hours, on the first flight out at 5:50."

"I can tell you need to sleep, *koukla*."

"I'm too excited. I can sleep on the plane. The trip will take about nine hours, including the layovers."

Diane made sympathetic-mom noises.

"Momma, you'll never guess what happened. Celeste has a boyfriend. He'll come too. Can I even say *boyfriend* when we're thirty years old? Yeesh. You should see them. No, don't. It's awful."

She held the phone out and frowned at it. "Stop laughing. Seriously. Now, I'm sending you a treasure."

"You found a treasure? Where? How?"

"Yes, we did indeed." Katina went on to describe her experiences during the last few days. It made her heart happy to hear the excitement in her mother's voice. However, she wondered when the advice would start, because she knew as sure as summer days were humid in the South, it would.

"My sweet girl, I'm sure you know what I'd do. Use it for a good cause."

"How? Sell it?"

Diane's blinker began to tick-tick. Tick-tick. "I'm almost at the mission. We can plan a fundraiser and use the bracelet as the main prize. No, better yet, *you* can plan it when you get back."

"A fundraiser?" *Good Lord, what have I gotten myself into? Parties? Galas? Pass.*

The car door opened, and wind hit the speaker of her mother's phone. "To support a child's love of archeology." The car door slammed shut. "Your father and I will bid on it if you want to keep it."

"Maybe." Katina meant *probably not.*

"Think about it. I've got to go now."

"Okay, thank you, Momma. We'll have even more fun in Rhodes. I've called to let Kostas know we're coming."

"From what your father told me it is not such an easy thing you must do in Rhodes. Be careful."

Grrrr. "Of course, I will. Daddy shouldn't have told you."

"Your father worries."

"Yes, he does, just like you,"

"Goodbye, Tina *mou.*"

Katina said her goodbyes and put the phone back into her purse. *A scholarship does sound like a great idea.* She remembered the first time she went on a dig with her father in Turkey. Men and women troweling a patch of ground, surrounded by toppled pillars and walls, for days. The trowel was replaced by brushes. Finally, a delicate mosaic of the Goddess Diane was revealed.

They poured water on the entire rectangle. It looked like a beautiful carpet with images of dogs, deer, and clouds. Diane, the Huntress, had her bow pulled back, an arrow ready to fly. The colored tiles, protected from the elements by the soil, were as vibrant that day as when the workers laid them. Katina pretended she wore a toga and ate grapes on a large block of granite.

I couldn't have seen that without Daddy. A less fortunate kid could have the same experience. I think Momma dragged me into her world. "Lord, help me." She crossed herself.

Katina went over to the bed. Celeste's eyes moved back and forth under delicate lids. Her lips were pursed as if in a kiss. *Do I sleep with such sweetness? I need to ask Jim.*

"Okay, husband, please answer." She entered his number. Her heart sank as it went immediately to voicemail, even though she expected it would.

"Hello, again, it's me. I hope you're okay. It would be wonderful if you could give me a call or send me a text. Bye."

She went to her side of the bed and folded her clothes, then tossed them haphazardly into her suitcase. She got into bed, dragged one of the blankets off Celeste-the-cover-hog, and whispered, "I've got to get some sleep."

A toilet flushed in the next room. Katina blocked the noise by covering her head with the blanket. After doing some Zen breathing, she concentrated on sweet things like hugs from her husband and kisses from her dearest darlings in the whole world, Pippen and Sadie.

~ * ~

The world quaked around her. Coming out of her warm sleep, Katina heard Celeste as she continued to shake her. "Get up. The cab's here."

Katina shot up in bed. "I just closed my eyes two and a half minutes ago. Drat it all, Celeste. I'm sorry. I'll brush my teeth and be ready in a second."

A laugh, like the sound of tinkling wind chimes, erupted from Celeste. "That's okay. I was just teasing you. We have an hour. Aubrey's downstairs having coffee. He came early."

As she closed the bathroom door, Katina mumbled, "I wish Jim was coming instead."

Chapter Twenty

Rhodes at Last

Katina's return to Rhodes answered a desire that remained in the depth of her heart. Her exhaustion lifted as she turned the knob to her penthouse apartment in the Mitsis Grand Hotel. She placed her bags next to the door and gazed at her home-away-from-home. She loved its mix of ultra-modernity and Greek influences. The foyer was a semi-circle of slender Corinthian columns. Within it, tiny tiles of azure, turquoise, aqua, and deep-blue marble were inlaid to form a porpoise leaping from the ocean.

A white marble floor and a twenty-foot wall of windows gave the expansive living room airiness. Glee filled her as Katina made her way to the sliding glass doors. She passed white leather furniture and colorful Turkish carpets. Pillows and fresh flowers, in shades of lemon yellow, tangerine, and a few splashes of red, added more layers of loveliness.

As she opened the doors, the soft sound of the waves and the salty sea's fragrance assailed her senses. She closed her eyes as the warm breeze lifted strands of hair and raised chill bumps of pleasure on her arms.

The spell was broken by luggage banging accompanied by Celeste and Aubrey's voices in the foyer. Katina joined them, ready to help with their bags.

"It's a small elevator, isn't it? Come on in."

All gazes turned as Kostas Menos, the house manager for the Papamissios's penthouses, entered the room.

"I thought I heard you. *Yassas*, Katina. Welcome home. Helena and I are so happy you're here."

She extricated herself from his warm hug. "Oh, Kostas. I'm so happy to see you. I wasn't sure you'd be here."

He wagged his finger. "I wouldn't miss your homecoming. Rest yourselves. How about some food and wine?"

"Let me help, for goodness' sake," she said, following closely. "I've been sitting for hours."

Celeste and Aubrey joined in offering their assistance.

"No, thank you all. This old man can handle it." Kostas rushed out of the room, then returned moments later with a large platter of delicious assorted *mezes*, which he set in the middle of the coffee table. "Helena prepared a small feast."

Katina leaned over the tray to admire the bounty. Her mouth watered as she smelled the mint, onion, and lemon that made up the ingredients of the small meatballs named *keftedakia*. She loved the crispy phyllo of the cheese-filled *tiropites*. *Dolmathes,* grape leaves stuffed with rice and lamb, soaked in lemon and olive oil, were also on the platter.

Celeste sent a warm glance to Kostas as she leaned over to enjoy the aromas and admire the variety of delicacies.

Katina remembered the time she told Celeste about a particularly mean tale. Kostas was saved from being the ugliest person on Rhodes by the presence of his wife, Helena. As the story went, one of the innumerable gold feral cats that roamed the narrow streets of the island, died of fright as it looked upon her face. They both had dark, pitted skin and deep-set, almost black, eyes. Their noses were large and hooked, coming to a point at the end. They could have passed for brother and sister. Katina had finished the story by saying, "Everyone who knows them thinks they're beautiful. They have honest hearts. Celeste, their love for God and all he created humbles me."

Celeste's sweetness to this beloved person made Katina's protective heart happy.

Celeste looked into Kostas's gentle black eyes. "Hello, Kostas. I don't know if you remember me, but I'm Celeste, Katina's friend from school. This is wonderful. Should I start with the vegetables and cheese or the hot bits of yumminess?"

"Yumminess? What is this?" Not waiting for an answer, he turned in Celeste's direction. "Yes, of course, I remember you, Miss Daly. I always start from the outside and work my way in. You will see Katina picks her favorites and leaves the rest for you. She was a naughty child, and her parents were too lenient."

Katina enjoyed his teasing. "Don't believe Kostas. He was the one who taught me which ones were the best. Didn't you?"

"Perhaps that is so, but how could I not spoil the most beautiful *koritsaki* on the island."

"What's a *kor-koritsaki*? Is that Greek for kitten perhaps?" Aubrey stuffed a whole triangle of the spinach and cheese pastry called *spanakopita* into his mouth.

She wondered if he knew how time-consuming those were to make. "It means baby girl." She walked over to Kostas and fiddled with the elderly man's hair.

He swatted her hands away. "Leave me be, *koukla mou*. You are still a pest."

"And you hate having your perfect hair messed up. That's why I do it." She winked. "Don't tell Helena; she'll give me the evil-eye."

"She saves those for me." Kostas gave a sigh of happiness. "And I love her so. You are tired. Eat, drink, then rest. When would you like Helena to have breakfast for you?"

"I forget how pampered I am here. When do y'all want breakfast?"

"Oh, I don't know. Aubrey? When do you want to get up?" Celeste put a bite of tomato and feta into his mouth. She dabbed at a tiny drip of tomato juice on his lip.

Those two would take an hour to decide, so Katina ventured, "How about 8:30, Kostas? I can't wait to give Helena a great, big Atlanta hug."

The old man went to the kitchen mumbling, "They cannot be any better than a good Greek hug."

She laughed. Greek hugs were the best. "Celeste, I'm going to skip the wine. I know it's early, but I need to go to bed now. I didn't sleep at all on the plane." She stretched and rolled her head from side-to-side. Her neck made those yucky crackling noises. "We have a lot to do tomorrow. Sweetie, you know which room is yours?"

Katina didn't mention where she wanted Aubrey to sleep—in a hotel down the street. As she left, the two lovebirds snuggled on the couch. Celeste's cell phone rang, but she didn't answer it. Perhaps she was too tired to care.

~ * ~

The morning was idyllic, as most were on the island of Rhodes. Katina wore a jewel-blue bikini and a sheer, white wrap, and sipped her sweet espresso on the balcony. Helena sat close and beamed with pleasure.

Katina filled her lungs with the sea air while memories filled her mind. "Remember when Papa gave me permission to swim in the ocean with you?"

Like most people that lived by the shore, Helena spent a few hours every summer day swimming. Katina was six years old at that time. She'd been torn between running headlong and splashing about like the other children or entering cautiously as her father had advised. His voice was still in her head. *Just because you took lessons in Atlanta does not mean you can swim the same way in the ocean, daughter.* Since he'd left that morning to spend the summer in Egypt, she'd ignored the warning and rushed into the sea as fast as her skinny legs could carry her.

The warm water splashed her knees, quickly lapping at the bottom of her swimsuit.

Helena yelled, "*Epistrefei*. Come back. This is not a pool, *koukla mou*."

Katina ignored her second warning of the day and shouted with joy at the exact time a wave swept her up and propelled her down into the stony bottom. She stood gagging and coughing.

Remembering the taste of that briny water, Katina groaned.

"I do. You ran like a lamb after its mother, but every day after that, we would float and swim for hours."

Katina yearned to slide into the sea that minute. "My arms and legs ache to go. Maybe later, Helena *mou*."

"If you have time," Helena said. "That would be, what would you say, awesome?"

A familiar man walked onto the patio. He was about 6' 1" with dark blond, curly hair. His light green eyes took in his surroundings.

Helena shot up straight and demanded, "Who is this man?"

Katina touched Helena's arm. "It's okay. I know him." She turned her attention to her surprise guest. "Well my goodness. Hi there. This is Bobby Daly. He's Celeste's brother."

Helena gave a sharp nod of acknowledgement. "Does Celeste know you're here?" She didn't wait for a response, got up and went past him. "I will make more coffee."

He ignored her rudeness and flashed his crooked grin. "Yep. I called her last night. Where have you guys been? You were supposed to be here yesterday." He whispered, "I was about to shake her hand. I don't think she likes me."

Katina whispered back, "Don't worry about it. She'll come around." She continued at normal volume. "We were having fun as usual. Have a seat. I'm glad you could come. Celeste misses you. Did she tell you we were in Scotland?"

"Yeah, she did. What were you guys doing there?" he asked, as he sat in Helena's vacated chair.

His green eyes were bright and his expression sharp. Katina wondered why he didn't seem the least bit jet lagged. Most people were for the first few days. "Well. Umm. Vacation stuff. Did you bring a girlfriend? Speaking of that, did you know Celeste has a boyfriend? His name's Aubrey."

"No, uh, she didn't, but that's not—"

"Is that Celeste?" Katina looked toward the doors and changed the subject again. "Come on. Let's get some breakfast." She rose and led the way.

Bobby had no other option but to follow.

I'm getting good at this diversion and secret stuff. All that damn practice in Dalkeith. She crossed herself for cussing and chuckled.

As they entered, Helena motioned with her hand. "Maybe you could help me in the kitchen. This young man can sit in the living room and have a cup of good Greek coffee." She handed him a demitasse. "Come with me, *koukla.* I want to show you something."

The kitchen was as large and industrial as those found in restaurants. Its one nod to luxury was the white marble of the island. The other countertops were stainless steel, as were the two refrigerators, the two dishwashers, and the Vulcan gas range.

Katina had never had a party, but if she did, the kitchen would be ready.

"Tina, Kostas said that man rang the doorbell and just walked in without a *yassas.* How do you say that in English?"

She laughed at this wonderful woman. "I would say, 'He walked into the house without a how-do-you-do.'"

"*Yassas* is faster. Anyways, Kostas did not know if he should let him in. This world is crazy now. I should use my evil-eye on him." Helena raised the gold chain that hung around her neck.

On it, dangled a small gold cross. Also attached to the chain was a glass bead with a blue dot in its center. The evil-eye. Mythical and ineffectual. Maybe.

"Oh Helena, I've missed you so much. You make me remember how special being Greek is."

"Speaking of that, do you want a big American breakfast or one of ours? I have the *psomi* cut," she indicated the bread board loaded with a medium heavy Greek bread, "and the tomatoes and cheese ready. Do you want eggs or meat? I have everything."

"I'm starved. Let's have it all."

"Good." Helena got the pans out for the bacon and eggs. "I am so happy you are here. Kostas complained that I sang like a chicken with a broken wing this morning. I told him I was happy because our Tina was home. That man doesn't appreciate me."

"Well, he said Papa sounds like a bull in love when *he* sings, but I don't think Kostas has ever seen a bull."

"Okay, missy. We have been to Spain. He has seen a bull and those big bells that hang between their legs going bong-bong, bong-bong."

Katina almost spit out a sip of coffee. "Do you mean balls?"

"Yes, I think so. They would not bong, would they?"

Katina giggled and hugged the woman who was sometimes more

of a mother than her own. "I love you and Kostas so much."

Helena patted her on the cheek. "We love you too. Now, let me work. You make me embarrassed. Go. Keep an eye on that man in the living room."

Chapter Twenty-One

What's Up With Bobby?

Celeste sat next to Bobby at the table on the balcony, under the shade of its huge blue and white striped umbrella. Deep grooves creased the space between his brows. He worried too much, but he was a detective, and that wasn't an easy job.

"You seem pretty good, kind of tense though. I read about the arrest in the *Times*. Are you still keyed up about that?"

Bobby picked at a cuticle. "Not much. It went pretty well. My partner's informant came through for him. I wasn't expecting an arrest so fast." He opened his mouth, then closed it. "Okay. I didn't come all the way over here for this, but…" He paused as a distinct look of chagrin came over his features. "You know I'd never ask for a favor unless it was real important, right?"

"I guess." His nervousness made Celeste want to pick her own cuticles, but they were still perfect from the manicure she'd given herself the week before.

Bits of blood popped up around his thumbnail, so he switched to fiddling with his coffee cup. "I know I haven't been as smart with my inheritance as you."

She stopped in mid-sip of her coffee and sat up straight at the sudden change of topic. "The real estate market was in an upswing at the time, and I—"

"Yeah, well." He raised his hand. "I didn't have time to do that. I need money to pay off my car. I want to buy an apartment, and I won't qualify if I still have a car payment."

Phew. That's not so bad. "Good thinking. It's better than throwing rent money away every month, isn't it?"

"Exactly."

She wondered how far she could question his finances without annoying him. "So how much do you need? Is the car close to being paid off?"

He bit his bottom lip. "Not quite. I refinanced it. I owe $35,000." He turned worried eyes to Celeste. "That's not too much, is it? Can you help your little brother out?"

"I want to come up with some good options here but, I don't

have $35,000 just laying around. I live on a tight budget, you know." Her stomach turned at parting with any of her hard-earned savings. "Do you want me to loan you the whole thing?"

Bobby put his forearms on the table and clasped his hands together. "I've never—"

"You've never asked for anything before." She folded her hands around her brother's. "Is that what you were going to say?"

He shrugged and nodded, looking about twelve years old and adorable.

"Even though you've received some of the city's top honors, cops don't get bonuses and aren't paid what they deserve." She squeezed his hands. "I'd be happy to help. I'm very proud of you. Mom and Dad are too. Since the day you were born." She released his hands and gave him a playful punch on his arm. "You were the prettiest baby at the hospital. Everyone thought those luxurious eyelashes and big eyes belonged to a girl."

"Hey, knock it off. I've never been pretty a day in my life." He pointed to a crescent-shaped scar a fraction of an inch away from his left eye. "See that? I got it saving your life when you were eight. I've been deformed ever since."

She laughed at his obvious exaggeration. "Sure, sure. If you call being hit by the swing I was on, as you walked behind it, saving my life." She leaned close and hugged him. "I love you."

A tight smile crossed his face. "You're a good person. Thank you."

"Don't mention it, and I mean that for real. Don't tell Mom and Dad."

"Oh, I won't. You can count on that." Bobby turned to the sound of people talking in the interior of the apartment. "It must be breakfast time. Here's Tina, and this must be Aubrey." He stood and held out his hand. "Good to meet you. I'm Bobby. The better of my parents' two children."

"Naturally. Pleasure's all mine." Aubrey returned the shake.

Katina placed some napkins and silverware around the table, then slid into a chair that Bobby held out. She put a napkin in her lap. "Hi, everyone. Glad you're here. How'd you sleep, Celeste?"

"Greater than great." She puckered her lips and received a kiss from Aubrey. "That was very sweet. I like it."

Helena rolled a breakfast cart onto the balcony.

Katina rose and placed the dishes of food in the middle of the table. "Isn't this scrumptious?"

"Yes, it is." Celeste said. "Thank you, Helena."

The men echoed her thanks and selected whatever delicacy was closest.

"Y'all stop." Katina sat back down and sent a scolding glance toward each man, but the edges of her mouth twitched up. She could not hide her enjoyment. "In Greece, it's the right, nay the *duty,* of the hostess to serve her guests."

Aubrey and Bobby chuckled. Celeste applauded. "Bravo, Katina. It's time you practiced your hostess skills."

"Thank you. Men, it's quite different than in the States." Katina placed food on various dishes and handed them around. "It falls upon my shoulders to overfeed you. In fact, I must do this to the point of ridiculousness and possible anger on your part."

Bobby finished his eggs in two bites, leaned forward and held out his plate for more. "So, how was Scotland? It must have been pretty damn good if you picked up this Brit here."

"Scotland was beautiful, and I didn't pick up a Brit. I met Aubrey that year I studied in England."

"You never mentioned him before. Did Mom and Dad know?"

Celeste's cheeks heated. "No and no. Come on. Let's have a nice breakfast, okay? No more third degree, Detective Daly."

He acquiesced with a flash of the disarming smile that had gotten him in, and out, of trouble. "Fine. If Katina's job is to act as hostess, I thought I should do my job as a brother. Anyway, I'll corner him later." He laughed and leaned away from a swat Celeste sent his way. "What're we going to do? Wanna go swimming this afternoon?"

Katina glanced at her swimsuit. "Good question. I'll take a few laps in the pool, and then Celeste and I are going to do some exploring." She went to the pool's edge. "Maybe you men can keep yourselves busy this morning, and we can meet up at the beach later." Her entrance into the crystalline water was almost soundless.

Celeste looked from Aubrey to Bobby. "Are you two okay with sight-seeing together?"

Bobby chortled. "No offense, but I'd rather hang out with you and Katina."

"*I'd* rather spend the day with you. Bobby doesn't need to tag along." Aubrey put his arm around Celeste's shoulders and kissed her cheek.

Giving them a stony look, Bobby said, "So... He just waltzes in here with that weird accent and takes over?"

What's up with Bobby? He's never acted like this before. "That's rude, don't you think? And Aubrey, that's not what Tina had in mind."

Katina appeared, dripping wet. "What's not what I had in

mind?"

Bobby said, "Tina doesn't like him either, you know. The three of us can hang out. Aubrey can fend for himself."

There he goes again. So aggressive. Angry. "What's your problem?"

Katina toweled her hair and cocked her head in confusion. "I don't like who? What're you talking about?"

Celeste glared at everyone around her. "This is ridiculous."

"Why are you mad, Celeste?"

"I'm mad because I've about had it with both of you, that's why."

"Who? What'd I do?" Katina had raised her voice to match the tenor of Celeste's.

Okay. You asked for it, girlfriend. "Bobby's right, Tina. I've seen how you are around Aubrey. I've also heard you complain about him under your breath. You can't believe no one hears you."

"I'd deny it, but I don't think I'd get away with it," Katina said. "This time."

Celeste didn't fall for her friend's attempt at cuteness. "You're damn right you won't. I can't believe my brother and my best friend are acting like children. Good God. Aubrey and I will spend the day together, and you two can do whatever you want."

Katina gave Celeste the you're-supposed-to-go-with-me look, to which Celeste responded with the fat-chance look.

"You mean it's either him or me?" Katina covered her mouth and spoke through her fingers. "Did I just say that out loud?" She moved her hand away and waved it dismissively. "I can go by myself. No biggie."

Bobby pushed his chair back and stood with the fanfare of an English knight of the realm. "Katina, I'd love to spend the day with you. Celeste doesn't appreciate the concern of a loving brother."

"Get over yourself, Bobby." Celeste tossed her napkin on the table. "You're confusing concern with rudeness. I don't need your protection. Knock it off."

Bobby threw up his hands in supplication. "I was just kidding. You and Aubrey can have fun by yourselves. Katina and I will have a good time too, won't we?"

"I'd rather go alone."

Bobby lowered his sugar-coated voice as he said, "I would love to come. Please?" He batted his eyelashes.

Will Tina fall for his charm?

"I wanted this to be just us." Katina stomped toward the living room. "You can come, Bobby."

Ooh. Look at that walk. Didn't fall for your charm, brother. At least you can go with her. Lord, please help them get along so I can have a nice day.

Chapter Twenty-Two

Guess Who Shows Up?

Katina was still discombobulated. She wanted to stay mad at Celeste, but her exuberance for the reconnaissance mission was too strong. *I'm so close now.* She prayed the pieces would come together.

The first puzzle piece was crucial. Katha's diary told her she needed to figure out where Gerard hid the key. She needed it to open the room to the treasure. If not, she'd have to figure out a way to break in the door.

Next was John Sinclair's map. It showed the section of the palace where the icons should be. The layout was etched in her memory now.

Those were two main pieces, but there were more. She just didn't know what they were, yet.

Katina and Bobby headed south on the shoreline street of Akti Miaouu toward one part of the fortified, outer walls meant to keep the medieval city and palace safe from invaders.

She side-stepped a young couple who held hands and each other's gaze so deeply they were oblivious to their surroundings. "Speaking of too much public displays of affection. Celeste sure got grouchy, didn't she? I've never seen her like that. Okay, that's a lie, but she's a patient person. Okay. That's a lie too. Forget it."

"Were we speaking of that?" Bobby chuckled as he looked toward the lapping waves. He turned his attention to the to the small businesses that lined the other side of the street. "Yeah, she's complicated. I'm trying to wrap my head around this guy, Aubrey. Is he a jerk or am I off-base?"

"I'm not sure yet. He's kind of grabby." She enjoyed watching people, mostly women, stare at Bobby.

He seemed to know when this happened; his head would tilt, and he would sometimes pause his stride. He was a detective and had a heightened sense of danger, though.

Or he was a little vain. "What do you see when you look at the store windows? I've seen people on TV do that. It's like you're checking on a tail."

"Goes back to my football days. I needed to know where

everyone was always on the field. It just stuck with me. I don't need to do it as a detective. I just walk around crime scenes and ask a lot of questions. Street cops, on the other hand…"

"Sure, you're not looking at yourself because you're so handsome?"

He threw a companionable arm around her shoulders. "You're right about that."

She poked him in the ribs and was relieved when his arm dropped.

"Ouch," he yipped. "I bruise easily, you know." He gave her a cheeky grin. "So, what'd Aubrey grab?"

"A picture."

Bobby followed her lead as she turned down Dimokratias street. "Why didn't you let him see it? What's the big deal?"

"The big deal is, he did it one too many times. He's pushy. He apologized, so I forgave him, but only for Celeste's sake."

"I'm pushy too. It's a cop thing." He leaned close and flashed a quick smile. "Don't tell anyone."

Katina gave a quick nod. "Gotcha. It would be nice if you didn't do that around me. I'm kinda over it." She pointed down the street. "We're heading to the northwest entrance, to the Ampuaz Gate of the fortress wall. It's very old, but not original."

"Are we just going to shop?" Bobby grinned. "I like to shop."

His goofy expression and expensive shirt indicated the veracity of his statement.

"Oh, I don't know. I haven't been to the palace in seems like forever. It's one of the few examples of Gothic architecture in all of Greece. Is that okay? You might like it."

"I guess." His grin had turned downward but appeared content. "Did the Greeks build all this?"

She nodded, glad he was showing some interest. "You might say that Greeks performed the labor."

"That's an interesting distinction. What do you mean? Were they slaves or what?"

"Good question. When the Knights conquered Rhodes in the 1300s, the Greeks decided to stay and built the Catholic churches and buildings used by the knights. They also reused Greek church sites. They made a pretty good living."

A cooling breeze swirled around them. She brushed the hair off her face and raised it from her neck for a blessed moment. "That was nice… Anyway, then the Persians came and rebuilt structures they damaged in the war. They turned most of the Catholic churches into mosques. Look around. You can see a lot of Persian influences." She pointed to the arch and peak of a window across the street.

Bobby shielded his eyes and squinted. "You're right. I saw the differences but didn't think much about it."

"Yep. But it didn't stop there. Christians eventually got the island back—" *Good grief.*

Bobby's attention was drawn by a young woman who wore a slinky, white T-shirt and tight shorts.

When his gaze returned, Katina continued, "Everything was in horrible condition because the Greeks were poor. Couldn't afford to rebuild. Italy took possession in the 1900s. Remember, they're Catholics, and this island meant a lot to their history too. Thank God for them, because they put a ton of money into restoration. I'll take you to a small church. You'll see both influences in it."

"Okay, but I have to warn you, I may not, umm, appreciate your level of knowledge. At least I can try."

A man with a tourist's map hiding his face, plowed into Katina.

She cried out as she tripped over her own feet and fell to the ground.

Bobby said, "Hey. Watch where you're going, jerk."

Both men grabbed one of her arms and lifted her to her feet. Katina, twisted legs and panting, righted herself. There were pebbles and drops of blood covering her palm.

"That's gonna sting." A half a second later, she nodded. "Yep. It's stinging." She puckered her lips to blow on her wound as a gray and yellow linen hanky was placed into her unhurt hand.

A deep and distinctive voice said, "I'm very sorry. I should know better than to walk around with a map in my face."

"George!"

"Please take this."

Katina looked from the man's face to the handkerchief he held and back. "Hi. You're the one that helped me in New York. I was in a car. You're the hero. I bonked my fore—"

"Yes! Yes, of course." The man held out his hand. "So, we meet again. My name is Maxwell Blackmarr. I'm terribly sorry I knocked you down."

Bobby interceded and shook the outstretched hand, simultaneously nudging Maxwell's shoulder to turn him around. "Nice to meet you, Mr. Blackmarr. See ya."

"Bobby, I haven't thanked him yet." She held up her hand. "Hi. My name's Katina. Thank you so much—"

"The man knocked you down." Bobby's face contracted into

irritation. "You don't need to thank him. Come on. Let's go." He took her arm to lead her away.

She stared at Maxwell's face as she shook off Bobby's grasping hand. "What are you doing here? Good grief. Who would've thought?"

"Yes, who would have thought. I'm here on business, as usual. Do you know much about the area? I need to get to St. Catherine's, and I'm a bit turned around."

Maxwell's charisma oozed. His statement wasn't anything special, not charming, but the way he spoke, the cadence perhaps, set him apart. He looked at her as if he understood something deep and essential.

She managed to say, "Really? That's in Old Town. We're headed there now. Why don't you come with us?"

Bobby scowled. "I'm sure he'll be fine. We need to—"

"Excellent." Maxwell's smile broadened as if he just realized he'd won a prize. "I'm usually great with directions, but the street signs are impossible to read."

"Yes, unless you know the Greek alphabet. I'd be happy to help you." She stared into his deep brown eyes that sparkled with flecks of green.

"Terrific. You can tell me all about yourself as we go."

Her hand itched to put a finger in his dimple. Instead, she walked toward the fortress, pressing the hanky against her palm. "Maybe I shouldn't tell you this, Maxwell, but…" Katina giggled. "I thought you were George Clooney. Can you believe that?" She burst out laughing. "I'm such an idiot. You do kind of remind me of him."

"Not me," Bobby said.

Chapter Twenty-Three

The Hunt for The Cross is On

Maxwell's gait was long and slow, that of someone who was assured of his station and comfortable in his surroundings. When he spoke, his accent was upper Manhattan. "Katina. Katina Bason. Lovely name. Even lovelier lady. Tell me, what happened to you after the fender-bender? Wish I had had time to help more than I did, but I had a terribly important meeting. You're no worse for wear, I see."

She touched her forehead. She remembered the warning her father had given, and she was still confused about the loss of her purse. "Oh, don't worry about that." She drew Maxwell's attention away from her accident by asking, "Did you know that this is also known as the Street of the Knights? It leads us right to the Palace of the Grand Master, up there to the right. It's a Byzantine museum now."

A museum I won't be able to peruse at will with them around, drat it.

Katina and Maxwell, with Bobby following far behind, passed stone buildings and shops that sold pieces of copper cookware, ceramics, and a never-ending supply of jewelry. Maxwell didn't stop once to buy anything, nor did Bobby. They were either cognizant of Katina's quest or had no interest in trinkets.

As they approached the palace entrance, Maxwell asked about the ruins across the street. Partial, crumpled walls and a few steps that led to nowhere were surrounded by piles of dirt and rubble.

"Those ruins are from different historical periods." Katina pointed to a free-standing block stone wall. "That was the Catholic Church of St. John. The Grand Masters burials were there. The Greeks call it the Church of *Aghios Ioannis*." She teased, "Try saying that three times fast." The love to educate was strong. She needed to impart what she knew. She hoped they wanted to learn. "So many wars, so many died for such a minuscule parcel of land. We're standing in the spot where the Temple of the Sun God stood thousands of years ago. The church and the palace were built on parts of their remains."

She regarded her companions. Bobby, Mister Grumpy, sat on a pile of stones, checking something out on his cellphone. Maxwell seemed very interested though, so she continued, "This happened over and over, country after country. History wasn't so much destroyed as *replaced* by either a more modern version of worship and architecture or a history rewritten to better tell a story of the victors."

"Incredible. I haven't been here before, so I didn't know what to expect. How do you know so much?"

She gave a dismissive wave. "I'm Greek. It's what we do. If we can afford it, we go back to the old country. That means we come to the town of our ancestors."

He took her arm and led the way to the palace door. In a low, unhurried voice, he said, "The old country, hmm? What about the new country? You didn't tell me about Manhattan and your head wound."

Lulled by the tempo of his speech, she jumped as Bobby's more strident voice broke in.

"What's he talking about?" He blocked their progress into the building. His piercing green eyes searched her face. He took her chin in his fingers and turned her head this way and that inspecting her hairline. "Slight bruising. What happened?"

So much attention over a bump. A tiny cut. She took a few steps back and fluffed her hair. "My goodness, you two. Celeste's car was rear-ended, and I hurt my head. A teeny bit. Bobby, you're acting like a cop." She forced a laugh. "Don't be such worry-warts." She lied as she said, "I might have punched the guy for damaging Celeste's car. She loves it like a baby."

He grinned. "You couldn't hurt a bug."

"I kill bugs all the time. Hate them. I can be vicious."

Bobby and Maxwell's expressions were amused as Katina raised her hands like a boxer. Maxwell murmured, "You don't have to be the tough guy. I'll take care of any pests that may cross your path."

He's so gallant, just like George Clooney. "No one's ever pledged to kill a bug for me. Being nine feet tall seems to intimidate men. I'm not the type to bring out their protective side."

Maxwell looked her up and down, and gave a deep, seductive, chuckle. "I'd say you're about five feet ten inches of loveliness. That's pretty perfect in my book."

Bobby gave a derisive laugh. "Oh my God. Are you serious, man?"

Katina didn't know what to say. These two men were not playing nicely. *It's time to punt.* "Come on. Let's go check this out." They walked through the entrance that was between two magnificent stone towers, complete with classic gothic turrets. She stopped at a sign that read:

Rhodes from early times to the Turkish conquest

(1522) is housed in various rooms on the ground floor of the palace.

Fully inside, she turned around in a slow circle. "Aren't these gorgeous? I love the arched buttresses of dark wood." She indicated the far wall. "See that tapestry? Maxwell, if you stood next to it, you'd be dwarfed. Its size is deceiving because the ceilings are so tall."

Maxwell whistled between his teeth, quiet and high-pitched. "It's massive. Is the tapestry original?"

"Unfortunately, no. Remember across the street? In 1856, an ammunition pile stored at the church blew up. Most of the rooms on this floor were destroyed. Everything in them too, of course."

"The room looks perfect. Who rebuilt it?" Maxwell asked.

Her enthusiasm grew. "I told Bobby that the Italians played a large part. They got the island after World War I, as part of the Paris Peace Treaty. It was a good thing because they repaired this building, and many more for that matter, around 1940, using mosaics of the Hellenistic and Roman period. The Italians, umm, retrieved some of them from the island of Kos. I bet they want 'em back." She paused in her lesson. *Am I teaching or being a good hostess? Doesn't matter. This is fun. Oh… Now I miss my class and my students. I wonder how many kids I'll get this fall. If I have a job. Professor Crenshaw.*

Katina groaned at her mind's pathetic turn. "Come on. It gets better." She turned to the left, walked across a lovely mosaic as millions had done over the years, and entered a small room. "Knights came here from all over Europe. Each group had their own meeting room. The crest above this door shows that this is a room used by the Knights of Malta. Can you imagine their pious discussions about God and country or their frantic planning during the blockade? Very cool, don't you think?"

"Hmm… Indeed." Maxwell took in the small, empty room. He didn't sound terribly impressed though.

Bobby walked in and seemed even less impressed. "Did you and Celeste spend your vacations looking at stuff like this? God, how boring."

"Are you serious?" Katina demanded.

He cleared his throat. "Sorry. That came out wrong. I just thought you were doing something fun, like enjoying the beach and pubs. That's what I'd do anyway. Now that I think about it, is that what you did all these years? No wonder you both stayed single for so long."

She gasped at the insult. *Holy crap. This guy can be mean.*

Maxwell glanced at her, then glared at Bobby. "Wow. You must like the taste of your foot. Why don't you give it a rest, huh? I don't know who Celeste is, but if she's like Katina, she's enchanting." He lightly grasped Katina's hand. "Let's continue your most informative tour. You are a knowledgeable guide." He put his arm around her shoulders and led the way out of the room.

Bobby scowled at them as they passed.

"Maxwell, you are a very sensitive man. And very chivalrous. I think I'll like getting to know you."

Bobby said under his breath, "Whatever. He's a dick. You'll find out soon enough, I guess."

She stopped short. "Maybe you need to take a break. Get a beer somewhere."

He shot back, "Good idea."

As he left, she shook her head at his animosity. She'd only been around him a few times, but he'd always been fun and friendly. "I don't know what bee flew up his pants."

The room they were about to enter had been easily recognizable on the map. As she approached a door, butterflies took flight in her stomach. If correct, there would be a flight of stairs behind another door.

"Let's look in this chapel. It's rather plain, but just imagine the knights kneeling in prayer five times a day." Katina took special interest in the two wooden doors at the front of the chapel. One was situated to the left of the altar. The other was on a side wall.

Her mind raced, but she forced herself to be nonchalant. "You know, the master architect, Vittorio Mesturino, used the original blueprints to rebuild this after the destruction from the blast. This part of the building is essentially the same. I can't say these are the actual doors, but…"

She started to open the door against the altar wall. It scraped against the stone floor, and she froze. She squeaked and slapped a hand over her mouth. With a quiet voice, she continued, "I didn't mean to open it. I figured it'd be locked. God, I hope there isn't a camera. I'll be arrested and thrown in the hoosegow." She closed the door as softly as possible and scurried over to Maxwell, taking his elbow in her hands. "Maybe we should leave. Let's go to the courtyard. I like to picture what happened there: The Knights of Rhodes in ragged red tunics with dirty, white crosses and armor beaten so badly it was hardly wearable. And think about the Sultan Suleiman. I wonder what he really looked like as he took command of the island. Did he march around demanding this or that, or was he very business-like, issuing orders as needed?"

A slow smile spread across Maxwell's face. He nodded and tucked her hand into his side. He leaned down to her ear. "Those times must have been as fascinating as I find you. Everyone around here thinks you're as beautiful as I do."

She glanced about and found no one stared. "I doubt that, Maxwell. They just wonder where I get my tennis shoes."

"You are truly amusing. One of the most charming and unusual women I've ever met."

Admiring the faded colors, but still sharp images of the frescoes by Gaudenzi and Vellan, she said absently, "Why? Because I have big feet?"

His laughter bounced off the stone walls of the long hallway they walked down. "Those are good feet, and more to the point, you think people look down there when all your beauty is up here." His forefinger traced a line from just below her earlobe, down her neck, to just above her collarbone.

She swayed into him as he put his other arm around her shoulders for just a second before reality proverbially gave a smart whack to knock it off. Removing his arm, she warned, "Stop. My momma would say you're fresh."

"She would?"

"Yes, and my daddy would shoot you."

He lifted her left hand. "And your husband?"

The banter was fun and sort of how she joked with Jim. "He wouldn't have to do anything because you'd be a hurtin' puppy, as he would say. My husband's six-feet-four inches tall. People don't mess with him."

Maxwell dropped her hand and bowed. "Can't blame me though."

"I was only kidding. He wants me to widen my circle of friends. Says I'm too much of an introvert. Your gallantry may be a little much for him to take though."

"Point taken." He led her in the direction of the courtyard.

A few American teenagers rushed past them, down the stairway, bumping Katina as they passed. "They have way too much energy."

They entered the sunshine of the courtyard. He put a hand up to shield his eyes and scanned its expanse. Statues of Roman emperors lined the walls. Other magnificent marble pieces dotted the area.

An old woman in a loose black dress and a black kerchief covering white hair leaned over the railing and glared at the teenagers. "Quiet."

"She's not fooling around," Katina warned.

As the youths ran for the exit, Maxwell said, "Glad they're gone. Now I can admire the proportions of the design in peace. It makes the area even more regal, doesn't it? Befitting of a king, I'd say. I suppose you're imagining your knights in mock battles as they prepare for war."

"Well, Sultan Suleiman was kind of a king. He was immensely powerful, and admired, truth be told. When he conquered the island, he could have killed everyone and kept the land for its strategic location. Instead, he gave a ship to the knights, allowing them to leave immediately, and religious freedom to the Greek Christians who stayed." She studied a stairway leading to an upper level of rooms bordering the open yard. "I have to say, that's better than some Christians did— I hesitate to judge any of their actions. It would be too easy to pick a side because I'm Christian. I think all those battles were over finance and power, and they used religion as an excuse."

"I agree. Money and power are aphrodisiacs for the morally corrupt." Maxwell's attention wandered from one end of the area to the other. His countenance was casual and content. "You seem to have a particular interest in the layout."

Oh my gosh. I want to tell him just a bit.

She braided hair as she thought. *He makes me feel safe and protected, really. Was it the handkerchiefs he gave me? I don't know.* She unbraided her work. *He'll never connect any dots anyway.*

"Well, a young and brave knight worked up somewhere at the top of those stairs. I read about him recently. The Sultan Suleiman's chambers were over there to the left."

"Did he have a name? Was he famous?"

"It was Gerard something. Not well-known at all."

Maxwell's step hesitated for just a second. "Come again?"

"His name was Gerard. He was a scribe." She laughed. "You seem shocked. Was he a long lost relative or something?"

"Well, no." He shooed a buzzing fly away from his ear. "I doubt it. I have some French in my background. I've always assumed my great-grands were milkmaids, butchers, maybe a candlestick maker." With another swat, he said, "Damn it."

The old woman marched toward them, the scarf flapping behind her. She scowled the whole way. "You quiet too. Bad, bad people."

He waved an airy hand and bowed his apologies for them both. "Let's go."

Sharing her passion with someone new was rare and pleasurable. He was far more receptive than Bobby.

They climbed the stairs and explored the rooms on the loggia level. "Not too much to see. I hope you're not bored." They entered the fifth room on the right. "You know a little about me. Tell me about you."

Maxwell's gaze darted from Katina's face to the bare stone walls and back. "Well, I'm here on business, as I said. I work in Manhattan. That work takes me around the world. London, Paris; I'm in merchandising. Always on the hunt for the newest fad to mass produce and market. I'm making inroads with a Chinese company as a major supplier."

They entered the sixth room. "So, if I googled you, it would say 'World Trader' next to your name?"

"I'm incredibly unknown, to tell the truth. I work in the background." He dropped his chin and gave a sly grin. "It makes it easier to go into markets and spy."

She thought about the spy comment as they explored more offices on that level. "Let's head back down. I'm hot."

Though he wiped a great deal of sweat from the back of his neck, he seemed reluctant to leave.

"Come on. I need to go. I should find Bobby, if he's still around."

"Do you have to go?" Maxwell couldn't have taken the steps any slower as he followed her. "Wouldn't you like to join me for lunch and a tour of St. Catherine's? You were going to show me how to get there, remember?"

She glanced over her shoulder, willing him to hurry. "I'm sorry, I can't. I need to get back and make a few phone calls. Nice to meet you."

"You are a beguiling lady." His voice deepened. "You've grabbed my attention with the history and my heart with your sweetness."

Good Lord, he's something. At the bottom of the stairs, she stopped and addressed him head on. "You're very nice, but I'm a very married woman, remember? My friends are probably waiting for me. I'll point you in the right direction. It's down the street, not too far." With long strides, she rushed to the exit and onto the street. "It's down there." She indicated the direction with a toss of her head. She thrust out her hand. "It's been a pleasure. I'm sure I'll see you again. It's a small island."

He took her hand in his, turned it over, and kissed the rapid pulse of her inner wrist. "I'm sure we will, Katina. I just relocated to the St. Nicholas Hotel on Ippodamou. It's quainter than the large hotel I was in. I've been way too forward and have abused your friendly help. I should be shot. Wait, we've had that discussion. My sincere apologies to you, your father, and your husband."

His eyes held a unique sincerity that instilled a sense of belief and trust in her.

"Please, I'd like to invite you and your friends to dinner this evening. I don't know anyone here, so it would make my stay so much nicer."

"I-I don't know." She rubbed her skin. "You have to stop with the kissing-the-wrist action. We do *not* do that in Atlanta. It makes me more nervous than a turkey at Thanksgiving."

"For someone so well-traveled and educated, you sure have some cute Southern sayings. They just pop out of you at the most unexpected times."

The heat of an uncomfortable blush came upon her. "Well, I guess, you can take the girl out of the South, etcetera, etcetera."

"It's wonderful." He laid a gentle hand on her arm. "Can I count on your Southern hospitality, and your friends, to help a lonely traveler out once again? Please. Join me at Tamam's at 8:00. I've read it's fantastic. Again, I'm terribly sorry if I was too forward. I'm rarely so effusive."

Katina appreciated his honesty. "If you can be a friend, then, yes, I think we can make it. Celeste and I love Tamam's." She smiled. "We'll have a great time, I think. I'll make the reservations."

He headed toward the street Katina indicated saying, "Till this evening, Miss Katina. I look forward to it."

Chapter Twenty-Four

Katina Avoids Confrontation, Even Within Herself

Six pairs of eyes bore into Katina as she entered the apartment. "What. What'd I do?"

Celeste, Aubrey, and Bobby's laughter bounced off the marble in the room, coming back at Katina in a wave. Celeste wagged her finger. "Girl, Bobby was telling us about your conquest."

"He doesn't know what he's talking about. I changed my mind. I don't want a brother. They're brats." Another round of laughter only annoyed Katina more. "Y'all just stop."

"Number one," Bobby said, "it didn't take a detective to know that Maxwell guy was hot for you. Number two, brothers are awesome. If we weren't around, there'd be nothing to make you girls look like the goody-two-shoes you are." He made the joke, but his demeanor had an edge.

"Well, whatever. You're a tattletale. Nope. Strike that. There's nothing to tell." Katina walked into the kitchen in a huff as her guests continued to tease. She returned with a glass of Chablis and plopped on the couch. "All right, people, enough. Celeste, what'd you do today?"

She cozied up to Aubrey on the other couch. "We strolled on the beach for a while. Splashed in the waves. Aubrey's never been to the Mediterranean before."

"Hard to believe, I know." He gathered Celeste in his arms for a squeeze and a kiss. "The sun has never been my friend."

Bobby, tanned and muscled, said, "I guess the red hair and freckles are a sign of cancer waiting to pop out."

Celeste gasped at his audacity. "That's a horrible thing to say. You're a terrible brat."

Katina slapped her leg at his wicked sense of humor. "Ha. He's right though."

"Tina, I'm gonna—" Celeste shook her fist but gave Katina a wink.

Be nice. Be helpful. Damn. I'm rotten at this stuff. Katina changed the subject. "Maxwell invited us to join him for dinner. Do you remember Tamam's, Celeste?"

"Yes. It's great." Celeste nodded to her left. "Bobby doesn't seem to like him though."

He doesn't like your boyfriend, either. Katina took a sip of the cool wine and ran the side of the sweating glass over her warm cheek. "He seems nice enough."

Bobby gave Aubrey and Celeste a this-girl-doesn't-know-what-hit-her look. "Too nice. Trust me."

"Maybe he acts that way to everyone," Katina said.

Three heads nodded. "Yeah. Sure."

"Forget it. We won't go." She flipped her hair to the back. "Y'all are ganging up on me." With her chin held high, Katina walked toward the balcony. Just before she arrived at the door, she tripped on the Persian carpet and spilled her wine across the marble floor. "Damn it. See? I'm a klutz. Proof." She grabbed a napkin from the table and wiped the spill, embarrassed and sad.

Celeste came over and dabbed at the few drops that were left. "You're not that awkward little girl."

Tears brimmed in Katina's eyes.

Her best friend's voice filled with sorrow as she said, "Sweetie..."

"I guess I don't see what you see. God. I'm thirty. I think I went from gangly to, to—wrinkled."

Celeste held Katina's hand as they entered the sunshine outside. "Can we talk about this?"

"I'm tired." She slouched into a lounge chair. "What's there to talk about?"

"About you," Celeste said, as she sat under an umbrella next to her.

"We *were* talking about me. We can change the subject anytime."

"It's a beautiful day. Chirping birds. Fluffy clouds. I think I see a cloud-penis or is it a cloud-ice cream cone over there? Listen. We've had a fun morning. We're relaxed. I bet if you talk about it, you'd feel better."

She harrumphed. *Girl talks. Don't like 'em. The penis cloud thing was good though.*

"I know Jim's told you how beautiful you are, hasn't he? Sometimes, men and women stare at you. Surely, you see that. Why do you think your self-image is so—not true?"

It's simple, but it's not.

Should I, no, that's not the real issue, is it? Can I, explain the heart of why I almost hate myself? Why I'm ugly? Why I think I can't do anything right? Not good enough? Even though I have a frickin' Ph.D.?

"You have no idea the importance of what I'm about to say."

"Please. Let me be here for you. Tell me. Everything."

She worried her wedding band round and around on her finger. "When I was little, I didn't understand the science of mirrors. I never heard that they reflected one's soul. However, I did learn they could reflect one image to myself and a different one to my nanny, Fotini. She would say stuff like, 'You have soiled your sheets. You have made your pretty dress ugly with mud. You have ruined your hair with that excuse for a braid.' Then, when I was about five, I was working in my backyard. I'd spent the first part of the afternoon cutting stems from flowering plants. And I spent the second part replanting them so more flowers would grow.

"Fotini came out, all red-faced, '*Oxi*. What have you done? You have ruined the garden.'

"I said, 'I wanted to help the gardener. He's home sick.' I remember twirling around and laughing at a bee landing on a flower. I said, 'See? More flowers can grow now.' She grabbed my hair and half-dragged me into the house. I screamed of course. I yelled that Momma said girls should be nice.

"Well, she got me to the bedroom and said, 'Look in that mirror. Tell me what you see.'

"I said something like, 'I see a pretty girl, with yellow ribbons, who is very sad.' I didn't know how to say, 'my eyes look like I'm hurt down to my soul'. That's what I would have said, because I'd actually spent the morning being the very best daughter I could be.

"Fotini screamed, 'You are wrong. I see an ugly girl whose eyes and mouth are too big for her skinny face. I see a child who would rather be dirty. Your mother would not approve, let me tell you.'"

"She was a totally crazy bitch, Tina! Did they fire her ass?"

"She didn't start out that way, I guess. But, yeah, they did." She turned toward the sea and let the breeze soothe her.

"You hurt now for the child who felt bad about herself, don't you?"

"I do, Dr. Phil. Is that bad?"

Celeste stroked a pretend mustache, à la the good doctor. "It takes time to get over childhood hurts." She quit all pretense and grew serious. "We all have them. Some are deeper than others. I dreaded the looks people gave me when I told them I was biracial. I still do."

Katina admired Celeste's golden skin, her amber, cat-like eyes shining in the light of day. "I never think of you as biracial. You're... how can I say this? A perfect blend of your mother's beauty and your father's handsomeness. Now that I think about it. I was going to say brains, but—"

Celeste laughed. "Stop it." She paused until Katina grinned. "You must've gotten *your* dad's brains. It sure wasn't his height. You were bean stalk tall. You were a loner and a single child. That's a tough combination. At least I had a brother. Lord was Bobby popular. He had a part-time job just to pay for his dates." A sly grin lit Celeste's somber eyes. "Now that I think about it, your parents wouldn't have let you date anyway."

"Are you kidding? You should have heard me as I explained all that to Jim. Good grief. I told him my instructions were to stay a virgin until I got married. Ha. His eyes about bugged out of his head."

"That's so funny."

"I told him I was 5' 8" when I was 14. Who was I supposed to go to a dance with? Lurch was busy that night."

"Lurch would have made time for you, if you'd asked. Too bad we didn't have boys at school."

Katina snorted. "My folks would have sent me somewhere else."

Celeste gave a decisive nod. "It all worked out for the best, didn't it? You were a great best friend. You are a beautiful woman and all proportion—"

Katina waved a royal hand. "You may continue…"

"I'm serious. One day, you'll see it. Just keep telling yourself that. Replace that lonely voice I know is ricocheting around in your head with thoughts of who you are *now*. Hopefully, you'll get it, before you *are* old and wrinkled, with boobs that hang to your knees."

She was relieved the talk turned to fun. "Hey. You were doing so well with the nice stuff until you blew it. You're going to have the same problem, you know. Except, yours are already closer to your knees. Shorty."

"You're awful." Celeste pretended to beat Katina.

Katina laughed and jumped up to dodge the playful attack.

Aubrey and Bobby must have heard the ruckus because they joined them on the deck.

"You're so damn big," Celeste yelled, "I can't throw you in the pool."

Katina skittered to the left. "Get your sister, Bobby. I'm about to toss her off the balcony. In two seconds. One—"

"Ladies. Ladies," Aubrey called.

Bobby said, "Hey, rule number one: never interrupt a girl fight. I've paid good money to see this."

"I give up y'all. I'm going to call Jim. We'll go for a swim in the sea when I'm finished."

Celeste threw a deck pillow at her brother and followed Katina into the penthouse. "Can we get something to eat?"

"Sure. Helena said there's lentil soup on the stove."

Celeste entered the kitchen and oohed. "The counters are full of goodies. I don't know where to start." She grunted as she opened the large refrigerator door. "Tina, there's more in here. I'm going to gain ten pounds."

Knowing her constant battle to keep her bottom from catching up to her top, Katina shook her head and wagged a finger. "Proportions. That's all I'm gonna say."

Both women turned when they heard Aubrey and Bobby's voices grow louder as they approached.

"Oops. I guess we need to feed them too." Katina made quick work of slicing bread and scooped two bowls of soup. "Celeste, those men are both yours. You feed 'em. I'm going to take my lunch to the bedroom."

"Gotcha." Celeste struggled with the refrigerator door again and grabbed some tea.

~ * ~

Katina placed the food on her white dressing table. She sat down and dialed Jim's number. A squeak escaped her lips, and she jumped up with such force it almost toppled her chair. "Jim. It's me. I can't believe it. I've been trying to call you for days. Are you okay?"

She paced the room as her husband yawned. *How could he?*

"Tina, my love, I'm so sorry. I was in the middle of nowhere. Stupid phone died, and I had to buy a new charger. I finally got all kinds of bings and dings."

"I left more than a few messages." She hoped he could hear the smile in her voice and that it wasn't a criticism.

"I'll listen to every one of them, promise. I'm glad Lexi's call woke me. I hung up with her a second ago. She was worried about *you*. Are you okay? Did you need me?"

"So far, pretty good." Katina mentally smacked her forehead. "I didn't think to call her. She could have called me though."

"We had a good chat and made some plans. Hey, let me tell you what I found. I followed some theropod tracks someone found in 2000. They're outside of a tiny town called Shell, in the Big Horn Basin, in a meter-thick layer of rock in the Gypsum Spring Formation."

She nodded while he spoke. "Umm-hmm." Love swelled within her. His deep voice evoked memories that made parts of her body tingle. *I missed this man.* She sat at the table and took a nibble of food. *I wish I enjoyed hearing about this stuff. Next, my sweet husband will tell me about some 170-million-year old creature that walked on two legs.*

"It rained like crazy here last week, so I thought I'd give this area a try instead of where I was. Sometimes, amazing pieces are uncovered by a deluge. Tina, I lucked out and found a whole animal this time. It's 170-million-years-old. You should—"

I was right. How can I be so right all the time? I wish I were dead wrong, just once. "Sweetheart?"

"—and see it. I'll let some students clean it."

"Darlin'?"

His voice grew more animated as he went on. "It took me three days to dig it up and a day to carry it out of the field to my car. It's times like these that I wish I brought other peop—"

"Jim!" Katina laughed. "Hey, we can talk about this sensational discovery when I get home. I have—"

"Listen to me go on." Jim sounded contrite. "Who wants to hear about bones, anyway? Tell me about what you're up to. Lexi said you went to New York. Then Scotland?"

She put a hand to her heart. "Oh my gosh. So much has happened. There have been car crashes, stolen purses and books, and riddles that Celeste and I solved. It's almost inconceivable." She thought about the experiences and how she had been alone for some of them. Katina murmured, "I wished I could have told you all about it as it happened. I know you go to some desolate places, but this trip is different. I needed you."

There. I said it. She got up and checked out the window for a cataclysmic event. No earthquake, no tornado, birds didn't fall from the sky. That wasn't so bad. "Everything's fine now, promise. A little bump on my head."

"Tina, I had no idea. Lexi told me about your father's accident. What happened to your head? This is why Lexi was worried. You should come home."

Now to the crux of my problem. He may be right to worry. Katina paced the bedroom. How could she explain the desire to go beyond what had limited her in the past: conformation, expectation, explanation. "I thought about it a lot last night. Dad and I getting hurt in car crashes. His warning to me. I went back and forth. It finally hit me that this is too important. I know you don't understand, but Jim, I was meant to find these things and return them to the church."

"Meant to? Come on."

Not handling the situation well at all, Katina tried a new tact. "Celeste's brother is here. He can take care of us."

"I disagree. Listen. It's good that you have a hobby. It makes you happy. I understand. This, however, is different. Tina, there are actual bad guys out there. They'll probably hurt you again to get whatever the hell you're after."

"It's not a hobby, Jim. It's my career. I need a huge article, a book preferably, to publish, to be recognized by the highest echelons in my field."

"It's not *that* important or you would have told me before," Jim said hotly.

"My career isn't important? I—" *He's right. Why didn't I tell him?* The answer came in a split second. *How am I supposed to say, 'Jim, you're super successful, and I'm not. I'm ashamed.'*

"The world won't stop turning if you take the smart and safe route."

"I know it won't. The point is, for the first time in my life *I* need to do something important. I've researched, read old books and manuscripts, traveled around, and had a pretty nice time. This *isn't* a nice time. I've never—"

She rested the phone on her chin and slowed her breathing. *What the hell am I doing? Could he be right? Could all of this be a horrible mistake? Can I get away with publishing what I already have?*

She closed her eyes and saw images of the car wrecks and a creep stealing books in Aubrey's office. *But what about the cross? I could find the treasure. No. It's not a mistake.* "Everything you say is true. I understand I could be hurt again."

"Christ, Tina. You could be killed, not just hurt. Go to the police. Go to a university there. Tell someone else what you're up to and let them figure it out."

In response to the utter desperation in his voice she replied, "Oh, sweetheart, I hate that I mentioned it. I hate that you're upset. I hate that you're not here. I know I'm being an idiot, but I have to do this. There are details I haven't had the chance to tell you."

He growled, "Like what? What the hell else is going on?"

"Nothing bad. Like how I'm the next Daughter of the Ancients, and there's a treasure from ancient Rhodes, and—"

"Are you kidding me, Katina? You think you're a daughter of something ancient? What the hell does that mean, and what does that have to do with this? It sounds like a load of crap."

"See? That's exactly why I didn't tell you any of this. It's not crap." Her pacing increased. *Oooh. He's done it now. He said it was crap. He's in so much trouble—Wait. Be calm.*

Puzzle pieces drifted about in her mind as she tried to work out facets of her life. One piece was in the shape of a broken heart. The others were shaped like tears and flowers. *Our first fight. Should I cry? Should I yell? How can I get him to calm down? Dang it. I should have dated more.* The pieces formed a heart with two entwined wedding rings in its center. *Be honest.*

Katina sat on the side of her bed and picked at the comforter. "I didn't find out about the Daughter of the Ancients part until after you left, and I *have* called you. It's real, Jim."

Holding back a sob, she tried to still her shaking hand and keep the small phone to her ear at the same time because she could barely hear what he said after he stopped yelling. Was his deeply measured tone better or more dangerous? She turned the speaker volume up and started when his voice boomed out of the phone and filled the room.

"...I can't stop you, Tina. I am not one of those husbands who try to control his wife. My dad didn't. I'm not. But damn it, my mom never did anything as hair-brained as this." He started to bellow again. "Be careful, for God's sake. Keep Celeste's brother close. Watch out for strangers. Don't ever be alone. Ever. Got that?"

"Yes, I will." She wiped her nose and nodded as if Jim could see her acquiescence. "I'll be safe. I'll stay with people, and I'll try not to get killed."

"Don't even joke about that."

"Okay. I tried to...to...lighten the situation. You know how I am. You're right. This is serious." She caressed the phone's screen as if it was Jim's cheek. "I promise I'll be fine."

"All right. I'm done preaching. I'm done yelling. I'm not done worrying." He took a slow, calming breath. "Tell me, did you miss me? What was in Scotland?"

Katina sprawled back, nestling her head in the down pillow and began her tale about Aubrey and the hidden books. All was right with the world by the time he learned of plans for a swim in the sea and dinner with her George Clooney surrogate was completed. She laughed at Jim's feigned jealousy and promised not to fall in love with the movie star.

"That'll be easy. Now, if he *was* George, and he *did* have the hots for me—"

There was a loud rap on the door. It swung open, bringing in a wave of Celeste's perfume. She poked her head in. "Are you all caught up? Wanna swim now?"

Katina held up her index finger and nodded.

"Tell your husband I said 'hello.'" With a wicked smile and a wink, she left.

"Celeste's wearing this pink and gold bikini. I wonder what it would be like to wear doll's clothes. Anyway, drive safely. I'll talk to you soon, okay?"

"Okay, sweetheart. I love you. I've missed you, you know? You, my dear wife, are perfect. Celeste is, well, smallish."

Katina laughed at his sense of the obvious. They at least had that in common. "I've missed you too. Bye now."

"Hey, wait. About the treasure. What are you going to do next?"

"Tonight, I'm going back to the palace, after it's closed. I need to find a key in Gerard's office. Hopefully, that won't take all night." She used her free hand to push her hair back, her nerves twitching with excitement. "If all goes well, I'll be back home before you know it."

"I hope so. You're killing me," he said. "I know you've run amok around the island for decades but take someone with you."

"I never ran amok, however, I promise to have someone with me at all times."

Chapter Twenty-Five

Thanks for Nothing

Rain, never a frequent occurrence in Rhodes, was overdue. Maxwell and his companion, Robert, strolled down dusty cobblestone streets. Feral cats panted under restaurant chairs. The men wore their linen shirts untucked, taking advantage of whatever offshore breeze could find its way through the winding streets of Old Town.

Maxwell did not approve of the patriotic moose printed on the front of Robert's well-tailored shirt. "I left Katina about twenty minutes ago. If all goes well, I'll have dinner with her tonight."

"Why? Why don't you get what you need and go back to the States? Getting too close may lead to trouble."

"Let me worry about it."

Their progress toward the Palace of the Grand Master was often blocked by meandering tourists with trinket-filled shopping bags that dangled from their arms.

Maxwell cursed as small arms wrapped around his knees. He took a step backward, away from the embrace, and almost fell. "What the hell are you doing kid?"

A child shouted in a high, squeaky voice, "Daddy, Daddy. I lost you." The sweaty child's watery-brown eyes grew large, and a wail formed in his mouth.

Maxwell knew what was about to happen and moaned, "Oh, God, no." With gentle but firm hands, he extricated himself from the unwanted grasp. "Little boy, let me go now."

"You're not my daddy. Where is he?" the boy cried.

Maxwell groaned again as heads turned in response to the boy's ear-shattering wail. He patted the child's damp head. "No, of course, I'm not your daddy. Now run along and find him." He searched the area for anyone who resembled this boy, then gave a little nudged in the middle of the boy's back. "Stop crying now. I'm sure you'll find him. Go on. He's probably right down—"

Appearing horrified at Maxwell's behavior, Robert said, "Christ. You can't just run the kid off. We can take him to a police station. It's not a big deal."

"We don't have a lot of time. I need to get to that dinner in a few hours."

"Yeah, I know but—"

"No buts," Maxwell said. "I have to find Katina's hidden room before she can. I told you there are too many places to search by myself. We need to split up."

He turned his attention back to the boy and made a concerted effort to appear kind and concerned as he tapped a nearby shopkeeper on the shoulder. "I'm terribly sorry to interrupt, but could you help us? He appears lost." Maxwell's voice was as slick as an oil spill.

With pitiful eyes and dirty hands on his hips, the boy exclaimed, "I am not lost. My daddy is, and I need to find him."

The clerk grinned and crouched. "Hello, little one. My name is Nicholas. You are a brave young man." He took the boy's hand. "Come with me. I will have my wife take you to the place where lost papas can be found. Okay?"

The boy sniffled and nodded. He looked back with fierceness in his miniature features as he entered the darkened shop. "This man is nice. You're mean." He used the palm of his hand to swipe at the dampness under his nose.

It made a tiny slushing noise that made Maxwell cringe. "My God. What the hell just happened?"

Robert laughed and slapped him on the shoulder. "You were almost a father. How'd it feel?"

Wiping sweat from his brow with a cotton handkerchief, Maxwell said, "Not good. Did you see his face when he noticed I wasn't his father? Tragic."

Robert scanned the street as they continued toward the museum. "Did you just say *tragic*? I was worried you'd drop-kick him back to the U.S."

"Good lord, no. I just don't know what the hell to do with people under the age of thirty. You probably won't believe it, but I thought he was kind of cute. Did you see the way he glared at me for pawning him off? That kid's pretty tough."

Maxwell and Robert entered the palace and made their way to the chapel. "Katina opened this door." He checked the hallway for passers-by one last time before taking Robert down the stairs. "I don't know if anyone's down here, so be quiet."

"You don't even know what floor to search."

"I know, damn it," Maxwell said. "We have a few hours though. It can't be that big. Now shut up."

Twenty minutes later, they stumbled and bumped into each other as they were pushed back through the chapel door, escorted by two large policemen. Maxwell was humiliated and furious. "We're terribly sorry. I needed a bathroom."

He and Robert continued to strain against their captor's grip as they were escorted up the stairs and out of the palace's main entrance. The guards released them and scowled. Their passports, confiscated soon after they were discovered, were handed back.

The larger of the two said, "You may not come back."

Maxwell opened his mouth but was interrupted by Robert's hand on his arm. "Let's go. It's not worth it. They'll never believe you needed to pee."

Maxwell vented his frustration the entire way back to his hotel. As they reached their destination, he shot, "I might have found it if you'd kept your big mouth shut."

Robert rubbed his reddened wrist. "This isn't my field of expertise. I gather information and arrange occurrences, for a price. You ought to know; you hired me."

"Jesus. Just shut up. I've got to think of another plan now. You've been an absolute waste of time and cost me a significant amount of money. Your information about Celeste and Katina was useless. You were always behind the curve."

Robert grabbed Maxwell's arm and turned him around. "Damn it, I can't control people's movements. I can only report them." His voice rose as he said, "*I* was the one who found out about Katina's trip to New York. *That* was worth everything you've paid me so far. At least I got Joey to Scotland in time."

Maxwell shook off the offending hand and continued to walk, forcing Robert to catch up. "Helluv a lot of good that did. Frankly, I don't need you and your services anymore."

Robert sputtered, "What the hell does that mean? You still owe me $10,000. I have people I need to pay. You can't just cut me out of this. Without me, you'd still be in New York."

"Shut up. You would have gotten the money *if* you helped me get the icon. Instead, you got me thrown out before I could find it."

"For Christ's sake, you don't even know if it's there, Maxwell."

"You're done here. You're off my payroll."

"I need that money, damn it." He muscled Maxwell into the shade cast by the hotel. "You. Owe. Me. Money." With each word, he jabbed his index finger in Maxwell's heaving chest.

His reaction to this physical and verbal assault was slow. His entire body stilled. All sound diminished. "I will not give you the full $10,000. You haven't earned it." He shouldered Robert out of the way. "Get out of my sight before I decide to destroy you. You are no longer needed here."

Robert half turned. "Go to hell, Maxwell."

Watching him retreat, Maxwell straightened his collar and checked the buttons on his shirt. He controlled his anger, but worry pounded in his head. *Shit. That might have been a mistake. He knows too much. I've got to get him off this island.*

He entered the great hall of his new hotel, the St. Nicholas. The suits of armor, antique tables, and chairs scattered about the lobby were barely noticeable. His footfalls created minute echoes down the hallway of the old monastery, with its worn stone floors, traversed countless times by black-robed monks.

He unlocked the dark, wooden door with the centuries-old skeleton key then entered his room, once an abbot's cell. The austerity fit his mood. The need for action was overpowering. He searched his phone for the number of Robert's actual boss.

"Damn it to hell." He threw the phone on the bedcover. "That's too risky. There's gotta be a better way to get rid of him."

Chapter Twenty-Six

Bobby's Mad, We're All Mad

Katina slid her favorite dark blue sheath dress over her head. Its gauzy edges floated as she moved. She chose sleek silver sandals and glided over to her vanity. Its surface was covered in gold necklaces, silver bangles, and crystal perfume bottles. She selected the tall, cut-glass bottle of Givenchy's *Ysatis*, then sprayed the air with a few pumps of this rich and intimate fragrance. It gave her such an immense pleasure to walk through the cloud of perfume.

The scent made her remember the first time she brought Celeste to Rhodes. They'd gone to the Valley of Butterflies in Theologos; a heavily wooded mountain path led them to a spring, cool and green. Plain, brown underwings of butterflies covered many surfaces of trees and bushes. A visitor clapped his hands so loudly it startled the people, but more so, the butterflies. She and Celeste gasped as the bright orange and black tops of thousands of wings fluttered and swirled wildly about. They were beyond spectacular.

Katina threw her bed covers up to the pillows and repeated the words of William Wordsworth. "'Oh. Pleasant, pleasant were the days, the time, when, in our childish plays, my sister Emmeline and I together chased the butterfly.'"

She turned her head toward the bedroom door. Angry and intense words were being exchanged. She gave the spread a final tug and walked slowly toward the living room.

Bobby said, "You go. Have fun. I'll be at Balsamico having a drink. I can see the women on the beach from there."

"Don't be like that. Aubrey is a very nice man. Once you get to know him better—"

"Not on my agenda, sis." His voice had gentled as he said, "Have a good time. I'll see you all in the morning."

While he closed the apartment door, Katina took the opportunity to go into the room. "Gracious, what'd Aubrey do this time?"

Celeste turned a sad face to her. "Nothing. Bobby just seemed to pick a fight. Very weird."

"Well, we won't let him spoil our night." Katina said the next in a whisper, "We'll go to the museum after dinner."

As if she'd taken a bite out of a lemon, Celeste grimaced. "Do I have to? Won't it be locked?"

Katina grinned at her partner-in-crime. "Don't forget, I spent a lot of time here as a kid. Jim said I ran amok. I didn't, but I know how to get into just about anywhere I want."

Celeste still looked dubious. "How will you find the right room?"

"Ah, my friend, I have my ways. We'll have fun, promise."

"I don't know, Tina. This is getting messy. I'm scared. I heard Jim yelling at you." She raised her hands in supplication. "He's right, you know. Can't we just tell someone and enjoy our time here?"

"Who is *someone*?" Katina jutted her chin toward the balcony and the residents of Rhodes beneath. "Who's going to know what we know?" She pointed a finger in the same direction. "Do you know someone who will bring the treasures to the churches where they belong? Who won't turn it over to the bankrupt government?"

"I don't, for one minute, believe the government would sell them, if that's what concerns you." Celeste's voice rose as a reflection of Katina's concern. "The country is full of treasures that remain untouched. Come on, Katina. Be reasonable."

She shook her head, denying the obvious but unwanted truth. "You don't believe in me. You don't believe we can do this, do you?"

"That's not it at all. I just don't want to get killed. I don't want you hurt either. Please, Tina. Don't do this."

Katina tilted her head and regarded Celeste.

Celeste, eyes full of worry, stood still and waited.

Their breathing, a reflection of their closeness, so often in rhythm with each other, was out of sync. Katina nodded in resignation. "I understand, my friend. I do." She gave Celeste a gentle hug and smiled. "Get that auburn-haired pain-in-the-ass, and let's have some good food." Katina rubbed her stomach. "I'm starved, as usual."

Chapter Twenty-Seven

Aubrey's So... Aubrey

Feeling gorgeous in a silk, black and yellow, Givenchy-knockoff minidress, Celeste took short, brisk strides across Katina's terrace toward Aubrey. The evening breeze lifted locks of his wavy hair. An ensemble of classic blue and white seersucker slacks and a crisp white shirt made him an almost perfect British gentleman.

He nuzzled her neck as his arms engulfed her in an embrace. "You smell delicious. Must we go? I can think of no less than three things I'd rather do with, and *to,* you this evening, especially since Bobby's out of the picture."

"I'm worried, Aubrey."

"But you weren't worried yesterday. Come on. Nothing's changed. Let her have her fun."

She turned to take in the magnificent view of the horizon. "That was before I heard Jim make absolute sense. No more cloak-and-dagger stuff. We were lucky that whoever stole your books at the palace didn't hurt us in the process. I can't stop thinking about that."

"Can't you talk her out of it? She listens to you." Aubrey ran his hands up and down her chilled arms. "You're the grown-up between the two of you."

Twisting out of his embrace, she snapped, "Stop it, Aubrey."

His hands flew up in surrender. "Sure, but stop what? Kissing you?" He grinned down at Celeste. "That would be impossible."

Ooh, that does it. She stomped her foot. "Stop making light of this, and please stop kissing me." Her voice had risen an octave. "I'm seriously worried. I tried to change her mind, but I couldn't. She's determined that this is for her and only her to do."

A flush spread across his cheeks. "Christ, I'm sorry, sweetheart. I must say, I don't think it's that dire of a situation. You are much too lovely for anyone to hurt." He nodded as if he had just decided how to save the situation. "How about this: we'll go with her, armed to the teeth with our intelligence and wit."

Celeste and moaned in frustration. "Can't you be serious? In Scotland, you tried to control everything. Remember taking the books from Tina?"

His mouth opened; a denial died on his lips before it could be uttered.

"How do you know there's nothing to worry about? Do you know who took the books? Maybe he's a really bad criminal."

Aubrey slapped a hand down his face. "What's got into you? I don't know he's not dangerous, but he didn't hurt us. Or come back for that matter. Now, please, tell me what's going on."

"I don't know." Celeste sniffed. "I do know that I'm scared, and your big idea is to bring intelligence and wit."

She allowed herself to be brought into an embrace. She laid her cheek on his chest, careful to have wiped her tears away first so his lovely shirt wouldn't get makeup stained. "I told her I didn't want to go, but I think we should. With or without our damn wit."

He lifted her chin and kissed her nose. "Then that's what we shall do. I had planned on accompanying her if I was invited. I know Katina was annoyed with my, how shall I say, enthusiasm over her discoveries. I'll endeavor to take the proverbial backseat and try to appear dangerous to all passersby. I'm half certain the building will be locked and guarded. We may not have a thing to worry about."

"Katina always has a way," she said, leading him into the apartment with a modicum of relief.

Chapter Twenty-Eight

Drinking and B&E's Don't Mix

Situated between a small motorbike shop and a well-appointed Orthodox bookstore was the unassuming entrance to the Tamam Restaurant. There, behind the busy street-level doors were businesses, while higher floors held apartments. Their narrow porches with white metal banisters didn't make the most welcoming site in this part of Rhodes. The more austere atmosphere was very different than the quaint, touristy establishments within the walls of Old Town. However, the proprietors, Andreas and Maria, their funny daughters, and most especially the terrific food, made this restaurant crazy popular. Reservations were not accepted, but the Papamissios family never needed them anyway. With a quick phone call, one of the ten tables were always made available.

The restaurant was a bustle of laughter, talking, and clanking of cutlery. There wasn't a single plate being smashed—no one could afford that anymore. The aromas of grilled meats and vegetables, marinated in lemon and oregano, were the perfect Greek stereotype.

Andreas, a nicely-rounded man with curly, dark hair and black, square glasses, ushered the small party of four next to the front window. Maria, a petite woman with brown hair, always in a tight bun, rushed out of the kitchen. She wore her usual black chef jacket and a huge smile.

In Greek, she cried, "*Yassas,* Katina. It has been more than a year. I think my friend, you grow more gorgeous." The way she said it sounded like 'gore juice.' "These are your friends? Is this tall, dark, and handsome man your husband, Jim?"

She wrapped Maria in a warm hug. She gave Andreas a quick double-cheeked kiss. "No, this is Maxwell. He's new to the island. I think you've met Celeste, and this is her boyfriend, Aubrey." Following Andreas's outstretched hand as an invitation to sit, Katina continued, "How are you and your lovely daughters? Are they married? Babies?"

Andreas shook his head and said in heavily-accented English, "My daughters will stay virgins and single until they die. We will adopt grandchildren."

Katina was so amused by the look of horror Aubrey and Maxwell exchanged, she played along, "Very smart, Andreas. That's the only course your wise daughters could take. How could any man compete with the love of a father like you?"

"Exactly what I have been telling them since they were twelve. I hope they believe me." He rubbed his hands together like a mad scientist. "Now Katina and guests, would you like to start with some wine and have some delicious *meze*? Katina? Would you like to order, or would you like me to overwhelm you? Is that the right word?"

Delighted to see him in all his rough and happy ways, she agreed. "I would be thrilled if you *impressed* us with the exquisite cuisine of your choice."

"Our Katina is back." He nodded and beamed at his wife with love. "Come, Maria, let's overwhelm her with something extra special."

Katina was at home and at peace. "Be ready for a small feast."

The evening started with glasses of wine and *Halloumi* cheese, tiny wild mushrooms in a wine sauce, and tender calamari. Course after course—small portions of peppered pork medallions, beef filet wrapped in aubergine, king prawns, and a special dish Maria called sea dream pasta—were delivered with a flourish. Each course was paired with a different wine.

After homemade ice cream topped with diced fruit, Katina requested that their hosts join them at the table. She raised her glass of Mastika and toasted the gourmet delight. Aubrey, Celeste, and Maxwell sounded a rousing, "Here. Here."

Maxwell followed up with a short missive himself. "Here's to Katina and her friends. Wish this evening would never end. You're all a delight. What a wonderful night. You all have been my godsend." He cleared his throat. "Good God, that was awful, but I did enjoy tonight. Without Katina's kindness, I'd have spent another night wandering the streets, alone and afraid."

Aubrey guffawed in response to Maxwell's heartfelt nonsense. "From the looks of the ladies in here, Maxwell, I doubt you'd have ever been alone and certainly not afraid." He slapped him on the back and raised a glass. "Kind of you to invite ush." Suddenly, Aubrey turned grayish-green. "Bloody hell. I seem to be a bit worshe for the wear." He stood and swayed to the right. "Celeste, maybe I should say goodnight. Would you mind terribly?"

~ * ~

Celeste, who'd enjoyed many glasses of Greek wine herself, stood and tried to right her much taller companion. "Oh, good grief, Aubrey. You didn't have to have so much to drink."

"You mean the free mistake-ee?" His slurred words highlighted the mispronunciation of the digestif. "What's a poor professor to do?"

He laughed and attempted a few wobbly steps to the door. He turned blurry eyes to Celeste. "Are you coming?"

She scurried over to him and whispered, "Aubrey, get a grip. We're supposed to go to the palace with Tina. She needs us."

He tried to appear contrite. "It did sound fun, didn't it?" He failed miserably when he burped and laughed.

Celeste put her hands on her hips. If he knew her better, he'd worry, maybe even run and hide. "I never thought this was about fun. We need to keep Tina safe." Her heart shifted again, and apprehension filled her voice. "I don't want to go without you. Aubrey…"

He held up a finger as if an idea of stupendous proportion just occurred to him. "Send Bobby. He's a dick. He'll go."

"What did you just call my brother?"

He doubled over, laughing soundlessly. "A dick. You know, short for detective." He slapped a knee. "It bloody well fits both ways, doesn't it?"

"You're drunk." Celeste pulled herself up to her full five-feet-three inches. "I'll get a cab to take us home. Go sit back down." With quick, uneven strides, she made her way over to Andreas, who laughed with customers at a table for two. She whispered in his ear.

He took in Aubrey's state and nodded, then excused himself from the guests and went to the kitchen, cell phone in hand.

It took more time than she liked to wind her way through the small restaurant, back to their table. The place was packed with too many crowded tables all of a sudden. "Aubrey here can't hold his liquor. Andreas is getting us a cab. Tina? Can I talk to you for a second?"

Katina rose and placed her paper napkin on the table. "Sure, sweetie."

They went to the door and stood with their heads together. "We can't go with you tonight. I'll ask Bobby."

Katina lifted the hair off her neck, then wrapped it in her fist. "I didn't want to get anyone else involved. Can't you come with me?"

"This has gone too far for me. I'm sorry. My poor idiot's eyes are drooping. He needs me. Take my brother. He's strong and brave," Celeste cajoled. "He'll be so much more helpful anyway."

"Fine, but I'm not happy. The only reason I'm agreeing is that I promised Jim I wouldn't go alone." She then murmured, "This stinks."

Celeste took a deep breath of relief. "I know. Just can't imagine why Aubrey got drunk. I would think he'd be right there, and I hate to admit it, butting you aside to get to the icon."

"It's odd, to say the least. Call Bobby. Tell him to meet me at the north entrance. That's the quickest way to get to the underground storerooms. I'll be waiting there at midnight."

Celeste grimaced. "Hopefully, he isn't so mad he turned off his phone." Andreas waved at her; the cab was there. She checked her watch. "It's 11:30. I'll call him on the way back to the apartment and get Aubrey to bed. He'll sleep by himself. I'm not gonna smell that disgusting breath all night."

"I don't blame you. It'll be like a skunk coming out of hibernation. Yeesh."

~ * ~

Katina was nervous and her excitement for the rest of the evening was building rapidly. It was time to get started—the final push to find Katha's treasure. She sat next to Maxwell and blurted, "Say. It's been such a pleasure. I need to get back to the apartment and catch up with my husband." She held out a hand for a quick shake, but he took it into his.

"I will see you soon, my dear." His gaze raked her body. His smile was wicked. "That I can promise you."

She jerked her hand back. A sheen of heat spread across her belly and nestled around her neck. "Um, sure. Thanks again, George—I mean Maxwell. Gotta go."

"You, my dear, can call me anything you want."

Her steps to the exit faltered. She whispered, "Oh-my-God, Oh-my-God, Oh-my-God."

His seductive laughter followed her as she left the restaurant. She gave a back-handed wave to Andreas and Maria with her left hand and crossed herself three times with her right.

Watching many a detective show, she knew that taking a cab to the scene of her future crimes was out. Instead, she hurried through dark but familiar neighborhoods, pondering the decisions that had gotten her to that place, at that time. Her love of Rhodes ran as deep as the Papamissios bloodline. A heretofore unknown conviction for achievement—the return of the painting of St. Paul which might be the very first icon ever created and the Cross of Rhodes—compelled a change in her very nature. This ideal drove her to be greater than herself and an expansion of the simple, lovely life she enjoyed.

Chapter Twenty-Nine

Will Katina's Luck Hold?

Katina checked her watch. It had taken her a half hour to walk from the restaurant to the fortress. She didn't have a schedule, but she liked to think this was a mission of such great importance that precision was key. Once inside the gate, she made her way through Old Town, side-stepping late-night diners and bar-hoppers. Greek and American dance music blared. She blended in with the tourists and townspeople alike.

She arrived at the quieter streets close to the Palace of the Grand Master after another five minutes. Lights no longer emanated from the closed shops on the street-level buildings. The full moon lit her way down the cobbled streets. The area was devoid of people and sound as she approached the entrance to the palace. The air was still and warm.

She paced, anxious for Bobby to show. *Should have changed into my breaking-into-palaces clothes. Mistake number one probably.*

Katina checked her watch again. *12:15. Where the heck are you, Bobby?*

She should've gotten his phone number before Celeste went back to the apartment. *Damn it. I'm going to have to wake her up. Serves her right for dumping me for him, again.* As her worry grew, the circles she walked became tighter until she stood still.

Before she could dial Celeste's number, the *1812 Overture* filled the air, announcing her presence to the world. The notes bounced off walls and echoed down the deserted street. *Damn, Damn, Damn.* She hit the talk button and blurted, "Hello?"

"Katina? It's—"

"Celeste, I was just about to call you. I don't have Bobby's number. Did you talk to him? Is he coming?"

"Katina, I—" Her friend's voice was strained.

"Didn't you call him?" A whimper from Celeste caused Katina to stifle her need for answers. Rustling came from the other end, as if the phone had brushed up against a piece of cloth. "Celeste? Are you there? What's going on?"

"Something bad happened. I can't tell you what it is, but I need you to help me."

"What can I do?" Katina asked.

"Can…Can you bring the painting to me?" Celeste's voice was ragged.

"Of course, if I can find it. What's the matter?"

She cried in earnest for a moment before catching her breath. "I can't t-tell you. You just must do it. And you can't go to the police for help. I know I told you you should, but for God's sake don't."

There was a muffled voice in the background.

"Okay, I'll t-tell her. Don't touch me! Tina? Call me back, and I'll tell you where you can bring it."

Katina yelled into the phone, "Are you all right? Just say yes or no. Are. You. Hurt?" A sob tore from her throat as the phone disconnected.

"Jesus, protect us all," she cried as she frantically searched for Bobby. He had to be close.

What the hell is going on, Celeste?

A block away, footsteps scraped. A man wearing a familiar white linen shirt sauntered into view. *That has to be him.* She whisper-yelled, "Bobby? Over here. Bobby, is that you?"

The man turned toward her. He walked out of the moon-shadow cast by a wall. She couldn't believe her eyes. "Maxwell. Thank God, it's you."

He jogged the few hundred yards toward her. "Katina, what in the world are you doing here? You were looking for Bobby?"

She held her hand out in a humble, pleading gesture. "Something terrible happened to my friend."

Maxwell took it in his. "You're crying. Which friend? Was there an accident?"

She swiped at a streak of tears. "No. It's Celeste."

"Is she hurt?"

Katina took an offered handkerchief and shook her head. "I don't know. She didn't say. She hung up before she could tell me." She wiped more tears from her eyes. "I need your help."

How am I supposed to tell him, and not tell him, at the same time? She wrung the hanky for a second. *I've got to calm down.*

"Celeste needs me to find something and bring it to her. It may be a tiny bit dangerous, and it's definitely illegal." She placed her palm on his chest. "Will you, anyway?"

As his muscles swelled under her touch, he placed a strong hand over hers. "I'm not sure how I can. Wouldn't the police be a better choice?"

Surprised that this gallant man, who was nicely muscled like a ball player, wouldn't even try, she removed her hand from under his. "I can't call them. No one can know what I'm doing." She faced the palace. "That's okay. Thanks anyway. I can handle it."

"God, Katina. This is crazy. I'm just an antiquities dealer. I guess I can steal a car. If the key's in the ignition."

She crossed her arms in front of her chest. "Thanks. You don't need to steal a car. Just come with me. I'll do all of the illegal stuff." She gave a sharp nod. "I need a lookout. That's all."

"From guards?"

"That's just it. I doubt there'll be any tonight. The government can't afford full-time staff. Besides, there's just a bunch of marble statues. Crooks would need a crane."

"Well... that makes sense, but—"

"No buts. It'll be okay. Don't worry about it." She led the way to a little-known side entrance she'd used as a kid. The door was the original wood, deteriorated with age. They were quiet for the three-minute walk. "If we get caught, just tell them I kidnapped you."

He ducked as if there was a swat team ready to pounce, then laughed. "You amaze me. Even though you're afraid, you try to make things easier for me, of all people, with a joke."

"Yeah, well." She pushed the door open with the side of her body. Its rusty hinges made a screeching noise. "Crap. Shhh," she said to the door. She pulled her satchel in front of her and squeezed through. "Stay close. I've got to get this done, fast. Then I have to help Celeste."

"Absolutely." He opened it wider to allow for his larger frame, causing the hinges to screech again.

The trek hadn't started very well at all. They cringed as they passed through the entrance. She stopped just inside of the large courtyard. They were protected from sight by a marble bust of an armored soldier. She scanned the vast emptiness of the upper loggia levels.

Their heavy breathing was the only sound. Convinced they were safe to proceed she sent a nod to Maxwell and darted across the expanse toward the stone staircase. Seconds later, she ascended them. *Almost there. All I have to do is find the key Gerard hid ... somewhere.*

She reached the top, panting from the exertion. She turned left and jogged to the second door down, following Katha's instructions. Her soft leather sandals were soundless.

As Maxwell joined her, she marveled at his calm and steady breathing. The man had stamina and nerves. "Is that Gerard's office?"

"You knew I was trying to find it?"

He shook his head. "No, but you looked around here earlier.

Remember? You told me about him."

He's right. I did. "I'll try to be quick." She nodded and went through the half-open door. The moon's glow, which was quite adequate in the courtyard, wasn't helpful in the windowless room. She retrieved a small flashlight from her bag and flipped the switch. A brilliant light filled the room.

"Ow!" Katina cried, from the pain of the sudden glare. She screwed the top until a tight beam shone on the far wall. "Crap, that's a bright light."

"I'll close the door, just in case."

Satisfied she wouldn't be seen, she swept the beam around the perimeter. The room was stark, devoid of artwork, as expected. A plain, heavy desk, made of dark wood, placed close to the far wall, was an obvious hiding place.

"Maybe I'll get lucky." Katina jerked the drawers out, checking the underside for anything unusual. She flashed the light in the hole created by the missing drawers. Finding nothing, she tugged at various boards on the top and sides. They creaked as they gave way to the pressure of her hands but yielded nothing.

"Where else?"

Maxwell tapped on the door. She covered the beam just as it cracked open. His quiet voice drifted in. "There's a guard downstairs. He's checking the courtyard."

The flashlight trembled in her hands, and the beam zig-zagged, as she studied the three walls. Her frustration grew with each second that passed. "Think, Katina."

"You have to hurry," Maxwell warned.

She lit the wall surrounding the entrance, careful to keep the light from being seen through the crack.

Set into the wall to the right of the door, was a carved symbol of the Freemason's famous Third Eye, surrounded by a compass. Of course. The Masons came to the aid of the Knights. Katha said, 'In plain sight.' *Gerard, you smart young man, no one would think twice about seeing that symbol.*

Maxwell cracked the door and whispered, "The guard's underneath us right now. He's talking on his cell phone."

"I think I found it. I just need a few more minutes."

Katina carried an old chair and positioned it under the symbol. As she eased her weight onto it and straddled her feet on each side, the chair quietly wobbled. *Okay, let's see what we have.* She felt its contours. *Where's the key, damn it?*

"The guard's coming up the stairs. I'll distract him if I have to."

She wiped sweat from her brow with the back of her hand as she studied the symbol closely. An odd shape was on one side of the compass. She dug her nails into the fragile plaster. Something popped out and spiraled toward the floor. She leaned out and snatched it in midair. Katina rolled her eyes and brought the object close to her chest as she climbed down. She inched the door wider and ordered, "Get in here."

Maxwell slid in sideways and closed the door with a quiet click of the handle.

Katina opened her hand and teared up. She held the life-changing key. She gave it a kiss before dropping it into the outer pocket of her satchel

Maxwell had his ear to the door's crack. He turned to her and mouthed, "He's opened the door next to us."

The guard's voice grew louder as he approached. She flattened herself against the wall. Maxwell followed suit. She held her breath and clutched his arm.

The door rocked, and a bang occurred simultaneously. The guard laughed, and his words receded as he continued down the walkway.

Her heart's wild pounding diminished as they waited, quiet and tense, for a few minutes before easing the door open. She peeked up and down the hall.

Maxwell said in a barely audible voice, "Why'd he hit our door? That was damn close."

"Tell me about it." She eased out the door and scanned the area. Nothing moved. She tip-toed over to the edge and searched the courtyard floor. All was quiet. "Let's go."

He followed her down the stairs. At the bottom, she gathered her flowing dress so she wouldn't trip on the hem. Like soldiers on a dangerous patrol, hunched and furtive, they made it to the other side and into the shadows.

"You were successful?"

"I was," she said, wanting to scream her success to the heavens.

"You're an amazing woman."

His finger trailed across her arm. She rubbed away the tingling sensation. "You've been, um, helpful yourself. Thanks."

"Where now?"

"The lower floor of the palace, where the chapel is." As she quickened her gait, her breath came out in short pants as her speed increased.

Now I have to locate the room. Katina and Maxwell took light steps into the main building and peered around each corner before proceeding. The guard was neither seen nor heard as they made their way to the stairs.

"What do we need to find?"

Katina entered the arched stone opening of the chapel and hurried over to the same wooden door she opened earlier in the day. "Can you lift it up and open it. I don't want it to scrape again."

Picturing the map she'd found in Scotland, she prayed Sinclair was correct and started down the stairs. "You need to know I was never going to keep what I find." She spoke even quieter in the close confines of the stairway.

Focused on the gravity of the task at hand, she only heard bits of Maxwell's reply, "But... give... to Celeste? Damn guards... down there."

On the top of the steps a few feet away was an owl made from small white and black, egg-shaped stones. She remembered the text in the diary. *Thank you, Katha.* With flashlight in hand, Katina withdrew the key from the satchel's small pocket. She scratched bits of plaster off, revealing more of the legend etched on one side. The top had the image of the owl, followed by three numbers and letters in a row: 2V 2D 2D.

He craned his neck to see but offered no ideas to their meaning.

She lowered her head as her mind recreated the map. The image she pictured broke into pieces. The floors and stairs realigned and brought new understanding. *These are directions. V. Vector? Veer? Doesn't make sense. D. Down. That seems reasonable.*

"I'm an idiot. Sir Pierre was French." She hit the home button on her phone and prayed she would have enough bars to Google French vocabulary. *One bar. Good enough.* She typed, 'words for directions in French.' A short list came up.

"You're very good at this, Katina."

"I know. I'm brilliant. V stands for *vers le bas*. We need to go down two *vers le bas.*"

"Excellent. Let's go down two *vers le bas*. What is it?" His eyes were alit with humor.

"Just come on." They descended two flights of stairs. At the bottom of the second, a hallway stretched from right to left. She let her mind clear. *D. Droit means right.*

The pieces of the map again filled her mind.

The first 2D. Time to take some right turns.

She turned and made her way to the end of the first hallway. She turned a second time. A row of closed wooden doors ran the length of both sides of the hall. It dead-ended after the fifth door.

Maxwell continued to follow at a discreet distance, keeping

whatever thoughts he had to himself.

Now for the second 2D. I need to go into the second door on the right. Lord? I hope I've understood this. If not, I'm going to need a miracle.

She stopped short. "I think this is the key to this room. Hopefully, I'll be just a few minutes. Could you guard the door again?"

"Of course, I will. Be careful."

She nodded and brought the key to her lips for a good luck kiss. As she inserted and turned it with a whispered, "Please. Please. Please." It stopped after a quarter turn. *No. It must be this door.*

Nudging her out of the way, he gave the key a forceful twist. It clicked as the lock's mechanisms moved into position.

"Thank you, Lord." She crossed herself and stepped back, looking at the door that would change her life and save Celeste's. "And, thank you, Maxwell. This is it."

Katina pushed it open and used the flashlight to scan the area. The room was small, ten-by-ten feet of emptiness, cool and dry. Katha didn't say which corner had the stone hatch.

The Sinclair manse was more difficult. Only needed to check four corners there.

With buoyed spirits, she kneeled by the closest corner. As with her previous attempts, she exerted all her strength. She jerked her right hand back in pain, then inspected a scrape down her palm. Using her dress, she blotted the tiny spots of blood.

Enough. Get moving.

She scurried to the next corner and tried again. Maxwell eased her over and gave it a good shove. As it moved, he grinned at her. "Glad my muscles could help."

The two-meter area rose, just as Katha described. "You did it. Now. Guard the hall. Please."

With flashlight in hand and satchel slung over her shoulder, Katina scampered down the stairs, lifting a hand to the ceiling to protect her head. Her voice quivered on, "Thank you, Katha. Please keep watch over me."

Katina took the last step, and the flashlight's narrow beam shone on the floor. As she entered the room it glinted off brass altar objects—goblets, incense burners, and heavy candlesticks—which were laid about on the floor and on top of wooden crates. She studied the items, searching for the Cross of Rhodes.

Fifteen feet away, she passed the beam over an inordinate splendor of riches. Before her wasn't the usual treasure seen in a movie, which was always highlighted by a massive beam of light from nowhere.

There were no chests full of pearls, sapphires, or rubies. Instead, there were historical riches, lost to the world for hundreds of years.

Greek Orthodox and Catholic icons were stacked around the room. The Catholic ones were realistic, graceful, and bold in color. They were so unlike the Orthodox, which were more darkly-shaded and mysterious.

Her gaze landed on a particularly famous Catholic icon. "Holy cow. Christ's Descent into Hell."

Christ had a golden halo and wore the pure white robes of the sinless. Deep azure and royal blue formed the background. A white castle was filled with the souls of Christians, depicted as naked bodies, reaching out in desperation to Christ, their Savior. He stood next to large vats filled with the souls of the fallen, boiling on top of fires. She moved closer, entranced by its rarity, the vivid colors, and the wicked serpents and demons waiting to consume the fallen.

Though it exceeded her idea of magnificent, Katina beheld the rest of the absolute fortune in art. Some paintings were three feet tall. Others were as large as five feet. *It's been centuries and they're still perfect.*

"You've found a treasure trove of art, haven't you? So rare. Many are medieval and some even older."

Katina stood with arms akimbo, not knowing what to make of this intrusion. She wasn't scared, but she certainly didn't expect him to come down. She moved the flashlight on him. His face was sharp, and his expression wasn't as gentle as his voice had been. "You were supposed to stand watch by the door."

Maxwell averted his face out of the beam's aim and ignored the statement. He went to the gilded frame of Christ's Descent and caressed it. His glance shifted from the painting to Katina. "Oh, I'm sorry. I didn't mean to startle you. You were gone longer than I expected." He lowered his chin and scolded her. "I got worried." He nodded toward the icon. "This is exquisite. Worth a fortune. Is this what you came here to get?" His expression was free of any avarice, though his words reeked of it.

"You weren't meant to see these. I know they're beautiful, but could you go back upstairs? Keep guard? I'll be up in a few minutes."

She took a deep breath as he seemed to think for a few seconds. His warm smile filled her with relief. "Thanks. You're terrific, Maxwell." Confident of his departure and lookout-man support, she continued the search for the cross and the painting of St. Paul.

Her head exploded in pain. She cried out and tumbled to the hard floor. Prostrate and dazed, she reached back and felt warm blood ooze from a small flap of torn skin on her scalp.

She laid her cheek upon her outstretched arm, powerless to shift away as Maxwell leaned over her.

"Where's the key to the outer door?"

Her skin crawled at his proximity. She inched her bloody fingers into a pocket of her dress, grasped the key, and tossed it toward the bastard.

"Thanks." He picked it up and walked to an old wooden box. He laid a small object on top. He hoisted the icon he had caressed moments before. As he left, he stopped just short of the doorway and studied the floor.

Her eyes barely focused as she watched him press the toe of his shoe down and twist it.

"You touched my heart, Katina. You're so very sweet. I almost decided to forget this. But I just can't afford to. I hope you understand." A small beam from another flashlight lit the staircase as he departed.

Chapter Thirty

Add Claustrophobia to the List

Katina's head throbbed as she drew out, "No... Don't do this... You're a good man." For the first time in her life, she was one hundred-percent dazed and confused. "He didn't have to hit me," she said. "A thief? The whole time?" Anger grew, but not at the obvious target.

She moaned. "How could I be that stupid? The hanky in New York. Bumping into me here. Just happened to be walking down the street tonight." She put a hand to her eyes. "I'm an idiot. Oh, Dad, you were right."

The impact of the hit had dislodged the flashlight from her hand. It lay a few feet away, the narrow beam pointed toward the back wall of the treasure room. All else was dark. As she rose onto an elbow, several sharp objects hurt her ribs. Her hand shook as she touched the fragmented fabric that disintegrated with her touch.

To reach the flashlight without making her head spin, she inched her body forward. She turned the top until the narrow beam broadened to light the whole room. A small bundle lay to her right. She anchored herself to stand, pushed herself up, and sat on her haunches, wondering what had been under her—musty, rotted material.

She moved a large piece of fabric away and gasped at what was hidden beneath. Bones. A skull was off to the side. She used her fist to stifle a scream. *What in God's name is this? Who is this?* She squirmed away, scared that this death might touch her in some way. Shivering, she wiped the dust of the dead person off her fingers.

"Hello?" she yelled then winced from the pain the effort caused. Toward the entrance, she called, "Help!"

Katina stood, pausing while the dizziness subsided. She gave a backward glance and shivered again. "They're only bones. That poor person can't hurt you." She tried to believe that was true.

She climbed the narrow staircase to the smaller outer room. The old wooden door leading to the hallway, and freedom, was closed. "Please don't have locked me in. Please, please, please," she whimpered. "I don't want to sit next to a dead body, or the skeleton of one."

Katina grabbed the handle and jerked it inward. She swayed, steadied herself, then pulled on the handle. "Don't do this to me!"

She remembered the brass candlesticks and went back down the stairs. The largest of them was by the wall on its side. She hefted it, surprised to find it hollow but still heavy. Blood was on the bottom edge—her blood.

"Damn you, Maxwell." She took it up and whacked the door. The thing bent a fraction. Trying again, it bent further. "Crap."

Katina tossed it onto the floor, defeated for the moment. The stupid thing made such a loud clank it hurt her ears. Helplessness and self-pity, rotten human traits, threatened. She fought back. *Someone will come when the palace opens.* She was unconvinced, picturing herself in those two rooms for days, cold and alone and sure that the flashlight batteries would quit any minute. Deep, cavernous darkness loomed.

"Don't think that way. Be positive. Be strong." Katina paced the area with slow, measured steps, keeping her head level to alleviate the effects of the head wound. "Be calm. And for damn sure, don't be a wimp." *Deep breaths.* In and slowly out. Over and over until the fear eased.

"I'm a genius!" She found her satchel, dumped the contents onto the floor, intent on finding her phone. "Why didn't I think of this sooner?"

"*Merde.*" Whipping the flashlight across the ground, she hoped it had fallen out. No luck. "Why'd you have to take my phone?" A fresh wave of anger welled. "Maxwell, get back here and let me out. Are. You. *Crazy.*"

As expected, he didn't open the door. With an irritated sigh, she said, "Get a grip. He's long gone."

She stomped back up to the main room and pounded on the door. Her palm started to bleed again.

"Blast."

She found a relatively clean spot on the hem of her dress to dab the blood. She sat there and listened for the guard—the man seemed to talk incessantly on the phone.

Thoughts about becoming a mummy, dried skin and bones, wrapped in swatches of stinky material took up some time. She wondered who the poor person laying on the floor below could be. Curiosity and a bit of bravery, mixed with an I-don't-have-anything-better-to-do attitude, replaced the fear. Descending the stairs, pausing at each step as the flashlight filled more of the room, she said, "Eww… I don't think I like this."

Katina continued in and took a few sideways steps. Squatting, she studied the remains, how the bones were arranged. The body had probably never been moved. He or she died right there.

Years of reading Kathy Reichs's books about forensic anthropology made her a pseudo-expert in the field of dead bodies. She was reminded of terms like *time of death*, TOD to the professionals, and *livor mortis*, not liver mortis as she'd thought for years. Reading about it and sitting next to it turned out to be different. The real-life skeleton caused a severe case of the heebie-jeebies.

Katina squatted and used her flashlight as a probe. "These bones are so small. Are you a female?" She studied the delicate brow of the skull. The chin was small with a gentle angle.

In her best Sherlock Holmes impression, she said, "What have we here?" She looked closer at an object that had flashed in the light. "A small, gold earring. A fish? No, it's a dolphin. Where's the other one?" She got on her hands and knees for a better angle to search. Within seconds, she'd found its mate, an owl.

A dolphin and an owl. The words in Katha's diary tickled the edges of Katina's memory. *What did it say? Her father gave Katha her mother's earrings. The dolphin would remind her of her freedom, and the owl would remind her of the wisdom she would need in life.* "Oh no. You can't be Katha." Katina drew the earrings protectively to her bosom. "Please, God. Please don't let this be her."

"I'm so sorry." Her eyes welled. "My God. How terrified you must have been."

Her hand shook as she touched the top of Katha's forehead. She stroked the cool, smooth surface. "I knew you didn't get to bring the Cross of Rhodes and the icon to the church, but I never would have thought you didn't even make it out of the room."

"How did the slab close on you?" Katha finished her diary and gave instructions to Gerard. He took the diary, and— As the reality of what must have happened struck Katina, she moaned. "Why would Gerard close the stone? Did he know you couldn't get out?"

She played out different scenarios in her head. "No. He couldn't have known. He carried out her instructions perfectly. Where's the painting of St. Paul? You'd have kept it close, I bet." As she followed the length of Katha's arm bones, she came upon a small bundle.

Hope replaced simple curiosity. Katina picked it up and peeled the delicate outer layers of gray material as if they were petals of a rose to reveal something better than a rudimentary painting. The artwork was the size of a book, painted on wood, with stylized brush strokes of his facial features, wise and strong, and the flowing robes he must have worn. She marveled at the centuries-old artistry of the people.

Katina said to Katha's remains, "Now I need to find your cross. If I ever get out of here, I'm going to take them back to your church. I promise." She studied the contents of the room.

Her gaze locked on a crate by the entrance. She remembered Maxwell's last few actions before he left her there. *He put something on top.* She walked over and found a small black knife. She put the flashlight on the lid and opened a blade that was dull yet deadly. A wave of revulsion filled her as she remembered how she once thought of him as a gentleman and how she had opened herself to depend on him. *Why didn't you kill me? You had the chance.*

And Jim wonders why I don't trust people.

After moments of disgust, the second thing he did crossed her mind. She pointed the flashlight to the floor. Where he had scuffed the toe of his shoe there was a dead bug. Smashed.

So, you whacked me on my head. Decided not to kill me. But you did kill something I'm afraid of. Seems like you aren't very comfortable being a rotten bastard after all. Must not have known what I was actually after. You would've torn this place apart to find the cross. That would have led you to enormous riches. But you didn't have the diary. Burnt Dad's car up, didn't you? Jerk. What else did you know? What other documents did you find?

Katina put her head back, closed her eyes, and tried to remember exactly what Henry Sinclair wrote in the first document they found in Manhattan. Ah. "...a message containing information about treasured icons..." *Did you find that document?*

She went back to Katha. "Where'd you hide the cross?"

Katina gingerly moved material and a few ribs and arm bones away from the center of what was once her body. She gasped as the corner of the Cross of Rhodes was revealed. She never expected to truly find it, to see gold that was once part of the torch of the Colossus of Rhodes.

"It's real!" She held it close to her heart and imagined what the young heroine thought about as she lay dying. Did she remember the sacrifices her mother made, her dutiful father, the wonderful Sir Pierre? Did she scream at Gerard for abandoning her?

She wanted to protect Katha's remains, as this young woman's own family and friends would have had they found her. Katina thought of her very best and only girlfriend. Anguish and worry flooded her mind as a sob of defeat escaped. She had no idea how she was going to rescue Celeste if she couldn't even rescue herself. Her chest seized. Hot tears fell as impotence overwhelmed her.

Katina focused her thoughts with all her might, clenching her fists like a child about to yell. *Jim, can you hear me? I really need you this time. If you can hear me, come find me, okay? Please, my love?*

Chapter Thirty-One

Where's Jim When She Needs Him?

The trip from Atlanta to Athens was interminable. Jim was too exhausted to sleep, and his butt hurt. He'd been on the hot, bleak bluffs of the North Dakota Badlands. He finished excavating the triceratops femur, fibula, tarsal, and the metatarsals four days ago. He lost interest in finding the phalanges three days ago. His appetite disappeared two days ago. Then he'd gotten the call from Lexi yesterday.

Instead of driving home, as he always did, making sure his finds made it safely back, he'd dropped his truck off at the Rapid City airport. He hopped on the first plane out to anywhere he could get a connecting flight to Atlanta.

His thoughts raced to a halt, and he came to an understanding: though Katina seemed happy, he couldn't get used to the distance she put between them. He'd never been married before, but that sure as hell wasn't how his parents did it.

The truth, *his truth*, hit him like a surge of air turbulence—the kind that made stomachs drop and heave. He should pay more attention to her, whether she wanted it or not. Her stories were hilarious. She moved with grace, when she didn't stumble over invisible obstacles, then laughed at herself afterward. So many precious moments. He couldn't imagine what else he'd missed, because she wanted it that way.

Did you warn me the day we were married? You said, 'I think I'm addicted to you, and I don't want to go through withdrawals.' Lord help me, I miss you, Tina. Even when we're together. Are you thinking about me? Do you ever need me?

He hadn't realized how lonely he was. He took a deep breath and mumbled, "Commuter planes suck." He was on the short hop between Athens and Rhodes.

He scratched his unshaven jaw as he peered down the aisle, hoping to see a flight attendant wheeling a cart containing some strong coffee and a cookie or two. Disappointed, he regarded his sleeping niece in the center seat. Her lids opened, and her gaze found his face. Caught in the act, he searched the aisle again.

"What are you looking at?" Lexi levered herself up from her crumpled position, stuck between her uncle and a rotund woman that wheezed with every breath.

"I need coffee. Maybe the attendant is brewing some."

She rolled her eyes. "Yeah. I don't think so. You were staring at me. I felt your eyes, you know."

Amazed that she could go from sleepy to sassy in two seconds, he barked a laugh. "How could you?"

Yawning, she tried to stretch her lanky form without bumping their row mate. "Apparently, the wheezing didn't bother you a bit, did it? I bet you could sleep through a tornado."

"I wouldn't know. Never had to try. To answer your question though, I was looking at your zygomatic bones, after I checked for coffee."

"My what? Why were you doing that? Is my mascara all over the place?" Lexi bent over. In a muffled voice, she said, "Where's my stupid bag?"

Jim waved a hand. "No, no. You won't be interested. Forget it."

She straightened. "Uncle Jim, you can't stare at someone's zydeco bones and not tell them why."

He grinned at her mispronunciation. He cleared his throat as if beginning a lecture. "*Zygomatic.* You have what are termed high cheekbones. That means you have pronounced zygomatic arches that form a pleasing symmetrical shape to your face." He stopped, and the corners of his mouth twitched as Lexi flopped her head onto her knees with the nimbleness that youth allows. "As I was saying, I was noting that you look like Katina."

"You're right." Lexi sat up straight and groaned. "I'm not interested." She pulled back the sleeve of her black twill jacket and took note of the time on her Luminox scuba watch, the Navy Seal model, like one of Katina's. She groaned louder. "Oh my God. The back of my head hurts, and I feel icky. Can I get up? I need to move."

"It'll take me a sec. I've got to get the kinks out of these old legs of mine. I'm still pretty—" Jim moaned a bit with the effort of rising, "—stiff from all those days in the field." As he stepped out of the way, he whispered, "Maybe you could go to the back and get coffee for us? I'm kinda scary right now. I should've shaved and put on decent clothes."

"You're clean, but that's about all I can say for you," she said, as she slid around him.

"No comments from the peanut gallery. I did the best I could. Get me some coffee, young'un."

She screwed up her face as if he'd spoken Chinese. "Comments from the peanut gallery?"

He shook his head and pointed to the back of the plane. "Coffee."

"Okay, just this once." She rounded her shoulders and arched her back in another moan-worthy stretch. That gained her the lascivious stare of a pimply-faced, teenaged boy. He averted his eyes after he caught Jim's glare. The boy scratched at his peach fuzz, trying to look nonchalant.

Jim nodded his approval and sat back down, rearranging his legs and booted feet. "Note to self: big feet don't fit in coach anymore." He closed his eyes for a quick rest. He hadn't known he'd finally fallen asleep until he jerked awake as his knee was jostled.

"I've got our coffee," she said, as she slid back into her seat.

Plane coffee, always bitter even when they boast a famous brand, was far from an enjoyable experience. Jim forced the brew down as he listened to Lexi rehash the need for their unexpected trip. He wasn't sure which soured his stomach the most.

"Like I said, Uncle Jim, I knew something was wrong with *Thea* Katina. Sometimes I can tell if people are in trouble."

"How exactly?"

Her mouth dropped open for a second. "O. M. G. There is no *exactly* about it. Thoughts just pop into my head." She looked over the restless woman, out the window, and into the blackness of the night. "One time, it was really terrible."

"Terrible?"

"It happened at the pool. We were waiting for our diving coach. She was an hour and a half late. I remember we were laying on lounge chairs. I said, out of the blue, 'She was raped last night.'" Lexi shivered and rubbed her arms.

Jim's stomach turned. He was speechless at the horrific statement.

"She was." Her voice was agitated. "How did I know that?"

He had never thought about having a psychic ability, let alone one that would show a young woman an evil event. "I don't know. I'm so sorry that happened to you."

She dropped her quivering chin to her chest. "Me, too. The other kids on the team thought I was horrible to say such a thing. When it turned out to be true, they said I was a friggin' weirdo."

"I believe you have a gift of some kind. They were the weird ones, not you."

He gave her time to recover from the memory. When she raised her head, he said, "I'm glad you called me. Sorry it took so long to get through to me."

He patted her hand. "I talked to Tina right after we got off the phone. She's with Celeste, her brother, and a boyfriend. The news wasn't good. If I had known what she was going to get into this summer, I might have taken her with me."

Lexi shook her head and chuckled. "That wouldn't have happened."

Glad her mood had improved, he cocked his head. "Hey, why not? She's done quite a few things with her father that weren't, um, five-star rated."

"That's true, but I can't see her giving up her vacation slash medieval research time to walk around the Badlands with you. Don't get me wrong; she loves you a ton, just not your dinosaurs, if you know what I mean."

"Yeah, it's not for everyone. I know she's a very determined woman. That's why I said *might*." Jim drank the last sip from his cup and regarded Lexi's dubious expression. *Kids.* "Okay. I get your point. Anyway, I don't know anything about Rhodes. I don't even know how to talk to the police, if we need to get them. Damn. I wish she would've called a university or a church official."

"I don't think she realizes there's badness close to her. It's not evil though."

"We talked about it. She knows something's not right." His beautiful, funny wife, so full of caution, and distrust of people in her everyday life worried him. *This stuff isn't in her wheelhouse. She's out of her league. Hell, I'm out of mine here.*

"Hopefully," Lexi said, "she's been careful. People can be jerks." She nudged his arm. "Hey, you look kind of sick. I bet she and her friends will be safe and sleeping in their cushy, satin-sheeted beds. We'll have to wake someone up though. I don't have a key."

He laid his head on the headrest and pictured Katina asleep, the sea air moving tendrils of hair on her pillow. He sighed. "Your lips to God's ears."

His mind drifted to Lexi's comment about loving him a ton, just not the dinosaurs. *I just published my book on new methods in biological archaeology, and Tina didn't even read it. She just said she was proud I was so mathematically gifted.*

Lexi hit on a rather crucial point. Tina had never wanted to go fossil hunting in the rich lands of northern Alabama or anywhere else for that matter. He couldn't suppress a moan. *Because of her father, Tina had decades of exposure to archaeology. So much of which was just scraping dirt from one small pile to a bigger pile. She doesn't care about Christopher Columbus. Christ. I bore her.* He gripped the empty Styrofoam coffee cup so hard it crumpled. *Things are going to change.*

Ten minutes later, the lights turned on in the plane's cabin. A loud bing-bing-bing sounded as the captain alerted the attendants to prepare for landing. People rustled around, gathering items to be thrown in the plastic bag being walked up and down the aisle. Lexi and Jim exchanged meaningful looks.

"This is it, Uncle Jim." She crossed herself three times.

The plane circled its descent for fifteen full minutes before it landed with a loud bump and the powerful sounds of the engines reversing their thrust. Taxiing took another five minutes. A final *bing* rang out.

The doors opened, and Jim did his best to get their carryon luggage down and position himself for a quick exit. He ground his teeth as he watched the first-class passengers and those close to the front exit. He started to sweat as the air got stale from the milling people with cell phones pressed to their ears, speaking in Greek.

"I'll call Katina. Tell her we're coming." They inched forward as Jim left a message. "Sweetheart, it's me. We're on our way to the apartment. Lexi said you'd love a surprise visit, so here we are. See you in about forty-five minutes. I love you so much. Bye." He struggled to return the phone to his back pocket in the confined space. "She must be asleep."

"I'll try Mr. Menos. We should've called someone when we were back in the States. The surprise idea was just dumb."

Jim had to agree. They shouldn't have tried to make their appearance seem anything other than what it was, a serious reaction to a potentially dangerous situation.

The pimply-faced boy watched with rapt attention as Lexi said to no one in particular, "Hey Siri." She waited a second, then continued, "Call Mr. Menos. Home."

With phone to her ear, she took a half-step forward. "Hello, Mr. Menos? Hi. It's Lexi, Katina's goddaughter. Yep, that's me. We're in, I mean, Uncle Jim and I are in... Katina's husband... Yes. We're in Rhodes. We're about to get off the plane... No, thanks. We'll get a cab, don't worry. I wanted to let you know we're here to surprise Katina, but I don't have a key. You will? Thank you. We appreciate it, and we're sorry for the last-minute call. We didn't plan this very well. I can't wait to see you too. Thanks... Bye."

She put her phone back in her satchel, exactly like the one Katina carried on her adventures—plain, black, and rugged. "He'll put the key in the vase by the door."

"Okay, Lexi. Let's go find my wife."

~ * ~

The airport was small, reflecting the number of travelers through it and available investment dollars the local government could afford. Having already suffered through the winding lines of customs in Athens, they walked directly to the green, frosted-glass doors exiting to the main terminal. The guard made everyone wait there. Jim ground his teeth at yet another delay. "What the hell are they—" His complaint died on his lips as the door slid open.

Lexi and Jim hurried to the first taxi in line. She threw her carryon into the trunk of a small Fiat, angering the Greek couple who were about to do the same. In Greek, Lexi begged forgiveness. Her pleading eyes went from husband to wife as they continued to complain.

She pointed at Jim. "His wife had a car accident, and she's in the hospital." They didn't move so she tried again, in Greek.

The man's snarl turned to concern; he lowered his suitcase and tried to assist Jim with his small bag.

The woman rushed over and stroked his arm. "Po, po, po."

Jim hated scenes and he hated the lie Lexi told, just not enough to turn down the cab. With stiff lips, he waved the help away and placed it in the trunk himself. As he got into the back seat, he growled at Lexi's impish expression. "You, young lady, are incorrigible."

"I remind myself of *Thea* Katina, too. You gotta love me."

He wiped the perspiration from his neck. He wished he'd had some shorts to put on. Digs required heavy pants and boots. "Using the aunt card again, I see. Rotten to the core."

Lexi acknowledged the compliment with a queenly nod. She retrieved her phone again and slid her finger across the screen a few times. "I'm going to open an application I developed for my programming class. I downloaded it to Katina's phone before she left."

"That's pretty sneaky. Does she know?"

"Nope. Well, she *did* accuse me of hacking her phone, but she doesn't know what I did." Her index finger tapped a few times. "She's not at the apartment."

"What?"

Traffic was heavy, cars honked, and their driver yelled, often. Lexi spoke louder. "She's not at the apartment. It's indicating Ippodamou Street."

Jim gripped the door's armrest when the driver took a sharp right. "If she's up, why didn't she answer?"

"You got me."

He peered closer at the phone. "Can you get an address?"

"No, sorry. I'll tell the driver to go to that street instead of the apartment. The display'll show us approaching."

Twenty minutes later, the cab drove slowly down the quiet street of Ippodamou. Lexi said, "*Etho*," to the driver. "Jim, we're here."

"I figured when he pulled to a stop. How much do I owe him?"

"Sixteen euros."

He took out a twenty and handed it to the driver. "Thanks."

The driver had a devious sparkle to his eye as he said in a light Greek accent, "Sure thing. Do you need me to wait?"

Jim eyes bugged out in a shocked response. Just what the driver probably wanted. He remained pleasant as he said, "We'll only be a few minutes."

Rhodes was a contradiction in architecture, as were many ancient cities. Plain, stucco-fronted buildings lined one side of the street. The massive fortress wall made of age and weather-roughened stone, hundreds of years old, lined the other. A few cars were parked along the road.

He threw open the car door. "This neighborhood looks rundown. Are you sure this is the place?"

The driver leaned over and pointed. "Yes. The entrance to the hotel is right over there. It's a nice place inside."

They strode to the stone-arched entrance and found a deep courtyard of sorts. Twinkling bulbs filled lush orange trees. The light was sufficient for them to make their way to the door.

Jim said, "I don't know why she's here at this hour, but…"

Following him in, Lexi said, "Uncle Jim, people don't go out to eat until 9:30 or 10:00 at night in Greece."

"Yeah, Tina told me that once. She's usually in bed by 10:00 though."

"I promise. Things are different here. You'll see."

The front desk was small compared to Atlanta hotels. The walls were made of huge blocks of limestone. The large room was an odd mixture of old and new. It had stands with medieval armor lining the wall and leather chairs in the middle. Wrought iron chandeliers were lit but only spread low light.

"It smells like a church." He wrinkled his nose. "Incense? Anyway, does that fancy app tell you where Katina is?"

Lexi looked crestfallen. "No. I'm sorry." Her face brightened. "Wait. I have a brilliant idea." She swiped and tapped her phone. The faint sound of the *1812 Overture* floated down a hallway to the right of where they stood.

"It's a fact. I'm a genius," she said, pumping her fist in the air.

His heart rate rose as he walked toward the music. "Yes, you are." He knocked on the first door to the left. The wooden boards were warped with age. The phone stopped ringing and silence remained.

"Something is definitely wrong here." He pounded on it.

The door burst open, revealing a tall man, with slicked-back dark hair, wearing stripped pajamas. "Can I help you?"

"Yes. I'm trying to find my wife." Jim shouldered his way past the man and looked around the stark room.

The walls were plain, like the lobby, but white drapes flowed inward as a breeze came through the window. A suitcase and the back of a large painting leaned against a wall. A business suit hung from a door to what must have been the bathroom. The room smelled of soap or shampoo.

"I just called her. I heard her ringtone."

"That was you? I'm afraid I might have Katina's phone." He searched through a small valise and handed a phone to Jim. "My name is Maxwell Blackmarr. A pleasure to meet you. You must be Jim."

"Yes. Hello." *So, this is George Clooney, huh?*

"Your wife's told me so much about you." He turned to Lexi and held out his hand. "Hi. I'm Maxwell."

Lexi put her own behind her back and gave a sharp nod. "I'm Lexi, *Thea* Katina's niece. Where is she?"

"If you'll excuse me for a moment to put on a robe. I feel rather indecent standing here in night clothes in front of a young lady."

She gave Jim an I-don't-like-this-guy-look as Maxwell retreated to the bathroom.

He shrugged in reply and studied the layout and contents of the room.

As Maxwell returned moments later, he said, "I had dinner with your wife, her lovely friend Celeste, and Celeste's boyfriend Aubrey just this evening. I sat next to Katina. I must have picked up her phone by mistake. They're all the same to me."

Lexi quirked an eyebrow at Jim, then said, "That's fine. I guess she's back at the apartment."

"I believe so. That Aubrey fellow was not holding his liquor well. I doubt they went anywhere else."

"Well, thanks for the phone."

"Not a problem." Maxwell chuckled. "She must have mine. If you don't mind, I'll pick it up in the morning before I catch my flight."

"Sure. Thanks again." Jim headed for the door and said to Lexi. "Let's go."

As they made their way to the cab, she said, "I don't like that guy. He gave me the creeps."

He opened the taxi door for Lexi. "He seemed all right to me. Definitely uncomfortable, but he was getting ready for bed." He then walked around and got into the other side. He rolled up a shirtsleeve as the taxi turned onto the street.

"If that's the case, why didn't he ask where Katina lives?"

He stopped mid-roll. "What the hell?"

Chapter Thirty-Two

Who'd a Thunk it?

Celeste could not fathom why she and Aubrey sat on Katina's couch in the middle of the night, with their hands bound behind their back. Aubrey's face was mottled red, and the veins on his neck bulged. He had a bruise growing on his cheek, and his shirt was ripped. Though she was unharmed, Celeste was furious and needed a drink.

"It'll be all right, Aubrey. Once he gets what he wants, he'll let us go." She wiggled and jerked her wrists apart, testing the strength of the constraints. "Ouch. Blast, that hurt."

He struggled against his own bindings, grunting with each tug. "All he's done is pace back and forth. Why does he think Katina will bring the icon back? How does he know she won't run right to the police?"

Tears of frustration filled Celeste's eyes. "I don't think he *is* sure. He seems scared."

"He's not scared. He's insane."

"God I hope not." She nodded at the shelf to their left. "I'm going to try to get that brass statue. It may have a sharp edge."

He got that sour look again. "Don't be ridiculous. He'll be back in a second. He just went to the bathroom, not for a God-damned drive."

"What else am I supposed to do? You expect me to have all the answers, and when I try to do something, you act like I'm an idiot. You're the one who ran for the door. If you had just kept your cool, we wouldn't be tied up."

Slow footsteps echoed down the marble-floored hallway. Celeste glimpsed the stupid shirt with the red, white, and blue moose. Bobby came into the room, carrying his third beer.

She said, "You need—"

"She's not an idiot, Aubrey," Bobby said. "You're such a dick."

Aubrey's mouth dropped open, and his face became beet red. "I'm not the one who's tied up his fucking sister. Celeste can't help you."

In just five long, menacing strides, Bobby covered the distance between them and grabbed Aubrey by the throat. "Shut your mouth. If you yell again, I'll put a stinkin' rag in it." His hand eased the pressure on Aubrey's windpipe. Mean red marks were left behind.

"Look what you did. You're not this guy, Bobby. Why are you doing this?" She searched his face for an answer only to see her brother's expression shift. *He's sneering at me. He's never done that.* With all the authority she could muster as his big sister, she demanded, "I don't know what I've done, but stop this. Now."

She reeled from the hostility that emanated from him and was desperate for some semblance of the younger brother back. She tried another tack. "I'll give you whatever you need. We—"

"Yep. I wondered when you'd get to that." He gulped his beer. His Adam's apple bounced with each swallow. "You'll give me what I want, huh? Well, *sis*, do you have $100,000 handy?"

Celeste cried out, "$100,000? Why do you need that much money?"

"You don't need to know," he snapped.

"I already said I'd loan you $35,000 for the car."

"That's nothing." He stormed to the open veranda doors and stood there, panting. During the next few minutes, his breathing slowed, and his stance loosened. He slouched and put his hands into his pockets, just like he did when he was a little boy in trouble.

"Bobby, what have you done?"

Her brother, a man whom many in the police force respected, bowed his head in disgrace.

Chapter Thirty-Three

Irrevocable Truths

The images played like a B movie, bad and full of bent-nosed New York mobsters, in Bobby's head. Mafia fucks. The day of the bust. So fierce it made the newspapers. The street was lined with broken bottles, soda cans, cigarette butts—anything and everything people tossed out their windows. Dirt swirled between rusty cars and trash cans. Traffic almost drowned his partner's voice. Bobby half-listened to Frankie's story. Something about his confidential informant making Mario Banino's arrest possible. How Frankie thought he'd make Detective First Grade out of it. *Fat chance.*

Blood pounded deep and hot within Bobby's chest. His focus was on the murdering piece of shit, Banino. The fat man in wrinkled, purple boxers, a soldier, the lowest ranking piece of scum, was dragged down the sidewalk. *Banino shouldn't have gotten nailed. I was supposed to steer the investigation away from him. Shit.*

Bobby scanned the street, searching for other members of Vito's crime family. The whole neighborhood stood around and gawked, took pictures with their phones, laughed, and called out obscenities. A kid, maybe thirteen or so, with a jagged scar across the olive skin of his forehead yelled, "Banino's gonna be the bitch behind bars."

More laughing. *Probably the most fun they've had in years.*

Banino's arms were about stretched from their sockets as he fought the grip of Perez, the arresting officer. The cocksucker screamed in his direction, "You owe Vito on two counts. You gave me up. Now you're a dead man!"

Bobby remained still, but he smelled his own sweat. *Never should have taken Vito's money. Worse than a loan shark.*

With a cop's cupped hand at the back of Banino's head as a shield, he was shoved into the back seat of the cruiser as he continued to scream. *Go ahead. Let him knock himself out.*

Bobby wanted to scream back, to defend himself. Instead, he stood there, legs spread, arms crossed. Mouth clamped shut.

Three hours after the arrest, two of Vito's men smashed in his apartment door. *Told 'em Frank collared Banino. Couldn't stop something I didn't know about. Told 'em I'd get the money when I could.*

That's why they hurt me.

Got my balls kicked in. Cleaned up the vomit when I could move again. Was gonna hire someone to kick in Frankie's head but didn't have any damn money.

Had to get some fast. Blackmarr came through. No one was supposed to get hurt.

As the thin clouds over the sea grew blacker against the full moon, the memories grew more immediate.

It should have gone better.

Blackmarr's fucking threats. I'll shoot him in the face when I get back. He'll be one dead dealer. Bobby pictured Blackmarr's head on the ground, a small caliber bullet hole in the middle of his forehead with a trickle of blood oozing toward the ground.

What the hell am I thinking? I'm not a murderer. Instinct warred with humanity.

Bobby remembered flashes of his days playing football. Popping steroids and pain killers. Didn't have any money back then. Gambling would have been a fun way to get it.

Celeste. His heart fell as she made a small sound that shouted despair.

I've fucked up big time.

Chapter Thirty-Four

No Easy Fix

Bobby turned his head in Celeste's direction. She dreaded what was to come, so unrecognizable was he. Had he spent the time reconsidering his actions or had his anger grown to a breaking point?

"I didn't invest what grandma gave me, like you did. I should have."

Celeste saw a heartbroken man, desperate to make whatever was wrong right again.

"I seem to have a problem." Bobby sat on a leather side chair close to her. He clasped his hands between his open legs and leaned forward as if in a casual conversation.

"I'm not the only smart one in the family." Celeste forced a small smile of encouragement. "You're a detective. The smartest people on the force. I've just been lucky. I haven't had the fun you've—"

Bobby slammed the beer bottle on the coffee table. The other bottles toppled over and rolled around. All semblance of contrition was gone. "See?" Bobby yelled. "That's just like you. You *did* have all the luck. It hasn't been fun, Celeste. It's been one shithole after another. I can't keep up with you."

"You never *had* to keep up with me. Bobby, what happened?"

His hands clenched and unclenched. "I used steroids in college. I always hurt. I was underweight. My muscles couldn't take 300-pound linebackers. The coaches told me it would all go away if I took the pills. I did. And it worked. But they were expensive." His anger evaporated again. "I was stupid."

A tear trickled down her cheek. She rubbed it on her shoulder.

Bobby cleared his throat and continued his story. "When I joined the force, I finally had honest money, a salary. I lived it up: poker games, booze, women. I gambled on anything." He started to pace back and forth. A trapped animal. His breathing was audible.

Celeste caught a flash of panic in his eyes as he looked away.

"Jesus Christ. I need to join fuckin' Gamblers Anonymous."

She wanted to keep him talking, to get it all out. "Do you have gambling debts? Is that why you need the money?"

Bobby's eyes were livid. His arms flailed. "Yes. What do you think this is all about?"

"Sorry." *He was always the golden child. He hadn't dealt with failure, never needed to learn how.* The times their mom and dad, even she, stepped in to help, tutoring, organizing his books and homework, getting him to practice and doctors' appointments on time, flashed through her mind. They all loved him unconditionally.

She leaned away from Aubrey and scooted toward Bobby. "I'll give it to you. Just let us go. Untie us. Help us find Tina. I'm sorry all that happened. I can—no, *we* can fix it, but, right now, Aubrey and I are scared, and Tina hasn't called back. Something must have gone wrong."

"Listen to her. She's right."

Celeste shot daggers at her boyfriend. "I think this is all a terrible mistake. Bobby wouldn't have done this if he wasn't desperate." *He's absolutely out of his mind.*

To Bobby, she said, "Maybe instead of keeping us here, we can all go find her."

"Not gonna happen, sis." Another instant, another mood. He stopped pacing and crossed his arms. "We'll wait," he said, with deadly calm.

"Mr. and Mrs. Menos are coming to make breakfast at seven. I don't know if they do a night check in here, but..."

A key turned in the door. Celeste wanted to groan and cheer at the same time. Instead, she was speechless.

Jim propelled himself through the door, his face full of worry. His powerful voice boomed, "Katina! Are you here?"

Chapter Thirty-Five

Reflections

Katina hadn't given up or given in. She did, however, give it a rest. She lay on the cold, stone floor of the small upper room, next to the door, with the flashlight off. The room was like the deepest point in a cave, devoid of light, beyond black, beyond any color that one associated with darkness.

To save the batteries, she ignored her impulse to keep the light bouncing off every surface. The only things she experienced during her sensory-deprivation trial was hearing her own moan, the dull pain in her head, and the fear that had started to overwhelm her. She had to turn the light back on or a panic might engulf her.

The ghosts lurking in every unseen corner needed to disappear, but finding the flashlight was more difficult than she expected. One pat, then two more, then a sweep of her hand across the floor found nothing. In a high voice of denial, she cried, "No, no, no, no. I put you right there. Oh my God."

Using her fingertips to delicately search around her, she felt nothing. Darkness became a heavy, stinking cloak. It weighed her down and captured her breath. Frantic, she swung her hand in quick, large arcs across the floor.

She connected with the flashlight and sent it skittering across the room.

"Nooo." She crept toward the far wall. Fear turned to shock as her hand grazed one of Katha's bones. Katina tremored in response. "Don't freak out. Katha's your friend. Do. Not. Freak. Out." She stilled, allowing her breath to slow.

With delicate strokes, she sampled the floor until the tips of her fingers touched the cool surface of the flashlight. Her sigh of relief echoed in the terrifying void as she took it firmly in her grip. She pushed the button and said, "Thank you, flashlight gods," but winced from the sudden brightness.

Her head wound began to pound, so she waited for her blood pressure and the subsequent pain to subside. Her shoulders slumped as she accepted that, at least for now, she wouldn't lose her mind.

Katina wiped bits of dirt from her arms and dress. After minutes of rest, the adrenaline left her nauseous. She became groggy either from the bump or another after-effect of terror. Rocking back and forth, she sang *Dust in the Wind* by Kansas. "All we are is dust in the wind." Over and over. Because she couldn't remember any other words.

Continuing to hum the morose, but appropriate tune, she checked out the icons stacked, one in front of another, around the edges of the room. Katina studied the three largest, with classically unyielding faces that fit her mood.

"You know what? I'm glad you're here to keep me company. With any luck, I'll have real people to talk to soon. No offense."

On stiff legs, she rose feeling just like old folks must, as they get out of bed in the morning. She stood in front of the paintings and nodded. "Hello, Saints. I'm Katina, Katha's friend." Working from left to right, Katina set the three side-by-side, facing her.

She stepped back to admire her work. "You'll do."

Sitting in the middle of the room, in front of the gallery of faces, she regarded two women and a man. On the left was the spectacular painting of the *Coronation of the Virgin*. Mother Mary was flanked by the Holy Trinity and cherubs. She was radiant in a red dress, over which a gold-brocaded blue mantle was placed. A white dove, with wings outstretched, was centered above the crown being placed on Mary's bent head.

The center icon was a painting of a beautiful man, Archangel Michael, threatening Satan with a sword. His leather-bound foot pressed the head of the personification of evil into mud and the flames of Hell. His blond hair shone, and blue robes swirled about in an unseen wind. His powerful wings, covering four feet of the canvas, were aloft and fully extended behind him.

Katina moved on to the last painting, Mary Magdalene. This Mary held the red egg, which she once presented to Tiberius Caesar in Rome, proclaiming that Jesus had risen. Mary Magdalene had been tormented by seven evil spirits from which she was eventually freed by the Lord Jesus. She was a brave, kind, and faithful young woman.

"Maybe if I think about you enough, you'll rub off on me, and I'll be brave."

All the saints overcame their broken spirits. She spoke to the people before her and the Lord around her. "I confess that I wanted to find and deliver the Cross of Rhodes and the Icon of St. Paul. I hope personal glory doesn't play a part in that. But Lord, if I have to die here, just know I tried to serve you and the memory of Katha."

Katina bowed her head and crossed herself. "In the name of the Father, and the Son, and the Holy Spirit, Amen." She wasn't convinced this prayer would help her now or after she died. Like Katha, she struggled with doubts.

Katina lay across the floor, rested her head on her arm, and contemplated her life. Her eyes closed, and images of Celeste tramping across the green countryside flashed through her mind. She pictured Jim's twinkling eyes and silly grin.

"I've let you both down. You begged me to stop this insanity. I should've listened."

Images and bits of reality combined as she grew more introspective.

She murmured as she fell asleep, "I'm a fool." Failure found its main target—her own heart.

Her mind's eye gazed at an ever-patient and lovely face.

Mother Mary said, "Yes my daughter?"

"You sound just like my momma."

Mary nodded her queenly head. "Dreams are interesting, are they not? What did you want to tell me?"

"Well, this is weird because now you look like her."

"And?"

"God this is hard, but here it goes. I wouldn't want to spend time with me either."

"Tina, my love, what are you saying?"

Katina's gaze shifted to the right. Celeste's face replaced Mary Magdalene's. It was still wise and strong.

Celeste said, "Tina told me she didn't appreciate the times you volunteered."

"I see. I asked my daughter to join me, but she was filled with different, more wonderful activities." Diane fluttered her hand like a bird flying away.

More wonderful activities. What a sweet thing to say. Guarded warmth filled Katina's heart. "I wish now I worked with you."

"You were a very shy child. Spending hours with strangers made you shake. I had hoped you would get to know them, and they you. But some things are just too difficult for sensitive young people."

Celeste piped in, "Yeah. I bet they have a name for that. Social anxiety of the adolescent brain, maybe."

Katina grinned at her friend's irreverence. "Stop it. My mom's trying to tell me something."

"You should google *Psychology For Dummies*. You'll see."

"What I did see was how she struggled to fit in. The children in our neighborhood had families who had been there for generations. They were not nice. They didn't invite her to their parties." Her mother leaned forward and pointed at Katina. "You were a good girl. I was very proud of you."

"Why?" She searched her mom's all-knowing eyes. After a moment, the truth of the love for a child dawned on her. "Just by being your daughter."

Two dark and ragged pieces of the puzzle of Katina's life flew out. One was the loneliness. The other was the strained relationship with her mother. Two fine and colorful pieces floated into their place.

Her mother glowed. "Now you understand. Now you can forgive yourself and forget. You are wonderful, and you have years ahead of you to become the woman you want to be."

With that said, the image of Diane reverted to the Virgin Mary.

Celeste said, "I tried to tell you. Love ya, girl."

Her image transformed into Mary Magdalene.

After a moment of sweet appreciation, Katina shifted her focus to the painting of the handsome Michael but found Jim instead. "I've failed you too. You asked to help me in the kitchen so many times. I turned you down flat."

"That you did. A new experience, for sure. My whole family helped out after dinner."

She pictured his hopeful smile recede as he left the room. *I was oblivious.* "You were always reaching out to me in one little way or another."

"Because I love you."

"Some people made me feel like I wasn't good enough. That's why I tried to do everything perfectly." Another piece, Fotini, exploded.

Jim shook his head. "My love, there isn't a perfect wife. Or a perfect husband."

"I wouldn't have understood if you told me last month, or last week, or yesterday for that matter. But, thank you." She regarded the painting of the Holy Mother. "Thank you too, Momma. And thanks for trying, Celeste. You may have ditched me, yet again, but you do care a lot." Her heart was light. Clarity brought a level of maturity previously unattainable.

Her heart was light from learning. Similar to what Celeste had experienced coming to terms with Aubrey, she too gained clarity of past hurts which brought a deeper level of maturity.

Understanding would bring forgiveness.

Katina woke enough to check her watch. *1:30.* Still a little queasy, she turned off the flashlight and closed her eyes, content to wait until the morning to start pounding on the blasted door again.

Chapter Thirty-Six

Meanwhile, Back at The Ranch

Almost there, sweetheart. Silence and lights flooded the apartment as Jim opened the door and strode into the living room. Celeste and Aubrey were on the couch with their hands behind their backs. Bobby stood close to them.

Jim dropped his luggage and advanced without a pause. "What's going on here?" The three flinched, either from the bang of the luggage or the command in his voice.

Bobby leaned out from behind Celeste's back and muttered a disgusted, "Son of a bitch."

"Thank God you're here, Jim," she said, as she brought her hands around and finished untying the ropes.

Aubrey shifted on the couch, making his wrists visible. "As they say, Bobby, 'The jig is up, you wanker.'"

"What the hell are you doing, Bobby?" Jim approached the group with Lexi on his heels. "Did you have them tied up?

"He sure—"

"Keep your mouth shut," Bobby ground out.

Aubrey shot back, "Not a chance." He rose, rubbing his wrist, and faced Jim. "Bobby was holding us hostage. He wanted Katina to give him some famous painting."

Jim paused to process this astounding information. *Hostage? Katina?* "What's he talking about?"

"I made a big mistake. Got in a bind." Bobby scraped his hand down his jaw.

"What bind? Is Katina in danger?" Jim demanded.

"She was trying to find a treasure," said Aubrey. "She was supposed to have someone with her for protection. I got drunk, so she thought Bobby was going to help. As you see, she needed protection from him. We all did."

The more Aubrey revealed, the angrier Jim became. He was supposed to keep her safe in life. He had failed, and now his love was missing. Rage filled him. He turned from Aubrey and punched Bobby in the mouth with hard, flat knuckles and a stiff wrist. The punch started in the tightening muscles of his stomach and finished with proper follow through, just like his brother taught him.

Bobby staggered back and used the couch to catch himself. He bared his teeth in an angry growl. He charged and delivered a left hook and a right jab. Then he stepped back and sent a vicious side kick to Jim's thigh.

His knee buckled from the pain so great he fell against a small side-chair. As it toppled, he grabbed the delicate arch of the back then used the leverage of his bent position to lunge toward Bobby and smash the chair against the side of his head.

Celeste and Lexi screamed as the two grappled again in a quagmire of curses and close-body punches. Bobby shoved Jim and took a martial arts stance, legs spread wide, the left leg leading, the right ready for a follow-up kick. His arms were up with fisted hands. They were positioned in the same left-right position of kinetic power waiting to be unleashed.

Jim wanted to kill the man who was supposed to have protected his wife more than anything he'd ever done until that point. But he wasn't a trained fighter. The adrenaline-fueled anger could only last so long. As he took in Bobby's attack stance, he was crushed by his own limited ability.

An instant later, maybe because his guard was down, Bobby leveled a lightning fast kick to the side of his head. He fell onto the couch, dazed and panting.

Bobby stood over him, fists and deadly feet ready.

When Jim's wits cleared, his humiliation lessened a fraction at the site of blood trickling from Bobby's mouth with each heavy exhalation. His muscles tensed, prepared to fight again.

Celeste cried out, "Enough." Aubrey tried to soothe her, but she pushed him away. "It's over, Bobby." She sent her brother a withering glare. "Are you done here?"

Bobby stepped back, wiped the blood from under his nose, and nodded. "Okay." He drew in a ragged breath and stormed toward the front door. "You win. I lose. End of story."

Jim stood and pointed a finger at Bobby's back. "Get back here. Explain yourself."

Celeste closed the distance between them in a few short strides. She threw a small hand out. "Let him go." She swiped at her tears and took a shaky breath. "Please. I'll get him into counseling. He's clearly out of his mind." She placed a hand on Jim's arm and searched his eyes.

"Your dear brother about killed me. My ears are still ringing."

"Believe it or not, that was a very controlled kick. I've seen him knock black belts out with it."

"Well, shit, Celeste. That makes me feel so much better." He tugged at the bottom of his shirt and glared at her. "Do you have any idea where Tina is?"

"No. She must still be trying to find the painting and cross."

"Alone?" he demanded.

"I guess." She ran her hands through her hair and dropped onto the couch. "Oh my God. This is crazy. Bobby could have just gone with her and taken it then. There's something else going on we don't know about."

Lexi had her arms wrapped around herself, leaning on a far wall. She pushed herself off and strode to the foyer. Her voice quivered. "This is ridiculous. I'm not sure what you grown-ups are up to, but what I do know is we need to find *Thea* Katina. I'll get my computer ready."

"You're right." Jim stood and went to the kitchen to get a damp towel. He returned with it pressed to the side of his head.

"I'm sorry you had to see that, Lexi. Bobby has some major problems. I had no idea." Celeste blew her nose and dabbed under her eyes. "How will your computer help?"

Lexi removed it from her carryon and put it on the dining room table. "I downloaded an app on *Thea's* phone. Mine has it too." She plugged the computer into a wall jack and opened it. "The problem is the phone app has limited capabilities. My computer has the full program. It can trace all her movements, and it has more memory to hold the data."

Celeste balled up the tissue and grabbed another. "I hope it works." Her eyes were full of shame. "Bobby made me call her with instructions. I bet I scared her to death. God. I still can't process what's happened."

"The tosser is going to jail for this, Celeste. I say we call the police while this young lady does whatever she's doing."

"I won't do it, and you better not either."

Aubrey's voice rose to demand, "He's got to pay for—"

"People!" Lexi interrupted. "Take your argument to the bedroom. I can't do this if y'all are yelling."

Celeste jerked a nod at Aubrey. "Come on." She stood and padded toward their bedroom. "We will *not* call the police."

On their way out, Aubrey and Celeste whispered fierce words, as Lexi tucked a leg under her, so much like Katina. "Uncle Jim?"

"What can I do to help?" A knot in his thigh muscle the size of a golf ball caused him to limp to the table.

"Nothing right now. I want to show you what I'm doing." She turned the computer toward him.

Jim dragged over another chair and stretched out his leg with a groan. As he rubbed the cramp, his thoughts went in three directions: the fight, Bobby's betrayal, and his wife. "Does Katina seem okay to you? Any feelings of danger?"

She closed her eyes for a moment. "No. None at all."

"Thank heavens." He exhaled and bowed his head in relief.

"Uncle Jim, I'm not Little Miss Psychic or anything."

His head snapped up. "What?" Her words sunk in. "I know, but you had good instances of intuition or whatever. I trust you." He put a heavy hand on her shoulder. His bleeding knuckles looked disgusting, so he removed it. "Sorry."

Lexi shrugged and continued to type. "Just so you know…"

"Message received." The numbers flashed, and pop-up windows moved in a rhythmic pulse. "What am I seeing?"

"The program is taking every sample of her waypoints and running them through positional algorithms I came up with."

"Complicated."

"Yeah, these things usually are. Hopefully, my parents are getting their money's worth from my higher education." She leaned in. "It's almost done."

He acknowledged the screen but still didn't have a clue what any of it meant. The display went back to the home screen. "Did it stop? What happened?"

"Wait for it… Wait for it…"

A pop-up window appeared, and a map, crowded with perimeter lines, came up. "This is a digitized representation of *Thea* Katina's movements tonight. As I said, it's been tracking her from the time she left Atlanta. It took me a while to cull only data points from the last few hours, minus the time we've had her phone. The code for my input windows isn't as elegant—"

"Elegant?"

Lexi massaged the back of her head. "It's a term computer geeks sometimes use. Not elegant means it isn't optimized. Not as user-friendly as it could be. It's not ready for sale, in other words."

"Got it." He touched a spot on the screen. "Can you enlarge the map around the hotel?"

"Yep." She used the directional arrows on the keyboard to zero in on Maxwell's hotel. "Okay. There it is." She tapped at the arrows.

"Now, let's move backward."

"I'm doing that. See?" She looked at Jim for confirmation.

"Sorry. My natural self is coming out." He gave her a half-hearted grin. "Must be the stress."

"Riiight. Can't be that you're bossy or anything."

"Just like your aunt."

"Why thank you. You are officially forgiven." Lexi searched the map. "This'll be tough. She could be anywhere along this path." She pointed to the green line that followed the streets back to old town.

"Celeste. Get in here," Jim yelled.

Aubrey and Celeste's raised voices ceased, and she scurried into the room. "What is it?" She joined them at the table. "What'd you find?"

"Too much," Jim volunteered.

"Come again?"

"What do you know about what Tina was doing?"

Her shoulders dropped, and she blew out a breath. "Almost everything."

He closed his eyes and counted to three. "Why didn't you tell us before we started?"

"I'm sorry. I was overwhelmed," she cried.

"Of course, you were." He shot a hand through his hair and shook his head. "What can you tell us?"

"Katha's diary mentioned the Palace of the Grand Master. Katina's trying to find a hidden room in it. She doesn't know exactly where it is. Well, she didn't before she left."

"Okay. I'll start there." Lexi brought up a search window and typed "address for Palace of the Grand Master" and hit return. The display changed to a picture of the palace and details about its location.

He groaned. "Yes. She told me about that too. I was so wiped out I didn't pay much attention until she started to tell me about the car wrecks and all."

Going back to her program, Lexi typed in the address. The map zeroed in on the palace. The green line was prominent. "I'll zoom in now. It'll show her movements as she walked around." She typed some more, and the green line turned into bars.

"This is amazing. It's like the 'I Lost My Phone' app," Celeste said.

Lexi shrugged and continued to work. "Sort of. It's how we tracked *Thea* Katina's phone to that Maxwell guy's hotel."

"Maxwell had her phone?"

"Yeah." Lexi said, as she perused the display for clues. "I don't trust that guy. He's too smooth." She explained what happened at the hotel.

"That's crazy," Celeste said. "Did he have a painting?"

Jim's stomach turned. *Maybe Lexi was right.* "One was leaning against the wall."

"He's truly treacherous. He could have killed you two. I'm sure he followed Katina to the treasure room. She was supposed to have someone with her, so if he did find her on the way to the palace, she might have asked him to help."

Remembering his instructions, *'Take someone with you', made him feel sick all over again.*

"Shit." She studied the map. "Where did the phone stop and double back? I bet Maxwell took it so she couldn't call for help. Then he left the way he came."

With an air of joviality, Aubrey walked up to them. "Brilliant."

"Not now, Aubrey. Go away," Celeste said, then pointed to the bedroom.

His lips curved down, and he turned on his heel. "Fine. Come and get me when you *geniuses* are done."

Lexi zoomed in on the map until the green dashes turned to tiny dots. "I found it. Celeste's right." She pressed a hand to her stomach. With the other, she used a finger to trace a small square on the screen. She typed another command. "4 minutes 37 seconds."

"What's that?" Jim asked.

"That's the amount of time the phone was in this small square. If this Max dude somehow fixed it so she's confined, trapped, or whatever, it has to be there or pretty close to it anyway."

"Fantastic," Celeste said. "Wait. It could take hours to figure out what floor though."

"No, it won't." His niece entered more commands. "I asked it to tell me the elevation of that point. That's the elevation of the building." She pointed to the number that popped up on her previous query. "That one is the elevation of the room. The difference is either above or below ground level."

A few key-strokes later, she said, "Got it. It's indicating a lower level. I'll send this data over to my phone. We can track her with another application. I call it 'You Can't Hide.' It coalesces the data from the computer. This'll be its first real trial run." She crossed herself and picked up her phone, swiped, and tapped. "Okay. It's there. Where are her car keys? We need to drive over."

"Should I come?" Celeste inquired as she retrieved the keys from the kitchen and handed them to Jim.

"We've got this. I think you have your own issues to deal with here. I must say, I've seen a new, um, commanding side of your personality. Good for you."

"It's always been there." She touched the rub marks on her wrists. "Wish I was a man sometimes, though. Good luck."

He nodded and addressed Lexi. "Ready?" He lifted her chin.

"You're pale. Are you okay?"

"I don't know. I'm dizzy and a bit queasy." She closed her eyes, as if taking stock of herself. "Must be jet lag. I'll be okay."

Studying her face, he asked, "Are you sure?"

With a far-away look in her eyes, she replied, "*Thea* Katina needs us."

Chapter Thirty-Seven

Shards Flew

Pure evil stood above Katina; Maxwell hit her with a club. Each swing ended with a low thud. Her brain was so sluggish she might have been drugged. Limp arms fended off the blows. Her body spasmed in anticipation of searing pain, but none came.

She woke from the nightmare, screaming. She pushed herself up and flipped the switch of the flashlight. The paintings, the cross, and Katha's bones were still there. There was another thud. Then another, and a bash, this time strong and cracking.

The outer door!

Katina stumbled on her dress as she ran to the stairs that led to the upper room.

Another bang resounded as if a bomb exploded. "Tina. Are you in there?"

Elation filled her at the sound of her dear husband's voice. "Yes. I'm here." Loud and continuous cracking threatened to drown her response.

The old door bulged with the loudest boom yet. He must have slammed his shoulder into the middle of it. "Just hold on, sweetheart!" Again, it cracked.

All she could think to do was jerk on the handle in a desperate attempt to help.

"I'm getting close. Stop what you're doing and stand back."

She moved to the side, wringing her hands. Helpless yet again, she hated that her only response could be verbal. "Okay, I'm out of the way."

With each thud, the wood splintered a little more.

A thin metal rod smashed through the center of the door. A hook grabbed the shards and pulled them away with a loud crack. The fissure grew larger as small chunks sprayed back toward Jim and flew close to her feet.

"*Thea* Katina, we'll get you out in a second!"

"Alexa!" Katina's body shook at the relentless destruction. Sweat beaded on her forehead and under her arms. Her head spun with anticipation.

The flashlight caught the beige of his shirt through the narrow gouge, a foot long now. The rod connected with another thwack. More splinters. The gap widened. Chunks flew. She lurched to the side as a piece flew past her head. She yelled encouragement with every blow. "I see you, sweetheart. You're doing great."

Jim's fingers tried to pry pieces out. "Crap." He stopped his tremendous efforts and gulped some air. "This wood's old but pretty damn strong." He gave a mighty yell as he hurled his body against the weakened panels. Finishing the job with a final blow, the door shattered.

Katina screamed and staggered backward as he fell to the ground in a huge heap.

"Let me help you." She knelt beside him and brushed bits of debris off his back and legs. She grunted as she tried to roll his two-hundred-pound body over.

He panted and laughed at her efforts as he sat up and shook the dust and small pieces of wood from his hair. "I can do it, sweetheart. How are you?"

Her response was to gasp at a bruise on the left side of his face and a large splinter embedded in his right cheek. Blood trickled toward his mouth. "Oh my God, you're hurt." She wrapped her arms around his broad shoulders and cried.

"I'm fine. I'm fine," he crooned,

"I can't believe you found me. I love you so much."

As his arms tightened around her, she gloried in the knowledge that he was there, and she was safe. She rubbed her cheek against the scratchy whiskers and smelled his maleness. His shudder caused her to instinctively draw him even closer to her heart. His tears mingled with hers. Her breath, his breath, became one for the split second before he crushed his open mouth onto hers. She moaned, tasting the salt of his sweat, tangling her tongue with his.

He pulled back a fraction to kiss her wet cheeks and eyes. "My sweetest love." He held her at arm's length with hands that were red from their harsh use. "Let me look at you." He scanned her face and arms. "Are you all right? Did Maxwell hurt you?"

The questions were slow to sink in. When they did, she was shocked to her core. "How did you know about him?"

His gaze bore into hers, demanding truth. "Did that son of a bitch hurt you?"

"No." She gave a loud, frustrated sigh. "Okay, Yes. But I'm mostly fine. How did you know he did this?" She gripped his shirt and gave it a shake. "How in the Sam Hill did you know I was here?"

His eyes softened, and he brushed a strand of hair from her face.

"Sam Hill, huh? Sounds like you're okay then. Come on. You're sitting on my legs, and they're starting to fall asleep."

"Glad you can tease me, but you didn't answer my question, oh by the way." All awkward arms and legs, she did her best to extricate herself. "Oomph." She flopped over onto her hands and knees. "Crap. I'm a klutz."

With a grunt, he lifted her by her upper arms. "You're not a klutz. Just tired. And, to answer your question, we went to the apartment. Celeste figured out what Maxwell did. Lexi here, our resident genius, found you."

As Lexi came into view, Katina exclaimed, "There you are," and threw her arms around Lexi's narrow shoulders. "Sweet girl, I am so glad to see you. Thank you, thank you, thank you." She drew back, dearly loving the fierce face that was before her. It reminded her of Iris, the Greek goddess of the messenger of the gods. "Let's get out of here. What do you think?"

"You bet. Boy, do we have a bunch of stuff to tell you."

"I bet you do. Like how you found me." Even though she was joyful and filled with success, tough questions needed to be answered soon.

"I can't believe we had to rescue you. It didn't start off all that badly. Uncle Jim and I talked with your dad. He told us what you were after. Radical. History changing stuff, *Thea*."

"Oh yeah." Katina took Lexi's hand and led them to the lower room. "I've lost my mind. I was about to leave without them."

Lexi's eyes rounded when Katina's flashlight lit the space. "Wow. Our church would love all this. Did you find the one you were looking for, or did Maxwell take it?"

"I did." Katina picked up the small bundle. "Maxwell didn't know about this one." She handed the most blessed icon to Lexi. "Do you remember visiting the bay where St. Paul preached? This painting depicts that."

After unwrapping it, she smirked. "It's not very fancy is it? Just a man in robes, a crescent beach, and a hill."

"No, it isn't, but someone painted it in a style ahead of its time, when he was here. This one's over a thousand years older than those fancy ones." Katina bent and retrieved the gold cross she'd hidden under Katha.

"That's the cross?" While backing away, she added, "Under the bones?"

"Yeah. It's quite a story, but I want to go now. I need to seal this room until I figure out what to do next." She handed the cross to Lexi.

"Can you put them in your bag? Be gentle. They're priceless."

"Of course."

Jim picked up the rod he'd used.

"A tire iron?" Katina asked.

"I left my battering ram back home."

Katina and Lexi rolled their eyes. They said simultaneously, "Riiight," and cracked up.

Back upstairs, it took a bit of time for Katina to figure out how to reverse-engineer the closing of the stone door. All it took was a gentle push of her hand and the darn thing slowly descended. She stared at the masterful design that ultimately caused the death of a martyr. Gerard must have bumped it.

The band of three walked up the stairs and through the destroyed door. Lexi asked, "Do you think anyone will notice the door?"

"Such a flare for the obvious," Katina replied.

"They may find our fingerprints. I don't think my sweet wife could tolerate being locked up for even a day after this."

"Holy cow. I never thought of that. I've touched just about everything in there. Crap. DNA. I forgot about that too." She stopped fluttering about. "Wait a minute. I doubt these floors way down here are checked very often, if ever anymore." She bit her lip as her stomach turned. The reality of her isolation became too true. She really could have ended up like Katha. *Stop it. That didn't happen. Move on, Tina.* "All right. A guard did come close to catching Maxwell and me, but that was upstairs."

"What?" Jim stopped in his tracks.

"Never mind. I'll tell you all about it later." She clasped his hand like she had been welded to it. She remembered the 2D puzzle as she led the way out. She wanted to tell the whole story but didn't have the energy to deal with all the details. So many emotions. Too many revelations about her life. "Can we walk faster?"

"Sure. What's going on?" His gaze darted around like a guilty criminal.

She ducked her head and whispered, "I have to go to the bathroom."

Jim and Lexi shared a chuckle at her expense as they hurried through the labyrinth back up to the main floor.

At the entrance to the men's room, Katina said, "You should go clean up that cut. Pull the sliver out. It makes my stomach hurt."

"You've been locked in a hidden room, for hours, with skeletal remains," he indicated his cheek, "and *this* makes your stomach hurt?"

"Well, yes. That was Katha. She's been gone a long time. And this is you. You're my husband, and you're bleeding."

He nodded. "That makes all the sense in the world, my love."

Lexi followed Katina and asked, "Are you sure you're all right? You can tell me."

Wiping the dirt from her cheeks with a paper towel, Katina said, "I'm fine, Lexi. He barely hit me. I promise."

"*Thea*. He hit you? I knew it."

Angry-man footsteps stomped into the tiny ladies' room. "I asked if you were hurt, Tina."

She squirmed under his worried perusal. "The jerk hit me on the head when I wasn't looking. Right here." She indicated the back of her head. "I would have whacked him back, but I was a little incapacitated."

"I'm going to break his neck," he said, as he touched the bump as gently as one might a baby's cheek. "Have you been dizzy? Nauseous?"

"Just a little. It's gone now." *Liar, liar, pants on fire.*

Lexi rubbed the back of her own head, then muttered, "Maybe it knocked some sense into her."

Katina and Jim said, "Lexi!"

"Well?" Her eyes were huge as she defended herself. "I'd be grounded for a year if I did what you did." She must have noticed they were still shocked. Her face gentled. "You have to admit that you aren't the getting-hit-on-the-head kind of researcher. You're too smart for that."

"Sweet-talking isn't going to work," Katina warned.

Lexi waved her hands. "I'm sorry, but, my God, this is crazy."

"She's got you there Tina."

"You're right." Katina threw away the towels with more force than necessary. "This trip really was crazy, so I'll let you scold me later. Let's go."

As they left the restroom, the distant voice of the guard echoed through the corridor. They darted back inside and listened. He seemed to be going in the opposite direction, so they rushed down two hallways, across the large room at the entrance and out of the palace. They were about to get into the car when a voice yelled, "*Stamata*."

"Holy cow, it's the guard. He told us to stop. Go. Go," Katina said.

"*Stamata*. Stop," the guard ordered, as he ran toward them.

They dove in. The engine roared to life. Jim's feet slipped off the clutch and pressed the gas. The car jerked, then stalled.

"Shit. Shit. Shit," he screamed, as he started the car again, this time with more finesse.

The guard was at the door of the palace, waving a cell phone, yelling again, "*Stamata.*"

Jim jerked the wheel and took off down the deserted street. "Sorry, ladies. I'm not very good at this getaway stuff."

Watching the receding figure as they drove away, Katina laughed and cried at the insanity of the situation.

Jim looked in his rearview mirror, exhaling a pent-up breath. "When this is over, my darling, you're going to have to teach me how to handle this kind of intrigue. I'm just a boring archaeologist and fossil collector."

"I can honestly say," she giggled again, "this is a one-time thing." She'd found what she was destined to find. This odyssey was almost over.

Her near hysteria calmed, but she and the others remained keyed up from the last few minutes. As Jim drove back to the apartment, he told his part of the story. Lexi, unusually subdued, described the part she played in the search.

"You were both so brave." she beamed at her talented niece. "You constantly amaze me. This time, it's for something good."

Katina laughed at the angry pout Lexi had on her face. "Thank you, darlin'. I love you very much."

Lexi gave a wan smile and mumbled, "Love you too." Then drawled sarcastically, "Darlin'."

Five minutes later, Jim parked the car in a haphazard manner in the lot. He came around to Katina's side and helped her out. If a passer-by didn't know better, they'd swear he was assisting a very pregnant woman outside a maternity ward. "Things may not be quiet when we get to the apartment."

"What do you mean?" she asked, glancing toward her penthouse.

He shrugged. "You'll see."

Her heart sank. She was completely self-centered. "I forgot all about Celeste. Is she okay?"

"You'll see soon enough," he repeated.

Chapter Thirty-Eight

What's a Life Worth?

Katina walked into an argument between Bobby, Celeste, and Aubrey that seemed worn out from use. Celeste and Aubrey were on opposite sides of the couch. Bobby sat on a side chair to the right.

Celeste pointed a finger at Bobby. "—and you have to promise to make major changes."

"I'm telling you right now, I'm a cop, and we don't get counsel—"

"Oh, thank God, you're back." She jumped to her feet and ran to Katina, wrapping her in a huge hug.

Katina wobbled from the force of it but righted them both and squeezed Celeste back with the enormity of someone who had a reprieve from a catastrophe. "Yes. I'm back. I'm back."

"Are you all right?" She gave Katina a little shake. "Where were you? What happened? What did Maxwell have to do with all of this?"

The wave of questions and sheer force of her concern overwhelmed Katina. Her head started to throb anew, and she was inordinately weary. "Let me come in and sit."

Celeste released her and dabbed her red eyes with a Kleenex. "Of course. I'm so sorry.

Jim put a supportive arm around Katina's back and guided her to the other armchair. She sat and hugged the yellow and blue throw that had laid across the cushion. Celeste and Aubrey were concerned. Bobby, on the other hand, stood and ambled to the balcony without saying a word.

"What the hell happened here?" Katina hid her shaking hands deeper into the soft folds. "The last I heard you were crying. You seemed terrified."

"Don't worry. All that's been resolved. Mostly." Celeste threw dagger-looks toward Jim. "I've been sick with worry. You could have called on your way back. What's the matter with you?" Her eyes swam with fresh tears as she sat on the couch and draped the butterscotch throw around her shoulders. "Blast. That was rude of me, Jim. I'm a mess."

"No problem. I should have called." He sat on the armrest of Katina's chair and ran gentle fingers up and down her neck. "As you probably can guess, we had a time of it."

"Those northern folks have a way with understatements, don't they?" Katina said.

Everyone laughed louder than that joke warranted. As the laughs turned to awkward chuckles, Katina took a deep breath and told her frightening and wonderful tale of the last hours of her life. She tried to be honest with every detail, even about her enlightening dream with the saints. "To steal a line, 'It was the best of times. It was the worst of times.' I love you all, more than ever. I am more determined to find the gold for the people of Rhodes than I was before."

"Because it's truly attainable now," Celeste said.

"Well, yeah. I think so, but Katha played a role also. I won't go into that, if you don't mind."

They nodded as if they understood, but they couldn't comprehend the spiritual connection she'd formed with the long-dead heroine. "Now. What happened, Celeste?"

Her friend groaned and rose, then ambled toward the balcony. "Bobby has some apologizing to do. Don't you, Bobby?" She waited with arms crossed. "Get in here."

He entered the room with head held high, his moose shirt droopy with dried sweat and a nervous Celeste beside him.

Katina waited for him to speak and wondered why Celeste didn't jump in as she usually would. *Lord, that man did not want to say a thing, but I can out-wait him. I'm a damn expert now.* Her patience flew out the door as she noticed pieces of furniture against a far wall.

"How'd the chair break? Bobby? Did you do this?" The room looked like it had haphazardly been put to rights. "Destroying my living room is why you didn't come help me?" She eyed Celeste. "What the hell happened in my apartment?"

With eyes sharp and mouth grim, Bobby left Celeste's side and moved toward her. "An apology is inadequate. All I can say is that I was desperate. None of this turned out anywhere close to the way it should have."

"How was *it* supposed to turn out?" Her glance passed over the room, then him. "What did you do?"

"Celeste's brother tied us up."

"Shut. Up. Aubrey."

Aubrey flew to his feet and advanced on Bobby. When he was an arm's length away, he took a swing at Bobby's face.

He ducked, spun Aubrey around, and pushed him back toward the couch. "Don't make me hit you, you English jerk. Sit down and shut up."

Aubrey stumbled but made his way, as bidden, shamefaced.

Though horrified, Katina used her hand to hold in a laugh. His embarrassment tickled a not-very-nice part of her personality.

Moving to sit with Aubrey, Celeste addressed her brother as she went, "Bobby, you don't have to be such an asshole."

This whole thing is just getting crazier by the second. What did Aubrey say? "What does he mean? Bobby tied you up? Literally?"

The man who had the room's attention, just gave a slight shrug.

"He was the one who made Celeste call you. He demanded the painting."

Her head whirled from the absurdity of the situation. The import of the conversation became apparent. She understood why Aubrey wanted to hit Bobby. Venom flowed through her veins. "You did *what?*"

"Like I said," he held up his hands as if she would attack him too, "things didn't work out the way they should have. I had to make sure I got the painting back here."

Lexi seethed. "You don't seem to get it. Maxwell hit Tina. She could have died down there."

"I didn't know he'd be there. Honestly."

"How the hell do you know Maxwell enough to know what he was going to do?" Katina snarled.

Lexi's body language indicated she was going to fly at his face with nails drawn.

Jim rose and stepped in between them. "I can't blame you, pipsqueak, but take a breather."

"Yes. We all need to." Celeste jumped up from the couch. "I'll get some drinks. Katina, you must be starved." She took Katina's hands in hers. "He did a horrible thing. Please. Let's take a moment. Then, let him explain. After he's finished, you and Lexi can punch him if you still want to."

"Okay. I'll wait, but I can't speak for Lexi," Katina ground out.

"I'll be right back." Celeste gave Katina's hand a final squeeze.

Her foot rocked back and forth agitatedly. *Relax my ass.* "Speak," Katina demanded.

Bobby sat in the chair he'd vacated earlier and put his hands between his knees. He stared at his feet. "I've been hooked on gambling for a few years now. I tried to control it. I... God-damn it's a long story." He shook his head in disgust. "Anyway, I started borrowing money from a man named Vito Leonardo."

As he relayed the story, Katina remembered a walk in the verdant valley with Celeste. *Vito 'The Lender.'* She remembered the article and picture Celeste had shown her. "That guy, Banino, the one you arrested, was yelling at *you*."

"Yeah. I was supposed to steer the investigation away from him, if I could. My partner tracked him and made the bust." Bobby's eyes pleaded for understanding. "I'm in a shit-load of trouble on all fronts. I was protecting Vito Leonardo's guys. He had me by the balls. Until I could pay him back, he pretty much told me what to do."

He leapt up and like a caged animal, paced back and forth, head low. "But I couldn't do it. I'm not a bad cop. I couldn't be owned like that anymore." He stopped and faced Katina. "That's when I got hooked up with Max."

She gasped.

Jim sat on the armrest, one hand fisted, the other gentle on hers. "We haven't heard about this yet. What about Maxwell? What'd you do for him?"

Bobby picked up a strand of blue worry beads on the coffee table. He moved one bead down the string, then another, making the tiny brass bell at the end tinkle each time.

Jim's presence kept her just on the right side of self-control, so she waited, as Celeste had wanted her to.

"I met Maxwell at one of those froo-froo art showings Celeste dragged me to. You were there, Katina. Last summer after you came back from England. He seemed normal. Asked about you two. Said he'd seen us together. I thought he wanted to ask one of you out. We talked about art stuff. Then we started discussing cards and gambling. That led to an invitation." Bobby took a moment, seeming to gather his thoughts. "Time passed, and I got to know Maxwell better. My debts were getting worse. A few weeks ago, he said he needed to know what you two were doing. Wouldn't tell me why. Said he'd give me $10,000 if I kept him informed."

Katina's brows shot up. "$10,000?" Celeste entered the living room, a tray of drinks in her hands. "Remember when you mentioned Bobby was keeping tabs on you?"

"I know. I'm sorry, Tina." Celeste looked reproachfully at her brother. The glasses clinked on the copper tray as she set it down. Aubrey was the only one who took a drink.

Bobby put a hand across his mouth, then rubbed his lips in a reflexive move to keep quiet.

Celeste had seen him do this a few times as a kid, being chewed out by their dad. Bobby would have loved to smart mouth back, but their father rarely roused himself. When he did, butts would be paddled hard if pushed at even a little bit.

Bobby continued, "I sort of headed up his team—"

"Team?"

He held out his hands, palms up. "Yes. Not a big deal. I just coordinated activities like—"

Katina stood and took two steps toward him, yelling, "You headed a team that crashed into your sister?" She balled her fists by her side. "And almost killed my father?"

He reared from the swing she threw toward him, but her husband grabbed her around the waist before it could connect. She pushed his arm off and snapped, "Why'd you stop me?"

"I'll do the punching. When did you turn into such a fighter?"

Her anger at Bobby spread around her in a wave of fury. "When I was hit on the head and trapped in a dungeon. That's when. How *could* you?"

Bobby looked at his sister plaintively.

"This is all on you, dude. Figure it out," Celeste said.

He nodded, frustration on his tired face. "First off. No one was supposed to get hurt. At all. This was supposed to be almost like a white-collar crime. You know? Art theft?"

"That's what they say in all the movies *where someone gets hurt*," Katina countered.

"God-damn, I know. I'm sorry about your father. Maxwell said he had a diary we had to get. Didn't sound like a big deal. It was just a diary, for fuck's sake. Max eventually said that once we got it, he would find some art the diary talked about. He didn't have much of a plan, and more importantly, there was a big chance he'd fail, because there were a lot of holes we couldn't fill. Like, when and where your dad would give it to you. So, a guy named Joey was supposed to handle you."

"Handle me? Is that what you just said?"

"Christ. Yes. He couldn't get it before you left New York, so I sent him to Scotland to maybe get the book there, if he had the chance."

She sat back in her chair. It was coming together. "The man at Dalkeith Castle."

Jim and Lexi exchanged glances but kept silent.

"That's where Tina and I found the directions to the room in the Grand Master's Palace. We can tell you about that later," Celeste said.

"Your ignoramus of a brother came to Rhodes to follow us around." She glared at Bobby. "Helena sensed you were rotten."

"I was only supposed to find out where you were going and what you knew, but Maxwell just couldn't stay away from you."

"Away from me or the treasure?"

Bobby shrugged. "I don't know. Both, I think. He talked about you all the time. Said something like, you were amazing and sweet. Stuff like that. It creeped me out." He gave Jim a don't-kill-the-messenger look. He turned his attention back to Katina. "I tried to keep him away from *you*, but that guy was determined. And you seemed to welcome his—"

"I did not," she protested with extreme vehemence.

He recoiled as if struck. "Sorry. Wrong word. Maxwell can be very, umm, charismatic. People either love him or hate him. Just depends on which side he wants to show. He can be ruthless, but I guess you know that now."

The room was quiet. Katina contemplated all that had transpired with Maxwell, how flattered she'd felt, then how betrayed. *So foolish.* She picked up a glass of red wine from the coffee table. The colors glinted ruby and berry as she swirled it. A fresh, fruity aroma rose. "I bet he's on his way to the airport now."

"Probably. Do you want to call the police?" Jim said.

Bobby's face turned gray as he took in an audible breath. "Please don't."

"No," Katina said. "Then I'd have to explain about the icons and breaking into the palace. That'd be a sticky situation at best. The church can handle all that eventually."

His color returned as he dropped into the side chair and watched Katina.

"Celeste doesn't want you in jail, but she didn't say anything about Maxwell. I could tell them after this is all resolved?"

After downing his drink, Aubrey slammed the glass on the table. "They should rot in jail here, then again back in the States. Katina, you can't let these guys get away with what they did. They're bloody criminals."

"That they are," Katina said. After taking another small sip, she handed her glass to Jim to share. "I'm going to take a shower. Maybe we can talk about what to do next later. I feel sick."

Everyone but Aubrey moved to aid Katina, but she waved them off.

"I'm fine. Thanks." She glared at Bobby one last time for the evening, one that turned out far more hideous than she could have ever imagined.

"I have to contact the church about the treasure and Katha's remains. I want her buried at St. George because that was where she was supposed to take the icon and cross. She sacrificed herself."

Chapter Thirty-Nine

Remorse, Penance, and The FBI

The plane from Paris to New York city was as crowded and noisy as the one he'd had to take to get to Athens. He was overwhelmed by it all.

Maxwell had little time to think about Katina the past week. His days and nights, and a hell of a lot of money, were spent obtaining the charter and bribes, both necessary expenditures, to get the most valuable artifact he'd ever possessed, out of Greece.

He stepped off the plane at JFK and was greeted by a man and a woman. Both wore gray suits, black service shoes, and flashed official badges.

They mumbled, "Welcome to the United States. We're the FBI. Would you mind coming with us, please? We have a few questions."

A hand grasped each of his elbows as Maxwell was ushered down corridors, past customs, and out a service door to a waiting government vehicle. He began to sweat as soon as an agent closed his door.

He'd spent the first ten minutes of the drive trying to appear cool and confident in his rumpled clothes, hiding the terror of his thoughts. *Holy Jesus, what do they have on me? How should I answer their questions? Am I going to crack like a pussy?* There were crimes, both small and not so small. Deals that flew under the radar and payments under the table. Tax evasion. International laws broken. The list was long.

Maxwell never rose above the antiquities hum. Deals were small. Clients were either anonymous or trusted regulars. Simple deduction led him to the obvious. He had to have been turned in by Katina Papamissios.

If that were true, she got out of the palace. *Good.* He liked her—a lot. He'd also pissed her off. She had a right. The blow to her head had not been gentle.

Traffic was heavy at 11:30 that night. They were in Manhattan, and Maxwell had no idea where they were going. He looked at his hands, not cuffed. A sharp pain hit his psyche—the guilt had returned. Maybe it had never left him. Maybe that's why he did what he did in Paris yesterday. Maybe that saved him on multiple fronts.

The car stopped in front a black skyscraper. A granite sign about forty-five feet tall stood guard in front. It had the seal of the United States on the top right, with 26 Federal Plaza in huge letters, announcing their location. He assumed this was the Manhattan headquarters of the FBI.

The agents ushered him into the building and badged him through. They went up an elevator and into a small office. His heart sank when the office turned out to be an interrogation room. He sat in one of three chairs surrounding a heavy desk. The door closed with a thud as the agents left. A four-foot bar was bolted to one of the nondescript walls.

He rubbed his wrist, gladder that he hadn't been cuffed than before, and took in a deep breath. It shuddered on the way out. A two-way mirror filled another wall. Katina wouldn't think he was much like George Clooney at that moment. He spent twenty minutes or so thinking about famous criminals named Maxwell and couldn't come up with one. Maxwell didn't want to be the first.

He shifted on his hip and relaxed his posture as the door opened. Two agents came in. An African-American man, in his thirties, a poster-boy for all things good and right about America, stood in silence. Next to him was a woman, about fifty-five with tight features and a compact frame. Her hair was salt-and-pepper in a loose bun that almost hid tiny silver earrings. She was the first to sit.

"I'm Special Agent Cornelia Holt. As I've already told you, you are not under arrest and are free to go at any time."

Maxwell didn't remember hearing this before. Thinking back, he didn't remember much of what the agents had said.

"This is Special Agent Dal Maision. Dalmatian. Ha. Don't ask him about his name. It's a sensitive subject, and yes, he feels great anger toward his parents." She searched Maxwell's face.

What the hell am I supposed to say to that?

"I usually get a grin from innocent people. I got nothing from you." Another pause. She turned to Maision. "Either this man has no sense of humor, or he's guilty of something."

Maision sauntered to the other chair and sat. "Maybe he's tired of the joke too." His eyes hadn't left Maxwell's face from the moment he walked in.

He hadn't seen him blink.

"My name's Dalton Maision. We're from the Theft, Forgery, and Trafficking of Antiquities division."

Maxwell kept his mouth shut and relaxed his face and back muscles. An old trick for looking innocent in front of the folks.

"We brought you here to ask you a few questions. You should

know, though, that you have the right to remain silent. Anything you say…"

His sight dimmed and white-noise filled his ears. *They're reading me my rights.*

"Did you get all that? Your face got kinda white."

He nodded his understanding.

Agent Maision raised a brow. A demand for actual words, Maxwell figured. "Yes, I understand." It sounded rough, but that's all he could manage.

"Good. Need some water?" Holt asked.

He wanted to say no, but nothing came out. He sat there with his mouth open like a fish on dry-dock.

Holt said with perky energy, "Again, we're not holding you for anything. If we were, you'd be handcuffed to that bar." She pointed to the wall.

He knew damn well where it was.

She continued, "Like we said, we aren't arresting you today."

"Today?" Maxwell mouthed. Prison bars seemed to slam shut somewhere close by. Thank God that sound was only in his mind. New sweat, oily in odor, broke out from pores he didn't know he had.

"You flew in from Charles de Gaulle?" Holt said.

He focused on her face. He searched for hints to where the conversation would go. He needed to say something. Innocent people help law enforcement. "Absolutely. Long flight and uneventful." He cleared his desert-dry throat.

"Would you like some water now?"

"Yes. Thank you." He slumped with relief.

A moment later, the door opened, and a young male agent, blond and pimply, put a bottle in the center of the table.

Holt addressed Maxwell, "They get younger and younger every year. Don't they?"

"I guess so." He shrugged and remembered to try to act cool. "So, what can I do for you?"

She gave a polite smile, nothing too big, just enough to put the average person more at ease. "We're checking into the recent discovery of an icon. Do you know anything about that?"

"Icons are discovered all the time. Russia. Serbia. Iran…"

"Yes, we know. We're hearing some chatter about one named 'Christ's Descent into Hell'."

Shit.

"Do you know anything about that one?" Maision asked.

"I've certainly heard about them. There are thousands out there.

Very common."

"Do you know about one that's particularly valuable. Recently turned up?" Maision leaned on the table. His serious expression turned impenetrable.

Damn. They can't arrest me. I didn't do anything wrong. "Are you talking about the icon I donated to the Catholic church in Paris?"

Holt opened the water bottle and slowly pushed it in front of Maxwell. "How 'bout that, Dal? I thought he might have forgotten his generosity."

Maxwell hesitated. Options, all useless, entered and exited the realm of possibility. He took a few gulps from the bottle. "The donation was supposed to be anonymous. How'd you find out?"

"We love the generous heart. Don't we, Dal? To answer your question, let me remind you that we *are* the FBI."

Maision nodded. Maxwell had yet to see him blink.

"Where'd you get it?" Holt asked.

"Someone delivered it to my hotel room in Paris." That part of the story was iffy at best.

"We don't believe you. Do we, Dal?"

Maision shook his head and leaned back in his chair. He rested his large hands on the table, so relaxed he might drum his fingers.

Maxwell gave his most winning smile and tried to feel a wave of goodness leave his body. "Wondrous things happen all the time. I was just one of the lucky ones." He waited for a blink. Nothing. "When a gift drops in my lap, I turn around and give a gift to someone else. They call it passing it forward or something. This time, I gave the same gift to the church. It belonged to them, at one time, I believe."

"Where were you prior to Paris?"

Mother of God. "What?"

"Where were you prior to Paris?" Maision asked again.

"On vacation in Rhodes."

"That in Greece?"

Maxwell nodded. "Exactly. Lovely country. Full of lovely people."

"Did you get thrown out of a building called the Palace of the Grand Master?" Holt asked.

How'd they know about all this? "I got lost. Had to use the john. The guards were rather rough with me."

"Were you alone?"

How much do I tell 'em? Do they know about Bobby? If I get caught lying about this, would they question my 'donation'? Maxwell took another swallow of water. He used his linen handkerchief to wipe the condensation from his palm. "I'm sorry. What was the question?"

"Were you alone?" Holt repeated.

"No. Some fellow was escorted out at the same time."

"Did you know him?" Maision said.

"No, but I'm sure he was an American."

"Why?"

"His accent."

Holt tilted her head like she was talking to an idiot. "Why would someone send you an icon? Why send it to you in Paris? Why not wait for you to get back to your home in New York?"

I'm going to fucking shoot myself when this is over. Didn't think of that. Didn't think they'd know about Rhodes. Didn't fucking think period. "Your guess—"

"My guess what?" she snapped.

"Sorry. Expression. Your guess is as good as mine. I don't know."

"You don't know what? If I know the expression?"

"No. I'm sorry, ma'am. I mean…" He finished the water and wiped his hand on his pant leg. "I mean I don't know why someone did that. Not a clue." Maxwell's gaze never left their faces.

Maision still hadn't blinked.

"The icon was delivered. I thought about keeping it, sure, but it was too historically significant."

"Where is your office?" Maision asked.

"My house."

Maision finally blinked. "Where do you keep your inventory?"

Oh, God.

"Do you have a store?" Maision added.

"No. I have a small storeroom. I don't keep much on hand at any given time. I do small trades. Dealers, dealing with other dealers. A few online trades. You know, just enough to keep a roof over my head."

Holt glanced at Maision. "Dal, we need that other young person. You know who I'm talking about?"

"You mean Soares, in computer forensics?" Maision said, then grinned.

Maxwell groaned.

Holt laughed and held up a finger. "That's the one. Call her when we're done here."

Maision sent him a squinting, sideways glance and smirked. "Got it."

Maxwell was usually the smartest one in the room, but those were rooms he chose, with people he carefully picked—those who would allow equal benefit from their dealings. That wasn't the case here.

The questioning went on like a ping-pong game. He lost every point. Some questions came so fast, they seemed to bounce off the walls.

Two hours later, he walked out of the FBI building with his balls trying to hide behind his prostate. The old phrase "when push comes to shove;" happened. It seemed he'd fallen into a sewer during a thunderstorm and was shoved up into a cesspool, because he stunk.

He looked at the business card Agent Holt had given him, just in case he remembered something else. *Riiight.*

A cab approached. Maxwell wondered if the agents called one for him.

He stepped into the street, and the vehicle came within inches of his legs and torso. The horn blared and sent his senses reeling.

He tried to re-center himself; to find a semblance of the man he was before *her* and the treasure in Rhodes. *Calm down for fuck's sake.*

While scratching at the days' growth of beard, he decided they couldn't prove he'd stolen anything. All they had was a donation to a church.

His spirits rose a fraction as he raised an arm to flag the next cab. It drove past.

Chapter Forty

The Long Walk Home

The hem of the priest's black robe brushed against Katina's sandaled foot as they left his small, tidy house in the countryside of Trianta, Rhodes, just a few kilometers from Panagia Filerimos.

Katina's heart raced. Her stomach was tight. She hadn't eaten all day. *This is it.*

A week of coordination, negotiation, and frustration had culminated in a successful plan to return the Cross of Rhodes and the Icon of St. Paul.

She wore a floor-length, jade-green dress that gathered at her right shoulder, held by a gold pin in the shape of a majestic Phoenix bird. Her braided hair was encircled at the crown of her head by a gold wreath of olive leaves. Escaped tendrils, dampened by the humidity and the moistness of her skin, clung to her neck and the top of her bare shoulders. Delicate earrings, one owl and one dolphin, hung from her earlobes.

She held the cross close to her heart, then handed the precious icon to a revered local Orthodox priest, Father Nikolaos. She raised her chin and took her first hesitant, but regal, steps forward. The day was overcast and quiet. A Sunday. God's day. She was doing God's work by completing Katha's duty.

The importance of it all filled Katina. A tear escaped. She wiped it away with one soft movement of her finger. *Now. For you, Katha. For all that you tried to do when you were so young.* She walked into the fresh air, taking a deep breath.

A few people stood about, some whispered, others were somber. The gathering quieted and watched her with great expectation. Father Nikolaos took her elbow and guided her forward, down the small road named Filerimou, toward the Monastery of Panagia Filerimos and the church of St. George, beneath.

"Come, Katina. It is time. They will follow."

Their presence was confusing, but she began the journey as encouraged. As they proceeded, Father Nikolaos's rich baritone voice sang out the beginning of an Orthodox chant. "*Kyrie Eleison...*" God have mercy, he sang, in Byzantine Greek.

As yards turned into a mile, more people joined the pilgrimage.

They left their homes by the road, wearing the traditional Dodecanesian costumes of Rhodes. The men wore simple black vests and pantaloons, with burgundy sashes at their waists. The women had black, sleeveless dresses over a simple white inner dress. All wore headscarves of various colors. The line of villagers lengthened behind the cross and the icon. The pilgrim's response to the chanting grew louder.

Katina whispered, "Do all these people know what we are doing?"

Father Nikolaos leaned in. "These families have lived here for hundreds of years, if not longer. Those who follow you have known about the Daughter of the Ancients. Your story has been passed down from generation to generation. They have been waiting for you, Katina."

With that, he resumed his deep, resonant singing for the last half mile up the winding hill. The tall, gray tower of the stone monastery and surrounding olive trees were in the distance.

As she approached, the skies lightened, a warm breeze stirred the blades of grass, and dust motes rose around their feet. From the church, chilling cries of peacocks were constant. Intertwined with the bird calls were harmonic voices, driven down the valley on the dry breezes.

They completed the steep incline to the top and turned the last bend. She gasped. The courtyard was filled with at least fifty Orthodox priests with robes of all the colors of the rainbow and more. They sung in ancient Greek as they called on God and sung his praises. Though the air was warm, chill bumps rose on her arms.

The chanting ceased. The birds were silent. The air stilled. All turned toward her. All crossed themselves, not for her arrival, but for the sacred artifacts that were to be presented. The small sea of ornately robed priests parted, allowing her and the priest to continue to the stoned archway of the monastery's small chapel.

Katina's heart pounded as she followed behind Father Nikolaos through the throng of holy men. Her eyes prickled as they adjusted to the darkness of the small interior chamber. By the far wall her parents waited with pride evident on their faces. She breathed deeply and sent them a smile of love and gratitude for traveling such a distance for this precious day.

Katina tore her attention away and made the sign of the cross. She turned her gaze to the simple icon of the Mother Mary against the wall by the small wooden altar and remembered that night of near horror. Those iconic images of hope, love, and perseverance influenced a fundamental change within her. They gave her inner strength and the ability to truly admit love into her life. *Because of that night, I am here,*

Katha.

The Ecumenical Patriarch of Constantinople, with long gray hair and beard, wore a bright purple, satin robe with gold filigree lining every seam.

He led the way to an anteroom and down a stone staircase. "I am Father Bartholomew. We go now to what remains of the Church of St. George."

Katina, never impressed with the hierarchy of any organization, figured she should call him "Your Eminence" or something, but she responded in Greek, "Thank you, Father."

Father Bartholomew continued in Greek also, "Do you know exactly what you need?"

"I look for the icon of the Resurrection of Christ." She remembered each word Katha had written in her diary:

There are symbols on the back of the cross. I will hold the cross up to the mosaic of the icon of the Resurrection of Christ, which I was told, also has symbols of a different nature, within the area that depict our Lord trampling upon the Gates of Hades. These symbols, joined with the illustrations on the icon, will show me the location of the rest of the gold. I do not know how this mystical event will unfold. I cannot imagine the mysterious process that will take place. I will trust that the Lord will show me the way.

Katina's breath quickened with each step she descended. Time both sped up and stood still. She was overwhelmed. *Will I be successful? Will I understand the images on the cross and the mosaic? Will I find the Ancient Treasure of Rhodes? My God, all the remaining gold from the flames of the Colossus. If I can, what will happen then? When will my responsibility here end?*

An ethereal reply swirled in answer to her questions. *"Yes, you can, Katina. You, and only you, were meant to do this. Trust in yourself. All will happen as it should, for the people of Rhodes, your home."*

Katha? Is that you? No answer came.

At the bottom of the staircase, they entered a large, chapel-like room. It had a small altar covered in a gold embroidered cloth. A wooden crucifix hung above. On either side, glorious mosaic- icons were mounted, rich in color and detail.

The one on the right was the Resurrection of Christ. With each small step taking her ever closer, the past and the future became the present. The icon held the image of Christ, standing upon the fallen gates of Hades, forming a cross for his feet. His arms were outstretched, inviting believers to follow in his steps. The white planks of the gates held symbols within the borders. Bones of the dead surrounded the gates.

These hinted of hidden meaning. Her gaze couldn't focus on just one thing and darted back and forth. Puzzles, always a comfort to her, now caused confusion.

A hand, soft yet firm, took her elbow. Father Bartholomew helped Katina raise the Cross of Rhodes up, higher and higher. She tilted the reverse side of the cross to the right, fitting it over the image of the gates.

"There. There!" she whispered. She pointed with her other hand. "It's happening."

The symbols and bones became pieces of a surreal puzzle. They rose into the air and swirled about in her imagination. Not a single crooked edge meshed with another. No pattern of color easily fell into place, as was so often the case for her.

"I don't understand." She bit her lip as she tried to hold in a cry of frustration. "I don't know what it means. I can't do this—"

"Calm yourself. It will come to you. Pray. Open your mind. Where would the people of ancient Rhodes bury a treasure meant to help them overcome the oppression of their invaders?" His voice became more melodic as he spoke. "Pray, Katina."

She closed her eyes. Her gut wrenched with worry of yet another failure. She let the heavy, woodsy incense that drifted in the air fill her lungs and give her peace. She drew her hands slowly down the sides of her face and neck, then settled them under her chin as she meditated, entering a zone she'd never attained in prior attempts. Through her nose, she took a deep breath.

Then, with great tenacity, Katina pushed her senses under a heavy, black cloak and exhaled all negativity. She stilled.

Guide my mind, dear Lord.

In her mind's eye, she made the fragments float. No pattern emerged. She added more puzzle pieces of many shapes and hues. *Guide me!* She gasped as the edges connected to form a square. A chunk of green was added, and a hill formed. Azure blue splashed across her vision. It was the sea to the north of where she stood! Between the two were pale columns, some standing, some toppled.

"I see the image of this acropolis. There are statues of two gods." The picture burst apart. She opened her eyes. The tension that had built over the last hours, making her muscles taut with anxiety, eased.

She faced Father Bartholomew. "It is so close, buried under the Doric temple to Zeus and Athena."

Father Bartholomew nodded although his eyes lacked joy or excitement. He looked at the icon and crossed himself three times. "God has truly blessed us, but what I need to accomplish now is a terribly difficult. I must determine the best way to distribute the benefits of this valuable property, all the while keeping the government at bay. May He now guide my every action."

A powerful presence surrounded and pressed into Katina. She was filled with the aura of golden light, sweet and peaceful. It burst from her body and joined with the light that was Katha. *God has blessed us.*

Father Bartholomew caught Katina around the waist as she collapsed. Her head lolled against his shoulder. He drew her up and held her until her mind cleared and her muscles gained strength.

He turned and guided her back up the stairs. "There is much still to do. The Church will decide how to retrieve this treasure. We must be discreet. The world must not know."

Katina didn't understand why not and couldn't form a coherent sentence to contradict him nor question his reasoning. Following him with hesitant steps, she ached to recapture the glorious feeling of light, to bask in its warmth and serenity, but Katha's presence was gone.

Are you at peace now?

No answer came.

"Father? And Katha? I believe it is her right to be buried here."

"I believe you are correct, Katina, but it is not that simple. Only clergy are buried on these grounds."

"Father," Katina protested. The muscles in her arms and hands tensed. "She may not be clergy, but she has served this—"

"Be calm, young lady. It will happen, I am sure. It will just take time. She has waited hundreds of years—"

"That's my point. She has waited—"

"And a few more weeks will not be hurtful. Her soul is already with our Lord. Be at peace."

She gazed at the Cross of Rhodes as they continued to the chapel above. The symbols were again just a series of scrolls. "I promised her."

Father Bartholomew remained silent.

Katina wanted assurances—no, she *needed* them. Katha's burial was more important to her than the gold from the flames of the Colossus. Entering the main chapel, she tried to quiet her restless spirit. Priests rushed forward. The stiff hems of their robes scraped across the floor. The noise turned into a din as their questions came at Father Bartholomew like bullets.

"Were you successful? Where is it?" Over and over, they asked with various levels of doubt and excitement.

Father Bartholomew raised his hand like her father used to, and called out, "Ειρήνη. Peace."

The priests quieted and retreated.

"All will be revealed. You must give us time."

The priests grumbled their vexation as they retreated.

He remained stoic. "All in God's time."

She breathed a sigh of relief, glad the priests' presence and the power of their curiosity and need for immediate answers was gone. Being taller than some in the crowded room, with a few peeks around this vestment, she saw her parents. They had remained by the altar. She pushed through the throng and all but fell into their waiting arms.

"Momma, Daddy, I did it." She erupted into tears.

Diane removed the hanky she had tucked into her sleeve and touched Katina's eyes and cheeks. Her mother's eyes, so filled with compassion, soothed Katina's frayed soul.

"There now, my most beautiful daughter. You have been successful. We are so proud of you, as always, my dear."

She nodded, finally believing that the words "We are so proud of you, as always" were indeed the truth. "Thank you."

The strong arms of her father gathered her close as he said, "Bravo. You have done well. You look exhausted, my dear. Can we go to the apartment or do they need you here? Helena and Kostas have a feast waiting."

"We can go." She gave a strong squeeze in return. "All of a sudden, I feel wonderful. I'm starving."

"Good girl. Please tell me I can drive us all back to the city. You don't have to walk back, do you?"

She laughed at his teasing. "I hope not. These sandals are sturdy, but that's a lot of miles."

They started toward the parking lot on the side of the building through the throngs of lively priests. Diane took Katina's right hand and placed something around her wrist.

It was the bracelet she found in Scotland. "Momma! I didn't decide what to do with it yet."

"I talked with Celeste. She explained, in detail, about what has occurred in the last week or so. My goodness, Tina, I had no idea the worlds you conquered on your vacations with that pretty friend of yours."

"Well, they're not all like this. I promise."

"I know, silly one, I know." Diane opened the back door of the black Mercedes. "I was teasing you. I've already called the Duke of Buccleuch. He insisted that you keep it and was especially pleased that you will use it for a philanthropic purpose. However, he would like you to call him."

They closed the car doors, and the engine came to life. Her father backed up and swerved, causing Katina and her mother to sway in the back seat.

"Slow down, Peter. I'll get car sick." Tsking, her mother re-centered herself in the seat. "Anyway, he said he'd like to talk about Lady Anne. Is she his wife?"

"Ha." Katina laughed. "I know exactly who she is and what he's after. He wants to find out if there really is a treasure hidden in Dalkeith Castle."

Diane's eyebrows shot up as she exclaimed, "Another one? Please say you are kidding."

They were thrown forward as Peter slammed on the brakes. He turned around and all but yelled, "Treasure? Katina. Are we going to find another treasure?"

She rolled her eyes but was glad life had returned to their version of normal. "Not you, Daddy. Celeste and I will find it."

Epilogue

With her big toe, Katina traced patterns in the hair on Jim's damp chest. Bubbles dropped off her foot into their marble tub, filled to the brim with lavender scented water. The tub sat in the middle of the bathroom, surrounded by a sudsy puddle. A crystal chandelier added bright warmth to the room's color palette of sea foam green, with accents of gold and cream. A bottle of Armand de Brignac Brut Champagne stood in a crystal bowl half-filled with melting ice.

Jim had just switched from humming *I'm Dreaming of a White Christmas* to *On My Own*, his favorite tune from *Les Misérables*. She had implemented a new rule last month. No Christmas carols after December and before November.

Because it was January, he was unhappy with the constraint on his love of all things Christmas, and thus inconsistent with its implementation.

"I read something profound today," she said, then sipped her flute of sparkling wine.

He stopped mid-hum. "What was that?"

"Francois De La Rochefoucauld wrote, 'Absence diminishes mediocre passions and increases great ones, as the wind extinguishes candles and fans fires.'"

While massaging her foot with slow, seductive strokes, he said, "Hmmm. Quite profound. Have your passions diminished since you left Rhodes?"

"Yes and no." She sighed with pleasure, a common occurrence since returning. "Yes, because I'm at peace with the outcome. The antiquities and gold have been returned to their rightful home. More importantly, Katha is in a crypt under St. George Church."

His legs shifted beside hers, and a toe tickled a spot close to her breast. A wicked grin spread across his face. She struggled to concentrate on her news. She gathered more bubbles close, covering her breasts, and pushed his foot down with an elbow. "I got word today that my manuscript was accepted. I'll be a full professor soon."

His look of seduction was replaced with pride. "That's fantastic. You're just now telling me?"

"That's the thing though." She moved a damp tendril behind an ear, exposing the owl dangling off her lobe. "In the spirit of full disclosure that we've adopted—"

"You mean explaining how we really think?"

"And what we need, yes, same thing. I'm afraid that now that I've achieved a greater success, like you, Momma, and Daddy, that I'll... I don't know... that the passion will be blown out."

Jim put his head back on the damp towel behind his neck and took a sip of wine. "Wow. That never occurred to me."

"Me either. That's just it. How can I top what I did?" Katina lowered herself until the water came up to her chin. "What do I do now?"

"What do people do when they finish writing a book?"

"I don't know. Get drunk?"

"That and..." He raised his eyebrows and waited.

"Start another book?"

"Exactly, Mrs. Bason."

"What should I call it? *Treasure of the Something-Something?*"

He grabbed a foot and bit her big toe. "Write the darn thing first."

Katina squealed, pulling her foot away. "Hey. Watch it." She waited until he looked into her eyes. "What if I want to start another project?"

"Fine with me. What'd you have in mind?"

"Knitting."

"Knitting?"

"A baby blanket."

He sat up so fast water splashed over the side of the tub, spreading the puddle that was already there. "You're kidding, right?"

"Nope." She smiled her biggest smile.

"Weren't you and Celeste returning to Scotland this summer?"

"That was the plan. I think only one of us will. Celeste might have to take a summer session, and Aubrey's still trying to find a position in New York. If things get sticky, and Bobby's out of the inpatient gambling addiction place, he can come."

"Aubrey is useless, and Bobby's a bat-shit crazy ex-cop."

"You're kinda right about Aubrey, but I don't think Bobby's crazy anymore. He promised he'd stay in outpatient therapy. He said he's going to get a private detective license. If I go, I might have to hire him for Celeste's sake. He has badass karate skills."

She rose from the tub, naked and proud.

Jim groaned and reflexively rubbed his leg. His gaze scanned every inch of her body and settled on her abdomen. "What about the baby?"

Katina wrapped herself in a fluffy towel and picked up the bottle of wine. She took sexy, hip-swaying steps into the bedroom and glanced back. "You mean the Maybe-Baby."

Acknowledgements

I would like to thank Kelli Keith, of Champagne Book Group, for being this book's champion. Kind regards are sent to the Colorado Springs Writers Group (CSWriters), principally Erik Johnson and group leader, Steven Janss, for the great support and friendship offered to me. Without it, my journey as a writer might not have succeeded.

I also thank those members of the critique groups of Madison County, Alabama, Huntsville Literary Association and Coffee and Critique headed by Eric Hamilton. They all always offered insightful comments. A special thank you goes out to FBI Special Agent Shayne E. Buchwald. Your expert feedback was invaluable!

As this book delves into matters religious, I would like to thank Kevin Millsaps, my former Greek Orthodox priest. As I've said many times, all that I learned about Orthodoxy's commitment to love and forgiveness, I've learned from you.

Thank you to all my Greek Church friends, especially Anastasia Jones, Joan Williams, and Paticia Jebeles. Also, dearest Popi and Mike Missios, Nely and Kostas Prapiadis, and Zinia Chatzibei, my most amazing hosts in Greece.

Lastly, sisters in my heart, Sharon Van Rensselaer and Fiona Kolodzy, and especially the brilliantly talented Carolyn Haines who gave me (along with hundreds of others) encouragement to write my dreams, I send you my most sincere thoughts of appreciation always.

About the Author

I am a retired software engineer and have traveled widely, including to the sites of this novel. Most of the year, I live in Alabama, close to my wonderful parents and older, ofttimes brattier brother, Kevin.

I spend the other part of the year either traveling Europe (as did Katina, though her hotels were often far nicer than mine) or in Florida, writing my next novel, which brings Katina and Lexy to Ireland on the hunt for The Lost Pearl.

My favorite author is James Lee Burke. The lyrical qualities of his prose are unmatched. His characters are crystal clear, virtuous, and dangerous, as are his locations. I can only hope to bring my characters to life as he does one day.

Donna loves to hear from her readers. You can find and connect with her at the links below.

Website/Blog: https://donnavanbraswell.com/
Twitter: https://twitter.com/DVanbraswell
Facebook: https://www.facebook.com/DVanBraswell
Instagram: https://www.instagram.com/donnavanbraswell/

What's next on your reading list?

Champagne Book Group promises to bring to readers fiction at its finest.

Discover your next
fine read at http://www.champagnebooks.com/!

We are delighted to invite you to receive exclusive rewards. Join our Facebook group for VIP savings, bonus content, early access to new ideas we've cooked up, learn about special events for our readers, and sneak peeks at our fabulous titles.

Join now.
https://www.facebook.com/groups/ChampagneBookClub/

Made in the USA
Middletown, DE
27 November 2022

15791768R00135